THE LOATHING

ILLICIT LOVE
BOOK TWO

ASHLEE ROSE

Ashlee Rose

Copyright © 2023 Ashlee Rose

First Edition

My dearest reader,

I'm glad you're here.
You're amazing, don't ever forget that.

Promise me one thing?

Do what makes you happy.
Do what makes your soul sing.
Love fiercely.
Dance in the rain.
Laugh, loudly.
You deserve infinite love and happiness.
You deserve to find your happily ever after.
You deserve it all.

Don't let anyone take away the fire in your belly, the love in your
heart and the purity of your soul.

Ily X

OTHER BOOKS BY ASHLEE ROSE

STANDALONES:

Unwanted

Promise Me

Savage Love

Tortured Hero

Something Worth Stealing

Dear Heart, You Screwed Me

Signed, Sealed, Baby

SERIES:

Something New

Something To Lose

Something Everlasting

DUET:

Love Always, Peyton

Forever Always, Knight

Way Back When Duet

NOVELLAS:

Welcome to Rosemont

Rekindle Us

Your Dirty Little Secret

A Savage Reunion

RISQUÉ READS:

Seeking Hallow

Craving Hex

Seducing Willow

Wanting Knox

ILLICIT LOVE SERIES

The Resentment

All available on Amazon Kindle Unlimited

Only suitable for 18+ due to nature of the books.

READERS NOTE:

Xavier, Royal, Amora and Reese are British, you may find some different phrases and spellings for certain words and scenarios, but please be advised these are grammatically correct for a British person.
Titus, Kaleb, Keaton, Nate and Connie are American.

All of the Illicit Love books are interconnected standalones and I do recommend reading them in order, although not necessary.

I strongly recommend you read Dear Heart, You Screwed Me (Reese and Killian) before the Illicit Love series so certain scenes and scenarios make a little more sense.
I also strongly recommend you read Savage Love (Xavier and Royal's story) to get an understanding of their characters, character development and their connection to this story.

TITUS KING

I STAND IN THE WARM SPRING AIR, INHALING DEEPLY AS I TIP MY head back and look at the clear night sky. This should have been an easy job; this should have been a straight swap over as such. But The Knight Brothers got to Amora before I even had a chance to. They blind-sided us and took her right from our grasps. Xavier is hunting them down and has promised that she will be on the next flight to America, but I'm not holding my breath, because if I do, I'll be dead.

I've told him he has a week.

A week to get her on that plane or the job is off.

I have my own shit to deal with, I don't need to be baby-sitting a twenty-one-year-old brat.

"Hey," I hear Nate's voice behind me, and I inhale deeply, "you coming back inside? They're doing the cake."

"Yeah, yeah, I'm coming," I grunt, turning round and walking back into the reception, I wrap my arm round Nate's shoulder as I plaster a smile onto my face. That's enough wallowing over Amora Archibald for one day.

I'll pick it back up again tomorrow.

AMORA ARCHIBALD

I knew the day was coming, it had been planned since my father took some nasty people down and brought them to justice. He knew he fucked up. He knew he messed with the wrong people.

But it was too late.

What's done is done.

All I had to do now was keep my head down and focus on my studies.

That was all I needed to do.

But yet, I didn't do what I was asked. No.

I was targeted, hunted and found myself the new obsession of The Knight Brothers.

That's when my whole world came tumbling down.

I'm now being sent some asshole from America, named Titus to watch over me twenty-four-seven, my freedom gone in a snap of the fingers, and my father is on a rampage because of what they're threatening to do.

Are you ready?

Are you sure?

Yes?

Then buckle the fuck up.

My father might be Xavier Archibald the third, but I am the spawn of him.

The Daughter of Satan.

I'm Amora Archibald, and this is my story.

CHAPTER ONE
AMORA

STANDING IN MY BEDROOM, I LOOK OUT THE LARGE, SASH windows overlooking the orchard. The mist sat just above the apple trees, a low cloud covering most of our grounds. The flowers were dead and wilted, the grass with a light dusting of frost, just over the tips. It was very picturesque, beautiful even. A heavy sigh left me as my eyes pulled from my view and dropped to the floor.

I couldn't quite believe this was happening. After being taken on my way home from work by two masked men who put a sack over my head, I knew it was them. They were sending my father a warning. They didn't lay a finger on me. I was taken to an unknown location before having the sack ripped from my head. But the cowards kept their masks on then offered me a cup of tea. That night, they dropped me home with a note telling my father what they promised to do next.

So now I was being sent a bodyguard to keep me safe in my own home. I was livid, but dad promised no one would get to me here again.

I would be safe.

I would be protected.

But what worried me the most, was if Xavier Archibald couldn't protect me, then who could? I had no clue what had happened, all I was told was that I was being looked after and may have to go away for a couple of months.

"Amora, darling..." I heard my mother's soft voice as she stepped into the room.

I spun quickly, my long, red hair swooshing as I did.

"Don't." My tone was clipped and short. "You could have stopped this..." I steadied my gaze on her. Her brows furrowed and her lips dipped down at the corners. My words upset her, but she and my father had upset me more.

"Amora, you know we are doing this with your best interest at heart."

"Cut the crap mum, seriously." I rolled my eyes, crossing my arms across my chest and walking for the door.

I bet Xander and Ezekiel wouldn't have been locked away with some bodyguard like a damsel in distress if this happened when they were my age.

But of course, daddy's little soldiers were grown and working for the family business.

I scoffed as I reached the top of the stairs, my father's icy glare on mine as he stood at the bottom, waiting for me. I looked like my mother did when she was my age, pale, almost translucent skin, and deep, fiery red hair. But my eyes? I had my father's. One ice blue, one a deep brown. My face was scattered in uneven freckles just like the constellation of stars on a clear night sky. They were mainly on my cheeks and across my nose. I was petite and slender.

"Amora," my father's strong, gritty British tone was thick as I ran my hand down the oak stair banister.

"Traitor." I snapped as I walked past and headed to find Betty. *Oh Betty.*

Walking into the large kitchen, I sunk into the chair at the end of the dining table as I drummed my fingers on the surface.

"Hello darling," Betty looked at me with sadness in her eyes, but her voice was upbeat as if she was trying to hide the pain she was feeling.

"Hey," a small smile crept onto my face as I looked at her, but my eyes were filling with tears.

My mother is a wonderful mother, but Betty was like the cool auntie that snuck alcohol into my bedroom when I shouldn't be having it. She was the best and I would most likely miss her the most. Betty turned to see my father and mother walk into the room, both with their heads held high, chins lifted, and their eyes cast down. You would think they were royalty; I think my mother forgets that she abdicated the throne for love. I rolled my eyes, shaking my head from side to side as I looked out the large, French patio doors that led to the gardens, a deep sigh leaving me.

"Betty, leave." My father snapped at her. Betty did as she was told and disappeared into the pantry. She was a lot frailer now and age wasn't on her side, but my father still treated her like he always had. Like a servant and not part of the family. It made me sick.

"You're so mean. Why do you talk to her like that?" I snapped back at him, my head spinning quickly so I was facing both of them. My eyes roaming up and down their bodies.

"It's done out of endearment. Betty knows my ways; I have never pretended to be something I am not."

"Well, I think you're rude."

My father shrugged his shoulders up, one corner of his lip turning up slightly as his eyes burned into mine.

"Stop with the attitude princess, it doesn't suit you." He

quipped as he dropped my mother's hand and walked over to me, pulling out a chair to sit down.

"I don't have an attitude, I am just annoyed that I must live with some giant, old, oversized nanny. You wouldn't have done this with your golden boys." I taunted.

"Amora," my father's tone was low and gruff as his eyes hooded slightly but I didn't miss the warning laced within his voice.

"What?" I scoffed, throwing myself back in my chair and crossing my arms across my chest like the bratty child I was being made out to be.

My father rolled his eyes so far in the back of his head, a tsk leaving him as he did.

"Tell me it isn't the truth." I still questioned him. I was annoyed that he was ignoring what I had originally asked.

"Amora," my mother snapped at me as if I had spat venomous words at my father.

"What!?" My voice was louder now as I bit back at her. My father growled as his different coloured eyes narrowed on me. "That fact that *Xavier* here cannot even answer my question pretty much sums it up and answers it for me." I smirk, my tongue darting out as I lick my upper lip trying to antagonize the situation. My mother shakes her head from side to side and I know she is disappointed in me.

"I was doubting our choice to bring protection here, but now I feel like we have made the right choice." Her tone was sharp and blunt as she waltzed over to the kettle and switched it on.

"Trying to keep me locked away like father done with you?" my tone was harsh, I didn't intend for it to come out the way it did, but I was so fucking angry with everything that was unfolding.

pressing the nipple into her mouth as she suckled hard, gulping down the milk.

"Slow down," I laugh, "you'll fill your little belly full of gas."

Her little, chubby hands clasped over mine and I felt my heartbeat sing under my skin. There was no greater love than your child.

Once she was fed, I sat on the couch and gripped her cheeks softly as I steadied her little wobble as I burped her softly. Satisfied that she had bought her gas up, I placed her against my chest and climbed the stairs to go and hunt for Sharon. I heard a rumble come from Arizona's diaper and I chuckled.

"Okay, lets change you first my little stinker before we go and ruin your mom's zen with your dirty diaper."

I nuzzle into her, inhaling her scent. Floating past the bathroom, I turn the corner into her nursery and lay her down on her changing mat.

"Once Mommy is done, I'll bathe you and get you all cleaned for bed, how about that?" I talk to her and she babbles away as I pop the buttons to her romper and reach for the baby wipes. "And, maybe tomorrow," I smile as she wriggles, waving her little arms around, her legs kicking. "We can go to the park, see the ducks? How about that?"

Wiping her clean, I dispose of the dirty diaper and get her dressed back in her soft pink romper. Gently picking her up, I snuggle her into my chest as I knock on the bathroom door softly "Mommy, guess who is awake and excited to see you," I hum through the door as I slowly slip it open only to find the bathroom completely empty.

My blood drains my face, my heart racing in my chest as I scan the room, frantic. My eyes dart back and forth.

"Sharon!?" I call out and I can feel Arizona squirming in my arms as she picks up on my emotions. Rushing from the bathroom, I run into our bedroom to see it empty. I lay

Arizona in the middle of our bed, "Stay there, baby," I coo, stepping away and pulling the closet door open to see her side completely empty. "She's left us," I can barely get the words out as I choke on my own breath, the air whooshing from my lungs as I gasp, and I hear Arizona's piercing cries fill the room.

I can't move, my back against the wall as I slide down it and drop my head into my hands as her screams get louder and all I can do is overthink of what may or may not have happened.

Drying myself off, I slip from my thoughts, and I float across to the large sink unit, squeezing toothpaste onto my brush as I stare at myself in the mirror, brushing my teeth. My spare hand rubs over my unruly hair, I need it cut. Dragging my hand down the side of my face and over the stubble. I look like shit. My eyes hollow and dull. My sleep schedule has been fucked the last couple of weeks as I've been working with Xavier fucking Archibald.

We're in completely different countries and time zones. He is in England, me in New York. He is five hours ahead of me, and he *always* wants to call at six in the morning, his time which is two a.m. my time. It doesn't matter how much I ask him to just push it back a couple of hours, he never does and seeing as he is *technically* my boss whilst I am on this case, I can hardly argue with the man. To be honest, I would be too scared to argue with him. He would put a bullet in my head. No hesitation and I can't risk that. I can't risk Arizona losing another parent. But I do find some peace in knowing that she would have three uncles and Connie, well, more like four uncles and two aunties now Killian seems that have floated into our group. He is a decent guy, took us a little while to warm up to him, but we

CHAPTER THREE
TITUS

WALKING BACK INTO THE ROOM, RELIEF SWEEPS OVER ME THAT MY bed is now empty. I don't do one night hook ups; I don't do one-night stands. I used to, two years after I accepted that Sharon was never coming back. It took me a long time to actually accept it, and now here we are, twenty-one years later and I've had my first one-night stand in what feels like a lifetime ago.

I went through a man-whore stage at the two-year mark, but after a few months, I wasn't interested in it anymore. I needed to focus on the most important thing in my life which was Arizona. I felt dirty after this morning and I may have scrubbed my skin a little harder than I should have because it now feels tender.

My phone beeps and I pat around for it on my quilt cover until I find it, my brows pinch when I see Kaleb's name.

I sigh, clicking the green button and lifting it to my ear.

"Yup," I grit, not that I have a problem with Kaleb, I am just a bear with a sore head and it's my own fault.

"Good morning sunshine," Kaleb chirps down the phone, "you sound rough," he chuckles, and I roll my eyes.

"Well, I had to drink myself into a coma because the sickly love declaration that I was behold to."

"You're such a grouch, that's what we should call you from now on, *Oscar the Grouch.*"

"And we should call you pussy whipped but hey, who am I to give you a new nickname?"

"Ouch," I hear his chuckle grow and Connie laughing in the background, and a smile pulls at my lips.

"What do I owe the pleasure?" I huff as I sit on the edge of the bed and rummage through my underwear drawer, letting out a heavier sigh as I notice my briefs drawer is running dangerously low.

"Just wanted to see how you were, you were in a pretty low place last night," I hear the ruffle off bed sheets and know he is getting out of bed to begin pacing.

"I'm fine, just over this Xavier shit now if I'm honest. Sounds like the dude doesn't know what he's doing. One minute she is about to get on the plane, then it's pushed back a few days. I told him he has a week. If she isn't on the plane in one week then I am done." I flop down on the bed. "I am exhausted with it all."

"I get it mate, just give him the week... if he is still fucking about then just leave it. It's not worth the stress."

I nod in agreement as if he can see me.

"Me and Connie are going to grab some lunch, you up for meeting us?" Kaleb asks as I hear him shuffling about.

"Oh yeah, like a third wheel kind of thing?"

"What's wrong with that?"

"Nothing," I quip, sitting back up slowly, "what time are you going?"

"About one? Does that work?"

I pull my phone from my ear, it's just turned seven.

"Yeah, but fuck, why are you up so early?"

"Connie woke me up with..."

I hang up and throw my phone into my unmade bed and shudder. I love Kaleb and Connie, but I don't want to know what Connie may or may not have woken him up with. My phone beeps with the restaurant where are meeting and I shake my head from side to side as a soft chuckle catches at the back of my throat.

When I finally get myself dressed and downstairs, Arizona is sitting at the breakfast bar with a bowl of granola. I smile, my heart warming in an instant.

"Morning Sunshine," I step closer to her and place a kiss on the top of her head, and she tuts.

"What? Too old to receive a kiss from your dad?" I place my hand over my heart and act wounded.

"A little, yeah," she quips, rolling her eyes as she goes back to scrolling on her phone. She truly is beautiful. Her curly black hair sits shoulder length, her piercing light green eyes hide behind thick, black rimmed glasses and her skin is a perfect mix of mine and her mother's. A ripple of old rage courses through my veins at the thought of her mother and how she could just abandon her daughter.

"Well, get used to it Sunshine because I will kiss you until my last dying breath," I wink and pop the coffee machine on. "Want one?" I ask.

She yawns, taking another spoonful of her granola.

"Yeah, please," she puts her phone face down and gives another yawn.

"Tired?"

"Exhausted, I've got a down day today and I'm back on for sixteen hours from tomorrow morning."

"Joys of being a medical intern," I smirk and hand her a cup of coffee.

"Thanks," she mutters, and I'm not sure if she is thanking me for the coffee or the remark about her being an intern. "My internship and studies are killing me, I know I am a super genius and I managed to skip a grade or two, but working and studying for my exams are making me permanently exhausted."

"You need a break," I say softly, and she scoffs.

"Yeah, I wish."

I shrug my shoulders up, "I'm third wheeling with Kaleb and Connie for lunch, want to come with?" I ask as I take a seat opposite her and take a mouthful of heaven in a cup.

"Why not take the busty blonde that snuck out this morning?" her own smirk pulling at her lips as she stares directly ahead, taking her own mouthful.

"You saw her then, huh?" I lift my brows high.

"Yup, I rolled in at six."

"Awesome."

"Look, you haven't got to sneak them out or worry about me. I'm twenty-one, I don't care who you bring home," she shrugs her shoulders up, "as long as they don't disturb my life, I honestly couldn't care less, dad." She stands from the breakfast bar, grabbing her phone and walking round towards me, wrapping her arms around my broad shoulders from behind, her cheek resting on mine.

"Night dad."

"Night, Sunshine," and before she can move, I turn quickly and peck a kiss on her cheek.

"Dad!" she shouts, pushing me away and taking her coffee upstairs.

I laugh until it fades, and I am sitting by myself, I look

at my watch and it's just turned nine. This morning is dragging, but I decide to finish my coffee then go to the office to kill some time until I am ready for my lunch date with Kaleb and his girlfriend.

Fuck my life.

CHAPTER FOUR
AMORA

"Amora!" my father's bellowing bounces off the walls, but I ignore him. I'm getting pretty good at that. "Amora!" he shouts again, and I roll my eyes.

"Go away!" my own voice loud as I lay on my bed, scrolling through my phone. "I am ignoring you! Stop shouting my name!"

But he doesn't listen, of course he doesn't. He comes barrelling through my bedroom door like the fucking wrecking ball that he is.

"Do you not understand what *go away* means?" I don't even lift my eyes to focus on him, I just continue aimlessly scrolling.

"Why are you so fucking stubborn?" he growls.

"Must be genetic," I side eye him, smirking but he doesn't return it.

"Do you not understand how serious this is? You could sit down and talk to me and your mother about this like an adult, you were quite proud to tell us you were an adult downstairs and that we're treating you as a child, yet who was the one who stormed to her room like a brat?" his vicious tongue whips at my skin but it doesn't affect me. I can deal with the wrath of my father; his harsh words don't bother me in the slightest.

"I don't want to sit down and talk, it would make no difference, would it? If I was to sit down and tell you how I felt, would anything change?" I ask and I sit up slowly, turning to face him, my eyes burning into his, but he looks away like a coward, his large hand brushing through his dirty blonde hair before he drops his head. "Exactly," I tut, shaking my head from side to side.

"Amora," his eyes lift to mine, darting back and forth between them and I see how his face softens. He steps cautiously towards me and sits next to me, his hand reaching for mine as he clasps them in his grip. "I love you, so much, as does your mother," he rasps, "I know this seems unfair, but I have always been very transparent with what I do. And unfortunately, I was tipped off incorrectly and I took the wrong person down and now, well, they're out for blood. And for some unknown reason, they're threatening me with you. I can't risk losing you," my father chokes, and my heart constricts in my chest.

"You're not going to lose me; what makes you think they're serious?"

"Because these people don't fuck about with shit like this." He rolls his lips. "You're an easy target, they want to hurt me and it would be too unsatisfying if they put a bullet in my head, so, they would come for you," he sighs and shifts his body slightly to face me, his head cocking to the side. "I can't lose you Amora."

"You're not going to lose me," I admit again but this time in a whisper, "and I hate arguing with you dad, but you're suffocating me and now you're telling me that I'm having a babysitter coming to look after me."

"Well, you were going to America," he rushes out and my eyes widen.

"What?!"

"But I couldn't have you that far away from me. At least with you being here, I know someone will always have eyes on you."

"Yeah," I roll my eyes, "you and mum, I don't know why we need a bodyguard, also, we have Xander and Ezekiel."

"No, I don't want to involve them. You all have targets on your back, your easy ransom to them, whereas by me hiring a bodyguard for you, I can get someone who will dedicate all of their focus on you," his grip tightens over my hand, "and I can't give you all of my focus. I need to find out why The Knight Brothers are sending these threats, best case scenario it's just a dud and nothing comes of it. But worst case..." he stalls, his eyes reaching mine.

"I know," I nod, running my tongue across my bottom lip. We sit in silence for a moment as the dust settles between us.

"Now, come downstairs. Your mother is all over the place with it all," his hand slips off mine and I look at how much my dad has aged in the last few years.

I nod, standing from the bed and following my dad down the narrow hallway until we reach the sweeping staircase. Letting my fingers glide down the banister until I am at the bottom. My dad disappears into the office, and I continue walking towards the kitchen that runs across the back of the house. My mum is standing by the French doors that lead out to the back garden, the wildflowers dancing in the soft spring breeze.

"Mum," I say softly, she turns round, her eyes red rimmed, tears threatening to escape as she holds a handkerchief under her nose.

"Oh, honey," relief swarms her as she rushes towards me, pulling me in for a hug. The softness of her lilac sweater pressing against my skin.

"I'm sorry," I mumble.

"For what?" she asks as she pulls away, her hands still holding onto the top of my arms.

"For the way I reacted, the things I said..."

"Amora," she tsks, smiling as a single tear escapes and runs down her cheek, "I would be concerned if you didn't act that way," a little scoff escapes her. "You are mine and your father's child after all, we are both fiery and stubborn and you," she presses her finger to the tip of my nose, "are a carbon copy of both of us, but just in one body... where mine and your father's emotions are split between the two of us, you have them all bottled up inside of you." Her head tilts to the side as her beautiful eyes bounce back and forth between mine, "Don't ever apologise for who you are," her arms wrap round my slender frame as she pulls me in for another hug but this time, she holds me a little tighter.

"I promise I'll behave."

My mum laughs, her whole body vibrating against mine.

"I don't want you to behave, just be a little more welcoming to your father's suggestions." A giggle bubbles out of me. "And don't make the bodyguard's life hell."

"Ugh," I groan, breaking away and pushing my hands into the back of my jeans pocket as I skate across to put the kettle on. "When is he coming?" I ask as I reach for three China cups.

"No idea, your father is meant to be sorting out the finer details this week apparently," she shrugs as she steps closer to me, but reaches for the fridge door and grabs the milk.

"He told me I was meant to be going to America," I slip out as I throw three tea bags into the cups.

"Yeah, that was never going to happen."

"I don't know, maybe it would have been easier to just cart me away," I shrug my shoulders up as the kettle clicks. Lifting it, I cover the tea bag with the scalding water, filling the three cups closely to the rim as my mum tops them all up with a little bit of milk.

"No," she shakes her head, "I need you to stay here, where I know you're safe."

I sigh, lifting my cup and grabbing my father's.

"Want me to take it?" she asks as she heads towards the sunroom.

"No, it's okay," I give her a tight smile and walk out of the kitchen and towards my father's office. I don't knock, just push the door open to see him sitting at his desk.

"I made you tea," I say softly as I place it on the desk in front of him, he gives me a little nod but a big smile.

"Thank you, love," he taps away on his computer.

"No worries," I turn to walk out the room when his phone begins buzzing.

"What?" my father grits out and I smile as I close the door behind me, letting it click into place.

Walking back through to the kitchen, the soft breeze dances across my skin and through my light pink chiffon blouse causing my skin to burst into goosebumps. Stepping outside, I let my head fall back as the sun beats down onto my pale skin. I enjoy this moment for a little while longer before I come back down to reality and see my mum sitting under the pergola. Smiling, I float over to her, the smell of the wild flowers filling my senses.

"Your father okay?" she asks as she takes a sip of her tea and I nod.

"Yeah, he just answered a call as I was leaving the office."

"I hope he will join us soon, the day is too beautiful to waste locked away in his office," and I hum in agreement. Once the early spring frost leaves, the weather flourishes.

I look over my shoulder at the small cottage that was once housed by the house keepers, but once Betty moved in, my father moved them into the village across and closer to my grandad's brother's castle. We have nothing to do with that side of the family, it's sometimes hard to remember that I have royal blood pumping through my veins.

"Is Betty okay?" I ask as I turn my attention back to the house, smirking knowing full well that Betty is currently walking towards us.

"Yeah, she's just Betty," my mother lifts her teacup to her lips as she takes a small mouthful, "It's hard to see the person who I've grown up with so frail," she sighs but then jumps when she gets a small tap round the back of her head.

"Ow!" she exclaims, turning to look to see Betty grinning.

"I am *not* frail," she shakes her head from side to side, her little hands placing on her hips.

"Well, you're not a spring chicken, are you?" my mother continues, and Betty's eyes widen and I let out a low laugh as I slide down in my chair.

Betty tuts and mumbles under her breath as she slips into the seat next to me.

"What a beautiful day," her voice slips into the breeze and I nod.

"It really is."

"Shame your father is going to lock you away."

"He isn't going to lock her away," my mother pipes up, her eyes closed as she enjoys the sound of the birds chirping softly in the distance.

"Okay love, if you say so," Betty chirps, giving me an elbow in the side and I laugh.

"He knows better than that," I roll my lips, my brows pinching as I squint a little when I see him approaching with his tea and a cup for Betty.

"Does he?" Betty quips just as my dad steps up into the pergola base.

"Does he what?" his eyes bounce between me and Betty, his hand stroking his beard that has a dusting of grey hairs scattered through.

"That you know better than to lock me away," I answer him seeing as Betty has become mute all of a sudden.

He says nothing, just brings his China cup to his lips and takes a mouthful, sticking his pinkie up in the air.

"Dad," aggravation rolls through me as I turn to look at him, his eyes meeting mine.

"Of course, I'm not going to lock you away," he snorts a laugh, his hand moving back to his beard.

I smile at Betty and throw her a wink, "See."

"Mmm, we will," she rattles as she takes a sip of her tea.

CHAPTER FIVE

TITUS

SITTING AT THE TABLE AT *SARA BETH'S* I WAIT FOR KALEB AND Connie. I feel awkward; Arizona had agreed to come with me but has a headache and ducked out of lunch so now I look like a loner sitting on my own. Twisting my wrist to face me, I check my watch and it has just turned quarter past. *They definitely said one.*

Didn't they?

I slip my phone out of my pocket and click on Kaleb's name when I see him and Connie rolling through the door laughing.

I roll my eyes as I shuffle out of the seat and stand, pulling Connie in for an embrace, kissing her on the cheek. Kaleb holds his hand out and I swat it away.

"Nice of you to join me," I groan, slipping back into the booth. "The waitress has been over three times asking me if I need anything."

"Sorry Titus, we got a little..." Connie blushes, her cheeks turning crimson.

"It's fine," I grit when I catch Killian and Reese out the corner of my eye.

"What are they doing here?" I ask, as I hold the menu.

"Oh," Connie says all surprised as she looks over her shoulder, her small dimples appearing as she tries to fight off her smile. "Must be a coincidence."

"Hmm, seems it," my jaw clenches as I shuffle further into the booth.

"Fancy seeing you here?" Reese giggles, her British accent strong as she slips in next to me, "Hi Titus."

I hold my hand up and wave, Killian slipping in next to her.

"I feel ambushed," I admit, my voice gravelly and low. "The day after your wedding and you decide to come here for lunch with us."

"Ambushed," Kaleb rolls his eyes as he rests his arm behind Connie.

"We don't go away until next week, we're going to Hawaii... I can't wait." Killian coughs, clearing his throat and Kaleb retracts his arm quickly from behind Connie.

I scoff a laugh, "Pussy," shaking my head from side to side as I scan the menu.

"Remember when I was meeting Harlen here and you turned up *Mr possessive*," Reese teases her husband, Killian, and he nods, his eyes glistening with happiness as he remembers the memory fondly.

"What are we eating? I need food." I interrupt the small memory of sappiness.

"The lobster roll is good," Reese pipes up, reaching over and pointing it out on my menu.

"Not sure on the lobster, doll."

"It is really good," she nods licking her lips, repeating her words again as if it'll make me choose the Lobster.

"Is that what you're going for, Buttercup?" Killian's

raspy voice floats over the table and I watch Connie roll her eyes as her dad pulls Reese closer to him.

"Ahem," Connie crosses her arms across her chest, "So you can *fondle* my best friend, but my boyfriend can't put his arm around me? How is that fair Killian?" her thick brows raise high in her head, her dark brown eyes burning into Killian and Kaleb sits looking at his menu with a boyish grin on his face.

"It's dad to you."

"It's Killian when you're being a douche."

"A douche?" Killian snorts, his head snapping up.

I roll my head back, groaning loudly.

"Seriously!" I slam my hand down on the table, "Please, I am hungover, extremely hangry... I just want some food," my voice stammers as I put on a forced cry as I finish my sentence. "If I wanted to watch a daughter and dad bicker, I would just stay home."

"Touché" Kaleb nods as his eyes continue to scan the menu as the rest of the table falls silent.

"Hi, welcome to *Sarabeth's,* what can I get ya'll?" the waitress pings her eyes to me, her chest rising and falling a little heavier as I watch the crimson dance across her cheeks.

"I'll have the sirloin burger and a Bloody Mary," I hand her the menu, "Actually, make that two Bloody Marys." I sit back, pulling my phone out and checking my messages. Nothing from Xavier but it had only been a day.

Everyone else orders the lobster rolls and cocktails. I am so hungry I could eat my own arm.

"I can't believe you're married," Connie gushes at her best friend, reaching over for her hand and smiling at her wedding rings.

"I know, it feels like we've been waiting a lifetime," she

sighs happily, turning to face Killian she places her hand on his cheek and he leans into it.

"Should have just stayed married the first time."

"What?" Connie's eyes widen and she chokes on her water, spluttering it out over the table. I scrunch my nose, turning it up as I reach for a table napkin and hand it to her.

"You were *married*?!" her eyes bug even more as she begins wiping her mouth and I smirk, shuffling back in my seat and turning my body as I am about to watch this unfold.

"Did we not tell her?" Reese gets flustered, running her hand up round the back of her neck, her finger twiddling with the thin gold chain that sits round her neck.

"Obviously not," Killian breathes out under his breath, pulling at his loose crew neck sweater and readjusting himself in the seat.

"You were *married!?*" she asks again, her eyes pinned on her dad and I pull my bottom lip between my teeth, my smile growing.

"Yeah," Reese nods, her hand now clasped over her other one, her fingers spinning her wedding band and engagement ring round her finger.

"And you didn't think to tell me?" Connie is fuming, her cheeks are red, her eyes are glued to her dad and I can see the rage seeping out of her.

"We did tell you, I am sure of it," Killian leans forward, reaching for her hand but Connie slips it off the table before he even has a chance.

"I think I would remember, you know, like when I found out Reese was pregnant with your baby but I only found out the baby was yours because you burst through the door like a mad man telling her you wouldn't be cut out of your baby's life," and I'm sure Connie's flustered voice was growing higher and higher as the seconds went on.

"Shit, Connie, I was sure we told you..." Reese reaches for her hand this time but Connie doesn't let her near her either.

"Well you didn't," she sits back in her seat, crossing her arms back across her chest and my eyes are volleying round the table.

Silence falls suddenly and I can feel the tension brewing. Shit. We don't need this. Connie has only just got them back in her life, things were going so well for her.

Kaleb looks at me for some words of wisdom but all I do is shrug my shoulders up slightly.

He presses his fingers across his lips as the waitress comes back with everyone's drinks. She passes me my two first, I mean, of course she does. I smirk at her, taking them and begin drinking as she dishes out the rest of the drinks to the hostile table.

She turns away, and scampers off.

"Look..." I say softly, my eyes scanning the four of them as I take a sip of my Bloody Mary. "Fuck, that hits the spot," I groan in appreciation, then pull out the celery and take a bite, causing a loud crunch to fill the awkward silence. "You have just got everything sorted, are you really going to let this *little* misunderstanding, or more so, miscommunication really set you back? I mean... so what if you didn't know that they were married. Is it really going to change anything? They're married, what happened between you all before is nothing but a distant memory. Don't push them away again, come on Connie... after *everything*."

She blinks a few times, drinking her mimosa. I wait on bated breath but she doesn't speak yet, it's as if she is trying to process everything. I reach my hand across and cover hers. "You've been through a lot; this..." I move my index finger between her and Killian, "it's a lot to digest, but it's just a small blip. Keep it as a blip," I give her a small smile, her eyes meet mine as she smiles back at me and I sit back, happy as a pig in shit that the little conflict was rectified quickly.

Reese and Killian both apologize to Connie, but she waves it off as if it wasn't a big deal.

"Now, onto more pressing matters... What the fuck am I going to do with a twenty-one-year-old girl who I need to keep safe?" my eyes bounce round the room as the waitress returns with our food.

WALKING THROUGH CENTRAL PARK WITH KALEB AND CONNIE, I enjoy the silence. I am working myself up at the thought of having Amora here with me, part of me regrets ever saying yes to Xavier, but like I said a few months back, if it was Arizona, I would be doing exactly the same. I would give my last breath if it meant saving her. Any dad would.

"Oh shit," Connie breathes, stopping in her tracks but her fingers are still laced through Kaleb's hand.

"What?" he asks her, his brows pulling before smoothing out quickly.

"They did tell me they got married," she gasps, her hand flying to her mouth, "well, Dad did..."

"Oh," I watch as Kaleb relaxes, his shoulders instantly dropping.

"When I found out that Dad was having a baby with her, he come over you know, to try and work it out with me and that's when he told me that he was tipsy and they got married." Her hand that was covering her lips now slowly makes its way up to her forehead, letting her head fall forward. "Shit," she whispers.

"It's okay, we will call them when we get home, you can explain..." I watch as Kaleb comforts her, pulling her close to him as his arm wraps round her back, his hand pressed into the small of her back that is covered with an oversized tee, covering most of her bike shorts. "You've had so much going on, things are going to get a little lost up there," he reassures her sweetly, pressing his lips to her forehead. "Come on baby, let's get you home," Kaleb glides his lips down then covers hers before he links his fingers back through hers and continues walking.

I want what they have.

An all-consuming love.

One day. One day I'll find the kind of love that my parents had.

But until then...

CHAPTER SIX
TITUS

TWENTY-ONE YEARS AGO

It had been one week.

One week since Sharon upped and left without a single word. It was pre-meditated. She knew what she was doing. It was all planned. I don't care about me, I'm a big boy, I'll lick my wounds for a while and I'll bounce back, but my daughter now has to grow up without a mother because she decided to leave. The fact that she completely emptied her closet—and later that night I found out that she emptied my bank account—she obviously wanted out.

What I don't understand is why she wouldn't tell me. I thought she cared about me, she could have sat me down and explained everything, if not for me, for Arizona.

"Okay, let's see if her phone pings," Nate pulled me from my thoughts, I just nodded as I wrapped my fingers round my hot cup of coffee.

Kaleb was bouncing Arizona softly on his knee, trying to occupy her while Keaton made her bottle. She wasn't in full screaming mode yet, but she would be. As each minute passed, her soft little sobs got that little bit louder.

We last pinged her location outside our house, I was ready to accept we wouldn't find her, but Nate wouldn't give up. And it wasn't until last night when he was sitting in my daughter's room at three a.m. feeding her that I realized that he wasn't doing it for me. He was doing it for her. No child should ever grow up without their mother, my only saving grace from this devastation was that Arizona would never remember her. The first few nights after Sharon left were hard. Arizona wanted the comfort from her mom, she needed to inhale her scent and have snuggles but Sharon didn't want to give it to her. She wanted to run. She wanted to escape this perfect life for some unknown reason. We lived in Long Island, on a beautiful suburban street. We had the white picket fence, the gorgeous yard... everything Sharon wanted, she got.

But now I was alone.

Bringing up a baby with my three best friends. If it wasn't for these guys, I wouldn't have gotten through this week.

But I did.

Because of them.

PRESENT DAY

I hadn't seen Arizona; I missed her this morning. I was still sleeping when she crawled through the door. She works until her hours are up, then she comes home and crashes. I miss spending time with her, but I love watching her chase her dream. She always wanted to be a doctor, I remember when she was a toddler I had to get her a little doctor's coat made and she wore it until it fell apart, and once it did, I bought her a new one.

She was the best damn doctor. My little ray of sunshine. She was the ray of sunshine I needed on my darkest days.

I had been checking my phone all morning, still no word from Xavier. He had three days to tell me what was happening. I hated not knowing, it was driving me insane.

Pulling up his number, I type him out a message.

> **Titus**
> Tick, tock, Xavier. I have a daughter and a life that I need to plan around, the world doesn't stop because you say so.

I hit send and wait to see if he reads it, it instantly turns to two ticks.

> **Xavier**
> Watch who you're talking to Titty. Change of plans, I need you in England.

My eyes widen, "What!?" I roar, my thumbs angrily dancing across the screen.

> **Titus**
> Like fuck, what am I going to do about my kid? Put Amora on the plane, or I'll send a fucking private jet to get her. Just get her here.

Again, he reads it instantly.

> **Xavier**
> Fuck you.

I slam my phone down on the wooden breakfast bar and tug at my hair, this man is insufferable.

Inhaling deeply, I pick my phone back up and type a response.

Titus
No, go fuck yourself.

Sliding my phone back onto the work surface, I open the refrigerator and grab a beer, twisting the cap off the top and taking a huge swig. My phone begins buzzing and dancing across the table. I sigh heavily as I watch his name flash on my screen.

I ignore it.

But he rings again.

And again.

"Fuck, this guy!" I shout to the empty room, slamming the beer bottle on the side, ignoring the fizz that threatened to overspill up the neck.

I click answer and wait for him to speak, but all I can hear is heavy breathing until eventually he speaks.

"Titty."

"Cunty," I smirk, reaching for my beer and bringing it to my lips.

"You want this job, right?" I hear the condescending tone dripping from his tongue.

"Not particularly, but you know, thought it might look good on the old resumé to work with an arrogant asshole who has his head shoved up his ass."

"Lovely," he grunts, "Anyway, Sunday. Does that work for you Titty?"

"No, it doesn't work for me, I have a daughter, what am I supposed to do?"

"Get her a babysitter."

"You're an asshole."

"I know, you've said that twice now."

The annoyance that is his voice is stirring something deep inside of me.

"You're annoying me."

"Thank you," I can hear the slither of a smile in his voice, he finds this amusing.

Silence falls between us.

"So, Sunday."

"No."

"Titty, I need you here for Amora. It's not safe. You have a daughter, so you've repeated throughout our communication today, put yourself in my shoes..."

"I did put myself in your shoes, hence why I accepted this fucking job. But the terms were that she was coming here."

"Yeah, well, things change, so do terms."

"No," I shake my head as if he can see me.

"I'll double the price."

"N..." I stammer, "what!?"

"That's how much I *need* you here. I don't fucking beg Tit, but this is as close as you'll get to hearing me *attempt* to beg."

I swallow, thickness coating my throat as I try and swallow again.

"You'll double it?"

"I will, if you get on the plane on Sunday and come to England. A car will be there waiting for you."

I contemplate his offer for a moment, rubbing my chin softly but the stubble causes a little friction against my skin.

"Fine, Sunday. Send me the details." And before he can respond, I cut the phone off.

"Asshole."

"Who's an asshole?" my ray of sunshine appears, her beautiful face full of pillow creases, as she yawns.

"Xavier, the prick I took a job for," I rub the knot out of my neck that seems to have suddenly appeared.

"Oh, is this the girl that is coming here?"

"*Was* coming here," I grit, my jaw clenched.

She floats over to the refrigerator and grabs a soft drink, unscrewing the cap. She is still wearing her pyjamas, yawning she brings the bottle to her lips.

"They want me to go to England."

She chokes on her drink, her eyes widening.

"England?"

"Yup," I sigh, pulling the bar stool out and slumping down in it, rubbing my temples trying to relieve the ache that is currently radiating there.

"And you're going?"

"Yeah, he is doubling the wage, I can't do that to the boys... be good to give the company a little cash injection."

"It makes sense," she nods, rubbing her lips together.

"I feel like there is a *but* coming."

"But... what about me?" she beams at me.

"Well, I haven't really thought about it... I did think maybe a nanny but..."

She shakes her head from side to side quickly, "No chance, no nanny."

"How about staying with Kaleb and Connie?"

She rolls her eyes at me, stepping over to me as she pulls out a stool and half sits on it.

"They're going to Hawaii with her dad and best friend,

they're your friends and you didn't even remember... you only saw them Sunday!"

"Look, I have a lot of stress," I hold out my hands, "Shit, right." Resting my elbows on the worksurface, I rest my head in my hands. "Wait, Connie and Kaleb are going too!? He didn't mention that."

"Oops, maybe you weren't meant to know," she shrugs apologetically and goes back to the fridge to put her soda away.

"Well, that leaves Nate or Keaton..."

"Really?"

"Really," I nod, I know which one I would prefer but I am hoping she will make the right choice.

"Have you asked them?"

"Just about to," I smirk, sliding my phone across the work surface and dialling Nate first. He answers on the first ring.

"Man," his voice is soft as I hear the tv cut off and Jeff the cat purring in his lap.

"Nate," I smile, tapping my fingers on the work surface.

"Everything okay?" his question is short and to the point, but there is a small slither of hesitancy in it.

"Yeah, just wanted a favor if that's okay..."

"Yeah, yeah, sure, what is it?"

"So, dickhead Xavier is making me go to England."

"Making you?" I hear him chuckle softly, "You're a big boy Titus, I'm sure you can tell him no."

"He is paying us double for me to go to the UK."

"Go; fucking get on the plane now and go."

"Exactly," I smirk, and my eyes move to Arizona who is eavesdropping, rotating her hand in front of me wanting me to get to the point.

"Could you have Arizona while I'm over there? Or you

stay here? I just don't really want to leave her on her own... she is only twenty-one." I was being over the top. I know I was... but still.

"I was assuming I was coming with you..." his tone was clipped, and I hear him moving around over the phone, the static growing before dropping out into silence once more.

"Oh, erm..."

"We need to know where these guys are moving from, where they're working and things... you can't do that without me and I'm sorry... the fact that Xavier has even had to call us shows that he has no one with my brains and skills to do it."

I open my mouth before quickly closing it again.

"You make a solid point," I see Arizona's eyes widen before she lets her head fall back.

"Suppose I better call Keaton then...." I sigh, giving Ari an apologetic look and she rolls her eyes but when her eyes land on mine, a smile is pulling at her lips showing her cute dimples and the divot in her chin appearing.

"Yeah... also, ask him if he can have Jeff."

"He is scared of cats..."

"Yeah, but Ari isn't, are you Ari?"

"She can't hear you..."

"Then put me on speaker dumbass." I huff, blowing out my cheeks as I pop my phone on speaker. "Ari, hon."

"Yes, Uncle Nate," she says sweetly and I smile.

"Will you look after Jeff at Uncle Keaton's for me?"

"Of course, well, if Keaton will have me."

"I'm sure he will."

"Then yes, I'll have Jeff."

"Thank you, angel."

I take him off speaker, "Right, let me call Keaton and see if he can watch Ari and Jeff."

"Make sure you mention Jeff, Titus, don't skim over that *minor* detail otherwise I'm going to get it in the neck when I turn up with him."

"I will mention it," I reassure him while shaking my head from side to side.

"Bye man," I cut the phone off and hover over Keaton's contact.

"Are you sure?" my eyes find hers.

"Yes, I won't be there much anyway."

"Okay," I inhale deeply and press the button. I love Keaton, but he is not someone you would want to look after your daughter. And yes, she's older I get that but she's still my baby. I am a little over protective.

"Well, hello Titus you grumpy fucker, what do I owe the pleasure?"

"Keaton, my favorite," I wink at Ari which makes her laugh as I press him onto speaker.

"What do you want?" his tone is annoyed already.

"I need a favor."

"If it's a hooker, I don't fuck them anymore, can't help you."

My eyes widen in fucking shock and Ari bursts into laughter.

"You stupid prick," I growl, my jaw clenched.

"Jokinggggg," he drags out the word, "What do you want?"

"I need you to have Arizona for a few weeks; you can either stay here or she can come to yours. You'll just need to make sure you're around if she is ever on call at the hospital and can't get a cab."

"Yeah, sure, no problem," I hear him groan a little and my ears prick at the sound.

"I'm warning you though, no lady friends in the house

44

while she is home, do you understand?"

"Scout's honor."

"I mean it Keaton, I'm being serious."

"And so am I."

"Okay, she has work on Sunday night, so she won't be home until Monday around six-ish, I'll grab a key from you at work for her, don't want her stranded if you forget."

"I'm not going to forget."

"Dude, you forgot her when you were babysitting her for me. You left her in the house as you got in the car."

"Did I drive off though?" he counter argues.

"No."

"Right."

"But you still left her in the house," I frown, looking at the phone like *what the fuck.*

"I was making sure the car was safe."

I scoff and let out a loud rumble of a laugh.

"Okay, thanks man, I really appreciate it."

"Sorry, you've not told me why?" Keaton snaps as I hear the sound of glasses clinking.

"I've got to go to England for Amora."

"How long for?"

"Hoping a few weeks."

"Why are you going there now?"

"Cause Xavier is a cunt," I shrug and I see the horrified look on Ari's face, "Cover your ears sweet pea, sorry," I say with a grimace and wince.

"Standard. Okay, but yes, I will watch your *little ray of sunshine,*" he teases her nickname on his tongue and it instantly gets my back up.

"Bye," I cut the phone off and smile up at Ari. "So, you're going to Uncle Keaton's,"

She nods then steps towards me.

"Dad…"

"Yes Sunshine."

"You didn't tell him about Jeff."

"Don't you worry about Jeff," I wink and pull her in for a hug. "Daddy will sort Jeff out."

CHAPTER SEVEN
AMORA

Sitting in the glass conservatory I stare at my blank canvas that sits on my easel. My father used to paint all the time when he was younger, but after his brother died... well, faked his death, he stopped. Grief became too overwhelming, but I seem to have been given his artistic streak.

Mixing up my pastel paints, I place my palette down on the windowsill for a moment whilst I pin my hair back with a clip. I hear footsteps behind me, and I instantly know it's my father.

"Hey baby girl," his hands wrap round my shoulders, his lips pressing to the top of my head. "What you going to paint?" he asks, looking at the blank canvas.

"I'm not sure yet," I admit, and I feel the reassuring squeeze on my shoulders.

"Don't force it, it'll come to you," he places another kiss on the top of my head and turns to walk out the room, but before he does, he stalls. "Oh, Titus is coming Sunday."

"Sunday?" I repeat, that's two days from now.

"Yup," his voice is flat.

"Okay, might as well enjoy my last two days of freedom then."

"Freedom," he scoffs, "Darling, you're not being kept prisoner."

"Sort of feels that way."

"Well, it's not *that* way," he gives me a stern nod then walks out of the room. Suddenly, I feel like I have lost the creative spark that was burning deep inside my belly and now nerves replace anything I did once feel.

Sighing, I stand from my easel and grab my palette. Floating towards the kitchen sink, I wash the paints off and watch as they melt away down the sink.

"Washing the paint off already?" my mother's voice pulls me from my empty thoughts, and I turn to look at her smiling.

"Changed my mind," I sort of shrug my shoulders up as I place the palette onto the draining board and let it dry.

"That's a shame, you haven't painted in so long, I was looking forward to seeing what you created."

"Maybe tomorrow," I give her a gentle nod, "I'm going to retire to my room."

"Is everything okay?" she asks.

But I can't even bring myself to mutter out the words, so I just give her a little *mmhm* before scarpering away and up to my room.

Pulling my floral sunflower dress from my body, I drop it to the floor as I walk into the bathroom. Turning on the tap, I let the hot water run and fill the tub. Tipping some salts into the bath, I watch as they dissolve into the water and all I can think about is sinking my body into the hot water and it washing away all the unwanted tension that I feel is slowly building inside of me.

Once the bath is filled, I pull my underwear from me

and discard of it in the laundry basket. Letting my hair fall from its clip, it curls around my face, framing it. Dipping my toes into the water, goosebumps erupt as the hot water burns over my skin, warming my blood and making my body temperature spike, but I welcome it.

Slipping under the water, I finally feel myself relax a little, the salt instantly calming me.

I am nervous about what my life will be like when Titus gets here, but I need to remember it's for my safety. Hopefully a few weeks and I'll be able to get some sort of normal in my life. I had to quit my studies of Art when this situation kicked off. I work for my uncle Carter in the city and I love it. But it's not what I want to do. I would love to be an artist, creating masterpieces from deep inside my heart and selling them to be hung in people's homes and even maybe a museum one day. But I know that this is just a blip in my life that will soon be over with. The bath quickly gets cold and as much as I want to stay here and shrivel into a prune, I know I need to get out. I feel like I am just existing, I'm not living. Not at the moment. Not until all of this shit with my father is over. He will not rest until he knows that I am safe. And for me to be safe, I need Titus here to watch over me.

I need my father to agree that Titus does not need to show up like a knight in shining armour, I do not need him to ride in on a white horse and save me. I do not need saving. I just need protecting. Just until whatever shit my father has got himself into is sorted.

Walking into the room I smile when I see a single white rose laid on the bed with a note.

I promise this will all be over soon, just take each day as it comes.
I love you, always.
Dad x

I smile and pick up the rose, bringing the soft petals to my lips. How can one of the most vicious men become so soft.

Placing the rose in the small vase that sits on my windowsill overlooking the orchard, I let out a blissful sigh. Pulling my pyjamas from the drawers, I drop the towel and slip into a short and cami set. I tug the stool from the dressing table and plop myself down when I hear my bedroom door go. I see my mother walking towards me in the reflection of the large, ornate mirror that sits on top of my dressing table.

"Hey my sweet girl," she smiles softly as she approaches, picking my father's note up off the bed and scoffs. "Your father did always love a note..." she stalls for a moment, "well, most of the time."

She places the note down on the bedspread and continues walking over to me. She reaches round me and grabs my golden hairbrush.

"May I?" and I nod, love swarming in my chest as my heart thumps against my chest.

Lifting the bristles to my hair, she starts at my crown and slowly brushes my long, fiery red hair.

"You remind me so much of myself at your age," she hums brushing through my knots.

"You were my age when you came to live with Dad wasn't you?"

"I wouldn't say *lived*," she lets out the smallest laugh

but then I see sadness glimpse over her face for just a moment before she is smiling wide again.

"Did you love dad when you first met him?" I ask, prying.

"There was something about him, I felt intimidated by him but also drawn to him. It didn't matter how much I didn't want to be near him, I couldn't help it. He was my *perfectly, imperfect.*"

My heart skips a beat at how her eyes light up as she speaks about my father. "Don't get me wrong, your father was no prince charming, he was a very vicious man, but something in him changed and he became a lot softer."

She half shrugs up, her smile a little sad. "But I loved him fiercely; I still do. I had no purpose in my life until your father. When I was sold to him," she pauses for a moment as she grabs a loose hair band and wraps it round her wrist. "He used to threaten me and tell me that I *had* to abdicate the throne, but in the end, the throne wasn't important to me. I didn't want him to be by my side all the time, to never be known as any more than a Prince because your father deserved so much more than that, but I couldn't give it to him if I was a Queen. He would always fall second best, and he was never meant to be second best."

"So, you abdicated for him."

She nods, smiling fondly.

"I would have given up the whole world for him if it meant I could love him."

"Really? You wanted to give up your whole life for him?"

"Darling, when you meet your soulmate, you would give up everything. I mean that, honestly, you would give up your last breath if it meant you could save them," she chokes on a sob, and I hadn't realised she has a tear running down her cheek.

"Mum are you okay?" concern roots through me and I turn to see her quietly sobbing.

"I am okay, just a lot of memories come flooding back, I am just so overwhelmed."

"Oh mum," I stand and wrap my arms around her holding tight, her arms enveloping me. She breaks away from me and ushers me to sit back down again. I sit, mum picking the brush back up again as she continues brushing my hair.

"Your father let me go, when I was kept prisoner," she pauses for a moment, her tongue licking across her top lip. I take a moment to study her, the soft wrinkles that are beginning to appear at the side of her eyes, the lines that run from her nose to the corner of her lips are a little deeper than before. I hate that her and my father are ageing, but it's part of the process of this shitty thing called life.

"I hate using the word prisoner, but at first, I was his prisoner. But things changed between us, we grew closer and I fell deeply and madly in love with him. He told me to go home, told me to leave and go and see my parents again and when I did, my father told me he was dying. I couldn't focus on anything but my father. I had to be ready to take my crown, to take my place in the royal line, but my father didn't want that life for me. He begged me with his dying wish that I lived my life in freedom. Once he passed, I knew I needed to go back to your father. He was my freedom, my home." She pauses as she places the brush down, bristle side up then begins French plaiting my hair.

"I came home, but couldn't find him anywhere. I still remember I was wearing my royal colours; I had a ball gown on and I flew home to him but he was nowhere to be seen. When I used to roam this house in secret, I found a little room hidden behind the book cases in his library, I saw that the door was open slightly and I just knew that your father was going to be down there. I moved slowly and found him on his knees, arms bound behind his back as his old right hand man Alan had a gun pointed at his head. I honestly felt like time froze, I forgot how to breathe but I managed to move my anchored legs and stand in front of him. I was ready to sacrifice myself for him, because that's how ferociously I loved him. But in a twist of fate, it was me that took the bullet. I thought that was it, I remember feeling so scared that he would have been shot as well, but as I went down I fired my own gun," she stalls, my eyes are wide, my mouth agape as shock ripples through me.

"You shot Alan!?" I gasped, covering my mouth.

"I did, but all to protect your father and I swear I have never shot another gun in my life..."

"You're a badass!" I gloat, my eyes wide and full of admiration for my mum.

She lets out a soft laugh as she ties the bottom of my hair, finishing it off.

"I have fallen slightly off topic, but what I am trying to say is, sometimes the most imperfect man for you turns out to be just your kind of perfect. Fall in love with someone that you would happily sacrifice yourself just to save them."

I roll my lips, nodding.

"Mum," I turn in my seat and I watch as she takes her own seat on the edge of the bed.

"Yeah?"

"We will be alright, won't we? Dad won't let anything bad happen, will he?"

And she looks through me for a moment, a ghost of a smile creeping onto her lips.

"Your father will *never* let anything bad happen;

remember... fall in love with someone that would happily sacrifice themself to save you."

I nod, palming a stray tear away when I hear my bedroom door creek open.

"Why are both my girls crying?" My father swoops in, scooping me and my mother up in one big embrace, holding onto us tight. "No tears, there is no reason for any tears," his lips press against the top of my head, then they move to my mother's. "I will fix this, I always fix everything." His voice wobbles slightly and it makes my chest ache heavily.

I just hope we all walk out of this.

"Where are the boys?" whispering, I hadn't seen Xander and Ezekiel since Monday night.

"Getting ready," is all my father says and I roll my lips, swallowing the burning bile that is crawling up my throat.

I feel like my brothers are getting armoured up for war, then it dawns on me.

That's exactly what they're doing.

They're getting ready for war.

CHAPTER EIGHT
TITUS

LUGGING MY SUITCASE OUT OF THE ATTIC, I THROW IT ONTO MY bed and place my hands on my hips. I have no idea what to pack, I have no idea what the weather is like in England. Here, spring is warm but not sticky hot like the summer here.

I tried searching for it on the internet, but each area of England has different weather.

Slipping my phone out of my suit pocket I open up messages and click on Xavier's name.

> **Titus**
> Hey, dipshit. I am packing my suitcase, what's the weather like?

It stays on read for a while which instantly annoys me. I sigh, slipping my sleeve up and seeing the time. It's ten a.m. here, so Xavier should be up and getting on with his day. I had so much to do before I left on Sunday, I had two days to get my work tied up, get Arizona settled at Keaton's along with Jeff and pack my bags. Oh, and I needed my hair cut.

My phone beeps and vibrates, and I see his response.

Xavier
It's raining cats and dogs : -)

And I swear I have never wanted to strangle and choke a man as much as Xavier. He makes my blood boil, no, he makes it boil *past* boiling point.

Huffing, I reach into my closet and grab jackets, jeans, shirts and suit pants. Throwing them into the open suitcase, I tug open the dresser drawer and throw handfuls of t-shirts and long-sleeved jersey tops. I'll have to get my shirts dry cleaned once over in England.

The closer the trip was getting, the more anxious I was getting about leaving. I didn't want to leave Arizona; I had never left her before. The thought weighs heavy in my chest and I find my hand rubbing over my heart to try and alleviate some of the ache.

Storming back to the closet, I crouch down and grab my shoes. Sneakers, boots and wingtips. That's it, I'm not taking loads with me. I'll do laundry and use what I have, worst comes to worst I'll have to go shopping.

"You okay dad?" I hear Arizona's soft voice float through the room and any stress or pent-up frustration I was feeling was now slowly leaving my body. She was my calm.

"Yeah, I think I've overpacked," I place my hands on my hips and turn to face her, "What do you think?" I smirk, watching as she looks around me and to my overflowing suitcase.

"Maybe a little," she holds her hand up, holding her thumb and index finger apart causing a small gap.

"I just have no idea what to expect," I admit, looking back at my suitcase and sigh.

"Want me to have a look? Maybe I can help?"

I give her a soft nod, not that I really need her help, but it's nice for her to offer and want to help so I let her do it. Makes her feel a little more important too.

She is too grown up, she always was. She mothered me from the moment she could, which was amazing really seeing as she didn't have a mother figure to look up to, it's just been me and her since. It took a lot for me to move from Long Island, but I knew we needed the fresh start, plus I wanted to be closer to the guys. We shared childcare between us with work, it made it a little easier that we owned our own business so we could take her in if really needed. It was hard, but we made it work. We got into a flow, a rhythm, a routine.

One day I spoke to a realtor, told them I wanted to live on the upper west side, central park side and she told me a wonderful ground floor apartment had just come on the market. Walking round it instantly felt like home. The high ceilings, the large sash windows, the backyard for Arizona. It had everything I wanted. I put an offer in only to be told that the upstairs apartment was on the market. Of course, I had to go and look and it just felt like both of the apartments would be the perfect home for the both of us. I got the architects in who said that the two apartments used to be a town house and the attic area was actually the third floor. I had no need for all of that space, so we went ahead and renovated it back to it's original build, minus the third floor.

We had stone-colored tiles throughout the hallway and into the kitchen, carpet in the living room and dining room and my office had a dark, oak wooden floor. The upstairs had bathrooms to each of the three bedrooms and one large master bathroom. I carpeted all the upstairs, I wanted to make it more homely upstairs for Arizona as she was growing up. The carpets were grey upstairs with white walls, very minimalistic but I changed my mind a lot when I came to décor, as did Arizona so we decided that we would keep most of the rooms similar.

We were happy here, it was our home and I never envisioned us leaving. I came to terms a long time ago after Sharon left that it would just be me and Arizona until she met the love of her life and left me. I never wanted to her to leave me, but I would never be bitter or push her away just because she wants to love someone other than me.

She asked once, when she was sixteen where her mom was and sure, I could have lied, but I didn't. I sat her down and explained the story, I didn't leave a single detail out. I never wanted her to think I lied to her. And if, by some miracle, Sharon decided to come back one day, Arizona would already know my side of the story, leaving Sharon to tell hers.

But honestly, I don't think she will ever come back. It's been twenty-one years and she has never shown up. No messages, no birthday cards, no Christmas cards. Nothing. She cut Arizona out of her life the second she decided to walk out that door.

But we got on with it.

Of course, we did.

I gave her enough love from just me, she will never go unloved. Ever. She is the love of my life; she will always be the love of my life.

I see her clicking her fingers in front of me, trying to gain my attention.

"Right," she huffs, putting her hands on her hips, "I think that's a little more organized, what do you think?" she asks as I look over at the suitcase that lay open on the bed. All my pants and jeans are folded into small little parcel rolls and piled next to each other. My tees and jerseys are neatly folded into little squares and placed in two tidy piles. My shirts are hanging along with my suit jackets.

"We can lay them on top in the morning, no point trying to squeeze them in now, but yeah, I think you're packed," she says with accomplishment strong in her voice.

"And are you packed?" I ask, wrapping my arm round her shoulders and dragging her into my hold.

"Ha!" she scoffs, her body shaking softly as she chuckles, "Not yet, I'll do it Sunday morning."

"Ari!" I bellow, "How can you be so organized with everything else but not yourself?" I ask and she shrugs her shoulders up. "No idea, but it works," she nudges into me before pressing on her toes and placing a kiss on my cheek.

"Now, go to work," she gives me a firm nod before she glides out of the room.

"Ugh, work," I drag my hand across my face and groan. "I need a vacation," I say to the empty room.

Grabbing my suit jacket that I folded over the back of the armchair in my bedroom, I pull it on. We had a meeting today with two new investors, one of them being Killian. I don't agree with mixing work and family, but who am I to say?

Grabbing my phone, I make my way downstairs and grab the cup of coffee Arizona had made me in a travel cup.

"Thank you, Sunshine," I smile, stepping towards her and placing a kiss on her forehead.

"Dad, the kisses need to stop," she swats me away.

"Never, you're my baby girl. I get to kiss you all the time," and I see her dimples appear as I walk out into the hallway, grabbing my car keys off the side. "I'll see you tonight, make sure you pack!" I call out and she shouts back.

"Yeah, yeah, see you tonight."

A laugh bubbles out of me as I open the front door and close it gently behind me. The wind is soft as it blows the cherry blossom petals off the trees that line the sidewalks. I love the cherry blossom trees, but they bloom for such a small amount of time before the confetti falls around us and leaving the branches stripped bare. Stepping down the steps that lead to my front door, I open the black iron gate and step onto the sidewalk. Unlocking my *Jeep*, I climb in. I could walk, but honestly, I can't be bothered. I'll just work extra hard in the gym tonight, burn of some extra calories. The drive is short, and I am grateful there isn't any traffic. This is my last workday in the office now until I am back in a few weeks. I say a few weeks but I have no idea how long I'll be there for, I am just hoping it's only a few weeks. I am not up for staying long term. My job is to keep her safe, just until Xavier has taken out the Knight brothers. The problem is, how long will it take him to do it. But from what I've heard on Xavier *'the fixer'* Archibald is that he is quick, precise, and clean as fuck. He leaves no trace so what baffles me is that he managed to fuck this up somehow and is now dealing with the repercussions of it all. Honestly, I've always had a feeling in my gut if something was off, and ninety-nine-point nine percent of the time, I am right.

And right now, with this situation, something in my gut feels off. I just don't know what.

Stepping up to the main door of the office, I press my key fob against the pad and push through the door. Waiting for the elevator, for some reason nerves ripple through me and it unsettles me. I wouldn't say I am nervous about going over to England, but I am apprehensive and a little unsettled about the whole thing. Leaving my life here in America, leaving my baby with Keaton. I have no doubt she will be okay; Ari can hold her own. But Keaton sometimes forgets where the line is, and when the line comes to my daughter, he needs to stay the fuck away.

The doors ping open, and I am greeted by Keaton, Kaleb, Nate and Killian. He seems to have just slotted right in, and as much as we were all a little apprehensive about it at first, it was like he was never not part of our entourage.

"Morning," my low, gruff voice floats over the room as I step closer to where they all are. Nate is hidden behind his three screens, his head popping up occasionally before ducking back down again. Keaton is sitting back in my chair, his feet up on my desk as he sits as if on a sun lounger. Killian and Kaleb are standing behind him, in light chatter amongst themselves. I have no idea how Killian can be so calm around Kaleb, but I suppose he saved Kaleb's life, and in doing so, Kaleb saved Connie right back.

"Morning," Nate's voice glides across the room and I see Kaleb pat Killian on the back before he steps closer to me.

"Why are you here today? You should be at home making the most of being a free man before Xavier gets his claws into you," Kaleb smirks, bringing me in for a hug.

"Couldn't leave without seeing you all now, could I?"

Kaleb and Keaton laugh, Killian gives a soft nod. And Nate? Well, he does nothing. I scoff.

"I have a few loose ends to tie up before I head off, but thinking we could all go for lunch, everyone free for that?"

"Yup," they all chorus in unison.

"Good," I stride towards Keaton and push his feet off my desk. "Now fuck off and go back into your own office," I growl but a wide smile is pressed against my lips. Keaton rolls his eyes so far in the back of his head as he slowly and sluggishly moves off my seat.

"This is why I didn't want an office; you two fuckers

wanted a big office, but yet me and Nate always find you hovering at our desks."

"Well, when you leave later, your desk is mine." Keaton snipes as he pulls the sleeves of his suit jacket down.

"Mmhmm," I hum as I take a seat in my chair, "Whatever you say sweetheart."

———————

THE MORNING WHIZZED PAST, I MANAGED TO GET STUCK IN AND DO everything I wanted. A stab of emotion radiates through my chest at walking out of the office for the last time for a while. I know it won't be forever, but I also didn't know when I was coming back. I was hoping it was a quick job. Get in, get the job done, get out.

We strolled through the bar of the small café lost in light chatter, the noise level increased as the busy café was brimming in friends, partners, colleagues all talking amongst each other. The ambient music crooned through the speakers making the guests talk at a lower level. The smell of aromatic coffee beans filled my nostrils, my thirst growing.

The young waitress walked towards us, tablet in hand as a large smile graced her face, her opal eyes bouncing between the five of us.

"Food and drinks?" her voice is high as she asked her question, I watch her for a moment as the blush creeps onto her cheeks a little more before she breaks eye contact and lets them fall to her tablet as her fingers tap away.

"Please," I say, clearing my throat as I do.

"No problem, follow me." her eyes slice to mine once more and I smirk. She turns quickly and I let my eyes roam over her body. She's curvy, her tight skinny jeans cling to her ass and toned thighs and I feel my cock stir in my pants. Did I really want another one-night stand? I felt disgusting this morning.

I feel a nudge in the back, looking over my shoulder I see Keaton shaking his head from side to side. "I've already got my eyes on her," he says quietly so only I can hear him, and I scoff a laugh.

"She didn't look at you once bro, I really don't think I have anything to worry about in that respect," I unbutton my suit jacket, sitting down with my ever-growing smirk beaming. I'm not going to pursue it; I just want Keaton to think I am. I like to torment that fucker.

She hands me a menu which I take, and I feel her linger a little longer. I feel Keaton's burning gaze on me and I take this opportunity to go ahead and fuck with him.

"I was wondering," I swallow as my eyes scan over the menu, and I can hear the soft chuckles of Killian and Kaleb. I let my eyes lift from the menu and I focus on Killian and Kaleb and watch their lips twitch in amusement. "What time you get off?" my eyes roam from my friends and I connect with her heated gaze.

"Four."

"Well, that sounds perfect. I'll pick you up?"

"Can't wait," her smile widening before she looks down at her tablet and I turn to look at a sour faced Keaton, I wink before rolling off my order.

"I can't wait for you to fuck off," Keaton scowls, lifting his glass to his lips as he takes a mouthful of his water.

"No one likes a sore loser, Keat," I smirk as I place my knife and fork on my empty plate.

"To be honest," Nate pipes up, pushing his plate away and linking his fingers together, "I don't think you would have stood a chance with her anyway Keaton," he shrugs his shoulders up as he reaches for his coffee, and I hear Kaleb roar with laughter.

"Gee, thanks," Keaton rolls his eyes, shaking his head from side to side, "What about you two dickheads? What did you think?" He asks, you can hear the irritation in his voice as his eyes bounce between Kaleb and Killian.

I watch as Killian looks at Kaleb and gives him a shrug when Kaleb leans forward.

"Yeah, sure. You stood more of a chance with her than Titus did," and Keaton's face lights up as he slowly turns his face to look at me to flip me off when my eyes slice past Keaton's to eye Kaleb who is shaking his head and mouthing "It was all you," to me which causes me to chuckle.

"WELL, I GUESS THIS IS GOODBYE THEN," I SAY WITH A DEEP, heavy sigh as my eyes move between my group of friends.

Kaleb shakes his head from side to side. "No man, it isn't a goodbye, it's a see you soon then," he gives a soft nod before stepping forward and pulling me in for a hug and it feels foreign for Kaleb. It's normally me pulling him in for a hug, not the other way round.

One by one the guys say bye, Killian gives me a firm handshake, Keaton gives me a firm pat on the back which causes me to cough, and Nate offers to walk with me. I lift the sleeve of my shirt and see it's two p.m.

"Keep me posted on anything new here; Kaleb, look after Connie. I know Killian will be keeping an eye on you anyway." I smirk, "Keaton, I'll see you a bit later when I drop Arizona and Jeff off."

"Jeff," Keaton's eyes widen when I feel Nate's hand swat me. "Who the fuck is Jeff?"

"My cat," Nate mutters as he pushes his glasses up his nose and I swear I see him stand a little taller. "But I don't need you to have him anymore," he says breezy when I feel his eyes on mine. "I've decided to stay, I've got some bits to sort out here... is that okay? Are you going to be okay?"

I laugh, "It's fine, I'm a big boy... I'm sure I can survive the big, bad, *old* wolf."

"Do you want me to have Arizona at mine?"

"No, she can stay with me. It's already sorted." Keaton snaps, his tone cold before he turns away from me. "I'll see you a bit later, enjoy your..." he coughs, letting his eyes fall, "evening." And with that he sulks off into the busy sidewalk.

"Think I've pissed him off?"

"A little bit," Kaleb laughs then swoops in for another hug.

"I think you're going to miss me." I smile as I hold onto him a little longer, and the truth was I was going to miss Kaleb the most. Yeah, we weren't blood related, but he was the brother I never had. It was only me until I found him, then he introduced me to the other two. But Kaleb was my best friend. I was his voice of reason; he was my conscious. I calmed him down in ways no one else could and I just hoped that he wouldn't *need* me while I was gone.

Ignoring the small ripple of anxiety that waved through me, I pulled away, giving him a soft slap on the cheek.

"I'll see you soon then."

"See you soon then," Kaleb smiles and Killian holds his hand up, giving me a small wave before they both turn and follow a sulking Keaton.

I inhale deeply, spinning on my heel as I face Nate. "I

want to get my hair cut; you want to walk with me? Or were you lying about wanting to walk with me?"

"Nah, I'll come with. Keaton was getting under my skin, and I didn't want to snap," he admits, running his hand round the back of his messy dirty blonde hair.

"Is something going on?" I ask as we begin to walk side by side.

"Not particularly, just someone from my past has popped up and I am trying to work out why I am feeling the way I am."

He doesn't look at me, just keeps his eyes forward.

"An ex?" I ask and I try and think back if I ever remember Nate having a long-term girlfriend. There have been flings and a couple of one-night stands, but never anyone serious.

"Something like that," he mumbles, and I know that is his way of letting me know that this conversation is over. "What time is your flight?" He asks as we beat the pavement.

"Early tomorrow morning, but I am leaving for the hotel later on tonight."

"I see," he hums. "Are you going to pick that girl up?" he stops, turning to face me.

"I don't think so, why? Do you think I should?"

He shrugs his shoulders up softly, "I just wondered, wasn't sure if you did it just to annoy Keaton."

I chuckle before I pick up my feet and begin walking again, Nate by my side.

"I did do it to piss Keaton off..." I sigh, "but then again I don't know... maybe I need to have some fun before I leave."

"I'm sure you'll be able to get some sort of..." He stops, rolling his lips as he thinks his next words carefully, "release while you're over there."

"Hmm, I'm not so sure about that. I honestly don't think Xavier will let me out of his sights. I'm there to keep watch on Amora, like twenty-four-seven... I'll probably have to piss myself because I won't be allowed a bathroom break," I laugh loudly but from what I have heard about Xavier, it wouldn't be out of the realms for him.

Nate stops outside *Apple* and I take a few steps forward before realizing.

"Need something?"

Nate shuffles awkwardly on his feet, pushing his hand through his hair as he looks over his shoulder.

"Just need to go and sort some bits out," he nods firmly, giving me a small smile.

"Okay man," I smile back when Nate holds his hand out for me to take. Clasping my hand round his, I give him a firm shake.

"I'll see you soon, then."

I give him a curt nod as I drop my hand from his. I turn and begin to walk away when he calls out my name.

"Yeah?"

"I'll keep an eye on Arizona for you," he nods, and I smile.

"Thank you," I shout back, his arm lifting as he holds his hand up. I inhale deeply and keep walking until I reach the barbers. Time for a new style.

CHAPTER NINE
AMORA

Walking through the gardens, I sigh when I reach the boat lake. The still water covering me in a blanket of calmness. The spring air still has a bite to it, but the wind feels warm on my skin as it dances through my hair. I close my eyes and let my head tip back as I lose myself for just a moment. My last day of freedom because my father got caught up in something he shouldn't have.

He told us he retired.

Told us that he was done in that world until *that* world caught up with him.

One. Last. Time.

He messed with the wrong family. I have no idea how it happened, but it did. And now I have to pay the consequences.

Lowering myself down, I sit on the edge of the decked, wooden pier and let my legs hang over the edge, my toes dipping into the cool water.

I feel myself relax when I hear the leaves rustling in the wind, the birds soft chirps singing as the warm sun beats down on my pale and pasty skin. If it was any warmer, I would burn. Me and my pale skin do not fare well in the summer.

Soft footsteps approach and I furrow my brow. I know they're not my father's. He has never been quiet and cautious in his life.

I don't open my eyes, not wanting this moment ruined.

"Hey baby," my mother's soft voice brushes over my skin and my lips turn at the corner slightly into a smile. Still, my eyes stay closed.

"Hey," and I can't stop the heavy breath that leaves me.

"That's a big sigh," she says softly as she sits down next to me, her hand on my thigh as she gives a gently squeeze through my jeans.

"I miss life when it was just..."

"Simple?" I feel my mother's shoulder knock into mine and I laugh softly.

"Yeah," I whisper, letting my head fall forward, my eyes locked on my hands that are placed in my lap.

"Life is never simple when it comes to your father," she smirks, letting her own feet slip into the cool water.

"I suppose it keeps this mundane life a little more exciting, right?"

"Exactly," she sighs, but it's not an unhappy sigh, it's a blissfully happy one. "Your father means well, I know you're annoyed about having some stranger here watching you but we're doing it all for the right reasons."

I hum in agreement.

"Don't be like that," and I can hear the hurt in my mother's tone.

"I'm not being like anything," I slowly turn to face her, the fine wrinkles round her eyes crease slightly, her ice blue eyes still full of glimmer and hope, I hate the fact that her and father are getting older. "But seems a little extreme... I don't understand why I need to be looked after in my own home," I shake my head from side to side.

"Well..." I see my mother's eyes flit from mine and across the lake and I know from her tone that I've been kept in the dark about something.

"Well?" I stammer over my words as my heart thrums in my chest.

"We just want you safe..." her eyes finally meet mine as I hang on every word that leaves her lips.

"I know," I whisper and for some reason I don't know why the rage is burning deep in my belly. I came out here to find my calm, but all I seem to be feeling is anger bubbling the longer I am sat here. Tears sting in my eyes but I refuse to cry.

"Titus will be here tomorrow morning, is there anything you would like to do..." I cut my mother off as I slice my eyes across to hers.

"You mean before you take my freedom?" my tone is harsh as I snap at her, and whether I meant to or not, it's too late. The spitefulness has already spilled out of me.

"Amora..." my mum reaches for my hand but I'm already up and walking away.

"Save it," I shout, my temper reaching boiling point.

I may look like my mother more than my father, apart from my eyes, but my temper is all Xavier.

My phone vibrates in my back pocket, and I see Arabella's name. The corner of my mouth lifts, reaching for it I look over my shoulder and see my mother's eyes pinned to me and I don't care that my chest aches. I can see the sadness in her eyes but the rage is too much.

"Hey," my tone is soft when I speak to my best friend.

"You okay?"

"Oh, I don't know, I've been better," I roll my eyes as I stomp back towards the house.

"It'll be okay, Daddy Xavi will fix it all."

"If he didn't fuck up in the first place, I wouldn't be in this position... of course golden boys, Xander and Ezekiel get to stay at home because..."

"Because they're not a threat. You are."

"So, you're saying because I am a girl, I'm a threat."

"It sucks, but..." she sighs, "yeah."

"Well, I'm not going to play ball, they want to get me a babysitter then I'll be a brat,"

I hear Arabella laugh. "He is going to wish he never took the job."

"Too right."

"I was going to ask you over, but honestly, my mood is awful, and I wouldn't want to put you through that," I smirk into the phone and my steps falter as I get to the steps of the back door.

"It's okay, we will have a night out once this is all over."

"That sounds amazing, give me something to look forward to."

"It's a date," she chimes, and I smile wide. "Call me tomorrow or something, you can let me know how hot your bodyguard is," and before I can respond, the phone goes dead.

I scoff, shaking my head softly before inhaling deeply and stalking into the house, my mood slowly creeping back into my sombre one.

I lay on my bed, earphones pushed in as music plays but I'm not listening. I am too lost in my own thoughts at how the next few weeks are going to go. I have no idea what my father has planned with Titus, all I know is he will be my personal bodyguard. No going out, no one coming into the house... The Knight Brothers know my father's whereabouts and what I don't understand is they would have already started the war if they wanted to so why now? Why is this suddenly a big deal. My father would never tell me the truth, he would keep me in the dark until the very last minute if he needed to. I know he means well and all he wants to do is protect me, but he isn't going to be here forever. What if the big bad men come after me again and he isn't here? What then?

Groaning, I roll onto my back and let my eyes pin to the ceiling.

The way my mother stammered over her words back at the lake has my mind reeling and I feel like something else is coming.

I don't hear the knock on the door, I am too far away in my head when I see it push open and my father with the same eyes as mine seek me out.

Lifting my head for a moment, I let it drop back down again as I pull the earphone from my ear and rest up on my elbows.

"Amora, darling," my father's voice is low and gruff as he sits on the edge of the bed.

"Yup," I roll my eyes. He doesn't turn his head to look at me and I watch as his shoulders sag.

"I'm sorry if I've hurt you by doing this," his voice is barely audible as he chokes out his words. "Everything I've done and everything I will continue to do is in the interest of my family. It may not seem fair to you, that you're the one who has to lose so much but it is necessary. The boys are older, they're going to work alongside me to stop these assholes from getting to you, but you, my sweet Amora..." he twists round, his knee bent up on the bed, his eyes pinning to mine, "I need you safe, and I can't personally do that hence why I have hired Titus."

I don't say anything, I ignore the burning in my throat from the lump that has wedged itself there, firmly.

"They owed me a favour, and that favour was guarding you twenty-four-seven until the threat is gone."

"And what if..."

"They'll be gone," my father nods firmly, his eyes hollow. He looks so God damn tired. He's aged, his dirty blonde hair now scattered with grey, his once thick beard looks thinner somehow with flecks of ginger and grey entwined through. His facial lines dig a little deeper showing his age, my once fiery father is slowly withering in front of me. "You're not going to like it—hell, you're going to hate it—but I need you to do this for me. I won't ask a lot from you in my lifetime, but this is one ask I am demanding of you," his voice is low, and I watch as he rolls his lips, his shoulders lifting high and dropping low as he intakes his breath.

"Okay," I whisper, unsure what I am agreeing to but for my father to sit here in front of me like a broken man is enough for me to agree to sign my life away if that's what he needed.

He stands, walking round the edge of the bed until he is standing next to my head and where I am laying, he says no more, my eyes lift to his causing my chin to lift and I watch as he bends, lowering his head down until he presses his lips against my forehead, lingering for a moment.

"I love you, petal,"

"I love you more," I whisper to the room, I hear a low hum before he stands. "Oh, and Dad," I call out and he turns to face me, can you say sorry to mum for me please?" I ignore the prick I feel behind my eyes.

"Darling, your mother understands more than you know..." he trails off for a moment, his eyes on me, "But of course I will." He gives a soft nod and I smile as I watch him walk out of my room. My erratic heart begins to slow, and I steady my trembling breath before gently sitting up and letting my legs hang over the side of the bed. I feel numb, but then again, I have no idea what to feel. I know my father has my best interests at heart, but I am also being kept out of the loop. His little bit of father daughter time just then and my mother stammering over her words earlier makes me wonder whether there is something going on in the background that I am not party to.

Annoyed by my own thoughts, I push up just as my bedroom door opens and I see Xander step towards me, his eyes pinned to mine.

"Hey," his voice is quiet, he takes another stride towards me before he looks over his shoulder sheepishly.

My eyes roam over him and if it wasn't for the age difference, you would think we were twins. We both have our mother's red hair and our father's eyes. One blue, one brown. They thought my eyes would stay blue but they began to change when I was four and now I match with Xander and my father.

"Hey," I mumble back as he stands tall, his hand rubbing the back of his head.

"Look, I just wanted to come and see if you were okay..." he takes another step closer.

"Oh, I am glorious," sarcasm drips from my tone and I walk towards him.

"Sarcasm doesn't suit you," he smirks, his eyes following me as I reach him.

"Well, that's just your opinion," I beam and go to push

past him but he doesn't let me, he wraps his long arm around me and pulls me in for a brotherly embrace.

"We've got you," he whispers into my hair, placing a kiss on the top of my head.

"I know," my brows furrow as I place my hands on his chest and push him away giving him a confused look. "What's going on?" I ask when I see Ezekiel round the corner and step into the room, his eyes moving between me and Xander.

"Hey, do I not get a hug?" he chimes, smirking as he bounds over, enveloping me in his arms. Ezekiel was a spitting image of my dad, just without the beard or his colour eyes. He had mother's ice blue colour.

"You all set?" Ezekiel asks as he looks round the room, his brows pinching.

"For the giant babysitter? Yeah, I think so," I shrug my shoulders up, as I look over my shoulder at my own room.

"He lands tomorrow morning," Xander's tone is sharp, and it doesn't go unnoticed.

"Dad is keeping me in the dark," I swallow thickly, my palms suddenly sweaty, "Is there anything I need to know?"

Ezekiel goes to open his mouth but soon shuts it quickly with Xander throws him dagger stares.

"Just that we will keep you safe, we will go to the ends of the earth to make sure you don't get hurt."

I nod.

"Everything will be okay though; we can get the Knight brothers easier this way and when they least expect it... well..."

"You'll kill them."

"Exactly," Ezekiel nods.

Anxiety swarms through me and I begin to panic.

"Hey, hey," Xander grabs me, pulling me into his chest

and I can hear the steady beat of his heart drumming in his chest. He holds me tightly so even if I wanted to move, I couldn't. "I promise you, this has all been planned out to the very last detail," Xander whispers which makes my skin prickle in goosebumps.

"Okay," I choke on threatening tears.

"We've got you, we promise," he says one last time before holding me tight again, and this time, Ezekiel wraps his arms round the both of us.

CHAPTER TEN

TITUS

STEPPING OUT ONTO THE SIDEWALK, I HEAD FOR HOME. I WAS still not sure if I wanted to meet the girl from the bar or not tonight, but part of me didn't want to stand her up because I wasn't a complete prick. Unlocking the door to my house, I pushed through and called out for Arizona.

"In the kitchen, Dad," she calls back and I smile, glad that I get to see her before she leaves for Keaton's. I would be lying if I said I wasn't apprehensive about leaving her in his hands, *but* I know she will be fine.

I turn the corner and into the kitchen when I hear Arizona's spoon hit the side of her China bowl.

"Oh my god," her eyes widen as she stares at me. "Where has all your hair gone?" I watch as her hand slowly moves to cover her mouth.

"I decided to make it a little lower maintenance."

"Well, it's certainly lower maintenance," she says with a grimace.

"Not a fan?"

"I'm sure it'll grow on me," she scrunches her nose up

before spooning cereal into her mouth. She would eat cereal morning, noon and night if she could.

I rub my hand over my short, soft black hair and smile, "I like it."

"It looks good, don't get me wrong it was just a little shock to the system, but it somehow makes you look younger," she cocks her head to the side and gives me a half smile.

"That's something then," I chuckle softly as I grab a beer from the fridge. Pulling a bar stool out next to her, I sit.

"I've got the option to go on a date tonight before I leave for the hotel," I say, bringing the bottle to my lips and taking a mouthful.

"Right..." I can feel her eyes burning into the side of my head.

"I don't know what to do," I shrug my shoulders up.

"Dad, I love that we're close and all, but I don't think you asking if you should..." she stalls for a moment as if she is choosing her words, "*fulfil* your needs is the kind of bonding I want, you know?"

I laugh, the bottle rim still pressed to my lips.

"Okay, fair play," I place my bottle on the countertop and sigh.

"I mean, a couple of drinks wouldn't hurt before your flight, right?" she finally says, and I turn to look at her, my brows lifting.

"I suppose not," I nod, facing forward once more and lifting my bottle to my lips, nodding my head to myself.

Silence fills the room for a few moments as Arizona finishes spooning her cereal hoops into her mouth then washes her bowl and spoon up.

"Shall we get you settled over at Keaton's? It's just you now... not Jeff," I swallow.

"Oh, okay, Nate not going now?" she spins, her fingers wrapped round the edge of the countertop as her back rests against it.

"Nope, something important has come up by the sounds of it and he needs to get it sorted."

Her lips roll as she gives a couple of soft nods. "I suppose we can go now then?"

"Come on then princess, let's get you dropped and settled at Keat's." I sigh, hating that I have to leave her, but I know she will be fine. Draining the rest of my beer bottle, I drop it in the trash can on my way out of the kitchen and head for her room.

———

LOADING MY JEEP UP, I HAVE NO IDEA WHAT SHE HAS PACKED BUT it's as if she isn't coming home.

"You're coming home, right?" I joke as I throw the last bag in the trunk.

"Of course, but I over packed. I have no idea what Keaton's laundry schedule is like so at least I have more than I need," she shrugs her shoulders up before she opens the passenger door and slips inside. I sigh, closing the trunk and hopping into the driver's side.

"I'm going to miss you, kid."

"And I'm going to miss you, but I think this will be good for us. You aren't the best at letting go..." she smirks, chewing on the inside of her cheek as I pull out onto the road.

"You're my baby, it's my job to always protect you," I say softly.

"I know Dad, and I love you for that, but you do also

have a life and I feel like you're not really *living* it you know?"

"You're my life," I grunt out.

"I'll always be in your life, but you deserve to find a little more... don't you think?"

I say nothing, rubbing my lips into a thin line as I turn the radio on and let my over thinking mind wander. Pulling up outside Keaton's I inhale deeply before cutting the engine.

"Have I upset you?" Arizona asks, turning to face me and my heart hurts. I give her a tight smile.

"No baby, but sometimes, the truth does hurt." I reach over and cup her hand in mine as I rub my thumb across the back of it and she smiles back at me, "You could never upset me, Ari."

Opening the trunk, I unload the car while Keaton stands at his doorway and just watches me as he takes a sip of his coffee.

Lugging it up the stairs to his front door, I scowl at him. "Thanks for the help," I scold, barging past him as Arizona stands just inside the door with her backpack on her shoulder.

"Do you need any help?" Keaton asks in a condescending tone, and it takes everything in me not to punch him in the throat.

"No thanks," I roll my eyes, and stand close to Arizona.

"You all set old man?" Keaton asks, sipping his coffee while keeping his eyes pinned to mine at all times.

"Not really, but a job's a job."

"Let's hope you don't fall for your client like ol' Kaleb did."

My mouth drops agape, my eyes widen as I just stare at him.

"What the fuck goes on in your head?" I question, my brows furrowing as I try and make sense of the stupidity of him.

"Not a lot, but, you know... it's not unheard of now is it," he wiggles his brows before turning and heading towards his kitchen. I hear Arizona give a heavy sigh and I am beginning to contemplate my choice of *babysitter*.

"I can take you to Nate's if you want," my voice is low as we follow Keaton.

"It'll be fine, you know what he is like," she smirks. "Always trying to get a rise out of people." I nod. "And you, *old man* fell right into his trap."

I scoff, shaking my head from side to side as Keaton gets two cups out for coffee.

DRIVING AWAY FROM KEATON'S MY HEART FELT LIKE IT WAS shattering in my chest. I hated that I had left her, and I know I have issues still feeling this way after twenty-one years, but it can't be helped. She is my pride and joy. My whole world revolves around her. It's been me and her, that is all she has known.

I sigh as I look at the time, still in two minds whether or not to pick the girl up or just go home, load the car up and head to the hotel then let a glass of whiskey comfort me.

Pulling up outside my house I decided on the latter, reaching for my phone I found her number and gave her a call explaining that I had to take a rain check. She was cool, and it helped ease my small amount of guilt at blowing her off.

After a quick shower, I dressed in jeans and a tee before dragging a hoodie over my head. I went through my bags another five times to make sure I had everything I needed. I knew that if I *had* forgot something, at least I could go and get bits over in England. Zipping my cases up again, I grab both of them and bump them down the stairs before grabbing my large duffel bag and backpack. I stilled as I opened the front door, the cool evening breeze blowing through, and I exhale slowly. I had no idea how long I was going to be gone for and I already felt slightly homesick.

But I needed to make sure Amora stayed safe. I had to remember why I took this job and let the fire in my belly burn. I was going to make sure I keep her safe.

As much as Arizona is my priority here, as soon as I am on English soil, Amora will be my priority.

I will protect her with all that I have.

I was hired for a reason; I know I'm good at my job, but I feel like for Xavier and Amora I need to be better. I need to be the best I can be.

The drive to the hotel was smooth, I hardly hit any traffic and I got lost in my country music. Not many people knew that it was my favorite. It was always a dream of mine when I was a teen to move out to the country a little more, but it seemed back then that the country life wasn't for me. I still would happily give all of this up to live in Montana in the mountains, or somewhere with an amazing view and live on a ranch with my daughter and maybe, a wife. But it seems my romantic days are over. I can't see me settling down and I am okay with that because I sacrificed all of that for Arizona.

I didn't unpack but made sure my travel clothes for tomorrow and my pyjamas were nestled on top of the duffle bag. I laid on the hotel bed, ankles crossed and back resting against the headboard as I went through the file again that Xavier had sent me. Something doesn't add up. I was told that Amora was taken by the brothers, but she was dumped back on his doorstep the next day with a note that said '*Remember the deal, Xavier. One night will turn into forever if you don't follow through.*'.

But Amora, as far as I am aware is still with Xavier and that's where I am hoping she will stay until I get there.

I have been kept in the dark pretty much since then, all I knew was that I needed to be there. I wanted to ask questions, but I thought it would be better to do it in person and face to face with Xavier when I am there.

I sigh, closing the file and reaching for my whiskey, I bring the rim of the thick glass to my lips and take a mouthful, an appreciative groan escaping me as the warm amber liquor coats my tongue before warming my throat.

Checking my phone, I tap out a quick message to Arizona wishing her goodnight, I wait for a moment or so to see if she replies but my message stays unread. I know her block of shifts rolls round tomorrow so I am hoping she is fast asleep.

Sleep doesn't come easy, but after a few more whiskeys, I soon drift off into a dreamless sleep.

MY ALARM SCREECHES, AND IT TAKES ME A MOMENT OR SO TO realize where I am. I slowly let my eyes scan the room and adjust to the dim sunlight that is peeping through the slatted blinds. Sighing, I throw the comforter back and head for the shower. I need to wake myself up. I feel groggy and I know it's because of the crappy night sleep I had plus the whiskeys that are currently splitting my head in two. Twisting the shower dial, I keep my hand running underneath it until it gets to the temperature I want. Pushing down my shorts, I kick them off and pull my tee over my head before stepping under the scalding water. I lather my skin and apprehension begins brewing deep inside of me. I can't help but feel like I am walking into a trap, but I don't know why. Trying to push the gut wrenching feeling back and deep inside of me, I rinse myself off and step out the shower. I don't hang about; I pull my clothes on and slip on my Hublot watch. I contemplate messaging Arizona but decide against it. I didn't want to interrupt her while she was working. I would text her once I am settled on the plane.

Once I am happy that everything is packed up, I give the room one last scope before slipping out the door and letting it softly close. Checking out, I grab my keys from the valet service and kick it towards the airport.

I had numerous feelings floating around but I was trying to drown all of them out by turning my music up so loud I was sure my ears were going to bleed. Pulling into the park and stay, I check in and hand my keys over.

"Mr. King," the concierge gives me a tight nod as he passes me a clipboard, tagging my keys.

I scan through it and sign at the bottom.

"And it's still okay for my friend to pick my car up in the next couple of days? I have no idea how long I am going to be away for."

"That's fine Mr. King, we will keep your bill running until your friend comes to collect it, Mr. Mills, isn't it?"

"Perfect. Yes, that's it." My voice is low as I hand him back the clipboard and turn on my heel. Swallowing down my nerves, I pace towards the terminal. This was my first time out of the country, my first time leaving my daughter behind and in the care of my friend. I felt ridiculous for being as anxious as I was, but it was understandable right? This was a big deal. She was my baby. Even at twenty-one.

It was all good until I was summoned over to England.

That wasn't the original plan. But Amora fills my mind and my heart sinks. If this was Arizona in this situation, I would do what was right for her, not anyone else. And that's what I needed to keep thinking. What if I was in this awful, shitty situation like Xavier was.

Shaking my head from side to side, the bright lights of the terminal hurt my eyes and I blink a few times to let my eyes adjust to the fluorescence. I stand, just watching the absolute chaos that is playing out in front of me. Dropping my chin, I head for my check in desk and ignore my palpitating heart that is currently dancing around in my hollow chest.

The line is fast moving and after a little while I move forward towards the young woman sitting there with a permanent smile on her face.

"Good morning, sir," she holds her hand out to take my passport, her eyes glance over it before putting it under a little scanner. "Boarding pass?" I hold up my phone and she scans it. "Perfect. Welcome Mr. King, I can see you are sitting in our business class area, you're in seat 4A, and flying into London Heathrow," she is still smiling as she taps her long, fake nails on the keyboard and prints out my tickets. "Pop your cases on for me, I'll tag them," she hits another button on her keyboard and prints a tag out, wrapping it round the suitcase. "Place your other bag on, your backpack is okay to go on the plane with you," she taps the same button and wraps another tag round. "That's all done for you, if you round the corner then head for the business suite, you can sit there until you're called for your flight," she passes me my passport and tickets.

"Thank you," I give her a curt nod and take my items. Following her instructions, it's a short walk-through security like a breeze, I continue forward and see the

ASHLEE ROSE

business lounge. I hand over my ticket to the guy at the door as they inspect it before he waves me through. I feel myself relax slightly knowing that I'm here now, the stressful side of it is done.

I take a seat, placing my backpack on the empty chair next to me as I reach for my phone.

"May I get you anything?" a young girl asks; she looks around Arizona's age. Her eyes are wide with hope and have a glint of pride coursing through them. She is upbeat, her hair perfectly styled and tied in a high ponytail, and she is dressed impeccably. A rarity in the younger generation.

Fuck. That makes me sound old.

"A black americano please," I say softly, my deep voice seems to echo round the large room, I keep my eyes on the menu as I scan it for food. "And I'll take two slices of toast." I hand her the menu.

"Certainly sir, I'll get that sorted for you," her skin reddens over her cheeks, and I clear my throat, looking away quickly.

I open my emails and sigh when I see my once clear inbox now heaving again. Most of them I've been copied in on and aren't for my attention.

My phone vibrates in my hand and I smile when I see Arizona's name pop up as a notification. Ignoring everything I was doing, I click on her message and my heart warms.

Arizona
Safe flight daddy, I miss you already. Come home soon xo.

My heart thumps in my chest, nausea rolls my stomach and I have to swallow down the lump that begins to form.

> **Titus**
> Not as much as I miss you, I'll be home as
> soon as the job is done. Love you X

Closing the messages, I reach for my laptop and pop my earphones in. I decide to lose myself in some work before my flight, the minutes are ticking by too slowly.

I don't look up as the young waitress places my coffee and toast in front of me, but I do give her a soft nod, so she doesn't think I am a rude asshole.

Because I'm not.

Well, I don't think I am.

Sitting back, I bring my coffee cup to my lips and take a small mouthful. My soul instantly happy from the grouchy bear it was a little while ago. I survive on coffee and to not have one this morning threw me a little. I have a routine I stick to at home but this morning I broke it.

I grab a slice of the buttery toast and take a bite, forcing myself to eat something. I want to crack on with work on the plane then read through the file Xavier sent over again so every single detail is planted in my brain. I don't want to risk missing anything, even though I think that Xavier hasn't told me everything.

Once finished, I have another cup of coffee and consume myself with my work until I am called for my flight.

CHAPTER ELEVEN
AMORA

Today's the day.

The day my babysitter comes to stay.

As much as I am against this, I am going to *try* and do right, at least for my father's sake. To see my father slip away in front of my eyes is enough to make me want to shut up and just follow the instructions.

It'll be a couple of months, if that.

If it's going to make my father happy and make him feel a little more at ease knowing that someone is always watching me, then I am happy.

Well. Sort of.

I smirk to myself as I pull my fiery red hair into a high ponytail, my loose curls tumbling down my back as I secure it with my hair tie.

Some may say I am being a pushover, but when your father is sitting in front of you basically close to tears something has to give.

But don't you worry, fiery Amora is still tucked safely inside ready to rear her ugly head when needed.

I dressed in jeans and a tee, the spring air was still had a certain coolness to it, but it was nice to see the sun shining more and more as the weeks went on. I sat at my large, ornate dressing table and flicked my lashes with mascara, then adding a light pink blush to my cheeks.

That's as far as I go when it comes to make-up.

Opening my door, I make my way downstairs to find my mother and father. Pushing into the kitchen I see them both sitting at the small table that sits to the left of the patio doors that opens onto the gardens. My father's hand is clasped over the top of my mother's. His eyes are pinned to her but she is looking forward, watching her meadow of flowers blowing in the soft wind.

"Morning," I say quietly, reaching for a teacup and tiptoeing over to where they were sitting.

"Morning darling," my mother turns, giving me a soft smile but I can see the worry in her eyes.

"Princess," my father croons, lifting his cup to his lips as he takes a mouthful.

"What time does Tyrone fly in?"

"Titus," my father grits.

"Oh, yes, Titus," I nod, rubbing my lips together as I try and hide my smirk. I lean forward, grabbing the tea pot and pouring myself a tea. Placing it down gently I add my milk and one cube of sugar.

"This afternoon," my father's voice is tight and I can't help but worry that something has developed.

"Is everything okay?" I ask, slowly lifting my cup to my lips as I take my own mouthful.

"Yes, darling," my mother gives me a reassuring nod. "Just enjoying the quiet."

"Okay." I take that as my cue to stop talking and just embrace this moment.

It lasts all of three minutes.

"I'm back to work on Monday," I gently say, reminding my father that I won't stay under lock and key when it comes to my job.

"I am fully aware Amora," my father's tone has bite to it.

"And Tyler can stay home, right? I'll be with Uncle Carter. Not forgetting Uncle Taron and Conor will be there somewhere," I try and sweet talk him, but who am I kidding.

"Titus," he snaps, his ice-cold glare on me.

I give him an apologetic shrug, my lips pursing into a smile and I see my mother give me the side eye, her own lips twitching.

"And no, *Titus* cannot stay home. We have been over this Amora and I'll be honest my patience is wearing thin."

I roll my lips, feeling guilty suddenly for antagonizing him. I nod, keeping silent. A loud sigh vibrates past his lips.

"I'm not a monster Amora, I know this is a shit situation to be in and I hate that I am having to put you in it, but this is the hand we've been dealt. I will get everything sorted and you can have your life back, but please, just do as you're told."

I still stay quiet. I have no words. I manage a gentle nod as I finish my cup of tea. My father's glare is still penetrating through me, but I don't look up. After what feels like an hour of silence another heavy sigh leaves him and I hear the sound of the wooden chair scraping along the tiles. He leans down, his fingers wrapped round the back of my mother's chair as she tilts her face up to face him. He lowers his lips over hers softly and suddenly I feel like I am intruding their private moment.

"I've got some work to do before I go to the airport later this afternoon," he sighs, "I'll see you soon, Red," his voice is low, and my mother's cheeks redden slightly. Turning my head quickly, I look out the window and focus on the soft rain that is hitting the panelled glass, the sound suddenly soothing.

"Bye Xavi," her quiet voice pulls me back into the room.

"Amora," my father's tone is still curt, I know I've made him angry.

"Bye Daddy," I just about manage, my voice tight as I pin my eyes to his.

He strolls over, his footsteps soft as he places a kiss on the top of my head. "I'll be back with *Titty*," I feel his smile spread across the top of my head and a low chuckle vibrate through him.

"Idiot," I scoff as he stands tall, his hands fisted in his pockets. "It's Titus," I roll my eyes and he laughs a little louder this time and I know all is forgiven.

For now.

I FEEL AT A LOSS AT WHAT TO DO WITH MYSELF. I HAVE BEEN unable to work since this fiasco with The Knight Brothers as my father didn't feel happy for me to go, but now, with Titus being here my work life *should* resume slightly.

I pace up and down the glass outbuilding where my easels and art supplies sit. I still can't imagine what this looked like before my mother moved in. She always told me this room was abandoned, but it led to the west wing of the house which used to be forbidden to her.

But now, there is no more separation. My mother and father had renovations done when we were all a lot younger to make the house as one and even though there are still two staircases, they both merge into the large, long landing and one leads down to the room that used to be my mother's cell, even though she never saw it like that. Maybe she did when she was my age; taken from her family due to her father's stupidity in gambling what little money they did have to the *cruellest man* in their kingdom, but as much as my father can be a dick, I can't see how *he* was known as the cruellest man.

I pick the skin around my nailbeds, my eyes scanning round the room. I have too much nervous energy bouncing around inside of me.

My thumb presses to my lips as I begin to nibble on my already short and bit to shit nails.

"Filthy habit," I hear Betty's frail voice from behind me.

I spin, dropping my thumb from my mouth and giving her a coy smile. I have no idea why she still insists on working for my mother and father, but I think it's because we are the only family she has. She never married and never had children, so she put her all into our family.

"Why are you pacing?" she asks, strolling towards me slowly.

"I feel a little unsettled," I nibble my bottom lip, "I don't know what to do to calm myself."

"You normally paint when your mind is heavy," her hand moves forward, wrapping her small and thin fingers round the top of my arm before trailing and lifting her other hand to my face, cupping it in a motherly manner, her cold skin against my warm skin making me flinch slightly.

"I just feel so conflicted, like I am constantly fighting with myself. My brain is screaming at me to lash out at my father for even putting me in this situation, but my heart won't allow it because as soon as I think about going for him, my heart makes my body heavy with guilt and I know he is kicking himself over doing whatever the fuck he done wrong."

"Language," Betty scolds as she drops my face from her touch.

"Sorry," I wince.

"You're such a mix of your parents. You have your dad's fiery temper, but you also remind me a lot of your mother when she was your age and how she always fought back with your father..." she trails off whilst she grabs my palette. "But your kind heart, that's all your mother."

I nod.

"Trust your father, he is never normally wrong. I know it's not what you want, but it's a small bump in your forever to give up... it'll pass so quickly, just like a moment. Before you know it, your father would have fixed what was wrong and things will go back to normal," she smiles softly as she hands me the palette. I take it, looking down and letting out a light sigh and when I look up, she has gone. Slipping my phone out my back pocket, I turn my music on and press the volume button up until it's at max volume and I lose myself in *Fast Car – Noelle Johnson*.

I squeeze out pastel colours and begin swiping them back and forth on the canvas. I have no idea what I am painting, just letting my emotions lead the way. I have no idea how long I have been sat here for when my earphone is pulled from my ear and I hear my father's voice.

"Amora, darling..." and I still. I place my paint brush on the small shelf at the bottom on the easel and slowly spin round to see my father standing in the doorway with his hands in his pockets, his eyes pinned to me. I swallow hard, my heart thumping in my chest so fast it makes my breath catch. The sun has set and the evening is beginning to draw in.

"Come," he steps closer to me, holding out his hand. I stand, inhaling deeply as I do and walk towards my father.

His eyes soften, the scar that runs over his left eye has faded so much in the last few years, the brown in his eyes is a deep brown, some days it almost looks black. Soft wrinkles appear at the corner of his eyes as he gives me a small smile.

He tucks a loose strand of my fiery hair behind my ear and I hear a soft snigger pass his lips.

"Your painting is beautiful," his eyes pass mine and I turn to look over my shoulder at the pretty pastel abstract painting that I have spent my afternoon on.

"It's not too bad... not my best," I shrug my shoulders up slightly and scoff a laugh.

"Titus is waiting in the library to meet you," my father's emotions change quickly and I see the hardness flash across his face, his eyes hooding.

I nod.

He moves forward, passing me quickly and I follow him like a lost little girl. Each step I take, I feel my stubbornness growing, my shoulders lifting a little more and my head is held high. If Titus thinks he is getting an obedient client, he is very much mistaken. We pass through the long but narrow hallway that runs adjacent to the lounge area. At the end of the hallway we pass the second flight of stairs that now joins both parts of the house together and within seconds, we're standing outside the library. I wait, willing for my father to turn round and give me a reassuring look, but he doesn't, and I feel my heart plummet into the depths of my chest. His hard and cold demeanour is guarding him, his walls up and ready to fight. I let me eyes fall to my feet, and that's where they stay.

A low growl vibrates in his throat as he pushes down the handle of the library door and I swear I forget how to breathe suddenly when my eyes move from the floor up to see the impeccably dressed man in front of me. Handsome, *very* handsome. And he is tall, *so* tall. If I had to guess, he would be around six foot six, six foot seven. His black hair is shaved short, his stubble is short and neat and joins up to his shaved sideburns. I feel my skin singe under his intense gaze from his ice blue eyes. My heart thumps.

"Amora," my father snaps me out of my hypnotic state and I finally manage to pull my eyes from Titus. "This is Titus," his tone is curt, and I give a gentle nod, and roll my shoulders back so I'm standing tall.

"It's a pleasure to meet you," I keep my tone sharp, my head held high as I move my eyes from my father and back to Titus.

"The pleasure is all mine, Amora," Titus' low voice rumbles, making my skin erupt in goosebumps and my lips part slightly, his eyes roam up and down my body and I don't miss the small smile that pulls at his lips.

"Okay, Amora, you're excused..." my father turns to face me, and his eyes find mine, he nods tightly and I say nothing else. Turning I walk out of the library and close the door behind me. Resting against the cool surface of the wooden door, my head falls back gently, and I rest it. My eyes flit from side to side as my mind and heart race at a million miles per hour.

Why did he have to hire an Adonis god?

I internally groan and head for my bedroom.

CHAPTER TWELVE
TITUS

I AM TIRED.

I slept on the plane, but it didn't feel enough. I feel like my world has been turned on its axis, the time zones already hurting my brain. I walk into the arrivals lounge and see a crowd of bored and unpleased strangers holding up signs. I yawn, scrubbing my hand down my face as I scan them until I see a sign that has my name scribbled in black marker. I drag my case along behind me, my eyes landing on who I am assuming is Xavier.

His dirty blonde hair is styled and tidy, flecks of grey shimmer out under the bright lights, he has a full beard, mixed with ginger and grey. He looks late fifties, early sixties if I was to put an age on him. My eyes finally meet his and I notice the difference in them. One is crystal blue, like the colour of the tropic oceans you see on vacation brochures, the other is darkest of browns and has a scar running from above his eyebrow down to his cheek. He is dressed in a dark grey suit and a crisp, white shirt with no crinkles showing at all.

"Xavier," I hold my hand out to shake his, but he looks down at it and scoffs, shaking his head from side to side.

"We don't need to do pleasantries *Titty*, let's just get home."

Titty!?

I snort, shaking my head from side to side. He is already walking off when I shrug my backpack up and throw my duffle bag over my shoulder while I drag my large and heavy suitcase.

"Thanks for the help, you ass." I grit, reluctantly following him.

We move to an underground parking garage when I see him unlock a red Porsche and I stand, my eyes wide.

"Um," I roll my lips, "I don't think all my luggage will fit."

"Who said you're coming with me?" Xavier spins and raises one of his brows.

"How am I getting to yours then?"

"Well, if you would have actually let me explain instead of jumping up my arse with your assumptions, you would have known that I have sorted you your *own* car." He reaches into his pocket and throws me a Jeep key and I smile.

"Thought you would be comfortable driving something you're used to..." he winks, opening the door and sliding into the Porsche Carrera 911.

A light chuckle leaves me as I unlock the black Jeep SUV next to him and load it up.

I climb in the righthand side of the vehicle and suddenly a wave of panic swarms me. I look over at Xavier who opens his window, and I open mine.

"Yeah?"

"Don't forget we drive on the lefthand side," and before

I can ask anything else, he pulls out of his space. It takes me a moment to get the Jeep started and into gear before I pull out and follow him out onto the road.

He must have a little bit of a conscious because he doesn't speed off into the early evening and leaving me to find my own way home. We pull off the motorway, marked the M25 and after what feels like hundreds of miles, we're pulling down small and narrow lanes. Xavier slows as he takes the corners in the now darkness, and I stay close. My eyes roam around at the emptiness that surrounds us, there are a few lights scattered in the distance but not many.

I see his blinker come on and I put mine on as he pulls across the road to the right and pulls outside tall, black, wrought iron gates. I slow to a complete halt and look up through my lashes as the gates begin to open to reveal a large, gothic looking manor house sitting proudly at the end of the driveway. The sound of the iron dragging along the shingled drive and I hear Xavier's tires crunch over the stones, and once he is through the gate, I take my foot off the brake and let the car roll forward as I follow him up the driveway when he pulls into a carport. I stay parked, waiting for him to tell me where to park and he signals for me to just pull behind him. I look to the side of the carport and see a ramp going underground and I am assuming it leads to a garage. Cutting the engine, I open the door and my heavy legs hit the ground. I feel exhausted.

Opening the trunk of the car, I get my luggage out and make my way up to the house. The house was lit up with up lights attached to the grey brick. There was a large archway and tucked inside was an iron door with a heavy knocker attached to it. It looked *beastly*. Like Xavier never wanted anyone here, it was like an iron fort he was trying to keep people out of.

He still doesn't help me with my luggage but I have succumbed the fact that he won't.

I wait as he slips his key into the lock and lets himself in, holding the door with his foot as I drag my sorry ass through.

"Thanks," I grumble and let my bags hit the floor by my feet as my eyes scan the inside of his house. The interior doesn't match the exterior and it's clear that his wife has decorated every inch of this home. She has taken it from a cold prison to a warm and inviting home.

"Follow me," he grunts, letting the front door shut as he kicks his shoes off and I follow his lead, then march up behind him with my case and bags. I let out a huff as we reach the top of the staircase and look to the left, then to the right. There are hallways leading in both directions.

"This way," he turns to the right down a narrow and dark corridor, portraits of men dressed in uniform filled the walls and it made me wonder if they were his ancestors. The hardwood, dark oak floorboards creak as we both walk across them until he stops outside a wooden door.

"This will be your room, you've got time if you want to freshen up. I also took the liberty in getting you a few suits so you had something presentable to wear when I introduce you to my family," his eyes fall to my cases, "because no doubt everything you have in that case is screwed up."

I nod, not even having the energy to come back with a response.

"I'll be back in twenty," his voice disinterested as he pops his sleeve up with his pinkie finger to look at the time before he disappears, closing the door behind him.

"What the fuck?" I groan, running my hand round the back of my neck, rubbing the ache that presents itself there.

I let my backpack fall from my shoulder and onto the floor, a loud thud echoes round the large room.

It's dated.

A deep cream paint wraps itself round the walls, a large, sashed window directly in front of me and I wonder what it looks out to. A queen-size four-poster-bed sits to my right, with white lace that hangs over the frame and is finished off with gold ribbon. It's clean in here, and it doesn't smell musty or damp. It just looks old. To my left is an ornate shabby chic dressing table with a large, gold mirror hanging on the wall above it. I see an open archway and my curiosity gets the better of me as I stroll slowly across to see a free-standing bath on gold legs, sitting under another large window. There looked to have been a shower recently installed over the other side of the bathroom which I was grateful for. I didn't mind taking a bath, but I was more of a shower guy. Sighing, I spin back around and pad into my bedroom and opened the closets to see six suits all hanging up neatly.

How the hell did he know my size?

My fingers grabbed the sleeve of a black designer suit and I decided I would wear that one. Pulling my sticky clothes off my body, I made my way to the bathroom to rinse the day off me and hopefully it wakes me up slightly too.

I pull my phone out and drop a message to Arizona to let her know that I am here safely. I've had a message from Kaleb asking if all is okay, so I replied and asked if it was him who gave Xavier my suit size; not that it matters, I just find it a little strange.

Once dry, I dress in the suit that Xavier picked out and it fits like a glove. I walk over to the mirror that hangs above the dressing table and give myself the once over.

Inhaling deeply, nerves ripple through me and just as I turn on my heel, there is a knock on the door.

I stroll over, slipping my Hublot onto my wrist and place my phone inside my suit jacket pocket. Opening the bedroom door, I see Xavier standing there with a resting face, his brows pulled and furrowed making his soft wrinkles harsh.

I wonder if he smiles.

"You look good, I approve," he gives me a nod, pushing his hand into his pocket as he stands up straight and begins walking towards the stairs. I close my bedroom door and follow him, taking long strides to catch up with him. I go to turn towards the stairs but he continues straight down a wider hallway, and I wonder why we're going this way. I keep quiet and just follow before we come to another large staircase. He heads down and at the bottom turns right and continuing down a narrow corridor. This house does not flow, it doesn't work, and I feel like this part of the house has been added on. He stills outside a room, looking over his shoulder at me then facing forward and pushing the handle down to reveal a stunning library. Floor to ceiling bookcases, ladders attached and so many books. I have to stop my jaw from opening, Arizona would love it here.

"Titus, take a seat," he shows me to a large leather chesterfield couch. The room smells of leather and oak.

I sit, fidgeting slightly my knees dropping apart, my hands hanging between them as I wait.

Xavier nods, disappearing out of the room and within moments he is back with a beautiful, red-haired woman wearing a long sleeve crew top and black pants. Her eyes are crystal blue, seeking mine out and I see her eyes widen slightly, her lips pursing into a smile as Xavier closes the door behind her.

"Titus," I stand, popping the button through my suit jacket and hold my hand out towards her.

Her eyes drop, her smile growing as her hand connects with mine. "This is my wife, Royal."

"Royal," I smile, my grip firm, "it's a pleasure to meet you," I clear my throat as I drop her hand.

"Ditto," she smiles, and I frown, my brows furrowed as my eyes bounce back and forth between Xavier and his wife. She lets out a small laugh, "It means *same*," she shrugs her shoulders up before turning to face Xavier. He looks down to her, his eyes softening and that's when I see it. The smile.

We fall into light conversation when I hear the library door click open as two older boys walk through the door, one is the spitting image of Xavier, the other Royal.

"Xander, Ezekiel," Xavier looks at his boys and I can see the pride radiate from him, "this is Titus, he will be looking after Amora."

The boys exchange a look then give their father a nod before they step forward and shake my hand. Nice to see they have manners.

Unlike their father.

"Do you have children?" Royal asks, her question throwing me slightly and I nod.

"Yes, a daughter, Arizona," I smile, "she's twenty-one."

"That's wonderful, what is she like?" she continues and gestures for me to sit back down on the sofa, she sits opposite me on a matching chesterfield.

"She is smart and beautiful, she is in med school..." my own pride is beaming from me now, I can't wipe the smile from my face. "She wants to be a doctor."

"Wow, and so young to be accepted into med school," Royal chimes.

"Over achiever—was two years ahead of her class."

"Smart girl," Xavier pipes up, "I'm assuming she gets that from her mother," and he smirks, giving me a wink and my smile slips for just a moment, but long enough for Royal to notice. I can see the concern on her face as she studies me.

"It's only me and Arizona, I raised her myself," and I swallow the bile that is clawing its way up my throat, burning my windpipe and I cough, trying to rid of the reminder of her betrayal. There is no way Xavier didn't know about Sharon. That was just an easy hit for him. I know he knows everything there is to know about me.

"Oh," I hear Royal say, and I can feel Xavier's eyes burning into me but I don't pull my eyes from Royal. I can see the sadness on her face.

"I don't want your pity," my tone comes out a little harsher than I intended, "I know it's easy to give, but I honestly don't need it. It's been twenty-one years, she didn't want to be part of mine and Arizona's life and I am happy with that."

"That's very brave of you," Royal gives a small smile.

Silence fills the room for a moment, "Has my husband offered you a drink, Titus?"

I shake my head from side to side.

"Xavi," she swats him on the arm and he scoffs a laugh, "Sorry about his tardiness, would you like one?"

"No, thank you," I smile at her, and sit back on the sofa.

"So, you have a daughter and I am assuming you understand the seriousness of this issue we're having?" She asks.

"Very much so, it's the reason I took the job," my eyes move from Royal, to their sons who haven't taken their eyes off me and finally, my eyes land on Xavier. "The thought of

Arizona going through something like this makes my blood run cold," I swallow thickly, rubbing my clammy hands together.

"At least we're all on the same page..." she waits a beat before speaking again. "Xavi," Royal turns to face her husband and I can't help but wonder why it's her asking all the questions.

"Red," his eyes sweep across to her, his fingers trailing across the top of her shoulders, and she leans into him.

"Can you go and get Amora please? I think it's best we go out the room whilst you are both introduced and once that is done, we can get down to business."

"I agree," Xavier's deep voice echoes around the room and I suddenly feel nervous again.

They stand and begin to walk towards the door before Royal stops and turns to face me once more, "Thank you for accepting our job offer, Titus," but before I can reply, she is gone.

I am sat alone for a while and I feel a little at a loss. I stand, pacing towards the back of the library to see a little nook in the corner where there is a tan leather high back chair, a small side table and *wuthering heights* sitting on the surface. I skim my fingers over the cover of the book before opening it up, turning the first page and seeing a handwritten note.

Red,
Forgive me for ruining your favourite book.
This is a first edition.
I love you with every fibre of my body.
Forever and always,
Your Xavier.

My lips pull at the corners at the note and I let the cover close before my eyes roam over the smaller bookcase that sits next to the chair. There are so many copies of the same books; first editions, second editions, limited covers, movie covers... Royal has them all. My eyes fixate on the authors as I let them sweep over the books.

Jane Austin.

Emily Brontë.

Charlotte Brontë.

Shakespeare.

Margaret Mitchell.

Arizona would be in heaven. I slip my phone from my inside suit pocket and snap a quick photo so I can show Arizona later. Putting my phone back, I fist my hands in my pockets and walk back towards the seating area when I see the handle wobble. I inhale deeply, standing tall, my shoulders back and I let me eyes stay pinned to the door and that's when I see her.

My lips part slightly, but I compose myself quickly. Her fiery red hair is sitting in a high and messy ponytail with long, wavy strands which have come loose and are hanging round her face. She has freckles dotted across her nose and cheeks and I can't help the smile that creeps onto my face when I see the pastel lilac paint that is smudged across her cheekbone. Her eyes match her father's, her left dark brown, her right crystal blue. She is a perfect mix of both of her parents, just like I am with mine. Her eyes widen as they sweep over me.

"Amora," Xavier snaps, his voice stern which seems to pull her eyes from me and they move to her father. "This is Titus," she gently nods towards me and I watch as she stands a little taller. Is it a warning? But then her eyes meet mine once more and I feel a sudden calmness.

"It's a pleasure to meet you," her voice is soft but I can hear the assertiveness to it. There is something about her voice that seems to cause the hairs on the back of my neck to stand and I feel a shiver dance across my spine but I manage compose myself.

"The pleasure is all mine, Amora," my voice is low as my eyes roam up and down her body one last time and a small smile pulls at the corner of my lips. I go to open my mouth once more but Xavier snipes in.

"Okay, Amora, you're excused..." she keeps quiet, nods and turns to walk away and within seconds she is out the room, the door closed again.

I am shocked at her obedience, she's submissive with her father and I honestly didn't think she would be. I was sure that she would give her father an attitude back, but she didn't even show that she may have that streak deep inside of her.

Maybe I have misjudged her.

"I trust all is well?" Xavier pulls me from my thoughts.

"All is fine," I nod.

"Good, then shall we go through the files then?"

I nod once more.

"Are you a brandy drinker? Or a whiskey?"

"I like both," I stand still, my hands still deep in the pockets of my suit.

"My kind of man," his stern face finally breaks slightly as he smiles and for some reason that small bit of interaction makes me smile myself.

We sit on the sofa, both in silence as we sip from the warm amber liquid.

"You look tired," the gruffness in Xavier's voice makes my eyes lift to meet his.

"I am exhausted," I admit, sighing as I take another mouthful.

Once Amora left, Royal came back into the library but without their sons this time. Xavier told me briefly that he was tipped off to take down Ryder Knight, he was one of the biggest drug runners in London and it seemed somebody wanted him out of the way, and when the job came in, it was from an anonymous source. Xavier showed up, followed instruction and did the job. But it wasn't until he was on his way home that he found out that he killed the wrong brother. He killed Bartholomew Knight, the boss of the underground crime world. He fucked with the wrong family. It didn't matter how much he tried to clean up the mess and fight his case, in their eyes, what's done is done. The wrong blood had been spilled and now Bartholomew's sons wanted their own blood. And they chose Amora.

Xavier had blood on his hands, and it didn't matter how much he washed them, he couldn't remove the stains. I could tell that Xavier wanted to tell me more, but he seemed to keep quiet while Royal was there and when she left, Xavier fell silent.

I didn't want to push; I can't even begin to imagine what he went through when this all happened.

"Go to bed, we can sort a plan out tomorrow, then work begins," he swallows the contents of his tumbler, placing it down on the table to the right of the sofa.

I finish my own drink and stand, placing it next to his.

"I'll see you in the morning, can you remember how to get back to your room?"

I nod.

"Night," Xavier says as he walks towards the door and leaves me sitting there alone.

"Night," I say to the empty room. I still for a moment, letting the last few hours sink in.

I've got to remember why I am here.

Got to remember why I took the job.

Sighing, I head for the door and then make my way to my bedroom.

Even though I did get lost a couple of times.

CHAPTER THIRTEEN
AMORA

I WAKE SUDDENLY, STARTLED WHEN I HEAR MY PHONE CHIRPING. Groaning, I turn and smash my hand down to silence it. Rolling on my back I let my eyes close again and just give myself a moment to wake up.

My phone goes again.

Hitting my fists into my duvet, I sit up and grab my phone to see Arabella's name. I answer, letting out a loud and dramatic sigh.

"What do you want?"

"God, you're really not a morning person are you?"

"I'm tired; took me ages to settle last night." I admit, turning to look at the sun trying to stream through the closed curtains.

"Why's that?"

"The babysitter arrived late last night."

"Oooo," she sings down the phone, "What is he like?"

"Not what I was expecting." I swallow, tearing my eyes from the morning and letting them drop into my duvet.

"Good or bad?"

I stay silent for a moment.

"Good."

"Is he hot?"

"He is old."

"Wait... how old?" I scoff a laugh, shaking my head from side to side. "Look, age gap is in at the moment... it's all the rage in my romance books."

"Well, newsflash, this isn't a romance book," I nibble on my bottom lip, "and I don't know how old, maybe mid-forties? I don't know."

"That's not old."

"It is when I'm twenty-five... it seems a little..."

"It sounds bloody hot, he would know how to..."

"Shut up," my cheeks flame red and I am mortified.

Arabella cackles down the phone.

"I'm so glad you are finding this funny."

"I know, it's brilliant."

I let her have a moment more as I stare at my bedroom door, I suppose I should go downstairs. I inhale deeply and hold it for a moment until I let it exhale slowly.

"Did you still want to meet in town? I saw a dress weeks ago and I am annoyed that I didn't get it."

"Please learn from this, you always do this," I groan.

"You know me so well... so, you game?"

"Yeah, twelve meet? I'll pick you up seeing as you still haven't learnt to drive."

"Why would I learn to drive when I have you?" and I smile.

"Exactly."

"See you at twelve."

"See you then." I hang the phone up and flop down on my bed. I turn to look at the fresh daffodils my mother put in my room yesterday, bringing a little bit of colour to my very dull room. Well, I don't think it's dull but to an outsider it probably is.

My walls are an off white, they almost have a cream feel to them in certain lights. My bedframe is a black metal, four poster queen-sized. I have black frames sitting on the wall opposite my bed with some of my abstract paintings. Most of my paintings just sit collecting dust, only a few have been put around the house. But that's more on my parents than me, I am quite happy having them sitting in the glass outbuilding under dustsheets.

My father swapped all my light switches from chrome to black, and I had off white bedding with cream and black scatter cushions.

Boring.

But I liked it and that's all that mattered.

A soft knock on my door has me sitting up, pulling the duvet up and round my chest.

"Amora, darling." my mother's soft voice breezes through the room, the wind dancing in the trees outside.

"Morning." I give a small smile as she enters my bedroom and pulls back my heavy, black curtains, letting the sun stream through the windows, lighting the room up.

"Breakfast is just being dished up; will you be joining us?" she asks as she begins trying to tidy my bed whilst I am still in it.

"Yes." I throw the covers back and slip my feet into my slippers as I stretch tall. I pad over towards my bathroom and grab my waffle dressing gown and wrap it round my frame.

I enter my room and see my bed all made up, cushions karate chopped in the middle, and I smile softly.

"I can make my own bed, you know." I wink.

"I know... I just..." my mum turns and spins to look at me.

"I know." I nod gently and I notice her eyes roam up and down my body, her brows furrow, "Do I need to get dressed?"

"Well," my mum clasps her hands together, her lips pursing into a pout as she tries to fight her smile. "I mean, it couldn't hurt... there is an extremely handsome young man downstairs and..."

"Fine," I roll my eyes, stomping into my walk-in wardrobe as I scan my clothes. My cheeks flush at how embarrassed I felt when I caught my reflection last night when I shut myself away in my room and I had lilac paint smeared into my cheek, my hair wild and loose.

I was a sight.

And not a good one.

"Is it warm out?" I call out.

"Not particularly, still got the British chill in the spring air."

"We need to move somewhere hot." I groan.

"I agree," my mother's voice drifts closer, and I turn to see her standing in the archway of my wardrobe.

"Why are you hovering?"

"Just because."

"Just because hmm?" I smirk as I pull a sage green seersucker tee and black skinny jeans. I take my clothes and my underwear into the bathroom and get washed and dressed. Brushing my teeth, I look at myself in the mirror and I can't help but smile a little, I feel like today is going to be a good day. I get to spend it with my friend, the sun is shining, what could dampen my mood?

"FOR GOD'S SAKE," I GROAN, PUTTING MY HEAD INTO MY HANDS, my elbows resting on the dining room table "I've had this planned for weeks," I seethe, lifting my head and settling my eyes on my father's. "Why can't I go by myself?"

"Because you have a target on your back, what don't you understand about this situation?" he tuts, shaking his head from side to side and my mother gives me an apologetic look.

"I hate this!" I shout, pushing my plate of food away from me and let my head fall back. I can feel all eyes on me, Xander's, Ezekiel's, my parents' and worse of all, Titus'.

"Sis, come on..."

"Fuck off." I spit at Ezekiel and his eyes widen and I hear a scoff of a laugh come from my father.

"Amora!" my mother's eyes are like saucers, and I can see the shock on her face. "Language!"

"Oh, stop it, we all swear, stop putting on a fucking show because we have a guest," and this time I hear Titus chuckle into his napkin.

"You either take Titus..."

"Or?" I challenge my father, crossing my arms in front of my chest and Xander rolls his eyes so far in the back of his head, I flip him off.

"Or you don't go," my father breaks his gaze from mine and picks his knife and fork up to continue eating.

"Fine, I won't go. I would rather go and choke on a bag of dicks then sit here any longer with you all."

My father's eyes widen as he chokes on his mouthful, the colour from my mother's cheeks drains and her mouth drops open in shock and I hear the low rumble of laughter coming from the direction of my brothers.

I push off the table, letting the chair fall and hit the floor before I turn and storm towards the door.

"Amora Mya Archibald, you get back here right now!" my father growls and instead of spinning to face him, I flip him off and slam the door behind me.

Fuck them all.

I SIT IN MY PAINTING ROOM, STARING AT THE CANVAS THAT I started yesterday, and I don't know if I even like it anymore. The pink, yellow and purple pastel colours begin to blur into one. It was giving me a beautiful sunset vibe... but now, now it looks like nothing but colours smudged together.

Scraping my hair from my face, I twist it round and grab a paintbrush, pushing it through my twisted bun to hold it in place. A few strands of red hair fall and frame my face. I sit back for a moment, tilting my head to the side as I look at my painting once more.

Something is missing.

"Wow." I hear a deep grumble from behind me and I quickly look over my shoulder, my eyes landing on Titus.

I snigger a laugh and turn back round to look at my painting. The silence fills the room until I hear the sound of his shoes moving across the tiles of the room.

"I just wanted to check in to see if you were okay..." I feel his breath on the back of my neck and I ignore the want to turn and look at him.

"I'm fine." I nod, swallowing thickly.

"It's okay if you're not..."

"I know it's okay, but I am fine," my tone a little harsh but I want him to know I am annoyed so he can run back off to daddy dearest and tell him.

"Okay." His voice trails off and the sound of a stool scuffing along the floor fills the room, him being in close proximity makes my breath catch in the back of my throat but I style it off with a small cough. His scent fills my nose, the smell of vanilla and woodsmoke surrounds me and I can't help breathing in a little deeper.

"If you still wanted to meet up with your friend, we can do that... I'll just hang back, you won't even know that I am there."

A whisper of a smile graces my lips as my eyes stay glued to my canvas.

"I'll know you're there."

"Subconsciously yes, but are you going to let your father's choices ruin your life for the foreseeable?"

I blink, turning to look at him and shake my head from side to side.

"Then tell your friend we will be there at noon," he gives a tight nod and stands, my eyes raking up his tall frame until they finally settle on his light, crystal blue eyes and then I watch as he walks out of the glass outbuilding and from my sight.

Turning back round, my lips twist into a smile.

SITTING IN THE BACK OF TITUS'S JEEP I AM A MILLION MILES AWAY as I look out at the scenery that is passing by my eyes.

I felt a little uneasy when I first got in the car knowing that Titus' first time driving on the left side of the road was late last night. I catch his eyes flicking up into the rear-view mirror and occasionally our gazes clash but I ignore the way my heart stutters in my chest.

There is something about Titus that pulls me in and I am confident it's his eyes. I feel like he is hiding so much behind those pretty blue eyes.

We slow as we approach Arabella's house, the oak gates slowly opening and the tires crunch on the gravelled drive.

"I won't be a moment," I say quietly as I open the passenger door and walk up the steps to their home, knocking on the door.

Turning back, I look over my shoulder and Titus' stare is pinned to me. My head snaps back round quickly when I hear the door open.

"Amora!" Conor beams, opening his arms wide and I fall into his embrace.

"Uncle Conor."

"Oh, Amora." Darcey's soft voice has my head lifting and I look at her, her green eyes narrowing as her smile grows.

"It's so good to see you," she grabs me from her husband's grips and pulls me in for a cuddle.

We break away when I see Arabella coming down the stairs wearing heavy black doc martens, shorts and an oversized tee tucked in the front.

"I heard you have a hot bodyguard... is that true?" Darcey asks me, giving me a wiggle of her perfectly shaped eyebrows.

I roll my eyes, swatting Arabella in the arm when she stands next to me.

"Ow!"

Conor's brows rise as he steps forward and onto the step of his front door, his eyes landing on Titus, and he lifts his arm to say hello.

I watch as Titus holds his hand up from the driver's seat, saying hi.

"Well, he is a dishy isn't he?"

"Mum!" Arabella scolds, rolling her eyes, "That's disgusting."

Darcey giggles as Conor pulls her close to him, kissing her on the lips.

"Ew, I'm out. See ya," Arabella shakes her head from side to side, disgusted by the public affection and storming past her mum and dad which only causes them both to laugh loudly.

"Have fun girls, be safe!" Conor calls after us as I turn and walk out the door and towards the waiting car.

Arabella opens the door, sliding across the back seat and I climb in after her.

"I'm Arabella," she holds her hand out and Titus turns in his seat, gripping her hand and giving it a soft shake.

"Pleasure."

"Oh, his accent," she sighs, sitting back in her chair and pulling her seatbelt across her chest.

My cheeks flame red, dipping my head so my hair tumbles down and round my face as I give her a glare.

Titus reverses and pulls back down the driveway when his eyes find mine again.

"What about you, Twilight, do you like my accent?"

"Twilight?" I screw my nose up and I see his dimples before his eyes focus on the junction where he needs to pull out, the sat nav talking to him. "I wouldn't say I like it... but I don't *dislike* it either." I shrug my shoulders up and turn my body to face Arabella.

"Have you read all the messages in the group?" she asks me, pulling her phone from her Dior canvas bag and starts scrolling.

"I haven't, I've not been on my phone since this morning..." I pause, slipping my own phone out and unlocking it, "Why, what have I missed?"

"Anais and Xander..."

"Of course. And what about now?"

"They just bicker constantly and the fact that Parker is on that conversation and everything that is going on with your family... just think it's a little insensitive," she shrugs her shoulders up as she continues scrolling.

"It's a distraction for us I suppose."

"Are your brothers coming next week? It is my birthday?"

"I doubt it hun, there is so much going on at home... and well." I sigh.

"That's a shame, Parker still hasn't said whether he is or not, but I'll hound his ass at work."

"Are these all your friends? Or family?" Titus asks as he begins to drive after pulling out at the junction.

"My parent's friends, well, more my mother's. My father just goes along with it for an easy life." I giggle, "But we're all friends with the original gang's kids..." I nod.

"Right, okay," he falls silent.

"Parker and Anais are Carter and Freya's children; me and Amora work for CPH." Arabella begins and I am sure Titus doesn't give two shits about all of this.

"CPH?"

"Cole Publishing House."

"Right, okay," Titus nods as if trying to keep up.

"Me and my little sister Lola are Conor and Darcey's kids... obviously," she beams. "Then you have Faith, Hope and Ryder... they are Taron and Luna's kids... Taron works on Carter's security, along with my dad," she keeps going and I just sit and listen. "Rafael is my Uncle's kiddo, but they live in Aspen."

"Oh, Aspen, never been but would love to." Titus pipes in and he seems so at ease out of my father's presence.

"Where are you from?"

"New York."

"That's on my bucket list, for sure."

"Me too," I sigh, "maybe one day, unless I'm dead... or kidnapped... again," I turn to look out the window and ignore the burn in my throat at the words that just left my mouth and I have to swallow the bile that rises.

"You're not going to die or get kidnapped," Arabella groans, "and what do you mean again?"

"You don't know that," I turn to face her, "and never mind... it's not important." I give her a reassuring smile, but it doesn't seem to ease the concerned look plastered on her face before turning my face back out the rolling green fields that are whizzing by.

"But I do." Titus' rasp pulls my eyes from the window, and I swallow the lump down my throat, his steady gaze on me.

The moment is ruined when the car begins to ring.

"Fuck," Titus groans, pressing the button to the car, answering my father's call. "Yup."

"Don't fucking *yup* me, where are you? Amora said she didn't want to go."

"Out with Amora."

"Sorry?" my father roars.

"I'm out with Amora; she changed her mind, and I thought it was okay as long as I was going with her," Titus smirks.

"I changed my fucking mind! If you still want a job, turn the fucking car round and bring her home... NOW."

"I'm sorry, I can't do that."

"You fucking do what I say."

I feel myself shrink in my chair.

"You hired me to do a job, so fuck off and let me do *my* job." Titus punches the red button with his finger on the screen cutting my father off before the phone begins to ring again.

A nervous laugh bubbles out of me and I cup my hand across my mouth.

"Seems I have an ally after all," I breathe out a sigh of relief as Titus pulls into an underground car park.

TITUS KEPT HIS WORD; HE STAYED CLOSE BUT NOT ENOUGH TO draw attention. His phone continued to ring until we pulled up on the drive and guilt knots in my stomach.

Titus pulls into the carport and my heart drums fast in my chest. He cuts the engine and opens his door, meeting me at my door as he opens it.

"I'm sorry," I manage, not able to look at him in the eyes.

"Why are you sorry?" his voice is calm as he waits for me to exit the car.

"Because you're going to get into shit with my father because I was being a brat," I slowly lift my eyes to level with his.

"I'm not going to get into shit, I'm a big boy... I think I can handle your father... plus, he needs me more than I need him at the moment so don't worry your pretty little head about it." He winks at me and I smile. "Plus, you're a grown woman... don't worry about him, I wouldn't let anyone get near you."

I nod, slipping out the car and ducking under his arm. I continue walking and don't look back behind him. I open the door, keeping my head down as I make my way upstairs and down to my bedroom. I expect Titus to follow, but he doesn't.

Dropping my bags on my bed, I flop down next to it and I wait for my father to come through my door like a wrecking ball.

Minutes pass, and nothing.

Slowly sitting up on my elbows, I keep my eyes pinned to the door but he doesn't come and for some reason, that instils more fear in me than him coming into my room.

Shuffling forward, I edge off the bed and walk cautiously to my door as I open it and look down the hallway.

Silence.

My stomach knots and I swallow hard. Stepping back into my room, I close my bedroom door and just wait.

CHAPTER FOURTEEN
XAVIER

I AM FUCKING ANGRY.

I pace up and down my office after calling the prick Titty for the hundredth time and the cunt ignores my calls again.

Gripping a handful of my hair, I tug at the root as I try and control my breathing but no matter what I do, I can't.

Who does he think he is? If I didn't need him so much I would put a bullet between his eyes.

I grunt and snigger at my thoughts.

I wouldn't really, my thoughts echo back.

"Maybe I would," I grit and when I hear the door to my office open, I spin, my brows knitted, jaw clenched when he walks through the door.

A cocky fucking grin on his face, his hands fisted into his pockets, and it takes everything in me to not wipe that smirk off his face with my fist.

Breathe.

"Well, decided to return, did we?" I run my finger along my bottom lip.

"Seems that way," he winks and steps closer to me.

And I swear to God, he makes my blood boil.

Wanker.

CHAPTER FIFTEEN
TITUS

I stand at the bottom of the stairs and watch as Amora walks up. The urge to follow and protect her is strong but my thoughts are snatched when I feel my phone vibrate in my pocket. Pulling it out, I see Arizona's name.

Smiling, I answer.

"Hey." I begin walking towards the back of the house.

"Hey dad, you okay? Sorry I've not called I've been swamped at work."

"That's okay sweetie, no need to explain. Are you okay? How's Keaton?"

She scoffs.

"Keaton is Keaton, but Dad, I'm fine. I don't even understand why I had to come here..."

"Where has this come from? You were fine with it when I said about it before."

"Because I didn't want to upset you." The line falls quiet, and I rub my hand over my short beard, my chest tight.

"You wouldn't have upset me," I clear my throat, I pace

back down the long hallway and stop at the bottom of the stairs, looking up to where Amora disappeared.

"I'm sorry," her voice is low.

"Don't be sorry, I'm sorry... I just thought—" she interrupts me.

"I know Dad, and I do get it... but I'm twenty-one, I would have been fine."

I inhale deeply knowing deep down she would be fine, it was me that wasn't fine. I couldn't let go. I still saw her as a young child, but she was growing into a beautiful young woman, just like Amora, and yet it seems me and Xavier have a little more in common when it comes to our parenting skills.

We both fucking suck.

"I've got to go, just about to get into bed."

"No worries sweetie, I'll speak to you soon yeah?"

"Yeah," she yawns.

"Night sweetness."

"Night Dad, love you."

"Love you more."

Pulling the phone from my ear, I inhale deeply and push my phone back into my suit pocket.

I pace back down the hallway and into Xavier's office. I don't knock, just push through the door.

He turns to face me, his expression stone cold, his brows furrow and I see his jaw clench and I can't help but smirk.

"Well, decided to return, did we?"

"Seems that way." I give him a sarcastic wink and step closer to him, closing the door behind me.

"Are we going to have a problem? Me and you?" He asks, walking over to his crystal decanter and pouring himself a whiskey. I raise my brows just as he narrows his eyes on me and I just shake my head from side to side. "Good."

I furrow my brows and then I raise them, lifting my chin slightly.

"Oh, sorry, I was saying no to the drink you were offering me, not your previous question."

"Don't get smart with me." Xavier stands tall, his steady eyes on mine as he lifts his tumbler to his lips.

"You can't keep her prisoner. Give her a little free reign; nothing is going to happen while I am with her."

"How can you be so sure?"

"Because I can." I grit, my own jaw clenching.

"I have no idea what these brothers are planning, all it would take is for one of us to drop the ball..."

"The ball isn't going to be dropped Xavier, I can promise you that. I have the team back home ready to hack into their phones, track our every move... but until then, let her be." I still, pulling out the chair opposite his desk and slumping into it. I feel exhausted, jet lag is kicking my ass but I'm not about to let it win.

His eyes pull from mine and they settle onto the file on his desk. He looks uneasy, as if he has the weight of the world on his shoulders, his mind racing at a million miles an hour.

It unnerves me.

"Do you have a plan? Has anything changed since I've been here?" I ask, not sure if I am overstepping but my priority is Amora, and if anything has changed then I have the right to know about it.

"A plan?" one of his brows raise and I don't miss the downturn of his lips, before he rubs them together and gives me a curt nod.

"Care to share?"

"You're a poet and you didn't know it..." he smirks, taking another mouthful of his drink and wincing at the burn. "I've made a deal with the Knight brothers..." he pauses, pulling his own seat out and slumping down into it. This has piqued my interest, I sit taller, shuffling to the edge of my seat, my legs open as I let my hands hang between them.

"What kind of deal?"

"It's on a need-to-know basis..."

"And let me guess, I don't need to know?"

"Bingo."

"When will I be privileged to this information then?" my tone is curt and I can't help that he gets my back up.

"When I'm ready. It's between me and them. Even Royal doesn't know."

"Must be bad then..." I mumble, sitting back in my chair deflated.

"Must be..." he repeats, trailing off and muttering something under his breath.

"Xavier?"

"What?"

"What is the point of me being here if you're not going to tell me anything?" I question, annoyance biting at me.

"I will tell you... just not yet." He shrugs his shoulders up.

"Is Amora safe?"

His eyes flick up to mine and I see the darkness dance through them, "For the moment." The crystal tumble rests on his bottom lip.

I swallow, my own nerves ripping through me.

"How long do I have?"

"Four weeks."

"Four weeks before I am due to leave?"

He shakes his head from side to side.

"Four weeks until what?"

"Until the deal."

And I don't know why, but my blood runs cold and my want to take Amora away from all of this is stronger than ever. I know what happened between Xavier and Royal. I know how her father sold her due to a gambling debt; he was a coward. Passing his daughter off to the man they called the *beast*... yet here I was, my skin prickling in goosebumps at the thought of him possibly doing the same to his daughter.

He wouldn't.

And even if he did, I sure as fuck wouldn't let him.

"What's the deal Xavier?" I ask, my voice a little more stern now and I feel the blood pumping through my veins, my heart thumping that little bit harder.

"Like I said before, it's on a need-to-know basis... and you don't need to know..." he taps his long finger on the side of his crystal glass slowly but he doesn't move his eyes from mine and I swear I see a fucking hint of a smile creep onto his lips.

"You're an asshole." I shake my head from side-to-side actual disgust lacing my tone, my face screwed up.

"Never claimed not to be," he takes another sip and the longer I am sitting here, the more frustrated I am getting.

"I don't get you." One of my brows raise and I steady my gaze on him, my eyes narrowing so all I can see is him.

"What's not to get? My priority is my family, it will *always* be my family. Everything I am doing is for them. I know it may not seem that way to you, *Titty*. But it's the truth." Xavier sits back in his chair, crossing his finger across his chest.

"I don't believe you." I shrug my shoulders up softly,

sitting back in my chair I let one of my legs cross over the other and link my fingers together as they rest in my lap.

"What do I care?" He sits back, his fucking finger tapping his glass again and I can hardly hear the noise it is making but it's enough to get my back up.

"Your daughter deserves to know her fate, Xavier." I shake my head again and now my head is dropped; I can't even look at him.

"And she will know when the time is right, but for now, *Titus*..." he trails off, and him actually saying my name correctly aggravates me more than the stupid nickname *Titty* that he has branded me with. "Do your fucking job," he barks, standing up and slamming his drink down on the table and I think he was expecting me to flinch.

"I'll do my job Xavier; you have no worries about that... you just might not like the way I do it." I snarl, turning on my heel and storming out of his office, slamming the door just for effect.

"What a dickhead." I sigh, scrubbing my face with my hand and suddenly I feel exhausted. I walk towards the kitchen, not expecting to see anyone, but Royal is standing there, leaning against the work surface as she stares out at the garden.

She looks a million miles away.

I turn slowly but it's too late. She noticed me.

"Hey, sorry you can come in... I was just thinking."

"I don't want to intrude," I hold my hands up, stepping back towards the door.

"Titus, it's fine... come in, I've not long boiled the kettle." She smiles at me, her eyes soft as she averts her gaze from mine, turning and reaching for two mugs. "Tea?"

"Please," I nod, stepping quietly back into the room and pulling a stool out to sit at the center island. The kitchen is big and runs along the back of the house. The floors are cream marble but look a little worn, the units are off white, and the countertops are wrapped in a black marble.

It looked as if it had been recently decorated, the walls a warm ivory.

"Do you take sugar?" Royal asks as she pours the water over the teabags, and I tilt my head to the side.

"I have no idea; I've never had an English breakfast tea." I admit, and she smiles.

"Let's do one sugar and some milk, see how you like it." I watch as she adds a dash of milk then stirs in a teaspoon of sugar. Walking it over to me, she passes it across the countertop, and I thank her.

"How's your day been?" she asks, pulling one of the stools out on the opposite side of the centre island and sits, her hands wrapped round her mug.

"Not too bad." I nod as I take a sip of my tea, my tongue darting out and licking my lips.

"And Amora, did she have a nice time?"

"I believe so, ma'am."

"Please, no ma'am," Royal shakes her head softly, loose strands of her red hair falling around her face before she catches it and tucks it back behind her ear, "just Royal."

"Okay, *just* Royal." My tone is laced with a little humour.

"Have you heard from your daughter?" she asks as she brings the mug to her lips.

"Funny enough, she called me about half an hour ago."

"Do you miss her?" Royal shuffles in her seat.

"Every second of every minute of every day." I sigh, sitting tall my own fingers wrapping round a mug. "This is a really good cup of tea." A snort of a laugh escapes me as I lift my mug to my lips once more, enjoying my drink.

"I'm glad you approve, nothing like a nice cup of tea to make everything better."

My eyes settle on her, and I can feel the nervous energy.

"Is everything okay?" I ask and I feel like I am overstepping.

"Not overly, but you know that because that's why you're here." She smiles but this time, her smile doesn't reach her eyes like it normally does.

"I won't let anything happen to her." I hate that I am making a promise I don't even know if I can keep because I have no idea what the fuck Xavier has up his sleeve. He is keeping me in the dark as much as Amora and I can't help but wonder if Royal knows anything at all.

I hear her inhale deeply.

"Xavier done good hiring you..." she trails off for a moment, her eyes downcast on her tea but I don't look away from her. "I know he can be difficult, trust me, I have the t-shirt to prove it... but he does mean well." She pauses for a moment, twisting her mug round slightly before she continues, "His priority is Amora, and he will put himself in the firing line before he lets anything or anyone get to her or his family. I know bits of his plan, but I don't know everything and as much as it infuriates me..." her light blue eyes finally lift and steady on mine, "I trust him wholeheartedly."

I swallow the thickness in my throat and give her a tight nod.

"I just hope I can too." I roll my lips and finish the last mouthful of my tea. "If you'll excuse me..." Royal nods at me, reaching for my cup before I even have the chance to place it in the kitchen sink. "Thank you for the tea," I say, standing and begin to walk towards the garden.

"You're most welcome." She turns and I hear the sound

of shuffling feet coming down the hallway. Nosiness gets the better of me when I look up and see a frail older lady heading towards the kitchen. "Betty," Royal walks over to her, leading her towards the large kitchen table that overlooks the impressive gardens. "I'll make you a cup of tea."

"Thank you darling, but I am more than capable of making myself one, thank you." I watch as Betty rolls her eyes and Royal laughs.

"I know you are, but it's nice for me to wait on you for a change." Royal's hand moved from Betty's shoulder as she walks away and pops the kettle on again. "In case you didn't know, Betty used to be my lady in waiting..." Royal looks over her shoulder and I see Betty sigh.

"Lady in waiting?" I ask, pushing my hands deep into my pant pockets.

"I was a Princess before I married Xavier; heir to the throne of Auradell."

My eyes widen slightly.

"You have royal blood?"

"Yup," Royal chimes, "but I abdicated the throne once my father died, it was his last dying wish..." she adds the milk to Betty's tea and I continue to listen. "It was always Xavier's plan to have me abdicate..." she stills for a moment as if trying to remember if I have heard this side of their fairy tale.

I nod giving her the signal that I do in fact know their story, just not the part of her actually being of royal stature or being made to abdicate.

He was a selfish fucker.

My back teeth grind as I listen.

"But as time went on, Xavier didn't want me to abdicate... but I had already made my choice. I fell in love with him and he was my life, my new plan... he was my fate. When my father fell ill suddenly, I felt it was my duty to continue with our original plan and for me to become Queen. But on my father's death bed, he didn't want to put that burden on me. He wanted me to live my life with the man I loved... he wanted me to have a small bit of normality after twenty-one years... and well..." she looks at Betty then back to me, "the rest is history."

"Wow," I rub my chin and I am in awe, "I feel like I should bow to you." A low chuckle leaves me and I watch Royal's cheeks flame.

"Don't be ridiculous," she waves me away and Betty beams.

"So who took your place? Do you have any siblings?"

She shakes her head from side to side.

"When I abdicated, the only rightful heir was my uncle so I gave it to him, and I got to live out my happily ever after, that's what my father would have wanted," and I see a glisten in her eye but she swipes the tear away before laughing and giving Betty her tea.

"You certainly did," I give her a tight smile, "and Betty, it was lovely to meet you."

I don't stick around. I feel like I have taken up enough of Royal's time. I only wanted to pace to get out of my head for a while, Xavier sure knows how to get in there and wind me up. He is a mastermind, the perfect puppeteer.

Don't get me wrong, I don't not believe his love for his wife and his family, it's obvious that he would die for any of them, but I don't understand how a man could be so cold hearted. He is horrid. In my opinion I don't think he even has one redeeming quality about him.

I continue through the flower garden, the sweet smell of pollen filling my senses. I look around at the brightly coloured flowers softly dancing in the spring breeze. I feel a million miles away. I continue forward, my shoes gliding across the soft grass when I spot a little picturesque cottage in the distance. I stop in my tracks. What a perfect setting. That would suit me, something like that. I wouldn't need the grand things in life, as long as I have Arizona and my friends close by... I would be happy. Waking up every morning, sitting on the decked porch area with a cup of coffee while I read the sports column, the birds chirping, the sound of the leaves rustling in the wind. Sounds like a little piece of heaven. I look behind me, the huge manor house sits proudly, and I can't help but wonder what this place was like before it had love filling it, before it had the touch of a woman and a little family making it a home. Shaking my thoughts away, I head towards the cottage and that's when I hear the sound of water. My feet waltz me across to a large boating lake, a long-decked pier overhanging the dark blue water. Walking out onto the decked area, I still for a moment just enjoying the calm. My eyes gaze out along the glistening water when I see a vibrant dragonfly. I watch as it dances and skates over the water's surface and I smile.

"Peaceful isn't it," I hear Amora's voice as it breezes over me, and I ignore the way the hairs on the back of my neck stand and the way her voice makes my skin tingle.

"Very." I don't turn to face her; I am too focused on what is in front of me.

"You found my favourite place, now I'm going to have to find a new one..." she is next to me and I feel her eyes on the side of my face. I look down at her and give her a wink.

"You can still have it, I'm just visiting." I let out a blissful sigh.

"Did you get in trouble?" she asks as she moves

forward, perching herself on the edge of the pier and leaning forward to pull her shoes off. I watch as she places them neatly beside her then dangles her feet over so her toes just dip into the water.

"Is that not cold?"

Her eyes meet mine as she looks over her shoulder before she shakes her head from side to side. "And don't avoid my question."

I smirk, kicking my own shoes and socks off before I sit down beside her, "Hope you don't mind me sitting next to you."

"Not at all," she lets her own breathy sigh out. Rolling my lips, I let my feet slip into the cool water and ignore the shudder that wants to vibrate through me.

"And in answer to your question..." I pause for a moment as I let my hands splay onto the decked area, "I didn't get in trouble."

"I don't believe you," she squints as she turns to face me, the low afternoon sun in her eyeline.

"That's your choice, Twilight." I give her a slow wink and I let out a low chuckle when I see her nose crinkle up in disgust.

"Why Twilight?"

"Why not?" I shrug.

I don't want to tell her it's because she is the last small bit of light before darkness blankets us all. She is that light. The twilight. The moment the day meets the night. The sun kisses the moon. The most beautiful time of day.

"Would you rather Princess?" I nudge into her softly and a small gasp escapes her before she twists her lips and a comfortable silence consumes us.

CHAPTER SIXTEEN
TITUS

"THE MAN'S LOST IT." I TUCK MY ARM BEHIND MY HEAD AS I REST on my bed, holding my phone with my spare hand.

"He is just being protective, I'm sure." Kaleb says, and Keaton agrees.

"Nah, I don't think he is... there is something else going on and I'll find out what it is."

"Detective King," Keaton jibes and I pull my arm from behind my head and flip him off.

Kaleb rolls his eyes, and Nate just stares into the screen.

"How's Amora?" Kaleb asks, shuffling in his seat when Connie appears on the screen.

"Hey Titus!" She beams down the phone and waves.

"Hey Sunshine, you okay?"

She nods, "Are you?"

"I'm not too bad," I yawn.

"How's the jetlag? I remember Reese really struggled."

"It's kicking my ass," I admit, scrubbing my face with my hand then dragging it down, letting my hands rub over my stubble.

"You'll find your feet again soon," she winks, "and I'm so sorry, totally gate-crashed your man chat."

"It's okay baby," Kaleb croons, reaching up and grabbing her cheeks in his hands as he covers her lips with his.

"Vomit," I hear Keaton spit, then pushes his finger towards the back of his throat pretending to gag.

"Don't be bitter Keaton, just because you're a loner."

"Erm, I think we're all actually loners apart from you, Kaleb."

"Speak for yourself," Keaton snorts.

My eyes move up to the small square where Nate's face is.

"Hey, guys, is Nate actually here or..."

I watch as their eyes scan over the screen.

"Nate?" I ask but his face is just frozen.

"Bet that little fucker has just put a screen grab there," Kaleb laughs loud.

I shake my head from side to side. "I miss you all," I groan.

"Ahhh sweetie, we miss you too," Keaton winks.

"I miss Arizona more."

"She is fine with me, I don't even think she misses you to be honest man," Keaton continues, popping a chip into his mouth and I watch the wide shit eating grin spreading across his face.

"Why are you even on here?" I snarl, narrowing my eyes on him.

"Ouch," he places his hands over his heart.

"Anyway," I focus on Kaleb, "Amora," I give him a little nod.

"How is she?" he asks.

"She's good, nothing how I expected which was a pleasant surprise."

"What did you expect?"

"Her to be a spoiled brat, just entitled to be honest," I sit up slowly, crossing my legs.

"Ooooo," Keaton chimes with a high-pitched tone, "does Titus have a little crush?"

And my eyes widen.

"No, god no!" I shake my head violently from side to side, "She's twenty-one, same as Arizona, no... no... hard pass."

"You didn't seem to have a problem with falling in love with a twenty-one-year-old, did you Kaleb?"

"Go and choke on your own cock you fucking prick."

My head falls back as a roar of a laugh rips through me, my sides hurting.

"Go fuck yourself," Keaton snaps, cutting the phone off so it's just me, Kaleb and the screen grab of Nate.

"Well, this has been wonderful but I am going to try and get some sleep," I yawn again, twisting my wrist round to look at the time.

"It's three p.m."

"It's eight p.m. here and I am so tired, so peace out. I'll catch up with you in the week."

"Okay, stay safe. And I know Keaton can be a bit of a douche, but Arizona is okay. You know that he would let you know if she wasn't, don't you?"

I nod, "Yeah bro, I know."

"Good, night Titus."

"Night Kaleb, night Connie..."

"Night Titus!" I hear Connie call out and I smile.

"Night Nate," my voice lazy before I cut the phone off and within minutes, I am gone.

Since a package arrived with a garter in it and a note that says *'time is running out, mostriciattola'* things have ramped up. Xavier is planning on putting Amora into lockdown. No more work, no more socializing. I get it, but I just feel like she is about to have the carpet ripped from beneath her and she is only going to react badly to it. I sigh, but what do I know? I'm just her bodyguard. Stepping closer to her room I pause for a moment, ignoring the hard drum of my heart in my chest. Lifting my hand, I knock.

"Amora," I knock again on her bedroom door and glance at my watch, "Amora!" my voice is a little louder now and I feel myself getting impatient. "Amora!" I shout again and knock harder when the bedroom door flies open, her brows knitted together.

"Give me a minute, Jesus," she huffs, grabbing her bag and closing her bedroom door and I don't miss the chance to inhale the scent that drifts past me as she stops in front of me, apricots and cocoa butter and I want to bottle it up so I have it forever.

"Don't bother me if you're late Twilight," I smirk, stepping aside and letting her pass me and follow her down to the car.

"We're not going to be late," she snaps, and I can tell her mood is going to be like this for the rest of the day. I get it, a twenty-one-year-old with a glorified babysitter. I would be pissed too.

"We will if you don't get your ass out the door," I chuckle as we make it to the bottom of the stairs, she bolts for the door, opens it quickly and lets it begin to close so it hits me in the shoulder.

My throat vibrates in a growl as my eyes narrow on her,

the little spitfire. She knows what she is doing, her eyes finding mine as she looks at me over her shoulder and winks.

"Oh how I was wrong about you... *brat*," I smirk back, unlocking the car and climbing straight into the driver's side and an annoyed Amora throws her hands in the air because she has to open her own door.

"Sorry, do you think you're royalty or something?" I tease as she slams the car door, hard. "Don't slam the car door Princess, I don't think daddy will be happy if you do."

"Just drive," she rolls her eyes before slipping out her phone and tapping away on the screen. The drive is quiet, I let the music on my phone play through the speakers and *Luke Combes* fills the car.

I pull into the underground garage of CPH and cut the engine. She jumps out before I am even out the car and walks as quick as her legs will take her towards the elevator.

"Is this how it's going to be today?" I shout across the garage but all I hear is my echo booming off the walls because Amora is long gone.

Locking the car, I pace towards the elevator when I see her standing there, holding her middle finger up as the doors begin to close. I jolt forward, pushing my foot into the doors and stop them and I watch as the smile slowly slips off her face.

"Too bad, Twilight," I scoff, pleased with myself as I rest my hands in front of myself and smile as we ride up to her floor.

"You're an irritant."

I roll my lips, letting my head drop as I try and hide my growing smile.

I have no idea why the sudden change in Amora's

mood, but I can't help but get that niggling feeling that Xavier has something to do with it. We have had a really good week and even though I am still considered a stranger to her, I feel like we have broken the awkward barrier.

I follow her out to her desk but keep five steps behind her and once she is sat down, I take her beige trench coat and walk it back towards the entrance and hang it up for her. I have no idea why I need to be here when she has extended family here, but alas, here I am.

I find it the longest eight hours, well, apart from when she goes for lunch. That's my favorite time of the day because it's just me and her. Most of the time we sit in silence, but I'm hoping today that I'll be able to get some information out of her.

"Morning Amora," a young man calls out as he walks past with piled up files.

"Morning Parker," she chirps waving, "I'll be up in a minute, let me just grab my bits."

"No problem!" Parker calls back and I furrow my brows which causes her icy stare on me.

"What?" she snaps.

"Nothing," I shrug, stepping back and sitting down at one of the empty desks out in the open plan part of the office and this is where I stay until I am summoned.

"Titus," Amora crosses the office towards me, then curls her finger at me to follow. Sighing, I stand and pop my button through my suit jacket and follow her down the hallway.

She stills outside an office, knocking gently then opening the door.

"Parker," she beams, Parker stands and walks round his desk towards Amora and wraps his arms around her frame, her smile widening and a pang of jealously runs through me.

I cough, clearing my throat and I see the agitated look on Amora's face. Parker scrunches his nose up; he has tousled auburn hair and bright sage eyes.

"You can leave," he holds his hand up towards his office door and I follow it with my eyes, looking over my shoulder then letting out a slow chuckle before my eyes burn into him.

"I don't think so," I shake my head from side to side, "I stay where Amora is, that's the rules kiddo."

"She's safe in here isn't she," he tugs on his white shirt cuff that sits under his grey suit jacket.

"She isn't safe anywhere," and I feel Amora's eyes burning into the side of my head, but I give no fucks.

"I said you can leave, you're dismissed," Parker stands a little taller, but he has nothing on me. He must be around five foot eight, maybe five foot nine at a push. I step forward and we're toe to toe, and I slowly crane my neck down to look at him, my lips pulling at one side as a smirk begins to spread.

"You're just a puppy dog in a big, old, city looking for your next pat on the head and getting a *good boy* from the alpha that you want to be." I say slow and low, "So *so* desperately."

I watch as his nostrils flare and I *love* that I am under his skin already.

"Be careful kiddo, don't want you pulling your neck while you're looking up at me,"

I hear a loud tut which I am assuming is from Amora. My eyes don't leave Parker's when I hear the office door shut a little harder than normal.

"Wow, I can smell the testosterone in here," and I realize it's Arabella's voice.

"These two are having a dick measuring contest," Amora scoffs and I snap out of my trance, turning to look at her.

"What the fuck?" I can't help the laugh that rolls out of me at her choice of words.

"Well, you might as well be," Amora crosses her arms across her chest, her white, silk blouse pulling slightly across her chest and my eyes slip from hers, for just a moment before I realize what I am doing. "You're both dickheads," she rolls her eyes, letting her arms drop to her side as she continues through a door in Parker's office which leads into a large board room. A deep oak gloss table sits proudly in the center and is surrounded by floor to ceiling windows overlooking London City.

"Wow," I mutter following Amora like a lost sheep, and I stand, hands fisted deep into my suit pockets as I stare out at the skyline.

"It's something isn't it," she breathes out, her smell invading my senses before I see her.

"Do you go into London a lot?" I ask, pulling my eyes from the beautiful city below me and face her, my eyes casting down.

"Used to," I watch as her happy smile slips, "but then..."

"But then." I roll my lips and turn my attention back to the view.

"Maybe when this is all over, I can take you into London... show you the best of the best."

"That would be epic," I rock back on my heels slightly then turn when I hear a deep voice.

"Dad," Parker nods towards the older man strolling into the boardroom. Parker is a younger version of his dad.

"Parker," he smiles, then turns towards Arabella and Amora.

"Ladies."

"Hi Uncle Carter," Amora bounds over to him and hugs him.

"It's good to see you."

"You too, you look great... I assume you're keeping well," he looks at her with such admiration and adoration.

She nods, breaking away from him while he embraces Arabella.

"And you are?" his eyes flick across the room to me.

"This is Titus, surely father of the year has filled you in?"

I watch as Carter's brows rise high then it seems realization sinks in.

"Oh, *Titty*."

I roll my eyes and Amora sniggers.

Carter steps towards me and holds his hand out, I reach forward, clasping his hand in mine and shake firmly.

"Nice to meet you, how is my wonderful friend Xavier treating you, hopefully well?"

"I think he would treat a dog better," I bark out and that causes Carter to laugh softly, and I join him. "Amora," I turn to face her and see her beautiful eyes drag to mine as they bounce back and forth, "where would you like me to wait?"

"You can stay here? Or do you have something you need to do?" her voice is soft.

"I have a couple of calls, but they can wait... I think I would prefer to just sit in, is that okay? I'm not encroaching in any way, am I?"

She shakes her head from side to side.

"Perfect," I say in a whisper.

"Do you need anything Titus?" Carter asks, looking over in my direction.

"I've got some emails to work on, I don't suppose you have a spare laptop laying around at all?" I ask, "Only if it's not too much trouble of course."

"Parker," Carter snaps at his son, and Parker scrambles to his father's side. "Go grab Titus a laptop please."

I half expect Parker to answer back, but he gives his dad a respectful nod, "Good boy," Carter praises and gives his son a pat on the back before he walks out the room and follows his daddy's orders like the good little dog he is.

"Thank you, I appreciate it."

"You fucker," Amora's eyes flutter shut before she tips her head down and smirks.

"What?" my brows pinch together, confused.

"You know what..." she sighs, turning and walking back towards the top of the table, pulling out her chair and sitting down.

I just stand, dumbfounded. I have no idea what she is on about.

I turn and then I let my smile creep onto my lips, I know *exactly* what I did. I take my own seat up the other end of the table and when I finally look up, I catch her eyes on me. My heart beats a little harder and I throw her a gentle wink and I don't miss the blush that creeps onto her cheeks as she looks away.

CHAPTER SEVENTEEN
AMORA

TWO WEEKS LATER

"WHAT?!" I SCREECH, SLAMMING MY HANDS DOWN ON MY father's desk.

"You heard me, no more work," I see my father's gaze lift from me and focus on something behind me and I know he is looking at Titus.

"Why? What has changed in the last two weeks that means I now can't go to work?"

"Drop it Amora, now." My father's voice is stern, and I know better than to continue but I can't bite my tongue. Something is going on, and either Titus doesn't know and is being kept in the dark or he is being ignorant.

"Tell me, come on... I'm a big girl, I'm sure I can handle it," my nostrils flare, my hands pressed firmly against his desk.

"It's just not safe Amora, after the package we received a couple of weeks back, I just don't think it's wise for you to go to work anymore. I promise I'm not hiding anything from you. Can you just trust me for one second of your life," my father's tone changes and I feel my skin prickle.

"I have trusted you, Daddy. More than I wish I did sometimes... but right now... no, I can't trust you," I shake my head from side to side, my stomach tightening, and nausea rolls through me. I swallow the tennis ball sized lump down with all my might and back out towards the entrance of the room, turning so my father doesn't see the tears that are beginning to fill in my eyes. He doesn't deserve my tears.

I try, but I can't not look at Titus as I pass him, and I see the harshness of his face slip when he sees the single tear that rolls down my cheek. I feel his fingers grab the thin material of my cardigan, but I pull my arm away and storm through the kitchen, ignoring the glances and worried gasps from the staff that are preparing dinner. I feel the burn in my throat, like an iron pole alight and burning in my windpipe causing me to gasp as I push out of the double French doors and into the heavy downpour of rain. I can hear his voice in the background calling after me, but I ignore him. I push forward, the rain belting onto my skin but it feels good. I scream loud, the air escaping my lungs until I can't scream anymore.

"Amora!" he shouts again, I shake my head from side to side and begin to run towards the lake.

"Leave me alone," I shout out but I can hear him behind me. His arm wraps around my waist and he pulls me back into him, my back hitting his chest hard.

"Get off me," I grit, my hands moving over his as I try with all my might to pull him from me.

"No," his voice is low, and his grip tightens.

"Please Titus." I plea, my voice breaking, "please just let me go, I need to be by myself..."

"I'm not going anywhere," his other arm wraps around me.

"I don't want you here, I don't *need* you here." I lash out at him.

"I know you don't but I am here, so let me," his voice is soft, not an ounce of anger to his tone at all.

My whole body shudders as I choke out the tears. Anger consumes me and my legs finally give out, buckling beneath me as I fall to the ground and Titus doesn't stop my fall. I let the rain fall down around me, my head tipping back as the tears still escape and roll down the side of my face, but now the rain washes them away.

"Amora," I hear Titus' voice.

He is always there. Five steps, four steps, three steps... it doesn't matter. He is always there whether I want him there or not.

I am angry. I am so fucking angry.

I ignore him.

"Twilight..." I feel his breath on my face, and when I open my eyes, his nose is inches from mine, his beautiful blue eyes scanning over me, his hands cup my face as he holds me still so I have no other choice but to look at him. He is on his knees dripping wet, the rain drops running down his nose and falling in between us and I feel my chin begin to wobble.

I feel humiliated.

My freedom slowly being taken, and I have no control over it.

He doesn't care.

Trust? I scoff, then choke on my own breath. How can I trust him? All he has done is lie to me.

And realisation hits me.

My worst fear is unfolding in front of me.

I'm a prisoner.

He is making me a prisoner in my own home.

The place I am meant to feel most safe, he is making a real-life hell.

Titus drops his hands from my face, and I instantly miss his touch. His hands slip down the side of my body before his long arms envelope around me and he pulls me into his lap and holds me there until I am ready.

We're both silent. Both soaking wet.

And I have never felt safer than I do right here, right now whilst wrapped in his embrace.

"I've got you, Twilight…" he says softly, his lips pressing into the top of my head and I listen to his racing heart that beats beneath his wet, white tee. "I've got you. You're my priority Amora. I am here for you and only you…" he breathes, and I feel another soft kiss on the top of my wet, red hair. I slowly lift my head from his chest, my wide, reddened and glassy eyes find his and my heart stutters in my chest.

"You promise?" I whisper, scared of these feelings that have slowly crept inside my chest and set up camp.

"I promise Twilight. It's all about you. I won't let anyone get to you, I won't let anyone upset you again…"

"Thank you," I sob, clinging onto his tee as my head drops, my forehead pressing against his chest as the tears begin to fall again and Titus holds me until I am ready to move.

It's just me and him.

I needed him more than I knew, and I hope he is true to his word, I hope I can trust him with everything I have and most importantly, I hope he keeps his promise. Because I am clinging onto that promise more than anything else he has said.

We have become closer; I mean, sure we have. He is the only person I am allowed to see outside of my family and there is something about Titus that draws me in like a moth to a flame, but what worries me is that the flame always fades by the time I get there. I tell him things I would never speak with anyone else, but I trust him.

I don't know why.

But I do.

Wholeheartedly.

After a hot shower and a set of fresh clothes, I am sitting quietly in my painting room, the heavy rain beating down on the glass roof and I find comfort in the sound. No other sound surrounds me apart from that. Candles are glowing on the low windowsills giving the room a calming ambience. I thought it may have helped but it hasn't. I am still upset, frustrated and angry. I exhale heavily as I look at my easel and what I have created. It's crap. I know it is. But it's annoying me at just how bad it is.

Dipping my paintbrush in the black paint, I swipe a large black line through it.

"Now it's ruined," I hear his voice and I try and twist my smile into a pout.

"It was already ruined," my tone is flat and I sigh heavily.

"I don't believe that all the paintings I have been privileged to see and not one of them have been bad."

I spin round quickly and startle myself at how delicious he looks. This is wrong. I should not be looking at my bodyguard this way.

"I never said they were bad..." my brow cocks high in

my forehead and I see his eyes widening, the panic setting in and I roll my lips. "Do you think my paintings are bad?" and I know it's cruel teasing him but it's too easy.

"No!" he rushes out the word as if it's burnt his tongue. "Amora," he breathes out, his light crystal blue eyes captivating me and pulling me in, "your paintings are far from bad, I'm in awe at how amazing they are," he steps a little closer and I let my eyes rake up and down his body, slowly as I take in this godly sight that is bestowed in front of me.

He was wearing cargo trousers, slate grey and a tight white t-shirt which clung to his broad shoulders and hugged his muscly biceps. He looked delicious and smelt heavenly, vanilla and woodsmoke.

"So you don't think my paintings are bad," I manage as he stops in front of me, his hand fisting into his pocket and he shakes his head.

"Not even this one behind me?"

"Not even that one behind you; to be honest, I think it might be my favourite of them all," his voice is low and barely audible, a hush of a whisper floating through me and making my heart pounce in my chest.

My cheeks pinch a crimson and I am grateful for the low light.

"Well, this one is yours if you want it," I shrug my shoulders up, spinning round on my stool as I look back at my canvas.

Greys, blues and a subtle hint of pastel pink and purple streaked through the colours like a horizon about to kiss the sunset.

"Reminds me of *twilight*," Titus' voice rasps and my skin prickles.

Silence crackles in the air, the room being filled with the sound of the rain once more.

Moments pass and my eyes are still fixated on my canvas when Titus finally sits down next to me, grabbing the stool from the other side of the room and perching next to me.

"What's going on in that pretty little head of yours?" he asks and I ignore the urge to look at him and keep my eyes pinned to where they are.

"Just my father unfortunately."

I hear Titus inhale, a slight whistle passing his lips.

"It's bad."

"It isn't bad, he is your father... I mean I do get the protectiveness, but I don't get the hiding things from you."

I shrug.

"I am just annoyed," I admit, tilting my head to the side still looking at my painting.

"And rightly so, you've had another part of your freedom taken, the life that you once had is slowly slipping from your grasp... trust me, I get it."

I turn slowly to look at him, his head dipping slightly so he is now looking up at me through his lashes.

"But I do see it from his perspective, he thinks he is doing the right thing... from what I know of your father and trust me, it isn't a lot... he is a very head strong and stubborn man. If he wants something, he doesn't care what he does to get it and if that means upsetting you then..."

I nod, swallowing the burn in my throat away.

"This is not how I expected to be spending my days..."

"I know, but it's just for a short while," I feel his hand on my shoulder as he gives me a reassuring squeeze, "and before you know it I'll be back on a plane to New York and getting on with my life too..."

"Do you miss home?" I ask, trying to change the subject because I don't want to cry again.

"I do, every single minute of every single day," Titus nods before letting his head hang, his feet shuffling along the tiled floors, his eyes pinned to the floor.

"Well, I'm hoping you get to go home sooner rather than later."

"Let's not hope it's *too* soon... you owe me a date in London," his head lifts as he throws me a soft wink and a smirk.

"Erm," I furrow my brow, rubbing my hand up and down my bare arm, "I don't think I called it a date."

"Oh," he seems taken aback, his voice a little higher than usual, "then what is it?" he sits tall, crossing his leg over the other and then linking his hand over the front of his leg.

"It's just a day out..."

"Shit, have I read this wrong?" he re-composes himself and suddenly I feel awful, my stomach flipping and my cheeks burn with humiliation.

"I mean..."

I link my fingers together and look down into my lap.

"Amora, love, I'm playing," his large hand slips across onto my thigh as he gives it a gentle but playful squeeze and I ignore the burning want for him to move his hand a little higher.

Oh my god what is wrong with me.

I let out an exaggerated giggle. "Got you," I double over, holding my stomach as I continue with this piss poor attempt at a laugh. "The messer become the messee."

"Hey," he sits back, a slight laugh bubbling out of him, "now that isn't fair."

"You should have seen your face," I try and calm my breathing whilst my heart is jack hammering in my chest.

"I'll get you back," and I can't help but hear the tease in his tone.

I ignore it.

I *must* ignore it.

I have never been like this before.

I need sleep.

And a wine or two.

One of the candles goes out and I inwardly groan.

"Shit," I huff, standing up when Titus stands next to me.

"I've got it," he ushers me to sit back down. I watch as he takes one of the still burning candles and lights the burnt out one and something in my chest warms, maybe my own glow?

Was Titus the candle to re light my soul? The one to bring me out of this darkness?

A small glimmer of hope ripples through me, but it was soon dampened by my subconscious.

Of course he isn't you silly, naïve, little girl.

He strolls back over and I shut my intrusive thoughts down in an instant. I stand for a moment, lifting the canvas off the easel and placing it softly down the side of where I am sitting, giving it a chance to actually dry. Reaching across, I stretch to get a new canvas and place it back on the easel then I sit for a moment and lose myself as I stare at the blank white surface.

"Feeling inspired?" Titus asks and I could honestly listen to his voice all day.

"I think so..." I lift one of my shoulders up as I reach for my palette.

"Does this mean I have inspired you?"

I scoff a laugh as I rummage through my many paint colours.

"Why do you think it's you that has inspired me?" I ask him but I don't turn to look at him as I collect golds, browns and nude colours. When he doesn't answer, I look at him over my shoulder and he raises his brows at my colour choices. "You've not inspired me," I snap a little too harshly and I didn't mean for my tone to come out as bitter as it did.

"Sorry," I rub my lips together before wiping my palette clean then adding the fresh paint.

"No need to apologise, it's okay if you don't want to admit that it was I that inspired you," he winks, "but in all seriousness..." he pauses for a moment and shuffles on the stool, "do you mind if I stay and watch?"

"Not at all, I might not get much done, but we will see."

"Do you have some sort of idea what you want to paint before you start working? Or does it come to you when you paint?"

I hum, reaching for some new brushes. "A bit of both really, if inspiration strikes," and I widen my eyes, "which it hasn't, I am just speaking hypothetically."

"Yes, of course," Titus closes his eyes, pouting his lips as he agrees with me but I know he is being sarcastic.

"So, yeah hypothetically speaking, if I am inspired there and then I can just paint and that's what I focus on. I see the image in my head and try to work as close to what I see as possible, but then sometimes I just paint." A small smile slips onto my lips, "That's my favourite kind, to just paint."

"Interesting..." he trails off for a moment, "but tonight you're inspired... so how are you going to paint me?"

"Oh, piss off," I snigger a laugh, swatting him with my hand and shaking my head from side to side, "you're unbelievable."

"Thank you," he sits a little taller, a smug as fuck smile on his face.

"That wasn't a compliment."

"Sure, sounded like one, baby."

He called me baby.

My heart skips and I swallow hard, ignoring the sudden pounding in my chest.

"Quiet, I'm working," I rush out and refuse to look at him. He is too distracting. Too beautifully handsome for his own good. Even if I wanted to, I wouldn't be able to paint something as devastatingly perfect as him.

"Okay," he whispers, pressing his finger to his lips and I giggle.

"Idiot."

Silence fills the large space when I hear his phone ringing. He looks at the caller ID and stands up slowly.

"Would you like a drink?" he asks, as he holds his phone close to his ear.

"Just a water please."

"Cool, I'll be back soon," he turns and walks away when I hear him say, "Hey, just give me a second," I wait until his voice has nearly disappeared to look over my shoulder and admire God's best creation until I'm met with his gaze, a smirk pulling at his lips before he disappears out of my eye line.

"Shit," I whisper, spinning back around in my chair as I begin to paint, feeling my creative spark course through me, and suddenly I feel a little more relaxed than I did an hour ago.

CHAPTER EIGHTEEN
TITUS

SOMETHING ABOUT AMORA DRAWS ME IN. LIKE A MOTH TO A flame.

Idiotic.

Reckless.

But tempting.

It seems the more time I spend with her, the more I am drawn to her. Me, moth. Amora, flame. We're devastation. But it doesn't matter how much I try and pull away I can't. Because of her and everything about her. Over the last few weeks, I have found that I have begun to love the calmness that surrounds her and I realize it's not just her. But her paintings too. I find the calm in them. I could sit and watch her paint for hours, just because I am lost in her imagination and her own calmness that it consumes me whole.

Stepping back into the glass out-building, I just stand in the doorway for a moment then slowly lean against the door frame as I bask in this moment. Her wild, red hair in loose ringlets, tumbled down her back and I smile as she twists it up and holds it in place with a paintbrush. Her sitting there, in her element, surrounded by all her work and a gentle glow from the candles while the rain pelts down onto the glass roof. This is a perfect moment.

Picture perfect.

Slipping my phone out of my full hand, I gently lift it and take a picture of her. It was too beautiful to miss out on. A small smile slips onto my lips and I stand for just a moment more before heading out towards the kitchen.

The house is quiet, and I am grateful because honestly, I wouldn't want Xavier to put a dampener on my mood. Opening the fridge, I grab two bottles of water for me and Amora. My phone call was short and sweet. It was just Arizona wishing me good night and letting me know about her day which I was grateful for. Closing the fridge, I turn to make my way back to Amora's studio but I hear Xavier's grumble coming from down the hall. I still for a moment, listening a little harder to see if I can make out what he is talking about but I can't. He is being quiet for a reason. I should head back to Amora, but my interest is piqued.

Cautiously walking down the hallway, I see his office door ajar, a soft glow from a lamp seeping out onto the floor. I still and press my back against the wall not wanting to step into the light and risk him seeing my shadow.

"I am," I hear Xavier rasp, "I'm happy to move the timeline slightly, things are falling into place now anyway so it should go smoothly..." he trails off and I edge closer. "I am sticking to the deal; this is the fucking deal. Don't test me, do you know what you're asking of me and have me do?" My brows furrow. "She's my daughter, she isn't something you can just take and keep for yourself. That wasn't the plan to begin with was it."

Heart hammering, blood pumping in my ears.

"I know," and I can hear the exasperation in his voice.

Shit.

"Fine," he grits, and I can imagine his jaw is wired tight. "One week," he finally says and I can hear the pain in his voice, "And the parcel that was delivered to my daughter's workplace... that wasn't discussed." Silence follows before I hear a loud bang, a painful roar filling the room and all I can imagine is that Xavier has flipped his desk over and is trashing the room.

I swallow the bile that is slowly seeping up my throat, my heart still jack hammering in my chest as I finally manage to pick up my feet and head towards my little Red.

My.

My little Red.

Stepping into the room, my eyes focus on the painting and the stunning golds that are wrapped around the brown and nude tones, entwining them together creating a beautiful abstract piece.

"Little Red," the nickname slips off my tongue involuntarily but I'm not mad about it.

She turns to face me, gold glitter paint flecked across her face making her pale skin glow in the low light of the room.

"Ty," her voice is low and it sounds heavenly falling from her lips. I continue forward, passing her the bottle of water and open my own. Sitting down next to her, I take a small mouthful. "What do you think?" she pulls her eyes from me and gazes at her painting but I am too busy being transfixed on her. The pride radiating from her, her aura shining bright. The way the gold flecks shimmer on her face in the soft light, her eyes glistening as she takes every part of her painting in, her hands clasped on her lap and her lips part as she waits for my response.

"It's beautiful," I mutter, but the truth was I wasn't

ASHLEE ROSE

talking about her painting. Shaking myself out of my head, I finally manage to tear my eyes from her and look at the painting she has been working on. "It's really something Amora," I smile, swallowing the sickly feeling that is threatening to rise back up from the pit of my stomach.

"Yeah?" her voice is soft and timid and it's like she is seeking my constant compliments, praising her.

"Yeah." My half smile pulls a little higher then I take another mouthful of my water hoping it gets rid of the dryness in my mouth.

"Would you rather this one than the one I ruined?" she spins fully to face me now and I scoff at the sight of her, she really is something.

"No," I shake my head from side to side, "I want the one that reminds me of the sun kissing the evening. The one where lightness meets the dark. The one that shows me twilight."

I don't miss the crimson that creeps onto her skin, the way her eyes bat down and flutter shut as her long dark lashes fan out. Or the freckles flecked against her skin that stand out more as they mix in with the glitter that she has painted with. And then there is her scent. Her intoxicating smell, apricots and cocoa mixed with paint.

I don't miss any of it.

She stretches up, a yawn escaping her as she reaches high and my greedy eyes skim down the side of her body as her soft sage tee rides up slightly and suddenly, I have the urge to put my hands on her, trailing my fingers over her pale skin and tracing out a trail that only I know is there.

"You ready for bed?" she rolls her head round, her neck clicking slightly.

"I am."

She stands slowly, giving her painting one last look

before she steps to the side and saunters over to where the candles are slowly beginning to dim. I can't pull my eyes from her even if I wanted to. Something has changed but I have no idea what. There is no denying that we have grown closer. She is my first thought of a morning and my last of a night. Even if I wanted to shut my thoughts down, I couldn't. But that is just it.

Thoughts.

They are just my thoughts.

She doesn't feel the same as me and I know deep down, I don't feel that way about her. Even if I did, I could never act on it. It's too wrong.

She is the same age as Arizona.

She's too young.

It would be wrong.

So very wrong.

She blows softly, the candles giving one last attempt at a flicker as they dance but they give into submission.

Finally standing, I follow her out and into the darkness of the house and stay behind her until she is at her room.

She opens her bedroom door, stepping inside then turning to face me. "Goodnight, Titus."

"Goodnight Amora," I manage before she saunters back and closes the door on me.

Doomed.

CHAPTER NINETEEN
AMORA

ANGER.

I hate anger.

But anger seems to be the only thing that has consumed me over the last few days and even painting hadn't helped. I found myself being so angry to the point of just sitting and staring at my canvas. It didn't matter how much I tried, nothing helped.

Until him.

The painting that I had worked on I ruined, and it still didn't make me feel better.

Titus sat next to me and didn't even really say much but him just being there helped.

I know it was all in my head, but I was sure we had a moment. To be honest, it was more than just *one* moment. It was the way he looked at me, each stare seemed to feel longer, more intimate. Like stolen moments. It was always when no one else was in the room or near us.

Stolen glances. My heart thumps in my chest. I adored the way my skin prickled in goosebumps every time he said my name, it sounded like heaven slipping off his tongue.

When he walked me to my room I had to stop myself from pressing up on my tiptoes and kissing him, wanting to know what his lips would feel like on mine, would our kiss be electrifying? Or would it be hot and messy with teeth clashing when desire just gets too much so that the fire rips through my soul, leaving me as nothing but ashes.

I feel the heat blossoming between my thighs at the thoughts. I wish I were more experienced; I wish I had the confidence to take a shot and if he shot me down then at least I tried. But I would be humiliated if I done it now and he pushed me away.

I slowly pace over to my bed, my fingertips gliding over the soft bedding when my mind wanders to Titus once more. I have no idea what hold this man has over me so suddenly and I am not sure if I like it or not.

It's as if I am in a chokehold that I didn't want to be in.

But not in a bad way.

Climbing onto the bed, I feel my bud pulsing and I know I need to rid this feeling. Titus is all I see, my fingers graze softly up my bare thigh, my lemon summer dress hitched slightly round my waist as my fingers continue their slow and torturous decent up my thighs to the spot that I so desperately need touching. Finally reaching the apex of my thighs, my fingers delicately brush against the thin material of my underwear and my breath hitches, a shaky breath leaving me as I do it again, my eyes fluttering shut when I hear a loud knock on my bedroom door.

"Amora," I hear Titus' voice float through the room and my eyes widen.

"Coming!" I rush out as I jump from the bed.

Yeah you wish my subconscious hisses at me and I ignore the little bitch and pull on my bedroom door, Titus' eyes move up to mine and I feel like my heart is jack hammering in my chest and I know for a fact that my cheeks are flaming red at the thought of what I was about to do before Titus knocked. He is wearing a sky-blue shirt with the two top buttons undone, his collar wide and I can see a glimpse of his glorious skin. His shirt is tucked into charcoal suit trousers, and he looks divine which makes my sex pulse a little more.

"Are you okay?" he asks, stepping into my room and placing his hand on my forehead. "You look a little warm," he breathes, his eyes searching my face, but I just didn't know what he was looking for.

"I'm fine," I swallow, willing for the dryness in my mouth to disappear and ignoring the heat that flows through my blood from his touch. I go to move past him, but he steps back in front of me.

"Are you sure?" his brows furrow, slowly stepping back away from me and leaning against the door frame.

"Yes," my tone has bite to it because the longer he stands here looking at me, the more I want his lips on mine, his hands in my hair as he shows me what it is like to be kissed.

"You're agitated, has something happened?" he asks again, his hand moving closer as his fingers wrap around my hip and I ignore the singe from his fingers on my skin.

"No Titus, please, can we just go? You obviously came here for a reason..." exasperation consumes me and suddenly I can't bear to be close to him. I am still reeling, and my senses are wired from being interrupted, my bud still pulsing as I squeeze my thighs together. My cheeks blush and I have no reason to let embarrassment suffocate me. He doesn't know what I was about to do. He has no idea that I was laying, wide legged and ready to pleasure myself just mere moments ago over thoughts of him.

"Dinner," his voice is low as his breath breezes over my face, and I don't miss the smell of bourbon.

I nod, rendered speechless so it's all I can manage. Titus moves to the side, letting me pass him and I keep my head down as we walk in silence towards the grand dining room.

"I only wanted to check if you were okay..." his voice is low as he walks beside me.

"And I told you that I am, so stop asking me." I snap my head up to look at him, willing for him to stop asking me.

He doesn't respond, just inhales deeply. We still for a moment outside the dining room when I feel his fingers brush against me and I flinch, my brain is screaming for me to pull my hand away, but I don't. I keep it where it is and enjoy the buzz of electricity that courses through me from his grazing fingertips.

"I am always here Amora; my loyalty lies with you. I made a promise to you, and I will honor that promise until I am sent away."

My breath catches in the back of my throat, my heart is galloping in my chest, forming a fast but steady beat and I am worried that he can see just how fast it is beating under my skin.

"I know," I just about manage before the dining room door is opened and Titus' fingers move from mine and slip inside his suit trouser pockets. My eyes scope the room and see my family sitting there, all their eyes on me.

Father. Mother. Xander. Ezekiel.

I swallow the lump down, stepping into the room and nodding at Christopher as I do. Christopher has worked for us since way before I was born. From what I have heard, he and my mother used to date in secret until my father came along and put a stop to that and as punishment for the both of them, Christopher was to work under my father, so he had to see my mother every single day.

Cruel, *cruel* bastard.

But Christopher got his happily ever after with Mabel, one of the kitchen hands. Her family lived in the cottage on the grounds but once her and Christopher were married, they moved just outside the grounds to raise a family.

My chair is pulled out for me, and I sit gracefully, and Titus is gestured to sit opposite me, but he declines, pulling the chair out beside me and sitting down.

"Evening," my father's gruff, deep voice fills the room and I give him a small smile. "How are you my angel?"

"Honestly?" I turn to face him and he gives me a silent nod, the awkwardness in the room suddenly thick. "I've been better," I rub my lips together, my palms running down my bare legs.

"I am hoping this will all be settled soon," he smiles towards me but his smile struggles to meet his eyes and it fills me with dread, my stomach knotting.

I nod. "It could have never got to this you know..." I pause for a moment and catch Xander staring at me.

"What's done is done," Ezekiel snaps at me and my brows pinch.

"Sorry?" my back is up, rage coursing through me. "That's okay for you *golden boy*. Nothing changes for you; your life stays the same. Yet *my* life gets turned upside down and I get told *what's done is done,*" I am seething, it doesn't matter how much I try and calm myself down, I am too far past that point.

"So," I hear Titus' upbeat tone echo round the room, his hand slipping under the table, and moving to my thigh and I feel the reassuring squeeze. I watch my mother's lips twist, her eyes cast down on her place setting. "How was everyone's day? Royal, what did you get up to?" Titus asks as dinner is placed in front of us. Stuffed chicken breast, green vegetables, and dauphinoise potatoes. "Well, this looks delicious," Titus hums, picking up his knife and fork and stabbing a carrot before pressing it to his lips and taking a bite. "Crunchy."

I nibble the inside of my lip.

"Thank you for asking Titus, that's really kind of you," my mother's eyes finally lift and cast across the table to Titus. "I had to run some errands," she nods softly, "then just done some gardening."

"You have a lovely garden, do you tend to it yourself?" Titus continues, cutting into his chicken.

"I do, I started when I first moved here when I was twenty-one," her cheeks blush slightly and I hear my father's growl.

"Yeah, when dad kidnapped you," I scoff as I continue to push my food around my plate as I hear my mother tut.

"Amora," my father's tone is sharp.

"What?" I snap.

"Enough," his eyes narrow on mine, but I hold his gaze not breaking away, willing for him to look away first.

"No, I am sick of the whispers, sick of the silence as soon as I walk into a room." I shake my head from side to side continuously.

"Amora, it isn't like that..."

"Then what is it like?" my brows raise high and my eyes bug out of my head.

"You don't need to worry about it, just trust me," my father hovers his fork above his plate with a string bean dangling from it.

I snigger, utter disbelief consuming me suddenly.

"How about you Ezekiel, Xander... good day?" Titus

continues and I watch as my father rolls his eyes, his jaw tight and clenched.

"It was alright," Xander shrugs and he takes a mouthful of potatoes.

"Same," Ezekiel's bored tone irritating me.

"I see," Titus nods, reaching for his water and taking a sip then popping it back on the table gently.

"You're annoying me," Xavier growls across the table.

"Why?" Titus looks at me, a smirk pulling at his lips before he faces my father again.

"You're asking too many questions," he pops his forkful into his mouth, chewing slowly whilst keeping his eyes pinned to my *bodyguard*.

"Well at least he is making the effort unlike *some people*," I mutter under my breath and Titus coughs.

"How are you Titus? Have you had a good day?" my mother asks, and I can hear the humour in her voice. My father's eyes cross over to my mother as he glares at her as if she has just told him that she is leaving him.

"I am wonderful thank you," he chimes, cutting into his chicken again, "honestly, Royal, thank you *so* much for asking," I try and hide the smile that is threatening knowing full well he is pissing my father off something chronic. "And my day, well, I got to spend it with your beautifully talented daughter, so yes, I have had a really, *really* good day."

A deep, rumbling growl echoes round the room and all eyes swiftly land on my father.

"Do you need some water Xavier? You sound like you're choking." Titus reaches for the jug of water, standing and pouring my father a glass. "Maybe slow down on the mouthfuls of food, no good for the digestive system," Titus gives my father a huge smile before sitting back in his seat and continuing to eat his food.

"I cannot wait to send you back on your fucking plane and back to America next week *Titty*."

Titus stops chewing, his eyes slowly lifting and resting on my father. My heart drops into my stomach and I gasp, choking on my inhale of breath.

"Xavier," my mother's tone is sharp.

"Dad…" Xander's voice is hushed, his head dipping as he tries to get my father's attention but it's no use, my father's sights are locked and loaded on Titus.

"My job isn't done yet," Titus responds, wiping his mouth with his napkin and letting it drop onto his plate.

"Your job is done when I tell you it's done."

Titus' hands drop into his lap, and now it's my turn to comfort him as I slowly slip my hand across to his, covering it with mine.

"So Amora is safe then?" I hear the low rumble in Titus' throat. "All threats are gone? I thought we had a *little* more time until then…" he pauses and my father's eyes widen slightly before narrowing into thin slits.

"We don't. You go Monday."

"So, three days?" Titus scoffs shaking his head.

"Three days," my father reaches for his glass and takes a mouthful of his water, "your money will be wired into your bank by the end of the day Monday," he says, giving a final nod.

I squeeze Titus' hand under the table, fear crippling me that he is being taken away from me.

"Everyone leave," my mother's voice calm and authoritative, but her tone is loud, my brothers standing up immediately. My mother very rarely gets angry, but when she does you know to listen.

"Sit down," my father grits, his fists balled.

"I said," my mother's blue eyes slice to my father's, her icy glare pinned to him, "everyone leave."

"Royal," my father warns.

"Out!" she shouts, and we all stand and move for the door, Titus closing it behind us.

"What the fuck is all that about?" I ask the three men in front of me but my question is aimed at Xander. My father tells Xander *everything*.

Ezekiel shrugs his shoulders up, his eyes moving between the three of us.

"Honestly Amora, I know nothing. Dad doesn't tell me shit like this," he turns to face Xander who won't look back at him.

"Xander..." I whisper, fear crippling me in an instant.

"I don't know a lot..." his voice is hushed, his eyes move behind me to the closed door before they meet mine.

"But you know something..." I swallow the bile back down.

He nods, then drops his head and I can hear the shaky breath that leaves him. Titus reaches forward, gripping his shoulder and giving him a reassuring squeeze.

"You're not safe Amora, the coast is most definitely not clear..." his eyes bounce between mine, "I don't know what sort of deal dad has struck with The Knight Brothers, but it's not a good one. I caught him crying last night in his office... it's big Amora and I am worried."

"It'll be okay," my voice cracks and I feel my chin begin to wobble, my bottom lip trembling and it doesn't matter how much I try and stop them, my eyes fill with tears.

"I won't let them near you," Titus reaches for me, tucking a loose strand of my hair behind my ear and I ignore the pull that I feel, the raw magnetism of the forcefield that surrounds us.

"You aren't going to be able to stop them Titus, not from thousands of miles away... you heard him," my voice rises, "he is sending you back on a plane in *three* days." My glassy eyes steady on his as I wait for him to say something.

"They can't take you if you're not here..."

Mine and my brothers heads snap round to look at Titus.

"What?" Ezekiel asks, his whole body turning to face him.

"Find me a safe place, I'll take Amora tonight, I'll keep her safe."

I watch as Ezekiel runs his hand round the back of his neck, his tell-tale sign that he is uncomfortable and anxious. He seeks out Xander's approval and permission all the god damn time. But I can't help but let hope bloom in my chest.

"We can find her somewhere can't we Xander?" and the desperation drips off Ezekiel's tongue, my chest tightening, my heart hurting.

Xander's eyes move between me and Titus and after what feels like a lifetime, he gives a heavy nod.

"Yeah, leave it with me. Pack your bags tonight, I'll find somewhere within the hour. I have enough people who owe me favours."

"Don't bring Carter and co into this," I warn, panicking that they may slip up.

"I'll try not to, but you haven't left me much time to sort something, they will be last resort," Xander steps towards me and pulls me into a hug, his arms tightening round me. "I promise, none of them will breathe a word of this." He reassures me, squeezing me tight again, "I'm not letting these fuckers take you," he steps away and then Ezekiel launches himself into me and Titus steadies me as Zeke nearly knocks me off my feet.

"I love you both, *so* much," I whisper trying to not let the tears escape.

"We love you too, kiddo," they both say in unison as Xander wraps his arms round me and Ezekiel.

CHAPTER TWENTY
TITUS

I HAVE NO IDEA WHAT THE FUCK HAPPENED LAST NIGHT, BUT Xander didn't pull through. I am not sure if Xavier caught wind of what we were planning but he is being antsy as fuck. I can see the rage practically bubbling out of him, one more degree higher and I swear he will have steam coming from his ears.

I pace up and down outside Amora's door waiting for her to emerge. She has been in a mood since early hours this morning when we were both camped up in her room waiting.

My phone pings and I can't stop the irritated sigh that escapes my lips. Slipping my phone out my pants pocket, I see a message from Arizona.

Arizona
Hey Dad, just checking in. You've been a
little quiet so just want to make sure you're
okay. I miss you xxx

I scrub my face, *shit*. I type out a quick response.

> **Titus**
> Hey Sunshine, so sorry. I am okay, I
> promise. Things just got a little complicated
> over here but hoping it all settles soon. I
> miss you so much. I hope work is going
> okay and Keaton isn't getting to you. I know
> how irritating he can be. I'll video call you in
> a few hours hopefully. Love you xxx

She reads it and responds with an *ily*.

I really do need to speak to Keaton, well, all of them really. I have completely fallen off the radar since being here. Consumed by a certain red headed beauty. My *little Red*. How can she have captivated me so much in such a short amount of time? It's just because we're spending so much time together. She is my job. My job is to protect her and that's what I will do. Until I know that she is out of harm's way and safe. I could never go there with her. She is the same age as my daughter. She is forbidden, no, she is impermissible.

She is pure.

Innocent.

Beautifully forbidden.

Perfectly impermissible.

Taboo.

The way my cock stirs in my jeans at the thought of her, the way her pale skin would feel under my touch, the way her lips would feel on mine and the way her moans would sound.

I shake my head from side to side, disgusted with myself.

"NO!" I shout, balling my hands into tight fists.

This is all because I am tired and wound up.

That's it.

Maybe I am hallucinating. What is sleep? Sleep hasn't come easy since I have been living here in England. Exhaustion hits me continuously, and even when I sleep I am restless.

The door pulls open and I see a frantic Amora, her eyes scanning up and down my body before they search my face for anything.

"Sorry, I didn't mean to startle you," I push my hands into my pockets and stand a little taller.

"You didn't startle me," she runs her tongue across her bottom lip slowly and my eyes cast down to watch, my lips part.

"What are we going to do?" she asks, stepping out of her room and into the narrow hallway, the scent of apricot and cocoa swarming me and I find myself inhaling deeply just so I can get my fix.

"We're going to go about our day until we hear from Xander..." I swallow, stepping back because suddenly she feels too close.

She nods, looking over her shoulder and sighing.

"Is there anything you want to do?" I ask as she closes her bedroom door and she begins walking. I follow.

"Can we go sit by the lake?" She spins to face me, her eyes lighting up, her smile wide and I melt at the dimples that present themselves.

Twenty-one.

Twenty-one.

"If that's what you want to do Twilight then that's what we will do," I smile back at her, my heart skipping a beat or two.

"Then, maybe we can go out on one of the boats. I've

got tingly fingers and that's normally when I know I want to paint."

"Tingly fingers, huh?" One of my brows cocks high.

"Mmhmm," she hums, turning as we reach the top of the stairs.

"Do you get tingly fingers with anything else?" the question is off my tongue before my brain has even caught up with what the fuck I have just said.

She gasps, looking over her shoulder at me and I can see the slight blush under her cheeks.

"That's for me to know and you to *maybe* find out Mr King," she breaks eye contact and I watch as she shakes her head side to side softly.

I scoff a laugh and follow her. The house is quiet and for some reason it makes me nervous.

We continue forward and into the kitchen where Xavier and Royal are sitting at the small table.

I hear Amora sigh heavily as she walks towards them.

"Morning darling," Royal's soft voice fills the room.

"Morning," Amora gives a curt nod and not making eye contact and I can see how quickly Royal's smile slips from her lips, and worry consumes her.

Xavier says nothing. His shoulders are rolled forward slightly, he is sitting as if he is ready for whatever is coming. He looks uncomfortable. I slowly walk past him and as much as I don't want to, I do look at him. His eyes are dark, hooded, haunted. He isn't looking at Royal, he is looking right through her as if she isn't even there.

"Morning Titus."

"Morning Mrs Archibald," I give her a slow smile as I still next to her but Amora is already out in the garden.

"Please, it's Royal, like it always has been," she gives me a little smile and I hear Xavier scoff.

"As you wish," I pause, "morning Royal," I tip my head slightly before following Amora out into the yard. She isn't very far and after a few long strides I have soon caught up with her. Her hands hang down by her side and I let my fingers spread slightly, willing our fingers to brush like they did yesterday and I can't help but wonder whether she felt the spark that coursed through me so harshly it made me flinch.

She stalls, her head tipping back and her eyes closing as she inhales the spring air.

"I feel free," she mutters quietly, my body turning to face her as I watch.

"Yeah?"

"Yeah." She sighs, "I know that sounds ridiculous..." she finally lets her head drop forward, then she turns to look at me.

I shake my head from side to side, "It doesn't sound ridiculous."

"Hmm, I think you're just being kind."

"Maybe," I shrug before she continues walking, I stay by her side.

Silence fills the void between us, the birds sing softly in the distance, and I can begin to hear the sound of the lake, only just, but I can hear it and I suddenly feel a million miles away once more.

We turn and walk down the deck, and I see her shoulders instantly drop and sag.

"Feel better?"

"Yes," she just about manages as she kicks her shoes off and walks barefoot down the deck. I stand and watch for just a moment, the way the sun beats down against the water, causing it to glisten and sparkle, her long, wavy red hair blowing softly in the breeze. Her skin somehow looks paler, but still just as beautiful. Her sundress sits midway on her milky thighs, her fingers playing with the hem of her dress. The breeze picks up suddenly and her scent consumes me once more and I feel myself stepping a little closer to her, even if I didn't want to, my legs just move, and I gravitate towards her.

She turns to look at me over her shoulder, a lopsided smile on her face but she faces forward too quickly, and I instantly miss it. She really is perfect. I don't even think perfect is a strong enough word to pin to her.

She is unblemished. Flawless.

Faultless.

I slip my phone out, lifting it slightly as I position it and snap a photo of her. It's too good of an opportunity to miss.

The way the sun is beating down, the reflection off the water beaming off her skin.

She is picture fucking perfect.

I drop the phone down and slide into my pictures and I see it. My fucking heart thumps in my chest and it scares me to death. Running my thumb over the screen, I feel a pang shoot from my chest down to my stomach causing it to twist and knot. Sighing, I push my phone back away.

I walk cautiously towards her, each step I close on her, my heart beats a little faster. A blissful sigh leaves me as I cast my eyes over the calm water.

"Have you swum in there before?" I ask, fisting one of my hands into my pocket, the other hanging beside me.

"Once or twice," she turns to look up at me and I've only just realised how short she is.

"Have you shrunk?" I playfully nudge into her and her nose scrunches, her brows crinkling. A deep chuckle leaves me, and I hear her giggle too. "In all seriousness, how short are you?" I scoff once more.

"Five foot four, so not short at all... you're just abnormally tall." She elbows me. I snort, tipping my head back as I rub where she nudged me. "Would you swim in there?" She asks, the breeze picking up slightly and dusting over my skin.

"Maybe when it's a little warmer, I don't feel acclimatized yet."

"Wimp."

I snap my head round to look at her.

"Wimp!?"

"Yeah, big guy, *wimp*."

She continues taunting me.

I reach for her, wrapping my arms around her waist as I lift her up, holding her over the water.

"Titus!" she screams, her fingers clutching at my shirt, "Put me down." I laugh, my grip tightening on her and ignore the burning that is scalding my fingertips from touching her.

"Please," she begs but she laughs.

"Okay Twilight, seeing as you asked so nicely," I step back, her body turns towards me, and my arms wrap tightly around her.

I take a moment, slowly putting her down and steadying her.

"Would you have really dropped me?" she asks all coy.

I shake my head from side to side, "No, darling, I wouldn't have."

She nods, bringing her thumb to her mouth as she nibbles on her nail.

"What are you thinking about?"

She inhales deeply, dropping her thumb from her lips.

"I have no idea what my father is planning, I'm worried and the fact that Xander knows something..."

"No one is getting to you," I pull her into me, holding her tight as her head rests against my chest and I pray she can't hear how fast my heart is racing. Craning my neck down, I place a kiss on the top of her head and breathe in her heavenly scent. "I'll get you away from here, your father hired me to protect you, and that's what I will do." The thought of being put on a plane in two days is crippling, I can't leave her. Not after I promised her.

I won't leave. He can't make me.

Holding her tighter, I feel her begin to tremble in my arms and I can hear the soft sobs that consume her.

"Hey, hey," I whisper, gliding my hand up her side and cupping her cheek, lifting her face to look at me. "No tears, there is no reason to cry," I give her a crooked smile, my thumb pad brushing against her cheek as I catch a rolling tear. Her skin is soft and in that moment all I want to do is let my fingers trace and roam over all of her.

"It's a lot for a twenty-one-year-old to go through..." I say softly.

I feel her stiffen in my arms, her eyes burning into mine.

"My daughter is twenty-one and I couldn't imagine..." she presses her finger against my lips to quieten me.

"He told you I was twenty-one?" her brows furrow and my eyes widen; I wrap my fingers round her wrist and pull her finger away from my mouth.

"You're not?"

"That arsehole," her head falls forward, so it's resting and pressing against my chest.

I keep my eyes pinned down on her and I feel anger bubble deep inside of me. Letting my hands trail up her body, I cup my hands round her face and tilt her head back, so she has no choice but to look at me.

"You're not twenty-one?" I ask again because for some reason, I can't seem to catch up. She shakes her head, her eyes filling with fresh, unshed tears and I watch as her chin wobbles.

"Why are you sad, Twilight?"

"It's frustration," she croaks, the crack in her voice evident.

"Well don't be frustrated, I will get this sorted," and before I realize what I am doing, I press my lips to her forehead, letting my eyes close for a moment as I try and calm myself down. "How old are you?" I mutter against her skin.

"Twenty-five."

I sigh, and I feel a little lighter somehow knowing that she is older than Arizona. The feelings that I was starting to feel towards her not as wrong as they should feel. I am angry at Xavier and feel like he only told me that she was the same age as my daughter so I couldn't say no. He made it personal. Made me feel more sympathetic towards the situation by making it about something we both have in common.

Daughters the same age.

"Your dad is a total dick isn't he," I sigh, and a small but soft chuckle comes out of me as my thumbs brush across her cheek once more before I drop her face from my grasp, and I instantly miss the feeling of her skin under my fingertips.

"So, your daughter, she's twenty-one?" Amora gives a small smile as she asks her question, her eyes glistening and I'm unsure if it is from the tears or the sun that is reflecting off the water. "What's she like?"

"Beautiful, strong willed, a kid genius." I scoff a laugh,

slipping my hands into my pockets so I can't reach for her like I so desperately want to. "She is in med school, a little earlier than she should be but then again she was always a few years ahead of her peers and graduated very early."

"She sounds perfect," Amora nods and sighs, "we haven't really spoken about your life before me..." she trails off and I don't miss the harsh swallow, her vein beating under her skin. "Bet you and your wife are proud as punch." I know exactly what she is thinking and why she purposefully asked that and that's when her beautiful blue and brown eyes drop from mine, and I instantly miss her gaze.

"Oh, no," I shake my head from side to side quickly, ripping the band aid off once again on my trauma that I have done so well on pushing as far down as I physically can.

"What?" her brows pinch, her lips parting and her eyes are on mine again making my heart pulse a little faster under my skin.

"There isn't a wife."

The top of her nose crinkles a little as she frowns a little deeper, forming fine creases in her forehead.

"There isn't a mother."

I swallow, my heart now racing and I swear I can feel beads of sweat sitting on my brow line. I have never, *ever* opened up about my history with Sharon. I have never cared about anyone enough to open up. But with Amora, I find myself wanting to willingly tell her everything. All of my secrets, all of my past and trauma... I want to give her everything so she can write it on her heart and lock it away.

"So it was..." she blinks a couple of times, her teeth drawing her bottom lip into her mouth.

"Just me and my daughter." I swallow thickly, the unwanted lump creeping up my throat.

"Oh," her voice quiet and her eyes fall from mine as she picks her nails.

"I had my friends helping me too, they were amazing and honestly I don't think I could have gotten through the first few months without them." I give a small nod, standing a little taller as I look over at the calm water and feel my heart begin to slow just a little.

Amora turns round, breaking her gaze from mine and walks back towards the edge of the wooden dock.

I stand for a moment, ignoring the pull that I feel to follow her. I inhale deeply, the thought of leaving her cripples me. I trust Xavier, I trust that he wouldn't put his daughter in harms way, but I also don't trust him. His daughter will always be his priority, along with his family and I get that. I do, because if this was Arizona, I would do whatever needed in a heartbeat to assure her safety. But it's the shadiness. The secret keeping. We're on the same team yet I am being kept out of the loop and not only that, being sent back on a plane away from the one woman who seems to have brought me back to life in the short amount of time I have been here.

My phone chimes in my pocket and I see Kaleb's name flash on the screen. Clicking answer, I lift the phone to my ear and turn on my heel, walking back towards the green lawn.

"Hey," I breathe down the phone, the intensity of the pull growing the further I walk away as if my body knows it's not right and I need to be by her side.

"Hey, I just wanted to check in. You've been quiet on us," I hear mutters in the background and I know he is with

Nate and Keaton. My brows furrow and I look down at my wrist, turning it to face me and checking the time.

"It's six thirty in the morning there, why are you all up so early?"

"We went to the gym early this morning with Killian, never again," I scoff a laugh, I can just visualize Kaleb being bossed around by Killian.

"Glad I missed that," I smirk, kicking the toe of my sneaker into the grass.

"How is it going over there?"

"Shit," I sigh, lifting my head and looking over my shoulder to check on Amora who is still staring into the distance.

"Want to elaborate?"

"Xavier is sending me home in two days, apparently my services are not required," I shrug my shoulders up softly as if Kaleb can see me.

"What?" his voice is low, and I hear a door shut softly in the background.

"Yup."

"Is Amora safe?"

"I don't believe so."

"And you're leaving?"

"Like fuck I am, I am waiting for her brother to find me a safehouse that I can take her to."

"Hey, you be careful... look what happened to me when I went to a safehouse," I can hear the smile in his voice.

"I'm not you," I shake my head, "but Xander is taking his time. I get he has to be careful because he works very closely with Xavier, but I need her out of here. I can't leave her."

"Bring her back to New York."

I scoff.

"If only."

"What? I can get a private jet on the tarmac tonight... you just need to get her to the airport."

"I don't know... I think it's too risky. I'm on Xavier's side, I don't want to piss him off any more than I have done."

"This is about Amora, not you or Xavier."

"I know that, dumbass." I sigh a little heavier, "But I don't think bringing her to New York is the best option. Xavier has a plan, and I know it involves the Knight brothers. He is indebted to them; they want Amora and honestly..." I pause, looking at her once more and taking another step forward, "I think he is giving her to them a lot easier than I first thought," I keep my voice low so only he can hear.

"Are you sure?"

"Ninety percent," I rub my lips together and let my hand knead the tension from the back of my neck.

"You heard something?"

"Just about a timeline moving up... he is being sketchy. I work for him. To protect her. And yet, he isn't telling me anything. The fucking look on his face when he told me that he was sending me back on a plane. It's personal. He doesn't want me here and I have no idea why... well I do, but it's beside the point..."

"What did you do?" I hear Kaleb growl down the phone.

"Nothing, I wind him up. I can't help the sarcasm that comes out my mouth when it comes to Xavier. I mean, I wouldn't tell him this, but I actually like him. He is an ass, but I like him."

"He just doesn't like you."

"Exactly," I slowly spin round, and Amora does it at the same time, giving me a small smile as she begins to walk towards me. "But it isn't about Xavier, it's about Amora," I rush out, "but if you, or Nate could help me with my request then I would be grateful. Far enough, but not too far."

"Okay."

"I'll call you later."

"Yeah, cool."

I cut the phone off just as Amora stops in front of me.

"You okay?" she asks, the soft breeze dancing in her hair and her scent fills my senses, giving me a rush of a high.

"Yeah, just my buddy back home," I say, following her lead and walking back through the gardens, but we turn in the opposite direction of the house.

"Still missing home?"

"A little, I miss my daughter most."

"I bet," her hands drop to her side, her fingers flexing open as my own hand hangs.

"Have you always lived in New York?"

"Moved to Long Island for a bit, but I am a New Yorker through and through." I smile at her, "I would love to see more of the world, England was on my bucket list..." I trail off.

"But babysitting a twenty-five-year-old wasn't," she laughs softly and damn, it's such a beautiful sound. I scoff a laugh back and shake my head.

"No, it wasn't, but I wouldn't change it for the damn world."

"Really?" she stops just before a large orchard full of apple trees, turning and facing me.

"Really," I nod.

I watch as her ivory skin reddens over her cheeks and her head dips down to break the eye contact with me and I instantly miss looking into the windows of her soul.

I stand, bewildered and dazed. I have no idea why I am feeling like this, everything is new and unfamiliar. I loved Sharon... *loved*. But it never consumed me like this? She wasn't my first and last thought of the day. I'm sure it's nothing more than just a little crush, I mean I'm not even sure if you can call it a crush because I hardly know her.

"You just going to stand there?" her voice floats over me, snapping me from my thoughts. She reaches up onto her tiptoes, her cream summer dress which is dotted with sky blue flowers, lifts up her thigh a little more and suddenly all I want to do is dig my fingers into her creamy ivory skin, just to feel her under my fingertips. I hear a light rustle and she plucks a bright, red apple from the branch, her feet back on the ground as she rubs the red skin of the apple on the cotton of her dress and instantly, I am jealous.

Of a fucking apple.

I scrub my face with my hand, letting out a soft but low groan.

She presses the apple to her rosy lips, a wide smile spreading across her face.

"You're trouble," I let my hands fall, squeezing my hand into a fist before flexing my fingers.

"I have no idea what you mean," she opens her mouth slowly and takes a bite of her apple, the crunch loud.

"I think you do," my eyes hood, my tongue running along my bottom lip, my teeth gripping and pulling it into my mouth slowly.

"Honestly," she rasps, her chest rising and falling a little faster, her fingers playing with the delicate frill detailing on her neckline of her dress.

I haven't even realized that we're in an apple orchard, surrounded by nothing but green trees and red apples.

"Honestly," I smirk, stepping towards her, reaching and grabbing my own apple.

"They're delicious," she breathes, her fingers that were once playing with the frills are now on her stomach, her fingers crumpling the thin material.

"I bet they are," I nod, rubbing my own apple against the material of my shirt then taking my own bite. Her eyes are wide, her mouth parted as she watches me.

I move another step closer, half expecting her to step back but she doesn't. She stays grounded to the grass beneath her.

"What do you think?" she asks in barely a whisper.

"Delicious." I nod, taking another bite and I hear her gasp.

We're standing toe to toe, my eyes darkening as I gaze into hers. I watch as they dart back and forth between mine. I slowly reach forward, wrapping my arm round her back and pull her a little closer to me, then let my hand glide up the side of her body until my fingers brush against the soft skin of her cheek, an electrifying jolt vibrates through me, my stomach knotting. Her eyes drop to my lips, silently begging me to kiss her, before they flick back up to mine and I feel overwhelmed, my heart jack hammering in my chest as my stomach fills with anticipation. Letting my fingers spread and move to hold her cheek, my thumb brushing over her full, red, rosy lips my own breath catches in the back of my throat, my lips edging closer to hers, my eyes falling to her mouth before they flutter shut. Our lips are just about to meet when my phone rings, causing Amora to jump, her apple falling from her laxed fingertips and it hits the floor causing a light thud.

I swoop back, fisting my phone from my pocket to see Xavier's name. I roll my eyes and lift the phone to my ear.

"Yes."

"Bring her home."

"Okay," I cut him off, shoving the phone into my back pocket.

Her wide eyes are glued to mine.

"We need to get back to the house," I just about manage to roll out the words.

She just nods, breaking her gaze from mine as she dips her head and walks past me and I fall back.

"Shit," I mumble under my breath, dropping my own apple to the floor and following her back into the house keeping five steps behind.

I continue forward, Amora doesn't look back at me. I fucked up. Did I? Did I read it all wrong? I watch as she rounds the corner, climbing the stairs and I am desperate to follow her but I have a niggling anger burning inside of me. I pause, stopping in my tracks and I watch as she disappears from my sight, and I instantly miss her. I turn to look at Xavier's closed office door, I lift my hand ready to knock but then decide against it. I push the handle down with force and let the door swing open, the sound of the door hitting the wall not making me flinch at all. Xavier is sitting at his desk, his eyes follow the door before they glide back to mine.

"What do I owe the pleasure?"

Rage burns through my veins.

"Twenty-one." I say through gritted teeth and I watch as one corner of his lip lifts slightly. "You told me she was twenty-one."

"Did I?" he reaches for his glass of red wine, sitting back in his chair and lifting the glass to his lips before taken a mouthful. He hums in appreciation, licking his lips and placing his glass gently down on a coaster.

"You did."

"What is the issue Titty?" his brows raise, "You're still getting paid for your time, I don't understand why you are pissed off about it."

"Because you lied. Do you have a moral compass? Because I don't think you do." I rub my lips together and take another step forward. "I would have come regardless of her age, because you asked me and I know what it is like to be a father, not to mention how much you helped my friend with his girlfriend Connie."

"So you felt indebted to me?" he links his fingers together, crossing one leg over the other

"Indebted? No."

"I've helped a lot of people Titus, it's my job. But you wanted to help if I remember rightly because yes, you have a daughter and I thought it would make sense for me to use someone who was in the same position as me. Young daughter, vulnerable..."

"Arizona isn't vulnerable."

"I wasn't talking about Arizona," his icy glare slices through me and I swallow. "Everything is finalized, your plane will leave tomorrow."

"You said three days."

"You leave tomorrow."

"Where is Amora going?" I swallow, the lump is wedged in my throat and is burning like hot coal.

"Amora is not your concern anymore."

"Amora is my priority."

"Not anymore."

"Xavier," my voice cracks, "don't give into them, please."

"Who says I've given into them?"

"Let me stay, I'll do whatever is needed... don't send me home."

"You're going home Titty."

"Push your feelings for me aside and think of your daughter..."

"I am thinking of Amora!" he snaps, interrupting me, standing from his desk and smashing his hands down into the desk.

"I don't think you are," I just about manage shaking my head from side to side, "but this is on you. I trust you know what you're doing, but I don't trust *you*. And neither will Amora after this."

"You have no idea," his eyes flare with anger, his breathing heavy and ragged.

"Sit down old man, you'll give yourself a heart attack."

I move closer to him, and he holds his hand up towards me, stopping me in my tracks.

"This isn't right Xavier... whatever they have made you do..." he sits slowly, his eyes finding mine and I can see the pain that he is battling inside, the fight that he is slowly losing as each day goes on.

"I hired you to protect Amora, you have done that. Your services are no longer required, Titus." He gives me a slow nod and I know there is no point even trying to argue with him.

I have to move forward with my plan. I will not allow him to do what he is planning. I know in my gut that something is wrong and my gut is never wrong.

"As you wish," I let out a defeated sigh and turn away and begin walking towards the door.

"Oh, and Titty," I smirk before turning to face him.

"Yes," my brows raise, my hands in my pockets.

"Don't ever fucking call me old man again."

I slip my hand from my pocket, pressing my two fingers to my brow line and salute him. "Whatever you say," I say with grimace, my lips pressing into a thin line and I turn and walk out of the room and towards my room.

I need to speak to Nate.

And then I need to speak to Amora.

CHAPTER TWENTY-ONE
AMORA

I'm pacing.

Up and down.

Down and up.

Replaying what happened only moments ago over and over.

The way his eyes devoured me. Raking up and down my body.

Did I tease a little bit? Yes.

Did I want him? Also yes.

The way we were so, *so* close to his lips being on mine. Consuming me wholly.

But once again, my father ruins it.

In an instant. He ruins it. Every. Single. Time.

I have never lost my virginity.

I have never been kissed because of that damn man.

I continue pacing. My hands in my hair as I tug at my root. My heart fluttering and skipping a beat in my chest occasionally when I think back to the way his hand cupped my cheek, my skin flaming under his touch. Could he feel it? Did he feel the same spark that ruptured inside of me as soon as he touched me?

Or was I another notch on the bedpost?

I still.

I turn, facing the window and overlooking the orchard that I was in only moments ago.

He doesn't seem like the 'notch on the bedpost' kind of guy, but then who was I kidding? I didn't know him from Adam.

He was my bodyguard.

And what did it matter now that my father was sending him home.

Whatever this was between us is no more.

My father has made sure of that.

The wicked man.

So cruelly wicked.

My heart thumps, my stomach churns.

He is leaving.

I'll never see him again.

The one man that made me feel something, anything, is leaving.

And what did I do?

I ran.

Because I am a coward.

I hear a click of my bedroom door and my head snaps round quickly praying it's him, but I only see my mother standing there.

"Amora, are you okay?" She asks as she glides towards me, head high, straight backed... the perfect posture. I suppose being a royal like she was, it was beaten into her how to act.

She was perfection.

"I'm fine," I nod, giving her a smile.

"Your father wants an early dinner tonight, to give Titus a send-off."

"But he doesn't leave for another two days..." I stammer over my words, my smile slipping and my eyes widen.

"He is being sent home tomorrow," my mother's voice is quiet and she can't even look me in the eyes.

"Tomorrow?" I whisper, my stomach flipping, my fingers clutching the material of my dress once more.

"Did you not know?" my mother steps towards me, her head tilting to the side.

I shake my head from side to side as she pulls me in close, holding me in a motherly embrace.

"Oh, Amora..." she whispers, her arms tightening round me.

"I..." I stutter, swallowing the large lump that has suddenly formed.

"I know sweetheart... I know," she reassures me and I know she understands what I want to say.

"Come, let's go make a cup of tea." She lets me go, stepping towards the door when I remember that Titus asked me my age.

"Mum..." my eyes pin to the back of her head, and when she spins, she has her beautiful smile proudly displayed, her blue eyes glistening.

"Yes darling?"

"Why did dad tell Titus I was twenty-one?"

Her smile falls, slipping almost instantly.

"What?" she whispers.

"He told Titus I was twenty-one... do you know why?"

"That bastard," she grits, "honestly, I love your father I really do, but I also would love to wrap my fingers round his neck and ring him to death."

I snort a laugh.

"You and me both. Why is he this way?" I ask, slumping down on the edge of my bed and sighing heavily.

"Your father is..."

"A dickhead?" I just about manage before a laugh bubbles out of me.

"Yes, that..." my mother walks back towards me and takes a seat next to me. "Your father is complex. He has had a lot of trauma and believe it or not, he isn't very trusting."

"Really?" sarcasm drips from my tongue and I smirk.

"Your father means well, Amora. I know it doesn't seem like it, but he does. Everything he is doing..."

"Is for me, for the family... blah blah blah," I make a childish tone, rolling my eyes.

"Amora."

"I'm just fed up of you making excuses for him."

And just by the look on my mother's face I know I have upset her.

"I'm sorry... I just..."

"I know," she sniffles, standing up then pretends to pick fluff off her cotton tee.

"Mum..." my voice breaks and she just gives me a smile.

"I'll see you downstairs," she turns, and I watch as she walks out the door but not closing it behind her.

I sigh, puffing out my cheeks as I flop down on my bed.

"Fuck," I sigh, my eyes pinned to the ceiling as I count to ten in my head, my heart is racing, my mind swirling.

"You okay Twilight?" his voice crashes through me, his thick accent, the gruffness... I feel heat swarm between my legs, my stomach knotting and burning with a need.

"Fine," I refuse to sit up, I refuse to look at him.

I am embarrassed and annoyingly, my cheeks burning with crimson give me away.

"Saying you're fine is basically saying you're not fine..."

I huff.

"I just wanted to come and check on you," I hear his voice get closer to me, my heart beating a little faster, my skin erupting in goosebumps and I adore these new feelings.

"I told you I am fine."

"You're not fine" I roll my eyes.

"Why do you care?" I push up onto my elbows, my brows furrow. I don't want to look at him, I will for my brain to not let me look at him, but my eyes betray me by devouring him whole. I will never get over just how handsome he is. The way he makes my heart sing. The way he makes my skin tingle in a way it never has before. "You're leaving tomorrow," I slice my eyes from him and flop back down onto the bed, ignoring the loud thumping in my ears.

"Do you think that's my choice, Amora?" and the sound of my name rolling off his tongue has my body reacting in a way it never has before. Heat swarms me in an instant.

"Do you think this is what I want? To leave you? To leave you before I have even had a chance to get to know you? A chance to kiss you... touch you... before I have even had a chance to...."

He pauses and I feel my eyes begin to glass over, tears threatening, and I am scared to blink because when I do, my tears will escape and render me guilty for feeling anything more than a mutual friendship.

"Amora, I don't want to leave... I swear to you. But I have no choice, your father has made sure of that," his voice cracks and I feel my heart drop from my chest.

"Then don't." I sit up, my red rimmed eyes volleying over to him and seeing his hard expression fade into concern.

"Baby," he whispers pacing over to me, his thumb wiping a rogue tear that slips down my cheek, catching it before it has a chance to fall into nothingness and dissolving.

"Please don't leave me," I whisper because saying those words out loud would break me.

"Little red..."

"Please Titus..." my voice cracks and I stand, my fingers wrapping round his shirt, clinging onto him as if he was the only thing that could save me, just like the oxygen I so urgently needed. I needed him like the air that I breathe.

Titus closes his eyes, his forehead pressing into mine and it doesn't matter how much I try to stop them, the tears fall.

"Please don't cry Twilight," he whispers, the thickness in his voice showing me that he is finding this just as hard as I am.

"Then don't leave me."

He opens his eyes, they burn into mine and I hadn't even noticed, but his hand is cupping my face, my fingers subconsciously wrap around his wrist, holding him there because his touch is the only thing that feels real to me, the only thing that reminds me of these feelings that this beautiful man makes me feel and the thought of never having his hands on my skin again makes me feel utterly devastated, to never know what it was like to kiss him, to have him see me as something other than a young damsel in distress that needs a knight to ride in on his white horse and save her from the burning kingdom at the hands of her father.

But the sad truth was, I would never know what that would feel like.

Because Titus wasn't going to be the one to save me.

"We've got to go for dinner," he whispers, lifting his hand from my face and I choke on my intake of breath at the loss of his touch.

I nod, unable to piece two words together.

How stupid was I to fall for the bodyguard.

How stupid was I to think that this would work out for me.

How stupid was I to think that my father wouldn't sabotage this at any given moment...

How stupid.

I walk alongside Titus, our fingers brushing just enough for me to be able to get the bolt of current that I so desperately crave, the tingling and stimulation radiating through to my core making heat blossom between my thighs. We don't exchange words, and with each step closer we get to the dining room the more my heart races in my chest.

This is last time I will sit next to him at the dinner table and I can hardly take it, how could I have been so silly to fall hard for a man I hardly know.

I never believed in love at first sight, but here I am, living proof that it happens.

We were just wrong time.

We were not meant to be together.

Our universes didn't align, our constellations not matching.

We were not meant to be.

I don't know what makes me pause outside my father's office, but I do and I hear his voice.

Stepping forward, the door is slightly ajar, and I peep through seeing my father pacing up and down his office, one of his fists balled, the other gripped round his phone.

"It's a deal Wolfe, you can come and collect her

tomorrow." I stumble back, my blood running cold at what I had just witnessed.

"Dad..." I hear Ezekiel's voice, and when I turn round to look at Titus his fists are balled, his jaw clenched and wound tight.

I shake my head from side to side as if in disbelief and that's when rage blurs my vision, a high pitch ringing echoes through my ears and I feel disorientated, but I know it's due to the rage. This is how it comes on, and once that red mist hits, everything else fades out. I am an Archibald after all.

"Amora," I hear Titus' voice but it feels as if it is a thousand miles away, just a distant echo. Even if I wanted to stop myself, I couldn't.

My eyes are wide and bloodshot. Hot, heavy breaths fill me making my nostrils flare. I am raging.

"You're giving me to them!?" I scream, breaking through the door to my father's office like a wrecking ball, Titus hot on my tail.

"Amora," my father's eyes dart from mine to Xander's.

"Did you know?" my voice comes out high pitched, lashing towards Xander. My eyes widening. "You were meant to *help* me." My voice is a plea, my heart shattering into a million pieces as Xander's eyes fall to the floor.

"I'm sorry," Xander rubs his lips together and gives me a glimpse of his remorse before his eyes are back on my father. Ezekiel is standing in the corner and I can see how pained he is, the fact that he obviously was kept out of the loop.

I should have asked Ezekiel for help. I should have never gone to Xander. What the hell was I thinking. I shake my head in disbelief as pain crushes through me, my chest suddenly feeling hollow and my breaths are sharp as I try to fill my burning lungs.

"Xavi," My mother's eyes widen as she pushes into the room and she hears the words that slip past my lips and I feel the air get knocked out of me when realisation finally sinks in, the red mist slowly clearing. My chest rises and falls with every fast and heavy breath. I feel Titus' hand wrap round my waist, splaying against my stomach as he pulls me back towards him and he makes me feel a sense of calm like waves softly crashing and lapping at the sandy shoreline.

"This wasn't the plan," my mother snaps and the panic is evident in her voice, my father stands from his desk, but she lurches herself forward and slaps my father hard round the cheek.

"Red," he grits, his hand rubbing out the sting that he is clearly feeling.

"No, don't Red me," she storms back towards me, "this wasn't what we agreed," her eyes dart back and forth from his and the longer she waits, the more her eyes fill with unshed tears.

"I'm doing what's right..."

"You're doing what my father done to me, something you promised you would never, *ever* do to our children... and look what you're doing," her face screws up and I don't miss the snarl in her tone, her tone is vicious.

"The deal is done, Royal." And my father can't even look at me or my mother, his eyes are on his desk.

"You're a fucking coward Xavier," she just about manages before she turns, sobbing and walking out the office and slamming the door so hard the frame shakes.

"I'm done." I shake my head at his complete betrayal. "I

loathe you Xavier," I manage, I can't even call him dad. I am sick to my stomach. My voice thick as I ignore the burning lump in my throat, silent tears threatening to fall down my cheeks. "Never in my wildest nightmares did I think you, *you*, my father would do something like this. You're just like grandad. Giving me away because of *your* mistake." My whole body begins to tremble, my chin wobbling as I sink my teeth into my bottom lip to try and stop the tears from falling. "You're dead to me," I choke out before uncontrollable sobs leave me, I turn and walk out of the office and I don't stop, I keep moving forward until I am outside in the rain, letting it belt down on my skin and I don't care. Déjà vu crashes through me at the thought that a few weeks ago I was running away, just like this. The hurt, the rain... I just didn't have the betrayal to this deep level. The heart splitting, stomach griping and wound tight hurt. Nausea swims through me making everything spin.

"Amora," I hear Titus' voice and I stop dead in my tracks as the rain continues to pour. My tears blend with the raindrops that are rolling down my cheeks and I don't palm them away.

"No," I mumble through sobs, "no..." I continue forward, my feet moving quicker underneath me before I am running, my feet pounding the ground.

I'm not running long when I feel Titus' fingers wrap around the top of my arm, stalling me but before I can say anything he pulls me round so I am facing him. My glassy eyes land on his, they volley back and forth between mine and I swear I feel the air shift. Both of his hands cup my face, his thumbs brushing against my cheeks as the water drips down his nose and falls between us.

"Titus..." I mumble, a low rumble of thunder rocks through the clouds, lightning cracking through the sky.

"I'm right here, I'm not going anywhere." He dips his head, looking up through his lashes.

I try and muster the words, I try to string a sentence together but before I even get a chance too, Titus is lifting my face up to look at him, letting his hands drop from my cheeks but his index finger and thumb grip onto my chin. The thunder roars again, the whole sky lighting up and I see just how blue his eyes are against early evening skies that are drawing in.

"Twilight..." his voice is low and it causes an ember to burn deep inside of me, his head tilts slightly and this is the moment I have been waiting for.

The perfect kiss.

Except this isn't the perfect time.

This wasn't how I imagined it.

But yet, it felt like everything. A perfectly imperfect moment.

My eyes flutter shut, my lips parting and within seconds Titus' lips are on mine, slanting over them and caressing them softly. There is no tongue, just soft, meaningful kisses and I feel myself melt, Titus' arm wrapping round my waist as he holds me up. My shaky hands glide up his wet shirt, clinging onto him and a soft moan slips into his mouth just as his tongue glides over mine and I feel my heart race so fast it feels like it's about to combust in my chest. Everything else around me blurs out, the once prominent thunder is now just a light rumble and the flashes of lightning that turn the dull sky almost purple seems like it's fading into nothing and all I can focus on is this moment.

All the hurt, the *resentment*, the *loathing*, and the *betrayal* all simmer deep inside of me because it's just me and him.

And I never want to forget this moment.

Titus breaks away, his eyes on my lips as his mouth pulls into a lazy smirk, and just as I am about to match his smile, his lips are back on mine in soft butterfly kisses.

"This was the perfect goodbye," I whisper between his kisses.

"This isn't goodbye Twilight," he mumbles, cupping my face once more, holding me in place. "I promise, this isn't goodbye."

"You promise?" my voice trembles, the thunder filling the warm evening, a sticky heat coating me.

"I promise you."

CHAPTER TWENTY-TWO
TITUS

MY FINGERS ARE LACED THROUGH HERS, THE TINGLES THAT SPREAD from my fingers to my hands, to my arms, to my chest and lastly... to my heart. My heart races under my skin, beating through my chest so hard as it thumps against my ribcage.

We walk in silence, but inside every fiber of my body is singing in a harmonious melody. As we round the corner, the dusk is setting in and it's my favourite time of the day. Twilight.

Our fingers gradually loosen from their tight links before they're just occasionally brushing until we're too far apart and I instantly miss her touch. Like an addict craving another hit. I crave her.

Constantly.

My skin itches.

My blood burns.

My mouth dry.

As soon as we're apart, I need her. The want is too much, and I count down the seconds until I am with her again, getting my fix.

We walk into the back of the house and through the quiet kitchen when I feel my phone buzz in my pocket. I ignore it until we are upstairs, tucked away and hidden from everyone's watch.

My hand scoops hers back up, bringing it slowly to my lips and I place a soft kiss on the back of her hand, her cheeks blushing, and I have come to realize how much I love when she blushes. Her freckles are dotted all over the bridge of her nose, her cheeks and some scatter up to her temples and all I want to do is kiss each and every one of them until my lips can map out every mark on her beautiful skin.

"Titus I'm scared," she admits, and I can hear the pain in her voice and fuck, my heart breaks that she is even in this situation.

"Baby," my voice is soft as I drop her hand from my lips and cup her face, holding her so she has no other option than to let her beautiful, yet unique eyes burn into mine. They glisten with unshed tears, and I don't want her to cry anymore, I don't want her father to cause any more pain to her than what he has already caused.

"I am awaiting Nate to call me back, and I promise you..." I stumble over my words, my heart thrashing in my chest as my eyes volley back and forth between hers. "I am not leaving you here."

I edge closer, my lips slanting over hers when I hear the sharp intake of breath that leaves her just as my lips cover hers.

"I promise Twilight," I whisper as I break away, "trust me..."

Her eyes flutter shut, a lone tear rolling down her cheeks as she does and my thumb is there, wiping it away and she nods, my hands still holding onto her face.

"Go into your room, pack a small bag of clothes and I'll leave a suitcase outside your door..."

She blinks up at me, her brows furrowing. "A suitcase?" she repeats, her voice quiet.

"Yes baby, I need to get you out and not cause any alarm. I only have tonight, I can't risk leaving it any longer."

She nods, staying silent.

"Pack what you need and leave the bag aside, then your father will think I am leaving with my suitcase and bags..."

"It won't work," she whispers against my lips.

"Trust me Amora..."

"Okay," she just about manages, her voice trembling.

I graze my lips over her forehead, pressing softly, my own eyes closing as I inhale her scent.

She opens her bedroom door, breaking out of my grasp and I hate that I am having to leave her already. I step behind her, my foot just over the door threshold.

"I'll be back at midnight; be ready, okay?" I don't want to seem demanding, but the sooner we are out, the better. "When your father looks back on the cameras which we both know he will, he will just see little old me dragging my suitcase up to my rental car. For all he knows I am on my way to the airport. He wants me gone, he isn't going to question me and by the time he comes for you..."

"I'll be gone," she whispers.

"You'll be gone," I nod, reaching for her hand and holding it tightly, my thumb brushing against her knuckles.

"Okay," her whisper is soft, her fingers from my grasp before her hand has fully left mine and I hate the emptiness that I feel.

"I'll see you soon, Amora."

"Goodnight Titus," she gives a little nod, stepping back from me and it takes all the strength in me to turn and walk away. I just hope she trusts me enough to come with me. I can't leave her here. I won't.

CHAPTER TWENTY-THREE
AMORA

I PACE UP AND DOWN MY BEDROOM, MY HEART JACKHAMMERING IN my chest, nausea ripping through me every second, the blood pumping in my ears suddenly giving me a sickly headache.

Was I an idiot for trusting Titus? Shall I stay here and just take whatever my father is planning on doing? Do I stay like the perfect daughter and do as he says?

No, no I can't.

I have to stand my ground. I cannot, I will not go with The Knight Brothers.

My father will need to find some other way to repay them for killing their father.

It was a mistake.

A careless one at that, but I am not paying for it.

Rushing through to my wardrobe, I have no idea where I am going, but I need to pack sensibly and suitably and for any possibility. I pull at my tees, summer dresses, jeans, yoga leggings, vests, and pyjamas. I look at my formal wear, half hesitant but decide against it. I feel like we will go somewhere secluded, away from prying eyes.

I pace into the bathroom, clearing my shelves of all my toiletries that I may need. I have no idea where Titus is planning on hiding me away but I want to make sure I have everything.

Nerves crash through me, making me second guess everything.

Maybe I am wrong.

Maybe I need to do this for my father, avenge his name for the mistake he made. It's only fair.

An eye for an eye.

What if they did do that literally and take my life to avenge their father?

How would Xavier act knowing that they've killed his only daughter? Broke down his walls to the point of complete weakness and strike him through the heart, taking him down with me? What if they haven't agreed a peaceful trade? What if they do want blood? That's what they threatened. My father has blood on his hands and he needs to clean them, but it doesn't matter what he promised to do to clean them, they weren't interested.

They wanted what he held most dear in his life.

The one thing he possessed that no one else has had.

The purest thing of all.

Me.

They would break me. In every, single, possible way and the fact that my father was willing to give them me, for that alone, makes my stomach roll with sickness. I feel nauseated, my mouth wet suddenly, and I have to swallow the bile back down to stop myself from being sick. I walk slowly back out to my room, almost floating as I feel as if I am having an out of body experience.

Sometimes I wish my mother kept her title, my father would never have been able to work under the crown, he would have been a prince, I a princess and secure and safe because I was of royal blood.

But no.

She gave it all up for him.

The sad thing was, even when my father begged her not to abdicate, her father did. She listened to her father, her King, her hero even after everything he done to her.

I love my father, so dearly, but I also loathe him in a way I can't even explain. Words would not do it justice to how much I dislike him.

I love him.

Adore him.

But I loathe him entirely.

Snapping away from my thoughts, I feel the burn in my throat, the sting in my eyes as I shove the remainder of my belongings in a duffel bag.

A small part of my life packed away and I have no idea how long I will have these items with me.

No idea how long I will be away from home.

Anger boils as I think back to Xander's face. After he promised to help me, but he sided with my father. Again.

Why am I even surprised? Why am I wasting my rage on him? Where Ezekiel, I should have gone with Ezekiel. He is quiet and calculated and would have never done what Xander did. But then Xander is so far up my father's ass, he practically cleans it. I scoff, shaking my head from side to side.

I zip up my bag then place my hands on my hips. My eyes trail over to my phone and I sigh. I have been such a crap friend... I haven't spoken to Parker or Arabella, not even Hope and Faith. They've been messaging on our group chat but I've just read and ignored. I've not been in the right headspace. I haven't even painted.

Painting.

My heart aches and I suddenly feel the tingles in my fingers. I twist my wrist to face me and look at the time. It's only just turned nine. I have a few hours, maybe I could paint.

Just one last time.

I look at the door, sighing when my mind talks me out of it.

I can't run the risk of running into my father or my mother, Xander or Ezekiel for that matter. I wouldn't be able to lie to them.

I am a terrible liar.

And then my father would make sure that I was never getting out of here unless it was on the arm of The Knight Brothers. I shudder, my skin prickling in a cold sweat at the thought of what my life is going to be like.

What if Titus fails? What if my father has already outsmarted him and knows exactly what he is up to? Or even worse, what if Titus has partnered up with my father and this is all just a ploy.

I couldn't bear the thought of being betrayed by Titus.

No, he wouldn't.

Would he?

Anger simmers once more inside of me, the rage I have become so accustomed to, yet with Titus I feel none of that. It is as if I am a completely different person when I am with him.

I have my father's sharp tongue, his sarcasm and his black heart at times, but I also have my mother's caring side, her empathy and sensitivity when I need it, but I always worry that my father's side will outweigh my mother's.

The devil on one shoulder.

The angel on the other.

I would always let the devil win.

Because that's how I have been raised.

I will always give into the darkness over the light.

My father was cruel, vicious. He didn't get to where he was being a kind-hearted person. For the right people, he loved fiercely. But for the wrong, he would kill you for even looking at him in the wrong way.

My father has been through a lot, and I know that. I know deep down his trauma makes him who he is today, but it's not an excuse to pass your daughter off because of his fuck up. That's what makes me angry.

That it is *his* mistake.

Yet I am paying for it.

I will be sacrificing *everything*.

This is what guts me the most, does he not see how this is going to affect me?

I begin pacing again.

Up and down.

I pick my skin around my nails, nibbling occasionally. Irritation and agitation swarm me. There is nothing else for me to do but wait. Yet waiting seems impossible.

Because I have no idea what I am waiting for exactly and apprehension is plaguing me.

But I will wait.

Because that is all I can do.

TITUS

"Nate?" my voice is quiet as I slip into my room, closing the door softly. No one comes over this side of the house where my room is situated. Amora has told me that this is where Xavier used to lock Royal away and it's hard to picture that because I can see, in his own fucked up way, how much he loves his wife.

"Hey, yeah you okay?" Nate's voice is chipper and it fills me with confidence that he has found somewhere.

"Yeah, I'm okay are you?" I ask, not really caring at this moment as I don't have time for 'how do you do's' but I was raised better than that.

"I'm great."

"Great," I respond, pacing the floor and I'm worried I am going to leave tread in the carpet where I am walking the same path.

"I have found you somewhere, when do you want to get there?"

"Tonight, where is it?"

"Somewhere called..." he pauses for a moment, and I can hear his fingers tapping on his keyboard, "the new forest."

"Sounds enchanting..." I scoff, one brow raised.

"It looks it, wild horses, secluded and nothing but quaint pubs and rolling green fields."

"Quaint," I stop pacing, my lips curling into a smile.

"I am just reading what it says here. Quaint."

"Never heard that word before."

"Me neither, okay, I have booked you in for two weeks is that enough?"

"I have no idea, but I have the option to extend right?"

"Seems that way," Nate hums down the phone.

"Okay, perfect, can you..." my phone buzzes while it is still up to my ear.

"Already done it." His playful tone doesn't go unnoticed, and I can't help smiling.

"Of course, you have."

"Be careful Titus."

"Always," I cut the phone off and pull up his message seeing the address and copying it into my maps, just over three hours from where we are. I look at my watch, it has just gone nine. I need to get packed up and drop the suitcase to Amora without being seen. Her mother always checks on her before bed, so I need to get it to her sooner rather than later.

I bend down, pulling my large suitcase from under the bed and unzipping it before emptying my sneakers and shoes from it. Zipping it back up, I stand and head for my door. Once open, I look up and down the narrow corridor before slipping out and walking towards Amora's room, my heart racing in my chest the entire time. I'm not worried about bumping into Xavier. I'm worried about what he would do to Amora if he caught me. What the fuck would I say? How would I even be able to explain it?

Shit.

Maybe this was a crazy idea.

Maybe I needed to give a little more thought to this than being so quick to think this is a good idea.

I haven't planned anything.

I haven't thought this through. I slow as I wheel the suitcase down the tiled hallway, trying to avoid every groove that may cause a noise and bring attention to my very poorly thought-out plan. I still, looking behind at Amora's painting room and my heart hurts that I am taking her away from the one thing she finds peace in. Maybe if I have time I can come back and collect some of her supplies... maybe.

My palms are sweaty as I approach the second set of stairs. I avoided the long corridor that leads straight from one side of the house to the other thinking this would be the better option but when I hear a commotion in the library I freeze. My feet are grounded to the floor and even if I wanted to move, I couldn't.

"Royal, please."

"Don't Royal please me," I hear Royal snap. "I am disgusted and disappointed in you. How could you?" her tone is sharp and I would hate to be Xavier.

"It's not as it seems, Red... I promise," and that's when I hear the sound of skin hitting skin.

Xavier lets out a low rumble and I can imagine he is having to bite his tongue and let himself cool.

"No? Because what I understand is that our daughter, our pride and joy, our young, *innocent* daughter is being given away to two brothers who let's be honest, are the mafia. Do you think that was the right thing to do? Do you think it was the right thing to try and clear your name? To try and get them to *forgive* you for spilling their father's blood."

Silence echoes round the room.

"The answer is no, Xavier."

"It's too late Royal."

Another slap against skin and this time I wince. Because I felt it.

"I am done with you Xavier."

"Red, please," I hear Xavier beg and I take that as my cue to leave. I walk quickly past the library, keeping my head down and climbing the stairs two at a time.

Whisking down the corridor to her room, my heartbeat quickens but it's not a panicked beat now. It's beating because it beats for her.

Its drumming along to the beat of hers, only hers.

I slow as I approach her room, inhaling deeply but exhaling slowly.

Knocking on her bedroom door three times, then twisting the handle and letting my head pop round the doorframe before my eyes find hers.

"Hey," she breathes, and I can see the relief on her face. I wait for her to invite me in, I'm cautious, hesitant. My greedy eyes roam up and down her body, the heart erupting deep inside of me and I have to try and ignore the ache that I feel between my legs as my cock hardens.

"Did you want to come in?" she asks and I don't miss the rasp in her voice, the way her cheeks have flamed a beautiful pink and I can't help but wonder if the rest of her skin will glow to that perfection.

"I would love to... but..."

"Oh, of course... yeah, no, it's fine," she shakes her head from side to side, her wavy red hair is pulled from her face and I can't help but fixate on every piece of her face, as if memorizing every single detail.

I snap out of it and guilt consumes me. Sliding the suitcase forward, her eyes drop from mine and to the suitcase.

"Just so I am clear..." she pauses, licking her lips, her beautiful eyes still firmly on the case. "You want me to get in there..." and finally, after what feels like a lifetime, her eyes are back on mine, and I feel whole again.

"Yes."

And that's when a laugh bubbles out of her, she covers her mouth with her small hand, and I let out a small scoff of a laugh.

"I thought you were joking about dragging me out in a suitcase," she says through her laughter, her eyes filling with tears.

"Amora, how am I meant to get you out with your father's security cameras?"

And suddenly, her laugh stops, her eyes widen, and her breath stutters from her continuous laughter only moments ago.

"Oh," she whispers, stepping further back and sitting on the end of her bed.

Inhaling heavily, I step across the threshold to her room and close the gap between us enjoying the crackle of the air that is so prominent.

I kneel in front of her, covering her hands with mine.

"I need you out of here, I need you with me, so I know you're safe. I can't do that if I am a thousand miles away from you in America, while you are wherever your father is sending you. If I have to take you out in a suitcase, then I will take you out in a suitcase," my voice is loud and stern, but I don't mean it to be.

She says nothing, she rubs her lips together and lets her eyes fall from mine. I don't miss the deep intake of breath she takes, her bottom lip quivering ever so slightly.

"If I could get you out any other way I would... this was not my first choice."

"What was your first choice?" she asks.

"Walking you straight out the front door," I smirk, rubbing my thumbs over the back of her hands.

"I think I prefer that option."

"So do I, but I have to ensure you get out without causing suspicion."

She nods.

"What happens when they realize I am gone?"

"They'll come searching, but trust me, I won't make it easy for them."

"Okay," she whispers.

"Okay," I give her a crooked smile, keeping my gaze pinned on her the whole time. Standing slowly, her hands are still in mine. Bending, I place a kiss on her forehead and linger for a moment longer.

"I'll see you at midnight."

"I'll see you at midnight," she repeats, and I finally let go before turning on my heel and walking away.

CHAPTER TWENTY-FOUR
AMORA

What the hell was I thinking agreeing to this? How did I end up being in the foetal position in a fucking suitcase. Yet here I am.

Curled up and in a suitcase as my bodyguard drags me along the driveway.

"So close..." he says softly, muttering under his breath. I try to ignore the panic that is clawing at my throat, the way my breathing has fastened so quickly I feel as if I may die from the lack of oxygen in this tiny and confined space. This is fine. Totally and completely fine.

Fuck.

This was not fine.

I was going to suffocate.

This was how I was going to die.

Cause of death: Suffocated by being smuggled out of family home in a suitcase by her bodyguard.

A SUITCASE.

I can't do this.

I feel around for the zip, but it's no use. I can't do anything from the inside.

Suddenly, I am being picked up and then placed gently on a hard surface.

I'm in the boot.

Okay, this is fine. I will be out in a few moments, my lungs filling with the fresh oxygen that they so desperately crave. The boot door shuts, and I wait.

Nothing.

Has he played me?

Oh my god.

He has played me.

"Titus," I whisper, tears burning, my throat lodged with a huge lump.

Nothing.

I hear another door slam and within seconds, the engine starts. A low, humming rumble vibrates through me and I hear the tyres crunch across the driveway.

Of course, Titus wouldn't have set me up.

He cares too much about me.

Doesn't he?

We keep moving forward and my nerves become more intensified, my stomach knots and tightens over and over.

"Not long Twilight, let me get out onto the back road and I'll get you out," I hear his voice and my nerves fade away, like the waves crashing against the sand. A once rogue wave was now an untroubled, tranquil wave breaking against the golden sand.

I nod as if he can see me, praying that it isn't too much longer. He is driving slow and cautious when all I want him to do is be a little reckless so I can be out of this situation.

I count slowly in my head, hoping by the time I get to ten I'll be able to breathe.

One.

Two.

Three.

Four.

Five.

The car stops abruptly, making me fall forward, the case hitting the back of the seats.

"Shit, baby are you okay?" his voice fills the car as he opens the boot and quickly unzips the suitcase.

I squint for a moment before taking a deep inhale and taking Titus' hand, the shock that consumes me makes my breath catch at the back of my throat.

"I'm fine," my chest heaves as I gasp on the air that surrounds me.

"Okay, okay, quick baby, get in the car." He helps me out, leading me into the car and shutting the passenger door. I inhale slowly, letting my eyes close for a moment and relief swarms me.

He kept his promise.

He is going to keep me safe.

My King.

We travel down the dark lanes, there is no lights so Titus drives slow on the unfamiliar roads. My eyes feel heavy, my breathes falling shorter as my body relaxes and I focus on the soft hum of country music that fills the car. I feel Titus' large hand slip between my legs, giving my thigh a gentle squeeze. I let my head fall back onto the headrest then turn to look at him, a slow smile creeps onto his lips and as much as I try with all my might to stay awake, I can't. I finally give in to sleep, my body falling heavy, and within seconds I am gone.

I wake, my eyes blurry as I try and sit up.

"Twilight," I hear Titus' quiet voice.

"Yeah" I nod, sitting upright and letting my eyes adjust.

"We're here."

Rubbing the sleep from my eyes, the headlights from Titus' jeep lighting up the idyllic and picturesque cottage that sits on a little bank on the border of a forest.

"It's pretty," I yawn, blinking when I pat myself for my phone.

"I've switched it off, we have new phones in the house, and all set up but we can't risk your father finding us otherwise this would have all been a waste of time," he leans across the centre of the car, his hand cupping my cheek and he gives me a lazy smile. He looks exhausted. His eyes dark and hollow.

"You look tired."

"I'm okay," his smile grows, "come, let's get inside."

I nod, rolling my lips and unstrapping myself.

"This is only temporary... couple of weeks max."

"Then what?"

"Don't you worry your pretty little head about it." But before I can ask any more, he is out the car and at my side.

Stepping out, I look up at him. "Don't ever make me get in a suitcase again," and I hear him scoff a laugh.

"I promise," he takes my hand and kisses the back of it.

"You are good at keeping promises."

"Twilight, I will never break a promise to you."

I swallow knowing that he can't make that promise. Promises always get broken whether they mean to or not.

It's just the way life is.

I ignore the sting in my eyes and follow him up the dark path, his fingers linked through mine so even if I wanted to, I couldn't let go.

He crouches down, lifting a small flowerpot and pulling out a key.

"Is this your place?" I ask a little confused.

"No, Nate sorted it..." he looks up over his shoulder at me and winks, "you'll be safe here."

"You hope."

Titus shakes his head from side to side, "I promised."

I keep quiet as he slips the key into the lock and pushes the door wide. Stepping in he turns the light on, and I am surprised how beautiful it is inside.

"Well, this is nice," he chimes, walking through the cottage and switching the lights on.

"It is," my voice is small, I feel such mixed emotions. I would have never run before Titus. I would have never turned my back and betray my father the way I have done... but what other option did I have?

I stop in my tracks and scan the quaint room. I am standing in the lounge which leads straight from the front door. To the left is a small kitchen that is separated from the lounge with just a single archway giving it an open plan feel. The lounge is painted cream, the furnishings a natural tweed with a matching bat winged reading chair. It has nothing on my little library at home, my perfect little nook and suddenly I feel homesick. Resting my hand on my stomach, I close my eyes for just a moment and remember why I have done this.

"Are you okay?" Titus' voice sweeps through the downstairs, and I nod. "There is a guestroom down here, the main bedroom is upstairs... I would rather you sleep upstairs."

"Okay," I sigh softly, giving the room one last look before I move forward down a narrow hallway where the stairs curl round and up to the first floor. I hear Titus' footsteps behind me reminding me that he will never be far away from me, like he is always five steps behind.

Pushing the door to my right, it opens onto a lilac and

white bedroom. The bed quilt seersucker with huge, white, fluffy show pillows.

Stepping into the room, my feet sink into the thick, luxurious white carpet and I feel like I am walking on clouds.

"I know it's not home…" Titus' deep voice vibrates through me, "but I hope it's okay," and my heart lurches from its chest.

"King…" I pause and turn to look at him, "Titus," I clear my throat.

"You can call me that, it is my surname after all," he smirks at me, wrapping his arm round me and pulling me into him and holding me close.

"This is perfect, I am so grateful," I swallow down the lump that is forming in my throat.

"Anything to ensure your safety." The low growl in his voice makes my heart race and suddenly, this is too intimate.

Placing my hands on his chest, I gently push back and pin my eyes to his. "I'm tired," I whisper.

"Okay," he dips his head, letting me go and stepping back, "I'll go and get your things from the car, I won't be long."

"I can do it…" I rush towards the door but he places his hands either side of the doorframe and shakes his head.

"I will go, you get into bed."

I give a weak smile and head towards the bed, tossing the pillows off and sitting against the headboard. I am glad I wore my pyjamas, so I don't have to worry about getting changed. As soon as Titus has gone, I feel as if I can't breathe. But not in a way that feels like he is suffocating me, but in a way that when he is not close, I can't physically breathe without him being near to me. I need him like the air I breathe.

Fiddling with my fingers, I glance at the small digital clock that sits on the bedside unit, it's nearly four a.m. and I wonder how long until they realise that I am gone.

Nerves ripple through me at the thought of how panicked they would be. I thought about writing my mother a letter, just to let her know that I was okay, but I didn't want to have to put her in a position where she has to lie to my father. I know she is angry with him, but she doesn't lie, especially not to my father. Not that he is controlling in any way; they're best friends and tell each other everything but it seems my mother is a little more sharing than my father has been.

How the fuck did my life become this complicated?

A little over a month ago I was living my best life, working in a job I loved, with friends I loved and in a home that I was safe in and with a family that would do anything for me.

And now I am in hiding with my bodyguard because my father has promised me to an enemy for spilt blood.

He never managed to tell me what his intentions were when I was with the brothers, but they couldn't be good.

A chill blanketed me and suddenly I felt cold. Pulling back the covers, I snuggled down under them and waited for Titus to come back, but he never made it before my body gave in to my exhaustion.

CHAPTER TWENTY-FIVE
XAVIER

"TICK, TOCK, FUCKER... IT'S TIME FOR YOU TO GO," I GROWL down the long hallway towards Titus' room. Nothing has brought me this much joy in a very long time. I whistle as I walk, my strides long until I am outside his room.

Now, do I give him the courtesy and knock or just tear the fuck in there and drag his ass out.

I like him. I do.

But at the same time, I don't.

He angers me because he counter argues with me all the time and annoyingly, he is only doing what I would.

Maybe we're more alike than I would like to admit.

Nope, I'm gonna pull the door off its hinges and wave bye bye whilst smiling and wrapping my arm round my baby girl.

Kicking the door down, I shout to the empty room, "Get the fuck out of my house," but my words soon disappear and fall on deaf ears.

"Titty?" I storm into the room then smash through the bathroom door. Nothing.

"Titty!" I scream, ripping open the wardrobe doors and

seeing everything gone. "Well..." I run my hand through the side of my head, fixing some loose strands of my blonde hair and pushing them back into place then pull on the bottom of my suit jacket. "Saves me a job," I mutter, my eyes slicing back towards the door.

Pacing out the room, I fist my phone from my pocket and check my message from Wolfe.

Fucking Wolfe.

"*Wolfie,*" I mimic in a childish voice.

Wolfe
We've decided, we want Amora tomorrow. Have her ready. Amora Knight... it has a nice ring to it, don't you think?

"Cunt," I rage, stopping and pummelling my fist into the wall before I let out a scream so loud it echoes down the hallway. I ignore the throbbing pain on my knuckles already because the pain in my gut is overwhelming everything else. The fact that I have to do this, and what's worse Amora thinks I have done it because I want to.

I have wanted to tell her the truth, but I can't.

I cannot and will not risk my plan being ruined because I am ready to fall to my knees and confess all.

I ignore the sting at the back of my eyes caused by a thousand tears but I won't let them fall. Passing the stairs, I continue towards Amora's room. I have no idea what I am going to say to her but I know that I need to push my emotion aside and be the cruel, vicious and heartless man she thinks I truly am.

Because that's what I am deep inside.

A monster.

A beast.

I may as well stay as this person, my wife hates me, my

daughter is about to hate me... soon I'll be all alone. Just like I was when I first met my Red.

Standing outside Amora's door, I inhale sharply as I lift my hand and knock softly on the door.

"Princess?" I call out as I push down the handle which reveals an empty room.

My face pales, my blood runs cold when I pace her room, pulling it apart bit by bit and suddenly it sinks in.

He fucking took her.

I am on my knees, my hands and head are pressed into the floor. I can't breathe. My chest hurts and all I can do is let out a choked scream every now and again.

"Xavi," I hear Red's soft voice and I can't even bear to look at her. "Xavier, what's happened?" I hear her footsteps closing in and my heart skips a beat.

I can't move.

"Sit up!" she demands, and I do as she says, pushing up onto my knees. Anger boils deep within me. She sits on the edge of Amora's bed and stares me down and fuck, is she beautiful.

"Amora is gone..." I finally managed and saying the words aloud cripple me. "Titus took her away... The Knight Brothers are coming for her..." I whisper waiting for her to say something.

"Good," she snaps, standing up.

"Good?" I rage, pushing to my feet and pull her to face me.

"Yes, good. I am glad Titus took her, now you can beat yourself up about it and deal with the consequences." She flicks her hair over her shoulder and begins to walk towards the door.

"This wasn't supposed to happen. I had a whole plan... he's fucked it. I have no idea what The Knight

Brothers will do when they turn up tomorrow and she isn't here."

"Tomorrow?" Royal spins round, her brows furrowed as her eyes narrow on mine.

"Tomorrow," I breathe, my voice thick and my heart thumps in my chest, a pain ripping through me as if my heart is being sliced in two.

"Xavier," she whispers, and she gives me this look, pure heartbreak and complete disgust. Disappointment floods her and I feel it in my soul. Her head falls forward and she shakes it from side to side. I have no words. They fail me completely.

"Royal," I hear Betty's voice, she glares at me on the floor with pure hatred and I swear that wench is going to outlive me.

CHAPTER TWENTY-SIX
TITUS

I LAY IN BED, MY EYES PINNED TO THE CEILING WHEN MY PHONE pings.

Nate
All okay? N x

I smile.

Titus
All in and settled. Thank you again for sorting this out for me. How is Arizona? I feel awful as I haven't spoken to her in a couple of days.

I watch as the dots appear.

Nate
She is fine. We explained that things escalated, and she seemed to understand. Keaton has hardly seen her; she has been so busy but her food is being eaten so he knows she is coming home lol.

I smile.

> **Titus**
> I miss you all. I can't wait to be back home with you all.

Nate
When will that be?

> **Titus**
> Soon. I hope. Soon. Once I know Amora is safe, I can take her back to Xavier and head home.

Nate
Okay, keep us posted. And keep your phone off, both of you. Stay safe x

I lock my burner phone and sigh, placing it face down on the table next to my bed. Sleep didn't come easy, and I was unsure if it was because I had so much going on in my mind or because I craved to be near Amora constantly. Rolling over, the sun peeks through the shutters and it forces me to get up. The cottage is quiet, and Amora hasn't come down from bed yet. I fight with myself if I should go and see if she is okay or just leave her be. A lot has happened over the last forty-eight hours, and I bet she is exhausted. Throwing back the comforter, I sit on the edge of the bed and scrub my face. I feel tired. Mentally tired.

I stand, grabbing my watch and my phone off the bedside table and type a message out to Arizona so she has my new number and letting her know that I'll videocall her later on.

I need to see her. I feel like it's been forever. Grabbing some sweatpants out of my suitcase, I pull them on and head towards the kitchen to make a coffee. I pause when I reach the countertop and see a kettle plugged into the switch on the wall.

"What the fuck is this?" my brows furrow as I lift the plastic kettle from its base, looking at it and popping the lid.

"That's a kettle, do you not have those in America?"

I spin round quickly, and my hungry eyes rake up and down Amora's body. She is wearing an oversized tee and nothing else. Her long legs are bare, and I can't help but think of how good they will feel locked around my waist. Her red hair is messy and tumbles over one shoulder. A small smile creeps onto my lips as I notice soft pillow creases in her rosy cheeks. I can't help but notice how my feelings have intensified since we've been alone, since I feel like I know her a little more. Maybe it's because I know she is twenty-five and nowhere near my daughter's age. But whatever the reason, I am fully aware that my feelings have grown for her. I swore I wouldn't let myself ever fall for a client. It was one of my rules but that was until her.

Until Amora.

"What do I do with it? I want coffee," I pull myself from my thoughts as I hold out the kettle for her to take and I don't miss how her eyes graze over my naked torso. I should have put a tee on but I didn't think she would have been awake just yet.

"You fill it with water and let it boil," she shakes her head from side to side and I don't miss the little laugh that bubbles from her as she steps foward and takes the kettle from me.

"I just want a coffee."

"And I'll make you one; well, if there is any coffee," she scrunches her nose up as she lets the cold water run from the faucet and then begins filling the kettle. I watch intently as she pops the kettle back on its base then pushes the small, plastic switch down.

"That's how you boil a kettle?" I ask, curling my fingers round the edge of the counter, letting the surface take my weight. She nods before spinning and I watch as she reaches up, opening the cupboard doors to look for mugs and I take my chance to let my hungry eyes sweep over her, the tee lifting slightly and revealing the curve of her ass cheek. Peachy and round and I have the urge to stalk over to her, fall to my knees and kiss the little crease under her cheeks before sinking my teeth into her skin.

"Do you take sugar?"

It's all I can think about.

Was it wrong?

"Titus?"

"Hm?" my cheeks pinch, my brows sitting high as I run my tongue across my lips.

She smirks, nibbling on that bottom lip of hers and I feel my insides swarm with heat, my cock throbbing.

"Do you take sugar?"

I shake my head.

"Milk?"

"I'll just have it black."

"Okay," her voice is soft and she turns back round and I watch her intently. It's not healthy how obsessed I have become with her.

Never in a million years did I think that I would be *that* guy... yet here I am.

I am desperate to feel her skin under my fingertips, to dig them a little deeper into her thighs and leave little marks showing that she belongs to me. The thought of her going to The Knight Brothers and being *their* property makes my skin crawl. I won't allow it.

She isn't going.

"Here," she pushes the mug into my hand, and I pull from my thoughts, clearing my throat as I follow her into the living area.

"How did you sleep?" I ask, trying to keep my mind from drifting back to my earlier thoughts.

"Not great," she shrugs her shoulders lifting slightly.

"No?"

She shakes her head from side to side, bringing both her legs up so her knees are near her chest and I have to try my hardest not to let my eyes drift down her body.

"Guilt has consumed me."

"Amora," my voice is quiet, I hate that she is the one who feels guilty when it should be her father that feels guilty. Not the other way round. "You have nothing to feel guilty for..." I trail off when I feel her eyes lock on mine, I swear the air shifts. The tension thick.

"He is going to be so angry," she inhales, nibbling on her bottom lip.

"He is, but he will come to realize that I have done this for all the right reasons."

"Have you though? I mean... if The Knight Brothers don't get me... then what? Will they come for my mother?" she sighs, "I feel like I'm just delaying the inevitable. This is happening..."

I shake my head in denial.

"Your father knows exactly what he is doing..."

"I'm not worried about what he is doing, they want blood Titus... if they don't get me..." She swallows and I can see the panic flash across her eyes and my heart twists.

"I promise..." I pause and she just gives a gentle nod.

"I know," she rubs her lips together and finally pulls her eyes from mine and suddenly I feel like I can breathe again.

———

Sitting on the edge of the bed, the morning has just disappeared. I hold my phone up and wait for it to connect. I feel like such a dick staring at my phone with a smile on my face waiting for Arizona to pop up. The phone makes a noise indicating it has connected but I can't see her.

"Sweetie?" I ask, my eyes searching the black screen.

"Dad, where are you?"

I look round the room, brows pinched before I am locked back on the phone.

"I'm here, sitting in the lodge."

"I can't see you…" she pauses, "have you got your camera turned on?"

I search the screen again.

"I think so, this is a new phone, so I have no idea what I am doing."

I hear her laugh and God do I miss her.

"Let me hang up and call you back, okay?"

"Okay," I nod as if she can see me and within seconds she is gone.

I inhale deeply and wait, my mind soon wandering to Amora. My phone vibrates in my hand, and I click answer.

There she is.

My beautiful ray of sunshine.

"Hey, my baby."

"Dad!" she pouts and frowns.

"I told you, you'll always be my baby."

"Can you not?" she rolls her eyes.

"Where is my happy Arizona?"

"I am right here, I am just swamped with work honestly, I don't ever feel rested."

I sigh.

"Can't you take some time off?"

She just laughs at me.

"Good one dad."

"What? You must be able to take paid leave?

"I'm an intern dad, I don't get vacation time."

"I don't believe that."

"Anyway," she huffs, "what's new with you, why are you doing an Uncle Kaleb and hiding a girl away?" her brow lifts and I feel the intensity in her gaze.

"I'm not doing a Kaleb," I tut, "things went a little south, this is just temporary."

"That's what Kaleb said," I hear Keaton shout from behind Arizona and her eyes widen.

"What are you doing there? Shouldn't you be at work?" I see Ari side eye Kaleb.

"Yeah, just had to pop home to see to something."

"Anyway, what is Amora like?" Arizona asked changing the subject swiftly.

"She's lovely," my smile widens, and I didn't even realize until Arizona picked me up on it.

"Dad... she's a client."

"I know that! It's not like that, she is just a good friend. We've become close over the last few weeks."

Just a friend.

Yeah okay, idiot.

A friend who you had an earth shattering, life altering kiss with.

A friend who you can't go a minute without thinking about.

"Dad, did you hear me?"

"Sorry?" I blink a few times.

"When are you going to be home?"

"Uh, I'm not sure yet darling, few more weeks I think."

"Okay," and I don't miss the small, exasperated sigh that leaves Arizona.

"Is everything okay?" concern laces my tone.

"Yeah, I just miss you that's all."

My heart throbs in my chest.

"I miss you too, so much." She gives a small smile, pushing her glasses up her nose.

"I'll be home as soon as I can."

"I know," she nods, "I'll speak to you soon okay?"

"Okay," I force a smile on my face.

"Bye Dad."

"Bye sweetheart," I swallow the lump and wait until she cuts me off because I didn't want her to see the tears that were pricking the back of my eyes like a million needles.

I felt homesick suddenly and I am a little annoyed that I didn't take Kaleb up on his offer of bringing Amora home to America, instead I am in the middle of a forest with no idea where I actually am.

I sit quietly for a moment and just contemplate the last couple of weeks, it has been one hell of a rollercoaster.

Opening a message to Nate, I type a quick note out.

> **Titus**
> Keep an eye on Xavier and his cameras…
> or should I say the fucking Knight brothers. I
> don't trust them and now I have taken the
> one thing they wanted I think we may have
> started a war.

I send then toss my phone onto the bed. Standing, I grab the neck of my tee from the back and with one arm pull it over my head in one swift move. I threw my old tee on when I went into my room to speak to Ari. I was desperate for a shower to wash last night off me. Stepping under hot water, I was grateful that there was a bathroom attached to my room. I didn't really want to go upstairs where no doubt Amora was getting dressed.

My cock throbs, the blood rushing down when I think about Amora in the shower, her beautiful skin covered in soap suds, her addicting scent of apricots and cocoa filling the steamy room. I scrub my skin until the pain distracts me from my inappropriate thoughts. I needed to jerk off, I had to relieve myself. I couldn't go on much longer in such proximity to her and ignore the growing temptation of everything I have wanted to do.

The need to kiss her again comes on strong, the want to touch her skin and let my fingers explore every inch of her is even more prominent than my need to kiss her.

The thought of any other man touching her is enough to make me see blind rage. I *hate* it.

Washing the suds off my skin, I turn the shower off and grab a towel and wrap it round my waist. Reaching for a hand towel, I run it over my hair and dry it before throwing it over my shoulder as I begin to brush my teeth. Once done, I pat my mouth dry and hang my hand towel up before I walk into my room. Whipping the towel from round my waist, I hold it over my semi-hard cock and dry my upper body. I grab a pair of grey *Boss* combat pants and a black *Essentials* tee and reach for a pair of boxers. I drop the towel when suddenly I hear a loud gasp.

"Oh my god, I am so sorry. Please, oh my god," Amora rushes out and my eyes widen as I turn to see her standing there with both hands over her eyes.

"Shit," I whisper, grabbing the towel that was on the floor and covering myself once more.

"I didn't see anything, Titus, I'm so..." I cut her off, I feel my skin slowly begin to heat and I know it isn't because I am embarrassed.

"It's fine," I let out a soft chuckle, "like you said, you didn't see anything..." I let my voice trail off.

"Exactly," and I can see just how red her skin is. "I'm going to..." she mutters, thumbing behind her before turning quickly and walking out the room, slamming the bedroom door behind her.

Once dressed, I hang my towel up and slowly open the bedroom door, my eyes searching the living area for Amora but she is nowhere to be seen.

"Amora?" I call out, padding through into the kitchen. Nothing.

I turn to look over my shoulder and up the stairs. Climbing two at a time, my heart begins to race but it soon slows when I see her sitting at her dressing table, brushing her long, red hair.

I lean against the door frame, my arms crossed across my broad chest and smirk.

"Little Red."

"Titus..." her cheeks flame red once more and I dip my head.

"It's okay, you didn't see anything..." I pin my gaze on hers and I want to see her admission. I know she saw me, she was just too embarrassed to admit it.

"I didn't," she rolls her lips.

"Then why are we still talking about it?"

Her breath catches in the back of her throat and it takes her a moment to turn her face away from me and focus on her own reflection.

"I'm going to cook tonight, grab a couple bottles of wine... unless there is anything else you like?"

"I like margaritas."

She licks her lips as if she is imagining the taste of the tequila-based cocktail on her tongue.

"Okay," my lips lift a little higher one side.

"With a chilli popped in it, salt round the rim..."

"Sounds spicy," I raise my brows.

"Spicy and delicious," her eyes float to mine in the reflection of her mirror.

"I can't wait to taste..." I lick my own lips now but not because I'm imagining the margarita... no, it's because I am imagining what she is going to taste like on my tongue.

My cock hardens and throbs.

"I'll see you downstairs," I just about manage before turning and heading downstairs, but I head straight for my bedroom, slamming it shut and jack myself off until I physically have no more to give.

I will get my obsession out of my head.

I have to.

CHAPTER TWENTY-SEVEN
AMORA

OH.

MY.

GOD.

My cheeks were flamed when I walked out of Titus' bedroom and scurried off to my room. The picture of him is replaying on repeat of him standing there, his towel dropped to the floor and *everything* on show. Shit.

A burn radiates through me, a delicious ache throbbing between my legs.

How am I going to live with him now? Now that I have seen him in all his glory.

I flick my lashes with mascara and try and push the images from my head, but it's no use. They are burned into my corneas. And honestly, I'm not mad about it.

I'm mad that I am not more experienced and brazen in a situation like this.

Arabella is confident in her relationships; she tells me all about it and I get a little jealous over what she has experienced.

I am over being a virgin. I'm not sentimental about losing my virginity, to be honest I would rather have it done and over with. Out of all of my friends, I'm the last one to lose it.

I had a pact with Parker—Carter and Freya's son—that if we were both still virgins by the time we were eighteen, we would lose it together... but he struck out of that pact when he lost his virginity on prom night.

I scoff a laugh. I didn't even get a chance to go back to my date's house, I was chaperoned home by father dearest so he could make sure I was home and safely tucked away in his iron fortress.

Placing my mascara down on the dressing table, I am swarmed with sadness and suddenly, I never noticed until now just how suffocating my father was.

I'm sure I will find someone one day, and then maybe I can finally lose my virginity and not get cock blocked every single time, and one day, hopefully, I'll be blessed with children of my own and understand just why my father is the way he is.

Maybe.

Or he is just a fucking psychopath.

I sigh, looking at my reflection and I can't even hide the sadness that consumes me. If this doesn't work out the way Titus has planned, I will be handed over to the Knight brothers and they wouldn't even hesitate to take my virtue. But I don't want them to take it, I don't want to go to the brothers as a virgin.

My head falls forward and I shake my head from side to side softly.

When did my life become this.

Pushing back, I stand and inhale deeply. I dress in a white, smock dress and slip my feet into my sandals. The weather has picked up and the cool spring air that once was has now been replaced by comfortable warmness.

I look over my shoulder at the burner phone that sits on my bedside table, a complete replica of the one that Titus took, but I don't have the urge to check it. This is one time in my life that I can be just who I am and not who they want me to be and I'm happy. I have no idea how long I am going to be here for, but until that moment, I am doing what makes me happy.

I SMILE WHEN I SEE TITUS SITTING ON THE SOFA LOOKING EVERY bit delicious. I know that one kiss meant nothing to him, but to me? It intoxicated me. Consuming every fibre inside of me that my nerve endings tingle every time I think about it.

But then again it was my first kiss so what do I know?

"Hey."

"Hey," I nibble my bottom lip, locking my fingers together as I stand a little awkwardly.

"You hungry?"

I shake my head from side to side, "I sorted myself something out before..." I pause, dropping my eyes.

"I see, I was going to run out to the store soon... thought we could pick something up for dinner? Maybe grab those margaritas you mentioned because they're all I am thinking about." His eyes lower, but they don't leave mine and I feel my stomach flip.

"That sounds good," I nod, lifting my head and slowly walking over to where he is sitting. I wait for a moment. His hand slips from his lap, his fingertips drumming on the soft cushion of the sofa, then slowly drawing shapes before drumming them again.

I kneel on the cushion, tucking my leg underneath me as I sit down next to Titus and suddenly my breaths draw shorter.

"I spoke to my daughter this morning," Titus says, and I'm not sure if he can feel the tension that is slowly brewing between us.

"How is she?" I ask, genuinely interested.

"She's good, busy with work," he nods, reaching forward and taking a mouthful of his water.

"Helps the days go a little quicker I suppose," I shrug my shoulders up.

"They must do, think she is missing me now though." He lets his eyes fall to between his legs, one of his hands holding his glass, the other resting on his thigh.

"It's been a long few weeks..." I swallow, feeling incredibly guilty, "I'm sorry I am keeping you from her, honestly, just take me home..." but I am stopped when Titus' hand is on my bare thigh, my skin erupting in tingles that shoot all the way to my toes.

"No," his voice is low, "I made you a promise Amora, and I am not going to break it."

"I just..."

"You just nothing," he gives me a small smile, "I'll leave when my job is done, you're my priority while I am here. You. No one else."

I lick my lips, nodding.

Silence falls over us and eventually, he moves his large hand from my burning skin, and I instantly miss the connection.

"Excuse me," I stand slowly, being mindful to make sure my dignity is shielded as I stand.

"Is everything okay?"

"Yes, get ready and we can go when I come back

downstairs," I turn to face away from him and disappear up the stairs. I had no reason to come up here other than to break thick tension that surrounds us. I stand with my back against the wall, inhaling deeply I hold my breath for five then breathe it back out once more.

I hate being this girl.

I want to feel the fire in my belly, I want my tongue to be sharp, but here I am, breathing in and out because my bodyguard touched my leg.

"Pathetic," I mutter under my breath. I close my eyes for a moment, vowing to leave this person behind.

I wasn't a damsel in distress. I was an Archibald.

Even if my father was a bit of a dickhead.

WALKING THROUGH THE AISLES OF THE SHOP, TITUS THREW ALL sorts into the trolley. I had no idea how long he thought we would be here for but by the looks of the contents, it seemed like months.

"Are you stocking up for hibernation or something?" I joke, nudging him with my elbow.

"Well, I don't know what you like... so I thought I would just grab enough so we always have something to grab."

"I like your thinking," I smile as we pass the biscuits. I reach up and grab a few packets of biscuits and drop them into the trolley.

"I like to have tea and biscuits," I answer Titus' confused look, "ohhh, of course. Because you have biscuits, but they're more like scones over here... these are more like cookies I suppose, but obviously not cookies," a laugh bubbles out of me.

"I'll have to give them I try," he winks before pushing forward and heading for the tills.

"Are we not getting margaritas?" I stop, his eyes finding mine as he looks over his shoulder at me before he looks round the large grocery store.

"Yeah, but from the liquor store, right?"

I shake my head from side to side, "Oh Titty," I scoff at the nickname my father gave him, "let me show you."

I lead him and stop at the alcohol aisle.

"I thought you had to go to a liquor store or something, I didn't know you could grab it from a grocery store like this."

"Is that how it is over in America?"

He shakes his head, and I can't stop my laugh.

"Then why did you think it was like that here, in England?" I ask as I lead him towards the alcohol.

"I have no idea, was just a guess."

"Pick your poison," I hold my arms out and the shelves that are stocked with alcohol.

"I am good with margaritas Twilight, are you?"

"Yup," I reach for two bottles of ready-made cocktails.

"We will make them ourselves..." he reaches out, wrapping his fingers round my wrist.

"I am happy with these," I shrug, "easier then? We can just pour and drink."

"Okay," his fingers uncurl from mine.

"We need some chillies," I place the bottles in the trolley and move forward back to the salad aisle.

Once we've paid and are done loading the car up, Titus opens the car door and I slip inside, "thank you," I mutter before he closes the door.

Titus taps the address back into the Sat Nav and soft

country music plays quietly in the background and I never realised how much I liked it.

"So, country music hm?" my voice is light as I tap my fingers to the strums of the guitar.

"Yeah, there is something about it, I don't know... I just sort of connect with it, does that make sense?" he asks, his own long finger tapping on the steering wheel to the subtle beat.

"Yeah, it does," I nod, "that's how I feel with painting," I sigh.

"I'm sorry you had to leave it all behind," and I can hear the sincerity in his voice, but I wave him off.

"It's fine, I'll get back to it one day," I shrug.

"You will," he smiles, "maybe you can come and visit me and my ranch when all this is over, I'll get you a painting room set up."

"You live on a ranch?" my eyes widen, and excitement fills my tummy.

"No," he shakes his head, and a low chuckle leaves him, "that's the dream, I am hoping that once my daughter chooses her specialty, I can look at doing it then. But we're a few years away from that," and I don't miss the small sigh that leaves him.

"One day," I reach across and place my hand on his that rests gently against his thigh.

"One day," he turns to face me, a sparkle in his eye that I have never noticed before. I remove my hand and let it rest on my lap, turning to face the window, a small gasp leaving me when I feel Titus' hand clasp mine tightly.

I try and hide the smile but it's useless.

I am smiling like a damn Cheshire cat.

THE EVENING WAS DRAWING IN, THE SUN READY TO DISAPPEAR AND the moon threatening to light up the sky with her fullness. There was something truly beautiful about the clear night sky, the stars twinkling alongside the light of the moon.

The small space of our living room was filled with more of Titus' country favourites and the one that was crooning through the speakers was called *Tennessee Orange* and my heart hummed along. I resonated with it so much given the situation I was in right now with Titus.

We snacked on cheese and bread with different relishes and pickles and now we're finishing it off with margaritas.

Titus hands me another one, the rim dusted in salt, a quarter chilli bobbing in the pale-yellow liquid, and I can't stop my tongue from darting out and licking my lips.

"Thank you," I beam, my cheeks constantly coloured in a red blush from the alcohol that is swimming through my veins.

"You're most welcome, you look very pretty sitting there," he takes a sip of his own margarita, his lips parted before he licks excess alcohol from them, and I don't miss the way his eyes rake up and down my body.

"You look very pretty too," I compliment him back and I watch as his smile widens showing me just how perfect his teeth are, he really is beautiful.

We fall silent as the music plays softly and I never want this moment to be over. It may not seem like much for an ordinary girl, but for me—who has always been kept on such a tight leash—this was everything and more.

"What are your dreams?" Titus interrupts the silence, his deep voice coating my whole body in goosebumps. "I told you mine, but I didn't ask you yours."

My eyes fall to my glass, a smile pulling at my lips.

"To be loved unconditionally, to have someone love me

with everything they have. A bit like how my father loves my mother, just not how it was in the beginning," a gentle laugh escapes me and I feel my heart begin to race in my chest. "I want a pretty farmhouse, far in the countryside where my kids can roam to their hearts content, where they can get dirty and be children." I sigh, "And of course, I would like to build the courage up to maybe sell my paintings at some point, but I am not good enough yet," I shake my head, my eyes still down, "but I feel that my dream is too far for me to reach now, that life I wanted and dreamt of will merely stay a dream. The Knight Brothers will get to me, and I will be forced to stay there, and my father has no doubt already agreed my hand in marriage to one of them. There is no other reason for them to want me. They might want to kill me, but honestly, I think they would have already got to me by now if that was the case." Sadness consumes me, and I feel my bottom lip tremble. I sink my teeth into it and bite down hard to try and stop the tears rolling down my cheeks. "I have to come to terms with a new dream," my voice quivers as I slowly lift my head up and my gaze lands on Titus, his eyes are dark and hooded and my heart skips a thumping beat making me cough.

"I will do everything in my power to get you as close to your dream as possible,"

I break my eye contact, suddenly looking at him is becoming too intimate. My head shakes from side to side as I tap my finger on the base of the cocktail glass.

"It's not your job anymore," my voice cracking and it's clear the alcohol I've consumed is beginning to affect me. I don't give him a chance to answer before I speak again. "Do you know what scares me the most..." I whisper, my throat feeling tight.

"What?" Titus edges closer, his breath on my face and

my breath catches in the back of my throat. I ignore the want to look at him, to lose myself in his crystal blue eyes.

"That I am going to lose myself, like I'll be a complete shadow of myself just fulfilling a role."

Titus reaches up and tucks a loose strand of my hair behind my ear and my breath begins to fasten, I don't miss the uneven heart beats that skip deep within in my chest.

"I want to promise that you won't feel that way, I want to promise that I'll be there to make sure you don't become a former version of yourself..." he pauses, and I don't miss the sharp inhale that he takes in, "but I won't promise something I cannot keep."

I swallow the lump that has formed quickly in my throat, willing for it to go because when I feel the burning presence of it, I know tears shortly follow and I hate being that girl. I hate crying.

"Hey, hey," his hand cups my face and I lean into his hold, the blaze that warms my cheek is addicting, my stomach knotting as I feel a burn in my lower stomach and a persistent ache between my legs. It's too much.

I stand quickly, "More drinks?" I rush out, grabbing the still nearly full glass from Titus and disappearing into the kitchen. My chest rises and falls quickly, my heart skipping beats as it races inside. Placing the glasses on the marbled worktop, I push my palms flat on the cool surface and let my head fall forward. Inhaling deeply, I try and calm the thumping heart in my chest.

"Amora," I hear Titus' deep voice float through the room, smothering my skin in goosebumps in an instant.

I spin quickly, plastering a wide smile across my face. Curling my fingers round the worktop behind me to steady myself.

"Yeah?"

"All okay?" he leans against the doorframe, crossing his arms across his chest as his eyes rake up and down my body. I am still wearing my cotton sundress and I can't help but let the heat of his gaze make my cheeks burn.

"Fine, I just needed a minute." I lick my lips and suddenly I am breathless.

"Did I do something to upset you?" he asks, and I can't help but stare at him. He really is something special. Muscular, broad, tall and handsome as hell.

"No, god no," I breathe out, shaking my head from side to side as he begins walking towards me.

My breath catches at the back of my throat as the gap between us is now nothing but a couple of centimetres.

Titus' head tilts to the side but I let my face drop, I don't know why but the intimacy just feels too much even if we were just having a conversation about our dreams. His finger presses into the bottom of my chin as he lifts my face slowly to look up at him.

"You're worrying me," his voice is low as he admits.

"Things just got a little..." I pause, licking my lips as I mull over my words for a moment.

"Serious?" one side of his mouth lifts, causing a lopsided smirk to play across his lips and I nod. "Then let's just pause the conversation where we left it, drink margaritas and worry about all the serious tomorrow, yeah?"

"Yeah," I smile and he lets his finger drop from my chin and reaches behind me for his drink, passing me mine as he steps back.

I thank him as I take it and bring the thin rimmed glass to my lips and take a small mouthful, the whole time our eyes are pinned to one another.

"How about a couple of tequila shots?" I ask as I pull the glass away and lick the salt from my lips slowly.

"Really?"

"Come on, let's forget the shit show that is my life and lets just get drunk," I shrug my shoulders up, "who knows how long we have until my father finds us."

Titus nods slowly.

"Let's do shots."

"Shots!" I shout before giggles bubble inside of me.

CHAPTER TWENTY-EIGHT
XAVIER

I PACE UP AND DOWN. RAGE IS COURSING THROUGH MY BLOOD AND I can't calm myself no matter what I do. Royal is still ignoring me. Ezekiel is upset with me and Xander is by my side like a loyal fucking lap dog.

"Father..." Xander says quietly as he steps behind me.

"What?" I snap, pushing my hand through my hair. Frustration fills me, inhaling heavily I turn to face him. "What?" I ask again, this time my tone a little softer.

"He couldn't have gone far with her, are we sure that Titus definitely played a part in this?"

"Was you not going to help him get away before?" I can't help the snarl that follows my vicious bite.

"It was just a ploy..." Xander steps away from me.

"But whatever you said whether or not it was a ploy, you planted a fucking seed in his head."

"She's my sister..."

"And she is my daughter and what I am doing is for *her*. Why does nobody see that?" I grab the root of my hair and tug.

"Because you're giving her to them! How is that helping her?"

"You said you trusted me."

"I do!" Xander's nostrils flare, his eyes widening as I see his own rage consuming him.

"Then fucking trust me," I growl as I pull my phone out of my pocket and press Tyson's name.

"Boss."

"CCTV, have you got it?"

"Already on our way."

I cut the phone off and slide the phone back into my pocket once more. Running my hand over my beard, I drag it slightly.

"Your mother is going to murder me in my sleep."

Xander sighs, "I wish you were joking," he scoffs.

"Me too, son. But your mother has a temper and I am on the receiving end of it." I can't help the smile that dances across my lips and Xander lets out a low chuckle, rubbing his hand round the back of his neck as if he is rubbing out a knot.

Silence falls when there is a knock on my office door.

"Yeah," I call out and see Tyson and his little bitch walking in with a laptop.

"Found anything?"

"Just take a look for yourself," Tyson places the laptop on the desk and opens it up before hitting play on the security camera.

"Oh, there he is, good old Titty," I scrub my face in annoyance at just seeing him on the screen and how much he has royally fucked up my well executed plan.

He was dragging along a suitcase, before lifting it and placing it in the boot.

"What am I looking at?" I ask as the screen flits to Titus pulling out the drive.

"Look again," Tyson says as he rewinds the clip that begins to play once more on the laptop screen. I squint, trying to see whatever the fuck he is trying to show me.

I watch again and watch as Titus pulls the suitcase across the gravelled drive and puts it carefully into the boot.

"I don't see it..." I admit, looking up at Tyson and he rolls his eyes.

"Watch again," he orders, rewinding it and pressing start again.

I edge closer and look at the small screen.

"Can you make the screen bigger?" and I hear Tyson sigh and mutter something under his breath.

"I might be a little bit blind but I'm not fucking deaf," I roar, standing up and narrowing my gaze on Tyson.

His eyes widen.

"Sorry," he holds his hands up in defence, "lemme see what I can do boss." He walks over to the screen, double tapping and making the screen full-size, "Better?" Tyson smirks.

"Don't be a condescending cunt Tyson," I side eye him and bend to look at the screen again and I hear Xander scoff a laugh. I look over at him, throwing him an icy glare. "Don't,"

Xander drops his head and stifles his laugh.

Little shit.

I turn my attention back to the screen and I watch.

And that's when I see it.

He *delicately* puts the suitcase in the back.

Any normal person would be a bit rougher with it maybe, but then I rewind again.

He turns back and looks down at the suitcase, his lips

moving but I am unable to hear a single fucking word he says.

"He put her in the fucking suitcase!" I bellow, grabbing the laptop and launching it across the room and I watch as it hits the wall, smashing before falling to the floor and the screen going black.

Royal bursts through the door, my bloodshot eyes wide and wild.

"Xavier, what's happened?" she asks frantic, her eyes moving between us all.

"Titus snuck Amora out in a fucking suitcase."

And that's when I see her fucking smirk.

"Well done Titus..." she presses her tongue into her cheek, hanging onto the door handle. "Titus 1, Xavier 0," she sings before slamming the office door shut.

"I love my wife, I love my wife," I repeat out loud as I close my eyes and try to control my temper and erratic heart. "I'm going to hunt him down and fucking take her back."

CHAPTER TWENTY-NINE
TITUS

I'M DRUNK.

How irresponsible of me.

And all I can do is smile at how beautiful she is.

My eyes are misty and I know it's because I have inhaled far too much tequila, and I am certain every time either one of us makes a fresh batch we add a little more in each time. But she is right.

These cocktails are delicious.

I want to taste them on her lips.

Savour every moment if I was to kiss her.

If.

Neither of us has spoken a word of our kiss the other night in the downpouring rain, yet it's all I have thought about.

She sighs and my brows raise.

"You okay?" I ask and I swear I am slurring.

"Mmhmm, just thinking."

"About?"

"How different my life is going to be in the next few weeks."

I grimace.

"My thoughts are a lot better than yours," I wink, taking a mouthful of my drink.

"Oh, yeah? Care to divulge?"

"I don't know..." I rub my hands over my stubble.

"Come on, that's not fair, let me know what you're thinking about... get me out of my head."

She edges forward, so she is practically sitting on top of me, her legs crossed and her eyes wide as she waits to hang on every single word that leaves my mouth and I smirk.

"I was just thinking about the time I kissed you..." I trail off and her cheeks burn, her eyes falling to her lap as she tries to hide her blush.

Reaching forward, I softly grip her chin with my thumb and index finger, lifting her face to look at me.

"Don't hide from me Twilight."

"I'm not hiding because of your admission," her brazenness taking over her once shy demeanour.

"Then why are you hiding?" I coax, hoping she will tell me.

I see her throat bob as she swallows, her eyes fixed on mine and my heart races under my skin.

"The kiss..."

"Was fucking epic," I scoff, letting my fingers fall from her chin and I instantly miss the tingle that ripples through my skin from touching her.

Her tongue darts out and runs across her bottom lip, her eyes gazing into mine.

"Was it?" she asks, and I can see the confusion that is furrowed upon her brow, uncertainty lacing her voice.

"Ouch," I chuckle, holding my hand across my heart, "I am wounded."

She leans forward and swats me before a small giggle slips past her lips.

"I didn't mean it in a bad way..."

"Then how did you mean it?"

"Well, I mean... I don't have anything to compare it to..."

It takes me a moment to register what she just said, and I am blaming the fucking alcohol. I blink a few times, replaying what she said over and over.

Well, I mean... I don't have anything to compare it to...

"Amora..." I whispered, edging closer to her.

"Titus?" she says so innocently.

"What do you mean?" I know what she means, I think. But I want to hear the words come from her lips. I want to see how the innocence colors her face in one of my favorite ways. The way the blush stands out against her milky skin, the way her freckles spread as she smiles.

She sighs before taking another mouthful of her cocktail.

My heart drums a little faster and I am adamant it is skipping beats, but she would never tell. I am good at keeping my cool, good at putting on my best poker face.

"I have..." she stammers, her beautiful eyes fluttering shut for a moment.

"You have...?" my voice falls quiet.

"You were..." she rubs her lips together.

I lick my lips.

"I was..." I can't help but tease her, my lips pull at one corner and lift into a smirk.

"You were my first kiss!" she blurts out, slapping her hand across her mouth and there it is, that pretty fucking blush pinking her cheeks.

"What?" I can't help the laugh that escapes me at the shock of her admission.

"I'm not repeating it," she shakes her head, fidgeting on the spot.

"I'm not asking you to repeat it, I just don't believe I was your first kiss."

"Well like I have said before, my father made sure to run any boy far, far away before they even got close. I am a twenty-five-year-old virgin for Christ's sake!" and her hand covers her mouth once more, her eyes bugging. She places her glass down on the coffee table then falls back, covering her face with a pillow.

She's a fucking virgin.

Shit.

"Oh my god, this is why I should not drink alcohol." Her voice is muffled by the pillow.

And that's when realization kicks in, her innocence shines through so brightly. How the hell could I have missed it. Because I was too infatuated with her to even notice.

Fuck.

I lean forward, lifting the pillow from her face with one of my hands and my eyes volley back and forth between hers. Placing both hands either side of her, resting them on the cushions of the couch and cocooning her in.

"Don't you ever hide from me Little Red," my voice is raspy, my heart is dancing in my chest. Her perfectly imperfect eyes stay pinned to mine and all I can think about doing is covering her lips with mine, but I can't.

I shouldn't.

"I can't believe you had never been kissed..." my voice is shaky as I hold myself up and over her, "until me."

"It's embarrassing."

"No Twilight, it's not embarrassing," I shake my head from side to side, edging my lips closer to her.

Amora's lips part, her eyes falling to my lips and I hesitate for a moment.

"Kiss me again," she whispers, her eyes slowly fluttering shut and I instantly miss her eyes.

I don't hesitate, I lower my lips until ours meet. Slowly, our mouths move in a rhythm before I tease my tongue, her arms lock round my neck and I take that as my cue to let my tongue sweep over hers before they're dancing together. Amora shifts beneath me, and her intoxicating scent consumes me before her legs part and I slip between them as if we were the perfect fit.

Letting my arms lower so my elbows are now resting on the soft surface my hands cup her face as our kiss intensifies, a small whimper passes her lips and I feel myself harden and rub against the seam of my jeans.

"Titus," she breaks away, whispering in a soft pant.

"Yeah baby?"

"I want you to be my first; take it from me. I'm not precious about it and I don't want to go to The Knight Brothers a virgin," I see a glimmer of tears fleck in her eyes and I can't even find the words to say. "I've not kept it because I want it to be special, I am fully aware that it's not going to be like that, but I am sick of having it hover over me and I am begging you, don't let it be them that take it."

"Okay," I whisper, hovering my lips over hers.

"You promise?" and I can hear the desperation in her voice.

"I promise, Twilight, I promise."

And I swore silently, that no matter how much I didn't want to have to take her innocence just to give her away, we both knew it was inevitable.

"But not like this…" I whisper before covering her lips with mine once more.

CHAPTER THIRTY

AMORA

I wake, tangled in the sheets and I am fully aware that I am not alone. Rolling, I see Titus still fully clothed and sleeping on top of the covers. A small smile graces my lips and I feel a humongous weight has been lifted from my shoulders. I've asked a lot of him, and I have no idea whether he agreed just to pacify me or whether he actually wanted to keep his promise.

I am hoping it was the latter.

Because I couldn't think of a better time to lose it.

Finally.

The heavy weight of my innocence gone.

Forever.

I know most girls want it to be special, candles and slow love making, but that isn't me. I have been ready since I was seventeen when I went to prom, but it didn't happen. And every other time it has even come close, daddy dearest fucks it up. And if it isn't father, it's Xander.

Father's little arse licker.

This is my chance.

ASHLEE ROSE

Rolling on my back, my heart begins to drum about what may or may not happen.

Turning my face to look out the window, the blinds are half slated and I can see the threat of the moonlight peeking through. I sit up slowly, careful not to wake Titus and I am grateful I don't feel too unwell after a night of drinking. My cheeks pinch crimson when I think back to what happened last night after my admission, after he laid his body on top of me and showed me just how good his kisses were.

Pushing open the blinds slightly, the star kissed skies are lightening slightly and it must be early hours of the morning. It won't be long until the pink skies dominate the horizon and the sun peeps up to say good morning. Letting the blinds slip back to their position, I spin and lean against the windowsill and just focus on Titus.

My mind drifts back to last night once more, *the way his stubble scratched against my skin, the way his lips trailed down my jaw and along to my collarbone. I placed my hands either side of his face and lifted his lips back towards mine, sealing them when my hips lifted, gyrating slowly against his evident bulge, the fly of his jeans rubbing just where it needed to, giving me the small bit of friction that I craved and so desperately wanted. I knew it was bad, alcohol was pumping through both of our veins, yet we couldn't seem to stop even if we wanted to. My soft whimpers escaped and vibrated through our kiss as I continued trying to rub myself against him.*

"Baby," he panted, his large hand wrapping round my slim hip, gripping tightly. "Not here, not like this," his earlier words slip past his lips and echo round the silent room.

"Okay, okay," I whisper, lifting my head up to meet his lips once more.

I rub my hand over my chest, trying to calm my erratic

heart at my thoughts. We were like two horny teens, but I wasn't even ashamed of my behaviour last night.

Tiptoeing quietly over towards the hallway and into the bathroom, I closed the door quietly and pressed my back against the wood.

Was I really going to do this? My thoughts ricocheted round my mind and I tried to shut them down. I needed out of my head. This wasn't a big deal. I wanted this. I asked him to take it from me. Washing my burning cheeks with cool water. I had no idea why Titus had this kind of effect on me. He was like a drug, my constant craving as well as my withdrawal. Running my toothbrush under the water, I stare back at my reflection. I like how I look when I am with Titus, and it kills me inside a little that I'll be without him soon.

We both knew this wasn't a permanent fixture, but a temporary one until my father found us.

He was like a bloodhound.

He would always find me.

No matter how far I ran. He would outrun me every single time.

He was a tracker.

I was the prey.

Letting my head fall forward, I shake it softly.

I wish I could say I am disappointed; I'm not.

I'm just numb to it all. Trying to block it all out.

Pacing back towards the bedroom, I slip back past the bed and walk round my side. My fingers find the hem of my silk black shorts as I fiddle. My eyes are glued to Titus when I see him stir, maybe he knows I am watching him. I panic, climbing back into bed quickly and cover myself up. I feel Titus' arm land over me, pulling me into him and his face nuzzling into my wild red hair. I don't move, but I feel my own eyes fall heavy again as I slip into a slumber.

Rolling over, sleep still full in my eyes Titus is awake, resting his elbow on the pillow and his head sitting on his hand.

"Morning Twilight," he smiles, leaning in and giving me a soft kiss on the forehead and I never thought forehead kisses would become a favourite of mine.

"I fell back asleep," I sigh, stretching up.

"When were you awake?" he asks, his brows furrowed.

"Early hours this morning," I yawn, rubbing my eyes.

"Obviously needed that sleep," he winks, his hand rubbing over my stomach, and I feel my insides knot and burn, the wanting ache between my legs blossoming and I am desperate to have his hands on me where no man ever has before.

"Obviously; think the margaritas helped..." I roll my lips and pull my eyes from his, letting them settle on the ceiling. My fucking heart is skipping beats.

"Do you remember much from last night?" he asks nonchalant.

Balls.

"Everything," I manage to breathe out, not quite sure why I have lost my voice.

"And you still want this?" Titus asks, and I can tell he is hesitant. I mean he is twice my age and I've asked him to take my purity.

I nod, unable to speak.

"Are you sure... because once... I mean... we're going to cross a line..."

"Do you not want this? Is this what you're doing?" I snap and then I grimace, wincing.

"Baby..." he coos, placing his hand on my cheek and

266

turning it so I have to look at him. "It's not like that... I know you say it's not *precious* to you, but it should be. It's not something you just *give* away." His voice trails off and I feel my agitation begin to rise.

"Just forget it," I sigh, pulling his hand from my face and roll over on my side to face the window and I know I am acting like a spoiled brat.

"Amora..." his voice is low and silky, his lips pressing to the shell of my ear and I feel the shivers dance up and down my back causing my skin to explode in goosebumps, but burning at the same time. "I don't want to forget it; I didn't mean it that way..." he pauses and I still ignore him. "I just wanted to make sure you were okay with this... that's all."

And guilt stings me.

I turn my head to face him, my face softening, my eyes falling to his lips.

"I have never been surer."

A hint of a smile graces his lips and silence consumes us for a while.

"Have you done anything before?" and my cheeks burn with humiliation, but I shake my head from side to side slowly.

His brows raise but he says nothing.

"I mean... I've touched myself... but," and suddenly I want to smother myself. His tongue darts out, licking the top of his lip and my insides quiver.

I let my eyes flutter shut, my breath catching at the back of my throat as his fingers trail across my bare thighs causing my sex to clench.

I feel his lips on mine, my eyes still closed as I try and steady my breathing. His kiss is soft until it isn't. Our lips crashing, teeth clashing and our tongues wild.

His fingers continue up the insides of my thighs and

just when I think his tips are going to slip into the inside of my shorts, he pauses as he lifts his lips from mine.

"It's not too late for you to change your mind."

"Shut up Titus," I groan, wrapping my hand round the back of his neck and pulling his lips back into mine.

His skilful fingers glide up to the edge of my silk shorts, playing with the hem for a moment and I am trying my hardest to control my breathing.

Our kiss breaks, his full lips fall to my jaw where he nips all the way to my ear lobe as he takes a soft bite, knotting my stomach and causing a pang of pleasure to shoot through me, straight to my heat.

"Titus," I whisper, bucking my hips up silently begging for him to touch me where I want him to.

"Patience Little Red."

The tips of his fingers brush gently across the front of my sex in a teasing manner and my breath quivers, my eyes locked on his. He lowers his lips back over mine as his fingertips slowly tease around my clit, but not rubbing me at all. I fidget, silently asking him to touch me where I needed him to.

"You're very impatient," he smirks against my lips as his fingers brush softly over my pussy lips.

"I want you," I whisper between our kisses.

"And I promise baby, you're going to get all of me," my whole body trembled at his promise and nerves crashed through me but not the kind that make you regret what you're about to do; no, the kind that makes your belly flutter with butterflies at what is coming next.

His fingers skimmed over my clit, a small whimper passing my lips and being muffled by our kiss. The way his fingers feel as they begin to slowly rub soft circles on my bud, my legs open wider for him, giving him better access.

His lips stay on mine, not once breaking away as his fingers work me up. I scrunch my fingers into his white shirt, a pant escaping as his fingers move a little faster now and this time, he lets his finger glide through my pussy and tease me with the tip of his finger and I feel myself stiffen, clenching between my legs.

"Relax baby," he whispers, "there is no way I will be fitting anywhere if you can't even take the tip of my finger. You're wet Twilight, let me in," he coaxes, his lips trailing down to my jaw, then my neck, sweeping them across my collar bone until they land on my breasts, his hot breath seeping through the thin, silk material as he nips my skin through it.

Bucking my hips up, his finger slips through my folds, dragging my arousal up to my clit as he rubs before slipping his finger inside of me fully and I lose my breath, my fingers wrapping round his shirt, my heart racing as if wild horses are galloping in my chest.

"Good girl, relax baby."

He stills for a moment, and I know I can take more but I am just taking a minute to adjust to the strange feeling. I have only ever got myself off by rubbing my clit, never by experimenting with anything else.

"Touch yourself, show me how you get yourself off," he rasps, his eyes leaving mine as he props himself up and watches his finger slowly pumping in and out of my pussy. My hand glides down my body, skimming over the silk of my cami vest top and over my lower stomach until it is hovering over my clit.

"There's a good girl, show me," his voice is husky and low as I press two fingers onto my clit and slowly rub to match the rhythm of his finger now slipping in and out of me with ease.

His eyes widen with delight as he watches before he turns to face me, a slow, sexy smirk lifting his lips. With his spare hand, he slips it under my top and bunches it, pushing it up round my neck to reveal my swollen breasts. He lowers his head down, covering my right nipple with his mouth, licking, and sucking when I feel a second fingertip threatening to fill me, but this time, I don't stiffen, I welcome it. Wanting to feel completely full. My fingers quicken as I rub my clit harder, the heat swarming me, tingles erupting over my skin as I feel my impending orgasm.

"Titus," I whisper, wanting to grab him but he is on my wrong side, my fingers still rubbing over my sensitive clit.

"I know Little Red, I know," I feel myself tighten, my hips lifting so I meet his every thrust into me with his two thick fingers. His lips lock around my nipple, sucking it into his mouth as he grabs a handful, squeezing and kneading and I feel the electricity bolt through me, I can hear how wet I am and it's turning me on, giving me the gentle push that I need to fall deep into the pleasure pool and sink to the depths of darkness.

"Shit," I just about manage, my back arching as he rubs that spot that no one ever has, my skin erupts in an ice blanket, my eyes roll in the back of my head.

"You like that baby?" he asks, his fingers pushing in and out harder now, my pussy aching, my stomach burning, and I can feel the tremble begin to vibrate through my legs.

"Yes," I moan, my spare hand clutching onto the bedsheet beneath me, scrunching it in my fingers tightly.

"Then let it go Twilight," he whispers, his lips pressing against my ear, and I do. I let it all go for him, my back arching and lifting from the bed as my orgasm explodes through me, my moans filling the room and suddenly, I see stars, my ears ringing as I ride my orgasm. My pussy riding his fingers because I physically cannot get enough of him.

Slipping his fingers from me, he lifts them to his lips and sucks on them and groans as he does.

"Fuck, you taste so fucking good," he rolls on top of me, smirking down at me before he crashes his lips onto mine and swipes his tongue through my lips. I pant, still coming down softly from the almighty high he just gave me.

I blush, covering my face with my hands and I hear Titus tut as he pulls them away.

"What have I said about you hiding, never hide yourself from me Little Red," his voice is silky.

"You have a dirty mouth," I whisper, struggling to get my words out.

"Oh baby, you've heard nothing yet."

I writhe beneath him, my body tingling all over as pleasure still zaps through me.

I knew it was going to feel good, but what I just experienced was out of this world. I give myself good orgasms I think, but Titus just showed me just how good it could be, and we have only just got started.

My heart aches a little at the thought of what we're about to do and why we are doing it but now was not the time to get lost in thought about what my future holds.

"You okay?" I hear the concern in Titus' voice and my heart constricts in my chest.

I nod, "I'm perfect," I admit, readjusting my top and covering my chest.

"Don't cover yourself up for me, I'm about to play," he smirks, placing a soft kiss on my lips before shuffling down my body. I take a sharp intake of breath before I hold it, waiting with bated breath to see what he is going to do next. This feels intimate.

A little too intimate.

But I am desperate to have his mouth somewhere no one else has been before.

His fingers slip into the side of my silk shorts and he slips them down my thighs slowly and I don't miss the low growl that vibrates in his throat.

"Do you know how much of a turn on it is that I am the first man to have touched you like this… to have tasted you…" I exhale a shaky breath slowly, his tongue swiping through my folds and I can't help but perch myself up on my elbows and watch as he flicks and sucks on my clit.

"Oh," I whisper, dropping my head back as pleasure courses through me.

CHAPTER THIRTY-ONE
TITUS

Fuck.

My cock rubs against my jeans, aching and heavy but this isn't about me. This is all about her. Keeping my promise, knowing full well it is one promise I can keep.

My eyes lift from her pussy and I look up to see her, lips parted, her eyes pinned on me and I give her a slow wink before I let my tongue circle over her clit a little faster and her hips buck.

"You're so greedy," I hum, letting one of my hands fall from her hip, my fingers gliding down the outside of her thighs and under before I am teasing two fingers at her tight opening, her pussy still glistening and wet from her orgasm earlier.

"Please," she whispers, begging me to fill her, to show her what it is like to be worshipped.

Softly and slowly pushing my fingers inside of her, my eyes roll at the feel of her and I can't wait to sink my cock inside of her, knowing full well I'll bust in three seconds.

All the girls before her were nothing.

My heart pounds harshly in my chest.

Pumping my fingers in and out of her, her arousal coating my fingers as I bring her close to another orgasm, her pussy clenching round my fingers as my tongue dances up and down her pussy before focusing on her clit, sucking it into my mouth and her beautiful moans fill the room and the hairs on the back of my neck stand. My cock is throbbing, and I can feel the precum that is sitting on the inside of my boxers.

"Titus," she mewls, her hand flying to my head, her nails scraping up and down my short hair because there is nothing for her to grab.

I groan, her hips bucking up and gyrating on my tongue. Pausing, I kneel back and look down at her. Her red hair wild, her eyes wide and hazy and her chest rising and falling. I lick my lips, her arousal coating them.

"What's wrong?" her innocence makes me smile.

"Nothing Twilight, just going to switch it up a bit," I wink at her, sitting up and reaching for her, I pull her into my lap, her legs falling either side of me as she straddles me. "Fuck, you are something else Little Red," I whisper against her lips as I kiss her, "I think I am addicted to you."

She blushes.

"Don't be getting shy now baby, I've just had my tongue buried in your pussy and I am not finished yet."

She grasps my face in her small hands and shuts me up by covering my mouth with hers, her tongue slipping past my lips and I groan at the way her tongue feels against mine. I still cannot believe that she has never been kissed or touched until me.

Possessiveness courses through me, lighting a fire a deep inside of me and suddenly my heart aches in my chest at the thought that what is next is fully out of my control.

We both know Xavier is going to send me back on the

plane the second he can and she will be taken away from me.

Don't go there Titus.

This was never the plan.

I was never meant to fall in love with her.

Love.

I need to get out of my head.

Holding onto her, I roll over, so she is sitting on top of me. A bubble of a giggle escapes her and fuck, it's a beautiful sound.

My fingers dig into the bare skin on her hips, holding her in place for a moment so I can just appreciate her. Everything about her is perfect. She is perfection.

She's too good for me.

Too pure.

But I am going to see this through.

For her.

If I can keep one promise, it'll be this one because honestly, I don't think any other promise I have said I can keep.

She wriggles over my evident bulge, pulling me out of my mind once more and I sink my teeth into my bottom lip, pulling it behind them before I slowly release it.

"You're going to make me cum if you carry on Little Red," and she gives me a slow, sexy smirk, her eyes darkening as she rolls her hips over me.

"Would that be so bad?" her sultry voice floats over me and I grip her hips a little harder, holding her where I want her as I lift my hips to meet her movements. I have no idea what the fuck has come over me, I'm like a horny teen but I don't care. I can't get enough of her and if this gets her off then I am all for it.

She pants, her hands pressing against my chest, her

head falling forward as she continues rubbing herself over my jeans, my cock rock solid and I am desperate for my own release.

"Baby," I rasp, the delicious build getting too much as her bare, soaked pussy rubs back and forth.

"I know," moaning, she leans down across my chest, and I crash my lips into hers meeting every roll of her hips when I feel my orgasm rip through me. I hold her still whilst I explode inside my boxers, my eyes closed, our lips still locked as my own moans vibrate through me.

Something in me snaps. I grab her, pulling her hot, wet cunt over my face and lower her down over me, my tongue burying inside her pussy before gliding it up to her clit, swirling and flicking my tongue. My eyes lift and I look up at her, her red hair has fallen around her face, her cheeks are reddened, and her hands are gripped into her thighs as she rocks over my tongue, riding my face. I move a hand round the curve of her ass, teasing my fingertips along the crease of her ass cheek then letting two fingers slip inside of her, pushing them in deep.

"Oh," she sings, and my cock hardens again.

Pulling them out to the tip, I tease once more before filling her again. Each thrust becomes harder and faster until I am fucking her with my fingers, her moans are the only noise filling the room and I swear I am in heaven.

Her pussy tightens round my fingers, and I nip at her clit before sucking it into my mouth and she cries out, her orgasm crashing through her. I lap her up, making sure not to waste a single drop of everything she gives me. I lift her up and lay her down next to me and all I can do is stare at her, resting my head on my hand as I prop myself up with my elbow.

Post orgasm glow smothering her, a sheen of sweat

glistening over her chest and her cheeks painting them in that pretty fucking red that I love.

"Damn," she pants, her hand on her stomach as she takes a moment to calm herself.

"Damn," I mimic, leaning down and brushing my lips against her forehead and inhaling her scent.

She shuffles slightly and I don't miss the wince that makes her brows pinch.

"You're sore," and suddenly I feel guilty.

"A good sore," she smiles, turning to face me and kissing me.

"Come, let's go get you cleaned up."

I stand from the bed, wrapping my arms around her as I carry her to the bathroom, turning the shower on where I take my time in washing every inch of her body.

I'm fucked.

CHAPTER THIRTY-TWO
XAVIER

"How has no one found them yet!?" my voice is loud as I shout, slamming my hand down on my desk. I haven't slept in what feels like a week, I keep playing the CCTV footage to see if I have missed anything, but there is nothing that gives me any indication of where that no-good cunt has taken *my* daughter.

He has no right.

I sigh, running my hand through my hair.

He does have a right.

I hired him to protect her and that's what he is doing.

And given any other circumstance, I would be fucking proud as punch, but in the circumstances I am currently in I need him to bring her home.

I try both their phones again, but they go straight through to voicemail. Of course, they are. Pressing Tyson's name, it doesn't even ring before he answers.

"Anything?"

"No boss."

"Fucking useless," I cut him off and drop my phone on the desk. "Cunt," I shake my head from side to side, fisting my hands in my pockets I walk slowly over towards the back of my office and I stare out over my grounds, my lips twitching into a small smile when I see Royal tending to her flower garden.

"How the fuck did I get here?" I groan, rubbing the kink out of the back of my neck. I am too stressed, I need to retire. As soon as I know she is safe and this is all finished with I am done.

I've said it for the last five years, but I am done.

Completely.

I hear a commotion and turn to see Xander being thrown through the door and he falls to his knees followed by cunt one and cunt two.

The Knight Brothers.

"Hello Xavier."

I turn to seek out Royal and that's when I see that she is no longer in the garden and my heart sinks.

I pull my suit jacket down, then pull on the sleeves walking over slow and steady towards them.

They don't scare me.

What's the worst they're going to do? Put a bullet through my skull like I did their father's.

Bullshit.

They're cowards. I would have been six feet under and cold months ago if that was the case.

They couldn't even run a piss up in a brewery let alone the crime world that their daddy dearest dominated before them.

I grab Xander's arm and drag him up. "Get the fuck up," I grit, dusting him down and pulling him by my side.

Ezekiel runs through the door, his eyes bouncing round the room at the situation.

"Go and find your mother," I bark at him, and he

scuttles away. I love Ezekiel but he wasn't made for situations like this. He is too soft and I'm not mad about it. I am glad he isn't heartless and ruthless like me and Xander are. Pain slices through me at the memory of my brother; Xander reminds me so much of him in some ways. *Xander* was a coward. Not like my boy.

"What do I owe the pleasure?" I ask, stepping forward.

"We've come to collect what is rightfully ours," Wolfe snarls, stepping closer to me so we're toe to toe.

"Well, that's going to be a bit of a problem," I admit, reaching out and picking a bit of lint off his shitty looking tweed jacket.

"And why is that?" Hunter pipes up, puffing his chest out and tilting his chin.

"You look like such a prick acting like that," I scoff, shaking my head.

Hunter rushes for me, but Wolfe holds his arm out to stop him.

"Not now, brother."

I smirk in Hunter's direction, winding him up a little more.

"You were saying?" Wolfe glared at me.

"She isn't here," I cross my arms over my chest, and I see Xander step slightly forward, so he is just in front of me.

My protective boy. Nothing like his uncle.

"Where the fuck is she?" Wolfe shouts and spit flies from his rancid mouth and onto my shirt.

I look down, disgust evident on my face as I reach for the napkin out of my top pocket of my suit and wipe it off.

"I wish I knew, I really do but I have no idea where she is."

"What!?" he hisses, and Hunter just glares at me.

"You heard me."

"I fucking heard you; I don't understand how you don't know where she is!"

"Her bodyguard snuck her out in a suitcase in the middle of the night," I shrug my shoulders up, "sneaky fucker that one," I point, wagging my finger at him.

Wolfe is the one that rushes for me now, grabbing the lapel of my suit jacket, clutching it. I have no idea what he is trying to do but I don't budge.

"What are you doing?" I scoff, looking down on him.

"Fuck off," he shoves into me and steps away, turning his back on me as he pushes his hand through his greasy hair.

"You have three days to get her back, if you don't..."

"Then what?" I sit on the edge of my desk, ankles crossed and link my fingers together and rest them on my lap.

"He'll put a bullet through your head," Hunter pipes up from behind Wolfe.

"Why are you answering for him? Is the big, *bad*, Wolfe not brave enough to say it?"

Wolfe turns and narrows his gaze on me.

"You have three days. If she isn't here and waiting for us, I'll take your family out one by one in front of you, and after you've pissed your pants because you're so scared and crying your eyes out like a little bitch watching the massacre that I would have caused, I'll finish you off."

"Oh stop it," I smirk, "I'll see you in three days." And with that, they storm out the office and once I know they're gone I clutch my chest.

Shit.

"Xander, get Kaleb on the phone."

"Sure thing."

I don't think I'll make it three days, I'm going to be done with a heart attack.

Within minutes Ezekiel returns with Royal and my heart slows.

"Baby," I push from the desk and rush to her, cupping her face in my hands as I check her over. "Did they hurt you?"

"Who?" she looks at me confused.

"The twat twins."

"I was with Betty in the kitchen," and I breathe out a sigh of relief, "they were here!?"

"Yeah, it's fine, I've sorted it."

"Dad," Xander walks over to me and hands me the phone.

"Kaleb."

"Yup."

"Tell your nerdy computer guy to tell me where the fuck your prick of a mate, Titty has taken my daughter."

"Why would I do that?"

"Because he has just put a fucking target on all of our heads!"

CHAPTER THIRTY-THREE
AMORA

I SIT QUIETLY AS I WATCH TITUS PACING UP AND DOWN OUT THE front on his phone. His hand is rubbing over the top of his head, his jaw is clenched and I can tell by his body language that this isn't a good conversation. I pick my nails and nibble on my bottom lip. I feel anxious and I know this has something to do with my father. It always has.

I hear the front door open and I sit up, dropping my hands into my lap and my eyes land on him as he walks through.

"Yeah no worries, I'll keep you updated," I hear him say as he paces into the lounge.

"Yeah, bye Nate," he sighs, turning his phone off and tossing it across the room to the sofa.

I stand, a little cautious of his mood because I have never seen Titus wound up like this.

"Are you okay?" I just about manage as I step towards him, closing the gap.

"I'm fine baby," he coos, wrapping his arms round my waist and lifting me effortlessly. My legs wrap round him as his lips brush against mine.

"Let me help you," I whisper against his lips.

"How Twilight, how do you want to help me?" he rasps.

"Teach me," I blush.

"Huh?" his brows pinch.

"Teach me to pleasure you..." my eyes bat down.

"Oh baby," he groans, tightening his grip round me as he backs me against the wall, his hips pressing into me, his tongue sweeping past my lips and I moan into his mouth, my hands clutching his face, my fingers linking behind his head.

"Teach me," I whisper, one of his fingers travelling underneath me as he rubs my clit through my shorts.

"Are you sure?" he rasps, his hand clutching my cheeks between his thumb and finger and I nod.

Letting me down slowly, my feet finally touch the floor and I place my hands on Titus' chest, pushing him back towards the sofa, our lips still locked. My hands skim down his hard, toned body as I grab the hem of his tee, but he beats me to it. His hand reaches behind him, grabbing the collar of his tee and pulling it over his head in one, swift move. And fuck. It was hot as fuck.

Not that I have much to go on, but.

A slow smile creeps onto his lips, his eyes heated and my hands are back on his warm skin and I feel the spark shoot through my fingertips.

My fingers glide down to his trousers and my fingers fumble with the button of his jeans. Tugging them down slightly, the nerves crash through me and my hands tremble slightly. His large hand wraps round my delicate wrist, my face lifting, my eyes widening.

"Slow baby, don't panic. Take your time," he leans forward, placing a soft kiss on my lips and I feel myself instantly relax.

I push him back and he falls into the sofa, and I let my eyes roam down his body, my eyes glisten when I see his hard cock bulging in his boxers. I slowly drop to my knees, grabbing my hair and putting it up in a high, messy bun.

"You look so god damn pretty on your knees," his voice is low and his hand reaches forward, gripping my chin as his tongue runs across his full bottom lip. "Nice and slow Little Red," he whispers, leaning forward so he can kiss me once more.

He leans back, his burning ice blue eyes on me the whole time, the apex between my thighs aching and I can feel my knickers getting wetter as the seconds go on.

Wrapping my fingers in the side of his boxers, I tug them down and my mouth dries when his hard cock springs from his boxers, resting on his lower stomach.

My lips part and I am trying to work out just how it is going to fit. I ignore my internal fear and keep lowering his boxers before I pull them off his ankles and nestle myself back between his legs.

I reach forward slowly, then let my fingers trace up and down the underneath of his beautiful cock.

"Wrap your fingers round me baby," he ushers, and I do as he asks, wrapping my fingers round his length and I watch him wince. "Not that tight, you'll strangle him," he chuckles, and I instantly let go feeling humiliated. "Little Red," he sighs, sitting up and taking my hand. "Let me show you," his hand guides mine back and I wrap my fingers round him once more, but not as hard this time.

"Glide your hand up and down baby," his hand sits over mine as he slowly moves mine. "Fuck, that's it," he lets go and sits back, his head tipping back as he groans.

I continue at the pace he showed me, not sure whether to speed up or stay as I am. I watch as a bead of cum sits on his thick head, leaning forward my tongue swipes across as I taste him for the first time and my cheeks flame.

Letting my hand sit at the base of his length, I part my lips and push them round the tip of him, before letting my lips slide down his velvety cock, taking as much of him as I can before pulling him back out.

"That felt so good," he moans, "do it again," he lifts his hips slightly and I do it again, my fingers still firmly wrapped round him. "Yes Twilight, fuck," he pants, his head dipped as he watches me and I feel the heat swarm between my legs, my stomach knotting as I try and ignore the desire that is burning through me.

My hand begins to move in rhythm with my mouth and I can't get enough of him.

I look up at him through my lashes and something in him snaps, his large hand moves forward, gripping onto my messy hair and holds me still as he lifts his hips, his cock slipping to the back of my throat as he fucks my mouth.

"I need you Little Red, so fucking bad," he lets me go, my heart is thrashing in my chest and my knickers are soaked, my pussy aching. "Look how much of a good girl you are, sucking my cock so well," I moan round him, my eyes fluttering shut for a moment.

He grabs me and lifts me onto his lap, his warm, hard cock sitting right where I so desperately need him.

I move my hips slowly, trying to relieve a little of the ache when Titus' hands cup my face, moving my lips towards his and I let my tongue dance with his.

My hand falls slowly and lands between my legs and I begin rubbing against my clit through my denim shorts but it's not nearly as satisfying as I need it to be.

"Take them off," Titus growls and I hop from his lap, standing in front of him as I unbutton them and slowly shimmy myself out of them and let them pool at my feet. "Sweet Jesus," his eyes roam over me and my whole body tingles. Reaching up, I take my hair from its bun and let it fall, cascading down past my ribs.

Standing in just a cropped tee and my white lace thong.

"Look how wet you are, did you like sucking my cock Little Red?" he licks his upper lip and I clench my pussy.

I nod, my whole body feels as if it is trembling with anticipation.

"I want you," I manage, my throat thick and I step forward, straddling over his lap. His large hands rest on my bare thighs, his fingers digging into my skin, and I feel the burn spread across my body before goosebumps erupt.

Slowly his fingers trace shapes on my bare skin and my breath catches at the back of my throat as they move closer and closer to where I want him.

Where I need him.

He smiles like a Cheshire cat when his fingers brush against the front of my lace knickers, teasing over my clit and I shudder. Everything feels so sensitive.

"You're so wet," he moans, pressing a little harder now, his fingertip rubbing my clit and my head falls back slightly, my hands moving behind me and gripping onto his thighs as my back arches, my hard nipples restricted against my cotton tee.

He shuffles, when I feel his teeth nip at my shirt as he tries to pull it up to get to where he wants me, his tongue flicking across my nipple, my skin pebbling as he sucks my full breast into his mouth, his spare hand kneading and squeezing as he continues to caress me.

"King," I whisper.

"Fuck, I love when you call my name, but love it even more when you moan King," he groans against the flesh of my breast, his hot breaths ragged as he moves across to give the same attention to my other breast.

My hips buck forward; I am needy.

I feel his thick finger wrap round my knickers, tugging them to the side, hard and I hear the rip of the delicate lace.

"I destroyed your panties," he growls, his eyes darken.

"I can get a new pair," I whisper, before I gasp when I feel two of his fingers slip into me.

"Is this what you want Little Red? My fingers slowly fucking you?" his voice low and seductive.

I nod, moans slipping past my lips as I lift my hips.

"You're such a good girl, you're doing so well," he praises, and I clench round his fingers. "I cannot wait to feel your tight virgin cunt around my cock, I don't think I am going to be able to let you go. Once I fuck you, you're mine Little Red, I will do whatever it takes to keep you," he whispers, and I block out the last bit because we both know this is a losing game. We will never win.

I reach between us, stroking his cock in my hand once more and he moans, "Baby, you need to stop, I want to be inside of you."

I feel a sting when he slips another finger inside of me, and I choke on my own breath as I take a sharp intake.

"You're doing so well, you can take it," he says softly as he slows down his pumps into me giving me a moment to adjust with his thumb brushing against my throbbing clit softly.

After a minute, he pumps into me hard and fast, my moans getting louder and my pussy clenches down over his fingers.

He slips them out of me, lifting me slightly as he lines his cock up and begins to rub it over my clit and teasing through my folds.

"Shit," I whisper, looking down between us and seeing his thick cock gliding through my spread pussy lips. I roll my hips, silently begging for him to take everything from me but he is too busy teasing me. "I am close," a silent plea, my fingers find my clit as I begin rubbing.

"You're so fucking beautiful," he moans, pressing the tip of his thick cock at my opening and I can't stop the gasp as he slowly slips into me, but only the tip, edging in and out of me.

"Fuck," he slowly drawls out the word, his jaw clenched as he pulls out then edges the tip back into me.

"Don't stop," I moan, my fingers rub over my swollen clit, and I am so close, my eyes begin to roll in the back of my head.

"Baby, I need to fuck you. I need to feel *all* of you," he slips out of me, "and this is a dangerous game," his throat is tight.

Panic floods me.

"Condom," I breathe.

"Go and check my bag in my room, my dick of a friend has no doubt hid some somewhere."

I nod, pushing off him and grabbing his boxers off the floor to cover myself up with as I slip them up my legs.

"They suit you, Little Red."

I give him a wink and rush into his room. My eyes dart round the room and I see a black duffel bag sitting by the wardrobes. Falling to my knees I unzip it and search round but it's empty. I huff, blowing up and my breath causes my hair to lift softly.

I look round the room once more but there is no other bag. I dive back in and find a small zipped up pocket inside. I unzip it and find a paper note.

Pulling it out, my brows crease as I unfold it and crinkle my nose when I see what is says.

A couple of condoms for you in case you get some English pussy.
Love Keaton X

"Ew," I shake my head, taking the silver foiled condom and folding the note up, holding onto it.

I rush back out to the lounge and toss the condom at him along with the note. Titus' brows raise as he unfolds the note, and his eyes widen before he shakes his head from side to side before they land on me.

"Your friend Keaton is disgusting by the way," I smirk, but he knows that. Pushing my hair from my face then push down Titus' boxers, discarding them.

"I don't want to do this here Twilight," he whispers, standing and scooping me up. "You're too good for the couch."

My heart drums in my chest as Titus carries me to his bedroom, kicking the door shut behind him and dropping me into the duvet.

CHAPTER THIRTY-FOUR
AMORA

Titus crawls over me, pulling me up and tugging my tee over my head and his hot mouth falls to by heaving chest, his lips locking round my hard nipples as he bites and tugs on my pert tits.

I watch, panting as he kneels back and he tears the condom wrapper with his teeth, his eyes not leaving me for a single second. Rolling the condom down his hard length, I quiver.

Kneeling between my spread legs, his fingers swirl at my opening and I let my hand dance down my bare stomach as I rub my clit, working myself back up to where I was before.

Slipping one, then two, and finally three fingers into me he fucks me slow with his fingers and I feel the pressure building. I don't want to come like this, I want his big, beautiful dick inside of me.

"King, please," I beg.

He slips out of me, his hands either side of my head, his arms encasing me as his lips brush against mine.

"Are you sure about this?" he asks one last time and I nod.

His beautiful eyes move down between our bodies, and he presses the tip of his cock at my opening and I feel myself tense slightly.

"You've already had the tip baby, relax or I'm not going to fit," he says quietly, his large hand rubbing and kneading my breast as he slowly pushes his hips forward, nudging into my tight opening.

"Oh," I just about manage as I feel him slip a little deeper and I clench.

"Don't squeeze baby, fuck," he squeezes his eyes shut, his jaw clenched. "You're so fucking tight." I watch as his head tips back and I look down to see he is only half in.

Tilting my hips slightly, meeting his slow thrusts into me and with each one he is hitting a little deeper.

"You're doing so well Little Red," he praises, his hand gripping my slim hip, his fingers digging into my skin.

"You're so big," I whisper, "shit," the sting burns as he pushes through the barrier and fills me completely with one last thrust. He stills for a moment giving my body a moment to adjust.

"Are you okay?" he asks, the veins bulging in his neck as he holds himself still.

"Yeah," I reassure him as he pulls out slowly and then moves back into me.

He takes his time, being gentle and making sure not to be too rough but it's not enough.

"King," I mewl, "I want you to fuck me," he stills for a moment. "I want to be sore, I want to be so sore that every time I move tomorrow all I remember is this moment and the way you fucked me."

He rears up, digging his fingers into the inside of my thighs and spreading my legs wider.

"Show me baby, fuck me the way you have been fantasising about fucking me," I smirk, and I hear a deep, primal growl.

He slips out to the tip; I feel the sting but I ignore it.

"You want it hard baby? You want me to show you just how much I have wanted to be inside your tight little cunt?" I moan at his dirty mouth.

"Yes, I want you to show me," I sink my teeth into my bottom lip, and I see the smirk that spreads across his lips.

He slams into me, hard and fast and I cry out. He does it again, his skin hitting my skin as he begins to pound into me, his cock slipping in and out of my pussy with ease and my eyes roll in the back of my head, my fingers finding my clit again as I begin to slowly rub as I watch Titus fucking me relentlessly, not holding back.

I watch as he pulls to the tip, leaving it there as he teases. "You want to be sore baby; you want to remember my cock every time you walk? Every time you sit?" he slams hard back into me, and I feel my pussy tighten, my fingers moving faster over my clit. His tip sits at my entrance, his fingers still digging into the skin on my thighs. "Every time you squeeze these pretty thighs together?" His cock hits me deep and I cry out, my legs beginning to tremble, and he pulls out again. "I hope you know what you've signed yourself up for, you want to be sore? I'll make you fucking sore," he growls slamming into me and I clench, the pressure building, my skin burning and my pussy aches, begging for release.

I lift my fingers from my swollen clit and Titus slows for just a moment as he spits on my pussy, then slaps my clit before he fucks me hard and fast, riding my pussy until I can't take it anymore. My fingers lower and I rub my clit, my hips meeting his every thrust until I am crying out, my orgasm exploding, coming hard and fast like a steam train and I swear I black out, my ears ringing with a high pitch noise. My back arches off the bed and that's when I feel Titus' fingers wrap round my throat as he continues to fuck me through my orgasm and I hear him roar, heavy, breathless pants leaving him as he pounds in and out of me as his own orgasm spills out of him, splitting him in two.

"Amora," he groans, his head tipping back as he loses himself completely.

He eventually slows, collapsing on top of me as his hands cradle my face.

"Well fuck," he scoffs, laughing slightly as he pushes my hair from my face.

"Well fuck," I blush, wrapping my legs round his large frame as my lips meet his, my whole world turned upside down in one moment, I am on a constant high and I never want to come down from it. He has ruined me.

In the best way.

"Are you okay?" he asks, concern lacing his voice, "I was a little rough," his face buries in the crook between my jaw and shoulder, and I feel the soft kisses he trails along my skin.

"I am perfect baby, thank you for showing me what it is like to be..." I nearly say *loved* but I stop myself, stumbling over my words for a moment.

"I will spend however long it takes to show you what it is like," his voice is muffled. "Come on, let's go get you cleaned up," he slowly rolls up but I shake my head from side to side.

"No, not yet. Just stay here with me. I don't want this moment to be over... not yet. Because as soon as this moment is over, it's back to real life and I'm not quite ready to step back into reality yet," I whisper because I am terrified of losing him.

"Okay Little Red, let's just stay for a while."

"Just for a while," I nod, sinking my teeth into my bottom lip to stop the tremble.

I had fallen so fucking hard for Titus King that it terrified me, but it terrified me in the best way possible.

THE NEXT FEW DAYS WERE SPENT EXPLORING EACH OTHER AND suddenly my mind drifts to last night.

"That's it, fuck, Little Red..." Titus' erotic groans fill the room as he guides me down his thick, hard, cock. "Look how well you take me," he praises as he fills me to the hilt. I still, letting my body get adjusted to just how deep he is in this position. I'm on top, legs straddled over his broad body, and I can feel every, single, inch of him.

Splaying my hands against his chest, I feel the steady beat of his heart underneath my fingertips.

I keep my eyes on him as I begin to slowly rock my hips over him as my eyes roll in the back of my head. Every bit of me feels over sensitive, his large, calloused hands grip into my hips and his fingers dig into my skin.

"You feel so good," his jaw is clenched tight as he lifts me slightly and he drifts his eyes down between our bodies watching as his cock slips in and out of me at a slow, delicious pace.

"Titus," I whisper, my voice quivering as I dig my nails into his soft skin and my hips rotate in circular motions a little faster now, trying to get all I can from him.

"I know baby," his soft, low voice breezes over me like a warm spring day but my skin explodes with goosebumps, my

skin pebbling under his touch. "I can't wait to fuck you hard, fast, rough..." he pants as he lifts me up his cock then slides me back down again. "Bring your knees up baby, I need more," he cranes his neck so he can get a better view of us. I do as he asks, bending my knees and letting my feet press into the soft mattress beneath me.

His hips rock harder and faster into me and I try with all I have to meet every single thrust.

"Oh," I moan as I feel that familiar, burning build up deep inside of my belly and I begin my chase for it. I have become addicted to the way he makes me feel, to the way my body reacts to him giving me just what I need. Just what he needs.

"Good girl; fuck your pussy looks so god damn pretty filled with me, you're so tight," he groans, his head tipping back as his own pleasure crashes over him like a tidal wave.

"Keep going Titus," I beg, my mouth dropping open as I watch his facial expression change with each stroke inside of me.

"I want you to come so fucking hard, I want you all over my cock," his teeth are clenched, his jaw tight as he holds me in place, pinning me to him as he slams into me over and over.

Everything aches and burns and I know I am close. Lifting a hand from his chest, I let my fingers press against my clit, rubbing in slow, gentle circles.

"One day Twilight, I am going to watch you get yourself off. Fuck, you look so beautiful," he whispers and the ache in my pussy intensifies.

"Titus," I moan out, my back arching and my spare hand moves behind me to grip onto his thick thighs, digging my nails into him the urge to mark him growing as each second passes.

"There's a good girl, let me feel you," he teases me with his words and his praise. I love being his good girl.

My pussy clenches around him and I feel his cock pulse inside of me.

"Harder, please," I pant out in-between his thrusts.

I love that I am being held tightly as he fucks me, bringing my orgasm teetering on the edge.

"Let it go baby, let me hear you sing my name."

My body stiffens and my orgasm rocks through me and I do as he asks, I sing his name as I ride out my high. My whole body relaxes and slumps as Titus thrusts into me one last time and I feel his cock jerk and pulse deep inside of me as he comes.

I look down at him, a giddy smile on my face and my heart swells in my chest.

"I'm never letting you go," he whispers, wrapping his fingers round the back on my neck and pulling me down so our lips meet, his tongue sweeping through mine before he rolls me on my back and fills me once more.

I snap out of it, my cheeks flushed, and I am needy for him once more. I am addicted to him. Like an addict chasing her next high. I'm the addict. Titus is my high.

Splashing my face with cold water, I pat the dry hand towel over my face and smile back at my reflection. I have a glow that I have never noticed before and it's all because of him.

CHAPTER THIRTY-FIVE
TITUS

I roll over, my arm reaching across for Amora but she isn't in the bed, all I find is an empty space. I slowly open my eyes, giving them a minute or two to adjust to the bright light.

I groan; rolling on my back I lift my arms above my head as a small smirk plays across my lips as my eyes flutter shut. The last few days have been everything and more and we spent the most of today in bed, naked and exploring each other's bodies. I couldn't get enough of her. My cock hardens at just the thought.

Suddenly I am pulled from my haze when I feel a large, hard slap across my cheek which cracks around the room.

"Wake up mother fucker," I hear the low tone of a familiar voice and when my eyes finally open, I see Xavier standing at the side of the bed, eyes narrowed on me and a jaw so tight and wound that his jaw must be aching. But before I could even ask what he was doing, he pushes his arm forward, gripping me round the throat and squeezing. "This is what you get for sleeping with my baby girl," and all I see is black.

CHAPTER THIRTY-SIX

AMORA

I walk quietly downstairs not wanting to wake Titus up and go to sneak into his room and back into bed before he has even realised that I have been gone but when I walk into the room, I see Titus laying, completely naked with his hand wrapped round his soft cock and my father standing next to the bed with a look pinned to me that could kill me.

"Dad," I gasp, my eyes moving from Titus to him, rage consuming me as I rush to my father. "What are you doing?!" I scream, shoving him in the chest hard but he doesn't move.

"Taking you home, pack your shit up... Now!"

"No, I'm not going," I slap his cheek, instantly regretting it when I feel the sting on my hand and see my father's eyes darken.

"Don't fucking push me," he grits, "if you don't come willingly, I will fucking drag you out of here. Do not test me."

"You wouldn't," I step back, my eyes widening when he follows me, closing the gap and his brows raising.

Before I can stop him, he grabs me and throws me over his shoulder walking me out to the waiting car and all I can do is scream for Titus.

But it's no use.

He is out cold.

CHAPTER THIRTY-SEVEN
TITUS

WHAT THE FUCK?

My eyes slowly open, my head rolling and I feel like I have been hit by a free rolling train. Everything aches, my head is pounding as if it's trapped in a vice.

"Wakey wakey," I hear his voice before my eyes land on him.

"Shit," I seethe, "what did you do to me?" I go to move my hands, but they're tied to a chair and then my eyes widen when I see that I am still completely naked.

"Really!?"

"Really," Xavier nods, sitting on the edge of his desk, ankles crossed as he takes a bite out his apple, a sinister smile spreading across his fucking face.

"Did you drug me?"

"Absolutely."

Shaking my head from side to side my stomach rolls with anxiety.

"Where is Amora?"

"Where she should be."

"You didn't." My blood runs cold and fear scratches at

my throat, I swallow the swollen lump that's wedged in my throat, but I cannot seem to clear it.

"I didn't have a choice," Xavier snaps.

"Xavier," I tsk, letting my head drop forward as I shake my head from side to side before I compose myself a little more and I don't care that I am sitting here butt naked. "You always have a choice."

And that's when I see something other than pure fucking hatred in his eyes. A flicker of sadness bounces through them before the darkness takes over.

He didn't want this.

"Xavier... we're on the same side..."

"We were until you had sex with my..." he pauses and closes his eyes, inhaling deeply and bringing his closed fist to his lips.

"About that..." I begin to speak but he holds his hand out to stop me, his eyes burning into mine.

"I don't want to hear it. We were on the same side before you snuck her out of my home; I've got to say... I am impressed. It took me a while but once your little friends found out the seriousness of this absolute shit show we were in, they were very quick to throw you under the bus." He smirks at me, "If I were you, I would be questioning where their loyalty lies..." I watch as he turns his back to me and paces towards the door of his office, grabbing my bag that I had packed and rummaging through it, he launches clothes at me as he does. "I've knocked ten thousand off your final bill because you were a cunt, don't do it again," he hisses, closing the gap between us. He reaches into his pocket and pulls out a pen knife before slipping the cool metal of the knife under the rope that is binding my wrist to the chair and slicing through them.

"I'll be back in ten, we've got a lot of work to do," he

winks, giving me one last slap on the cheek then disappears out the room.

I dress quickly in cargo pants and a tee, I feel like I have slept for days. My thoughts are constantly on Amora, and I just hope and fucking pray that Xavier has a good explanation for what he has done because in my head nothing makes sense.

I hate that I had her for just a short time, completely to myself. I'm not mad at Nate or the rest of the guys for giving up our location. I'm mad that I didn't make the most of my time with her, mad that I didn't take every ounce of her in.

I sigh, pushing my hands into my pockets, I wait.

CHAPTER THIRTY-EIGHT

AMORA

I PACE AND PACE UNTIL I DON'T KNOW WHAT ELSE TO DO WITH myself. With each stride I take, anger consumes me a little more. This was really happening. Realisation sinks in and my stomach bottoms out. I inhale sharply and I feel my blood boiling. I fall back and sit on the edge of the queen-sized bed which sits in a ridiculously sized bedroom, I stare at the plum-coloured walls. I focus on that colour as I try and push the anger from me. What is it going to change? Nothing.

What's done is done.

My eyes narrow on the plum wall. What a boring colour. My fingers tingle and the urge to paint my feelings onto a canvas are screaming inside of me, but I soon silence them.

I crinkle my nose and let out a heavy sigh.

The doorknob twists and my head snaps round to see who it is.

The Wolfe.

Or the Hunter.

Wolfe enters the room, sauntering along the wooden

floors. His greased black hair is slicked back, his defined jaw giving his face a certain edge but not in a good way. He isn't like the beautiful men I read in my books; he isn't handsome like Titus.

My heart squeezes in my chest.

"My sweet Amora," his voice is low, his hand reaching for me as his fingers glide down the side of my face and I freeze.

"I'm not yours," I snarl, jolting away because the feel of his fingers on my skin is enough to make acid burn up my throat.

"Don't be like that, it's not a nice way to treat your husband now, is it?"

I swallow, nerves ricocheting deep inside my stomach, but I don't let him know that. I don't even give him the satisfaction of changing my facial expression.

"I won't be nice to you; you want a perfect wife that obeys your every command like some perfectly trained dog?" I scoff, covering my mouth with my hand for a moment, "You won't get that with me, I won't do as you ask, I'll disobey your every command because I can. You want the perfect wife but I'm not perfect, far from it actually..." I pause for a moment, and I see Wolfe's eyes darting back and forth between mine. "Still want me?"

"Even more now," he winks then sits on the edge of the bed. I scoot over, careful not to wince as I do because I am sore, but I do not want to be anywhere near him.

"You will join me and my brother, Hunter for dinner at seven p.m.," he shuffles but I stay frozen to the spot.

"Will I?" I retort back.

"Yes."

I say nothing, rolling my lips.

"Is that going to be a problem?"

"A little yeah," I admit, letting out a breath.

"And why is that?"

"Because like I said before, I'm not obedient, I don't follow orders," I reply, rolling my eyes. "Are you a little thick?" I lick my lips and hide my smirk.

"Are you really going to put up a fight?"

"Absolutely," I snort, shaking my head from side to side.

"Then you're a damn fool," Wolfe snaps, his teeth grit and his jaw is wound tight.

"Maybe," I shrug, "rather be a fool than weak."

Wolfe says nothing, just stands.

"Can I ask something?" I pipe up as he begins to walk towards the bedroom door.

"Anything," he turns to face me.

"I'm assuming you go by nicknames. Because surely your mother and father... God rest his soul," I make a cross from my head to my chest and across to my shoulders, "wouldn't be as cruel to name you Wolfe and Hunter? Or is it Hunter and the Wolfe?" I smirk knowing full well I have gotten a rise from him.

"Fuck you Amora," he snarls, opening my bedroom door and slamming it shut.

I giggle before falling back and laying on the bed.

After a while, the silence becomes a little bit louder and my stomach twists. I miss Titus and I can't help but wonder where he is. Has my father hurt him? Or did he send him straight back home on a plane. The thought unnerves me and all I want is to be enveloped in his arms. We had only a moment together, but it felt like a lifetime. I crave so much more, but it will always stay a craving. I will become a Knight and have to live in the shadow of my former self. Any feelings that I once felt will be buried so deep inside of me they will never resurface.

I rub the ache out of my chest, and I feel the prick of tears begin to sting at the back of my eyes.

Never did I imagine I would be living like this.

Given away to be married off to my father's enemy.

All because my father made a mistake.

I feel a single tear roll down my cheek and disappear into the duvet beneath me. Running my index fingers under my waterline, I need to stop. I don't want to cry anymore.

Sniffling, I sit up and look down at my clothes. I am still wearing Titus' tee and a pair of my pyjama shorts. I have none of my belongings with me. Lifting Titus' shirt to my nose, I inhale his scent, closing my eyes and just for a moment imagining he is here with me. Sighing, my eyes flutter open and I am consumed with thoughts once more.

My father literally dropped me off on the door before speeding off into the distance and he didn't even say goodbye.

I want to think that he has something planned and that he hasn't actually left me here, but then again...

What if?

I HAVE NO IDEA HOW LONG IT HAS BEEN SINCE WOLFE CAME IN barking his orders, but I haven't heard from either of them. I stand, needing to stretch my legs so I head towards the walk-in wardrobe. Switching the light on, I see it filled with all the clothes you could ever want. Ballgowns. Summer dresses. Tees. Jeans. Denim dungarees. Skirts. Pyjamas... you want it? I've got it all hung and folded within these walls. Letting my fingertips glide along the different materials until they land on the dungarees. I tug my shorts down, letting them pool at my feet before I step out of them. Slipping the dungarees off their hanger, I slide them over my thighs and up my waist before letting the straps glide up my arms. I tuck the loose parts of Titus' tee inside and a lump forms thick and fast in my throat and my chest aches. I never want to take it off. If this is all I have left of him then it's all I've got to remember him by. My fingers trail over my parted lips and my stomach drops at the thought of not having his lips on mine anymore, having his fingers tracing over my skin, following the map that only he knows.

Swallowing the lump down, I turn and walk back into my bedroom. I stalk towards the door, stopping for a second but before I let my mind get the best of me, I open the door quickly and I'm surprised it's not locked. That's what I get for assuming he was going to lock me away like a prisoner. I shut my thoughts down and slip out onto the large landing area. There are eight doors in front of me and I want to know what is behind every single one. Just as I am about to open the one directly in front of me, I hear Wolfe's voice and my curiosity is piqued. Stepping quietly towards the large, winding staircase I stop at the top.

"She's not going to be easy," I hear him say and pride swarms me.

"We like a challenge though, right?" Hunter replies and I shudder.

"We do, but not with her. We need her on our side if she is going to eventually do what we need."

Hunter hums in agreement.

"So play nice, she's been betrayed by her father so we're all she has." My shoulders drop a little. "I hate him so imagine how she feels about him."

"I'm pretty much there with you," I whisper to myself and take a step down.

"I can be nice," and I can hear the seediness in Hunter's voice. I feel like me and Wolfe could maybe get along, but me and Hunter... I already despise the little prick.

"I mean it Hunter, don't fuck this up any more than it already has been, this is how we're going to get redemption for what *he* done to our father."

My skin erupts in goosebumps.

"And I can't fucking wait," Hunter booms and I grip onto the cool, black iron handrail.

I shake it off, holding my head high as I begin taking each step until I am in the grand entrance hall.

From how loud their voices were, I thought they would have been where I am standing now but they're nowhere to be seen. I continue forward down a long but narrow hallway. All of the walls are painted in that shitty colour, and I have no idea why they thought it would look nice, because it doesn't.

Scrunching my nose up, I push through double doors and end up in a large office. Sitting at the desk is Hunter and Wolfe.

They look very similar, except Wolfe is tall and slender, Hunter is shorter and stocky.

Both of their brown eyes lift and land on mine and I give them a sweet smile.

"What do we owe the pleasure?" Wolfe asks as he stands and makes his way towards me.

"I just needed to stretch my legs," I nod. "Thanks for the clothes, nice to wear something other than pyjamas," I lie. I would much rather be living in Titus' tee for the rest of my life.

"They suit you."

I feel Hunter's eyes on me and the guy gives me the serious creeps.

"I was wondering..." I pause for a moment and avert my gaze from cunty Hunty. "Do you have, or could you maybe get me an easel and some paints?" I make myself sick with this sweetness shit façade I have going on. I have never been sweet. Until Titus. But that was different. I was a completely different person with Titus.

I ignore the searing pain that slices through my heart and focus on Wolfe.

"We already have one, I had a studio sorted out for you as per your father's request... would you like me to show you?"

I nod, my heart skipping in my chest that my father asked for him to provide one... maybe he does have a plan after all.

CHAPTER THIRTY-NINE
TITUS

"She's going to hate you, you know that right?" I say before taking a sip of the coffee that Royal made me.

"My wife already loathes me, what's one more to the list," Xavier doesn't lift his eyes to meet mine.

"And that doesn't bother you?" I can't help but answer back and I am trying my hardest to keep the rumbling rage that is currently brewing deep inside of me at bay.

"Of course it does you silly prick, but it's done. Royal is stubborn, Amora even more so but I have to do this, this is what has been planned since the beginning and you had to come along and fuck it all up," he snarls, and I ball my fist in my lap.

"Well, if you hadn't kept me in the fucking dark then maybe we wouldn't be in this situation, but here we are so fucking tell me what it is you've got going on in that fucked up head of yours," my voice gradually getting louder as my anger begins to fill me.

"Don't you dare," Xavier growls at me across the desk, banging his hand on the surface.

"Or what?" I stand, jaw clenched, brows furrowed.

"I'll knock you out again," he smirks but doesn't stand to meet me and for some reason that winds me up more.

"Course you will, I think you had a little help from drugs for that didn't you old man..."

"Is that what you think?"

Now I am getting under his skin.

"Of course, the size of me compared to you... plus you had me at a disadvantage."

"I wouldn't say that... I had you at an advantage, got some awesome photos that I've pinged back to your group of *loyal* friends."

"You're a cunt."

"As are you Titty, as are you."

"My priority is Amora... it will always be Amora... now fucking tell me where she is and what this plan of yours is because honestly Xavier, the way you're going on makes me think that there has never been any plan. I still don't understand why you hired me, you practically begged me to look after her for you just to give in to The Knight Brothers and give her to them anyway? It doesn't make any sense," I shake my head from side to side as I slowly begin to sit down.

"If you hadn't run with her, the plan would have been explained," he pulls his eyes from whatever the fuck he is looking at on his laptop and steadies his cold gaze on mine. My eyes focus on his scar that runs under his left eye and down his cheek, finishing just before the left side of his nose.

"How did you get the scar?" I ask before my brain catches up.

"Why did your wife leave?"

My eyes widen and I scoff, "I was waiting for that one, anything else you want to know?"

"I know everything about you Titty."

"Scar?"

"A brawl."

"With?"

"No one important," and I can tell by his tone that it is someone important.

After a minute or two I answer his question. "I have no idea why... gave up asking that question a long time ago."

I hear Xavier sigh. "For the record..." he clears his throat, sitting back in his office chair and linking his fingers together, "I tried looking for her, I tried seeing if I could find anything that may have given you answers but..."

"I appreciate it," I give him a firm nod, cutting him off. And it's the truth. I did but that part of my life is over.

He nods back and I feel like we both have a mutual understanding.

"So, plan?"

"Mate, get off my case," he rolls his eyes in an over exaggerated manner and before I can answer the door swings open and his expression softens so I know it's Royal.

"Titus, would you like another drink? A cold compress for your bruising cheek and eye?" Royal asks.

"I would like a drink, I'm parched," Xavier pipes up but she just ignores him as if he isn't in the room and I roll my lips, trying to hold off my laugh.

"I'll take a water if that's okay?" I smile at her, and she takes my coffee cup.

"Are you hungry?" she asks.

"Fucking famished," Xavier answers but she doesn't look in his direction.

"I am okay, thank you," I turn to face Xavier and give him a wide grin.

"I'll be back in just a moment with a water and cold

compress," she reaches forward and places her hand on my shoulder, and I hear the deep rumbling growl that vibrates through Xavier.

She turns and walks out of the room, slamming the door as she does.

"She is so annoyed with you," a deep, throaty laugh escapes me but the more I try and hold it in, I can't.

"I'm glad you find it amusing."

"Oh, I do," my head falls back as more laughter erupts from me.

"If you want to know the plan I suggest you shut the fuck up," he shouts and I scoff, palming my cheek when I realise I have reduced myself to tears.

"Go on then, I'm all ears."

CHAPTER FORTY
AMORA

IT'S BEEN THREE DAYS SINCE I LAST SAW TITUS AND MY HEART IS cracking a little more every day. Staring at my dark grey, violet and black painting it looks as depressed as I feel.

Wolfe has left me alone which I am grateful for, and Hunter hasn't even breathed in my direction.

"Maybe add a little white... it won't be as heavy." I freeze; my heart jack hammering in my chest as I turn to see if my ears are deceiving me.

My eyes widen when I see Titus leant up against the door frame of my studio, wrapped in a light grey suit and a white crisp shirt which makes his crystal blue eyes shine like diamonds. I don't miss the bruise that is sitting pretty round his eyes and spreads down to his cheek bone.

"Titus," I choke, tears are streaming down my face as I run to him. I needed to be wrapped in his arms, my head on his chest so I could listen to see if his heart was racing as fast as mine then finally, feel his lips on mine. But none of that happens. He stops me. His fingers digging into the skin at the top of my arms and he shakes his head from side to side slowly, pulling his gaze from mine and my heart obliterates in my chest.

"We can't," he whispers, nudging me back slightly and I feel the air leave me as it is snatched from my lungs. "You're not mine anymore, Twilight."

"Don't, please don't do this... Titus," my chin wobbles, my bottom lip trembling and I couldn't even stop the tears if I wanted to.

"This was always the plan. I was hired to look after you, to protect you... that's what I am doing. I will be by your side every step of the way until you're married." He pauses and I can hear the thickness in his voice; he doesn't want this. "Then once you're married and I know you're okay... well, then I go back home to New York." I watch as his throat bobs and I can see the emotion that is spreading across his face.

"Titus," I whisper, reaching for his hand and our fingers just brush before he pulls them away.

"Please Amora..." he whispers back, "please let me do my job." I hear the crack in his voice and the tears roll down my face. I can't say anything else, so all I do is nod, over and over again.

"This just wasn't our time, Little Red. Maybe in another life, but not this one," and with those words said, he turned and walked out the studio and my legs buckle beneath me as I drop to the floor and sob silent tears.

TITUS

I watch her, sitting so subdued and sad and it destroys me. I don't let her know I am here until I hear a sigh leave her,

her head tilting slightly as she looks at the dark canvas she has painted.

My heart is ricocheting in my chest, blood pumps in my ears so loudly the sound is all I can hear.

"Maybe add a little white... it won't be as heavy," a small smile pulls at the corner of my lips but it's all façade because I am slowly dying on the inside, my heart splintering at the thought of what I am about to do. I see her whole body stiffen at my voice and I know she wasn't expecting it. She turns slowly, her eyes widening as they land on mine and I see the shock on her face. Her beautiful eyes roam over me and I see the relief swarm her, her shoulders visibly relaxing at the sight of me.

"Titus," I hear how choked she is as she says my name while running towards me and I don't miss the glisten of tears that are streaming down her cheeks, her arms reaching out for me when I have to stop her, my fingers pressing into the top of her arms. I ignore the burn that courses through me, ignore the way my heart begins galloping in my chest and the way my soul seeks hers out. But I have to stop her because if I hold her, I will never let her go and I'll want to throw this whole stupid ass plan out the window. I shake my head from side to side.

"We can't," I whisper, gently pushing her back from me because she is too close, and I am finding it impossible to breathe even though it is so much harder when she isn't next to me. I swallow down the burning lump in my throat and ignore the sting in my eyes from the tears that want to fall so desperately. "You're not mine anymore, Twilight."

I watch as the breath she inhales gets caught at the back of her throat.

"Don't, please don't do this... Titus," her chin wobbles, her bottom lip trembles and that's when I see the tears that begin to fall down her pretty face and I hate that I am the one who put them there.

Lie number one.

"This was always the plan. I was hired to look after you, to protect you... that's what I am doing. I will be by your side every step of the way until you're married." I pause because honestly, this is too fucking much. I try and hide my emotions the best I can, but I can see by the look on her face she isn't buying it. "Then once you're married and I know you're okay... well, then I go back home to New York." My throat bobs as I try and swallow the apple sized lump that has formed in my throat.

"Titus," she whispers because saying the words are too fucking painful. She reaches her hand forward, our fingertips brushing and I don't miss the way her touch brings me to life but I quickly pull them away as if they've just burned me.

"Please Amora..." I whisper, "please let me do my job," my voice cracks and I hate that I have done this to her.

She stays quiet, just nodding over and over.

Lie number two.

"This just wasn't our time, Little Red. Maybe in another life, but not this one," and my heart is fucking screaming at me, but I turn and walk away because if I stand in front of her any longer, I'll crumble. And I can't do that.

As soon as I am out of sight, I hear her cry.

Slipping my phone from my pocket, I type a message to Xavier.

> **Titus**
> I fucking hate you.

CHAPTER FORTY-ONE
AMORA

THE DAYS ARE ROLLING INTO ONE. I WAKE, BREATHE, EXIST, THEN sleep into a dreamless emptiness. Each one passing a little slower than the one before, but I am one step closer to being married to Wolfe.

A loveless marriage.

An unwanted husband.

A lonely wife.

I roll over, my eyes dry from the amount of tears I have shed; I am certain I have none left to cry. I hear a soft knock on the door, but I don't lift my eyes to see who it is. I don't need to. I feel him.

"Amora," his voice floats through the room but I gaze ahead, almost trance like.

"I'll be out in a minute," my voice is flat, I feel so unattached from myself, and I don't even know who I am anymore.

I'm wallowing and I am pathetic. I don't know how long I had waited, but finally I slowly push myself up from my bed, I sit on the edge and let my toes curl into the carpet.

Sighing, I stand and drag my heavy legs towards the door in hopes that Titus had left me, but who was I kidding. He has been my shadow. Five steps behind me at all times and even though I silently begged for him to come closer, he wouldn't.

How could someone I had such intense feelings for and shared such an intimate connection with suddenly feel like nothing more than a stranger. *Just* a person.

I ignore the twist in my chest, my heart ripping into nothing but tiny pieces and scattering throughout my body.

"Ready?" Titus asks, but I ignore him. We've hardly said more than twenty words to each other since he broke my heart and betrayed my trust. I have nothing to say to him. I shouldn't be angry with him, I know that deep down and that the person I loathe is my father, but he isn't here so the only one I have to take it out on is Titus.

So, he is going to get it.

Every last piece.

"Wolfe is expecting you for breakfast," Titus says as I near the stairs.

My fingers wrap round the balustrade, letting my hand glide as I make my way towards the dining room.

The door is opened for me, and I see Wolfe sitting at the head of the table, Hunter to the right of him. I hold my head a little higher as I walk towards them, pushing my heartache to the pit of my stomach. My chair is pulled out and I take a seat, placing my table napkin on my lap.

"Good morning wife," Wolfe rests his elbow on the table, chewing with his mouth closed as a small smirk spread across his lips. Snapping my head to face him, I narrow my gaze on his.

"Please don't call me that. I'm not your wife."

"Yet."

"My name is Amora to you, nothing else."

"Someone is agitated this morning," Hunter snipes and shakes his head.

"What gives you that impression?" I click my tongue to the roof of my mouth and steady my gaze on him.

He stops chewing, staring me down and I don't let my eyes move from him.

"We're really not that bad," he shrugs his shoulders, very blasé.

"I don't care, I don't want to be here but..." I roll my lips and look down at my smoked salmon, muffin and scrambled egg.

"Is everything okay?" I hear Titus ask and my skin flames.

"Fine," I snap. Truth was, I didn't like smoked salmon. The texture was enough to make me gag.

"Can you not speak to my wife?"

"I'm here for her, no one else but her. That was part of the deal you struck with her father so I will speak to her whenever I want to."

I hear Wolfe growl before responding, "You need to know your place."

I freeze.

"I know my place, don't try and intimidate me. I'll snap you in two if I needed to. Touch her without permission, I will kill you myself," Titus' voice is low and my heart races in my chest.

"Empty threats."

"Oh," Titus chuckles, "they're not empty, try it... I dare you," Titus' voice rumbles in his throat.

I slam my hands down on the table.

"Enough!" I look over my shoulder, my facial expression softening. "Titus, thank you... but I have this. I can look after myself," I give him a gentle nod and he closes his eyes. Snapping my head to face Wolfe, I narrow my gaze on him. "I don't need Titus making threats, I will kill you myself. Don't you even think about touching me. Everything will be on my terms, not yours. I am not a woman you can just use when you want. I have worth, don't think for a moment just because we're due to be married that I am your property to do what you want with, it doesn't work like that." My tongue is sharp and I wait for him to respond but he says nothing. "Do you understand?" I raise my eyebrows and he nods.

"And you," I look at Hunter, "I don't like you, like, at all. Don't think you can even look in my direction without my permission. When I am in the room with you, look at the floor, the wall, your dick for all I care. I do not want your beady, sleazy eyes on me, do I make myself clear?"

I hear Titus chuckle behind me, Wolfe sharing his own laughter.

"Understood."

"Good," I look back at my plate, my insides screaming with pride, "Oh and tell your cook I don't like smoked salmon." I push my plate away.

Wolfe whistles and a timid young man runs in. My eyes roam over him and his head is down the whole time until Wolfe clicks his fingers. My mouth drops open, my eyes wide at how he is treating this poor guy.

"He isn't a dog," I snap, my blood boiling. "Treat him with respect, how dare you,"

I stand in a rush, pushing my chair out and letting it fall back. "Hey," I tip my head down so I can look him in the eyes and his hazel ones find mine. "Don't let him treat you like that, you're worth so much more," I smile, reaching my hand out and touching the top of his arm. "What's your name?"

"Arlo," his voice is quiet.

"Arlo," I repeat, as I nod and smile, "from now on you only answer to me, okay? I'm Amora."

He stands a little taller and I drop my hand from his arm when I have Wolfe behind me, angry breathing down my neck but before I can turn round and deal with him, Titus pulls me out the way and stands tall in front of Wolfe, towering over him.

"Back the fuck up," Titus growls.

"Don't push me Titus, I wouldn't think twice about putting a bullet between those pretty blue eyes."

"You know full well I have full protection, you're not allowed to touch me... part of the deal unfortunately for you."

Wolfe continues breathing hot, ragged breaths out his nostrils.

"Come," I wrap my arm round Arlo, "let's leave these children and have a cup of tea," I smile, walking towards the kitchen. "And Arlo, I say softly as we walk into the hallway, "please let your chef know that I don't like smoked salmon. Scrambled eggs and the muffin will be adequate enough of a morning."

Arlo nods and I feel my shoulders relax as the door closes behind us, leaving Titus, Wolfe and Hunter to sort their shit out.

Sitting at my easel, I slip my earphones in and let *already gone – sleeping at last* float through my ears and I find myself painting a peaceful ocean, crystal blues, turquoises and opals all mixed in with the odd frothy white wave break. A mix of emotions flood me, I miss my mother. I didn't get to say goodbye and that's a pain that no daughter should have to feel. All because of my father's selfishness.

I'm sure Wolfe would let me see her, surely. If this is going to be my life, I've got to be allowed to see my family and friends. I was never given my phone back from Titus, I have no connection to what is outside these four walls.

I sit for a moment, gazing at the painting and it's like I'm there. My feet buried into the warm sand, nothing but the sound of the waves kissing the shore, breaking into nothing but calmness.

I still don't know how I got myself in this situation.

Fell for someone I shouldn't have; we both knew we were never going to get our happily ever after, but a small part of me thought we stood a chance. I thought my father would have fixed this and I could be free to love who I wanted to. But now I am living with a man I despise and the man I love. My hand has been sold to Wolfe for marriage, my purity and heart is with Titus and now I have to live in this grey world just existing. Every ounce of colour I once saw so brightly has now turned into dullness. He painted my world in a way only I could see, shades of colours only visible to me. My once beautiful kaleidoscope was now nothing but black, whites and greys. He was my perfect medley before.

Before this.

Before I fell into a world with no colour. Before I fell into a world of nothing but emptiness.

But now I am breaking into a thousand tiny pieces, I'm a mess.

Everything I saw with him I can't see with anybody else.

He has broken me but in the best possible way.

I am ruined.

Obliterated.

I will never feel pieced together without Titus. This new feeling of emptiness is something I have to get used to.

To never feel loved.

To never feel desired in a way Titus wanted me.

To never be craved.

My eyes close as I picture myself as the ocean, with each day that goes on, I break and crash into nothing against the one thing I want most in my life, but I'm never getting there. Instead, I retract back into the ocean, taking small pieces of the life I once had and sinking beneath the surface to live with nothing but darkness. My life on a loop. Never reaching the shore, never to feel the sand between my toes again. Our love crept up on me like a storm out at sea. Quick, strong and devastating all at the same time. We never really knew what was happening and when we did, it was ripped out from under us in an instant.

I should have never fallen for a man nearly twice my age who has a daughter a few years younger than me. But I did.

It was wrong. But we weren't wrong for each other. You have no control who you fall in love with, and I happened to fall in love with my bodyguard.

He was forbidden and so was I.

But he was the storm in my calm ocean.

Reckoning and devastating but I craved him constantly.

We were never to work.

My mind drifts back to the ocean waves breaking

against the sand and sinking back into never ending emptiness.

I'm the ocean.

Titus the sand.

The perfect match.

But never meant to be.

CHAPTER FORTY-TWO
TITUS

IT HAD BEEN A WEEK.

One whole week.

One week since I kissed her, held her, inhaled her heavenly scent.

One week since *everything* completely changed for me.

I knew I had fallen.

But fuck, did I fall.

Head over heels.

I know it's quick; fuck, I would be delusional if I didn't see what was happening right in front of me, but Amora has drawn me in. I have been blinded in this whirlwind, her love like a tornado. Destroying everything and anything in her path until she consumed me whole. I wouldn't have even been able to stop it if I wanted to. I didn't see it coming. No one would have.

We fell *that* fast.

If she ever asked me to hang the moon for her, I would hang it all. The moon, the stars, the galaxies and everything beyond.

Because she deserved it all.

She had my heart.

From the moment she said hello, I fell.

I know she's my soulmate, my person.

But now; now I have to watch her marry someone else. The one person who gave me back the light in my never-ending darkness wasn't mine anymore.

And with that, my light slowly burned back into darkness.

CHAPTER FORTY-THREE
AMORA

Walking the grounds, the sun is sitting low in the pink sky as dusk threatens. Titus is here, always five steps behind and I let my hands relax by my side, my fingers spreading slightly and I'm imagining his fingers are brushing mine, our own secret that no one else has to know.

"Titus."

"Yeah," and I instantly miss the *Little Red, Twilight... Baby.*

"Walk with me, please?" I stop, looking over my bare shoulder, my fingers playing with the frilly hem of my dusty, ditsy daisy pink sun dress, the frill of the straps sitting just off my shoulders and at the top of my arm.

"Of course," and as soon as he is close, I feel as if I can breathe properly for the first time in weeks.

"How are you?" my voice cracks a little, but I keep my eyes forward. My wavy, red hair blowing softly in the wind. I push it away from my face using my hand.

"I'm okay," his tone is flat and I know that he isn't okay. Neither of us are.

"That's good to hear," I nod as we continue through the

meadow, my fingers brushing along the wildflowers and long grass.

"And you?"

"I'm getting there," I admit, even though we both know it's a lie. I am not getting there; I'll never be there. How can you get over the love of your life?

He says nothing, there is nothing to say. We carry on forward and I stop for a moment, looking at my surroundings and I miss the lake back home.

My favourite place with my favourite person.

But now I'll have to find a new favourite place without him.

My chest aches and I ignore the need to rub it with my palm.

"How's your daughter getting on?" I ask as I begin walking again, my eyes falling between us and I notice his hand is relaxed and by his side.

"She's doing well, I spoke to her this morning. She is coming up for her break between shifts so hopefully she'll get some sleep and see her friends. Her job is quite lonely with her long hours so she isolates herself which I don't like, but what do I know?"

I scoff a laugh.

"I mean, fathers are a pain in the ass," I nudge into him, playfulness masking my sadness.

"But we mean well..." and that's when I feel his fingers brush against mine, my heart stuttering in my chest as my eyes flutter shut and I make sure I savour this moment because I don't know if I will ever get to feel the rush that is currently coursing through my veins, my blood thumping in my ears and my heart singing a song that only I can hear again.

"Some do," I finally give in, turning my face up to look at him and his eyes volley back and forth between mine.

"Your father cares for you Amora, so much," his voice breaks and I snatch my hand away, my brows furrowing in confusion.

"Since when did you and him become best friends?" I snap, crossing my arms across my chest.

"Amora."

I step back and away from him.

"We're not best friends, far from it... we both just have the same goal. To keep you safe."

"My father is not keeping me safe, how is sending me away to marry some fucked up psycho keeping me safe? For all I know, Wolfe could put a bullet through my head. Xavier doesn't know this person; he has done it to get the target off his back."

"Amora..." Titus tries to reel me back.

"My father is dead to me. Plan or not. You don't do that to someone you love. Break them in a way you never thought was possible," and now I don't know if I am talking about Titus or my father. "He vowed to never put any of us through what my grandfather did to my mother, but here we are. It's like déjà vu and I'm reliving this constant nightmare. This is my life. A prisoner here, married to someone from the crime world and I'm expected to sit like the good little wife, it won't be long before he wants more than a wife, he will want a mother for his children and who will I be if I refuse him? I'll be dead.

"I have no choice in this, my freedom was gone the moment he dropped me off and sped off into the darkness. I will be a Knight soon. Archibald will be stripped of me, and my father will have to live the rest of his lousy life knowing that he was my downfall. He will have this tied to him. A son-in-law he accepted all to save his life? Grandchildren from the man whose father he wrongly killed. How is this fair? How is this an acceptable thing to do? But what does it matter, because no doubt you have your payment, and as soon as I am legally bound to the devil inside that fortress you're out of here. That will lay on your conscious."

I see Titus' shoulders sag, his brows slowly digging into his skin.

"You let them win. You let my father influence you in doing this. You could have run with me; you didn't have to stop. Yet you did," tears are rolling down my cheeks, "it was me and you against the world... you gave up." My voice gives out, and I choke.

Turning, I keep on walking knowing that he is of course, just five steps behind.

BRUSHING THROUGH MY HAIR, I LOOK BACK AT MY REFLECTION. MY eyes are puffy, my cheeks are reddened, and my heart is broken.

The door handle twists, and I hold my breath, praying it's Titus but it's not.

It's my asshole husband to be.

"Amora," my name rolls off his tongue and the way it sounds makes my skin crawl.

"Wolfe," I challenge as I stare at him through the mirror.

"I have some business to attend to tomorrow in London, I'll get Siobhan, the housekeeper, to pack you a bag. You can come with me, then maybe we can go shopping? I'm sure you would like to pick some clothes that are more your taste."

I swallow.

"Thank you, but I'll stay here." I give him a fake smile and go back to brushing my hair.

"It wasn't a choice."

"Sorry?" I turn round so I am facing him. His dark eyes sweep over my body, and he drags his bottom lip between his teeth. I'm wearing a silk, thigh length nightie and a matching silk dressing gown. "Please don't look at me like that... it's gross."

He sniggers, looking over to the wall before his eyes are back on me, his head tilted to the right.

"I wasn't asking if you wanted to come, I was telling you. You're coming to London with me. I would like to introduce you to the circle, you will be a big part of this life, so my people need to know who the wife of Wolfe King is. What's a mafia king without his queen?"

"A tosser?" I shrug my shoulders up, then twist back round about to place my brush down when Wolfe is behind me, his fingers wrapping round my throat, his lips by my ear but he keeps his eyes pinned on me using the mirror.

"Be careful how you tread, *mostriciattola*."

"Did your father not teach you how to treat a lady? I don't think little monster is a very fitting name for your wife to be," I goad, smiling as he tightens his grip around my throat. "Also, I didn't know you were Italian, or are you trying to put on a little show? Pretending you're something you're not."

"*Little monster* is very fitting for you. You need to watch your tongue, it will get you in trouble one day," his lips nip at my ear, squeezing my throat a little tighter and I gasp.

The bedroom door bangs against the wall, and I watch as Wolfe's eyes lift from mine and focus on Titus.

"Let her go, I swear if there is one single mark on her,"

his voice booms around the room as he storms across the floor, his hand grabbing Wolfe's shoulder and pulling him off me before Titus has him pinned against the wall, his large hand clasping his skinny neck. "Don't you dare lay your hands on her," he seethes, and I stand from the dressing table, my fingers rubbing at the base of my neck, my eyes wide.

"She needs to learn her place," Wolfe grits and Titus lifts him, so his feet are off the floor.

"You need to understand what I am saying, do not lay a finger on her. I swear if one strand of hair is missing from her head, you're done for."

Wolfe laughs. "You really don't know who you're messing with."

"And neither do you, trust me."

Titus drops him and Wolfe falls to the floor.

"I will put a bullet in you."

"You really do like them empty threats, don't you?"

Titus rolls his eyes, stepping towards me and cupping my face in his large hands and my throat burns.

"Are you okay?" his eyes bounce back and forth between mine before he scopes my face and I nod, unable to breathe.

My eyes widen when I see Wolfe stalk over and Titus drops me, turning and standing in front of me.

"I suggest you walk away," Titus warns.

"I'm walking, get your bags packed little monster, we leave tomorrow," he grits, turns then walks out of the room.

I exhale a shaky breath and slowly sit on the edge of the bed.

"Leaving?" Titus' wide eyes land on mine, "Where are you going?"

"London."

"Like fuck, what for?"

"To introduce me to his *circle*," I whisper.

"He can get fucked, this hasn't been cleared." He rubs his hand over the top of his head.

"Titus..."

"Don't move, you are not to leave with him do you understand me?" and I nod feeling entirely numb.

"I'll be back Twilight," he whispers before he walks out the door.

Twilight.

My heart skips in my chest.

CHAPTER FORTY-FOUR
TITUS

I STORM DOWN THE HALLWAY, MY HEAVY STEPS ECHOING OFF THE walls. I am angry, so fucking angry that my blood is burning under my skin. Pulling my phone out, I click on Xavier's name and he answers on the first ring.

"What?"

"Don't what me Xavier, I am angry. I need out. We need to get her out," I keep my voice low as my feet pound the floor.

"What's happened?"

"He laid his fucking hands on her, grabbed her round the throat. If I was a few seconds later..." I pause, stopping and looking back towards her room. "He wants to take her to London to introduce her to his circle."

I hear the heavy exhale of Xavier.

"Go to London with her."

"Can't we get her out? I can't stand watching her like this."

"Titus, stick to the plan."

"What fucking plan?" I am near on hysterical now, my heart is galloping in my chest, the blood pumping in my ears, "I don't know what the plan is because you still haven't told me everything!"

"You know everything you need to know... for now. Tell cunt chops you're going to London with her. That was part of the deal. She moves, you follow. Five steps behind."

"But—"

"Goodbye Titus," and the line goes dead.

I clasp my phone tightly, my lips rubbing into a thin line as I inhale heavily. Moving forward, I rush down the stairs to find where the little weasel is hiding.

"Wolfie," I call out, giving him a little whistle like you would call a dog. Pushing the door of his office open, it's empty and my brows furrow. I turn to see Hunter standing in the doorway.

"Move," I growl.

"You're becoming a bit of a problem," he smirks, holding his arms out, stretching across to the frame.

"As are you," I step forward, my fists balled at my side.

"Who are you looking for?"

"Your asshole brother."

"He isn't here unfortunately," he licks his upper lip.

"Where is he?"

"London," his evil grin spreads across his face and I grab him by his shirt.

"He wasn't meant to be leaving until tomorrow," the panic is evident in my voice.

"Change of plans," he sniggers, and I pull him away from the door, discarding him to the floor like the piece of worthless trash that he is.

Running towards Amora's room, I am praying that Hunter is winding me up but when I kick through the door and see her room empty, I know he has taken her. How the fuck did he get her out *that* quick.

Fuck.

Pressing Xavier's name, I wait for half a second before he answers.

"Titty."

"He's taken her," I breathe out, my eyes pinned to the emptiness. "He's taken her," my voice barely audible as I cut Xavier off.

"What the fuck am I going to do?" I pace up and down, before twisting my wrist to check the time. Scrolling, I find Nate's number.

"I need your help," I wish I could hide the panic in my voice, but I can't. As the seconds tick past, I am losing my mind.

"What's happened?"

"Find Wolfe, I need to know where Amora is."

"Ping me over anything you have and I'll track him down. Are you okay?"

"I will be, god, I should have listened to Kaleb and just brought her home to New York," and I hear Nate sigh as he taps away on his keyboard.

"No you shouldn't have, because then you would have made this mess even messier, I have faith. You'll be home soon though... right?" I hear slight hesitation in his voice.

"I hope so... why, what's happened?" My brows raise, my hand dragging down my face.

"Nothing," his tone is clipped, "just wanting to know... it's been a while."

"Nate," I grit. I know this fucker better than I know myself.

"It's nothing, I mean, I was just wondering what the deal is with Amora... I mean..."

"I haven't even thought about it..." my hand moves to the back of my neck as I rub, letting my head roll back.

"We're not together, we haven't spoken about what comes after this... but she knows that once she is married to Wolfe, I am on my way home without her."

"Is that what you want?" Nate asks but his voice is low.

"Fuck no, the thought of her marrying..." I can't even finish my sentence without my chest tightening, a lump forming and lodging in my throat.

"It'll be okay," it's not much from Nate, it never is... but that is enough.

"Is Arizona, okay?" I change the subject because I feel as if I am suffocating.

"Yeah, we haven't seen much of her, but Keaton says she is getting on just fine."

"Well at least that's something."

"Yeah."

"I miss you all."

"And we miss you, now get the details over and I'll get back to you."

"Okay, bye."

"See ya."

And I just stare into the room.

Fuck. Fuck. Fuck!

CHAPTER FORTY-FIVE
AMORA

"You do realise you're not meant to go anywhere with me, without Titus?" I say, staring out of the back passenger window not wanting to look at Wolfe.

"You do realise," he pauses, and I feel his eyes on me, before he adverts his gaze to his driver "I don't give a fuck," and I hear the viciousness in his tone. Freezing when I feel his hand creeping onto my bare thigh. "You do realise," he continues in his sleazy voice, "you belong to me," his fingers glide higher and under the hem of my pastel blue and white sun dress.

I grab his wrist, stopping him from moving any higher and turn my face to look at him.

"You do realise you have no right to just touch me, I haven't given you permission."

"Since when did I need to ask my fiancée for permission?" he smirks, and I see the darkness flash in his eyes.

"Since I said so," I smile sweetly, pushing his hand away from me and off my skin.

"You will give yourself to me, if you don't..."

"You'll take it anyway?" I scoff, shaking my head.

"You got it in one."

"You touch me without my permission, I'll cut your hands off..." my tone is sharp, "and if your micro dick comes anywhere near me, I'll cut that off in your sleep. Are we clear?"

His arm flies up and he grips my cheeks, squeezing them hard until I taste blood. He's squeezing me so hard I have bitten the inside of my cheek. Wanker.

"Listen to me you little whore, I am trying to be nice, I am trying to be respectful, but you are making it very fucking difficult." He leans over me, his stale breath making me heave. "You're soon to be my wife, and the way I am feeling I'll have you dragged down that aisle by the end of the week so I would shut that pretty little mouth of yours and do as you're told."

Before I can respond, his lips are on mine, but I roll my lips tight, his tongue trying to make its way through as his other hand skims under the skirt of my dress.

My heart is racing under my chest.

I let my lips part just enough to let his tongue slip in and then I bite down, hard.

He retracts, roaring in anger and pain no doubt. My smile widens, my chest heaving up and down, but he soon slaps the smile off my face, the back of his hand striking me right across the cheek bone.

"You little slut, just you wait," he snarls as I hold my cheek, my eyes beginning to water as the tears threaten to fall but I blink them away. I will not cry in front of him.

We sit in the lavish suite of *The May Fair* and I am quiet. My cheek is bruised and throbbing and I know the bruise is already colouring my cheek. The power Wolfe Knight holds is scary. No one dares look at him in a certain way or decline any of his demands. Maybe I underestimated just how powerful he is.

"Make yourself at home," Wolfe says softly, and I have whiplash from his split personality. Jekyll and fucking Hyde.

"No thanks," I flip him off, stand and storm through the open planned hotel room, slamming the bedroom door behind me. I am so disappointed in myself and angry with Wolfe.

And I miss Titus.

My heart aches and I fall onto the bed, but I'm not by myself long when Wolfe enters the room.

"Go away you asshole," I lift my arms above my face and cross them over my face.

"Look," he starts before he pauses suddenly.

"Don't want to hear it."

"I have a meeting in an hour with some of my guys... you *need* to stay in here. Do you understand?"

"Very kind of you to ask," sarcasm drips from me and I know he never asked me, he told me thinking I was some obedient woman, "but I would have stayed in here anyway. You can make yourself comfortable out there because that's where you will be staying for the duration of our trip." I don't move, my breaths shallow.

"Is that so," he pushes his tongue into his cheek.

"It is, now please get out."

I know he is still hovering, but within moments, the door closes.

Once Wolfe walked out, I showered and dressed in a

fresh sage summer dress. It has ruffled thick straps, covered in small white daisies and flows from just under my waist. It's light and comfortable. My hair is pulled into a loose, messy bun. Strands fall and frame my face and I lose myself in one of my favourite authors, *L G Campbell's* book, *Rise Above* since he was kind enough to let my bring my Kindle with me.

There is a gentle breeze blowing through the window and I am grateful to be away and cool from a hot and sticky London city.

I hear the hotel door buzz, my eyes lifting for a moment, but I can hear Wolfe greeting them all and I roll my eyes. As if this is my life... this... there must be so much more than this.

But I guess I'll never know.

TITUS

As soon as Nate sent me Wolfe's location, I was racing it down the motorway. Fuck knows where Hunter was, so if he was meant to be keeping look out, he was doing a pretty crappy job. Doubt crosses my mind for just a split second when I think that maybe I was walking into a trap but then again, I didn't care. I needed to make sure she was okay.

I needed to see with my own eyes that he hadn't hurt her. That she was safe.

I saw *The May Fair* in my sights, and I slipped into a space outside. I didn't even look at the meter, just locked the car and run into the hotel, ignoring the doorman's greeting as I entered the building.

I stand in the lobby, looking around. Do I head straight to the suites or do I ask at the check in desk?

My phone beeped in my pocket, and I saw Nate's message.

Nate
Suite. First floor wing.

I walk quickly to the stairway and take them two at a time. Walking towards the suites, I knock on the first one and wait.

A short, stocky, butch man opens the door and I look straight through him to see Wolfe sitting there.

Pushing past him, I glower at Wolfe as I close the gap and his eyes widen.

"What the fuck are you doing here?" he stands from the table, banging his hands down.

"My job," I grit, searching the large space, "Amora!" I shout, pushing one of the doors open to see an empty room. "Amora!" I open the next door and see her curled up and her head buried within her book.

Her beautiful, perfectly imperfect eyes settle on mine, and it takes her a second to realize, her eyes widening slowly but then I notice her cheek and my fucking blood boils, and all thoughts of Xavier and his fucking plan leave my head as I realize I can't keep this façade up while she is hurting.

"Titus," she whispers, realization sinking in as she lifts her hand to cover her cheek.

I ball my fists, ready to turn but she is up and in front of me shaking her head. "Not now, please," she begs, and it takes everything in me to listen to her because I am more than angry. I have never felt a rage like the one that is currently brewing up deep inside of me like a tornado.

"Little Red..." her nickname slips off my tongue like a habit. Her small hands press against my chest, and I feel my heart drum beneath my skin, her wide eyes on me as she blinks.

"Please."

I inhale deeply, exhaling slowly.

Slowly lifting my hand, I bend two of my fingers as I gently stroke them across her angry looking cheek, her eyes closing as she winces.

"I'm going to kill him," I seethe.

"No..." she pauses, "you're not."

"Amora," I cup her face in my hands.

"Titus," she whispers and her scent floods me, my palms itching, fingers tingling to touch every part of her.

"I am mad," I press my forehead to hers.

"Then let me make you forget..." her voice like silk as it wraps round me.

Pulling back, my brows pinch but before I can say anything, her lips are on me. At first, I freeze but then everything in me screams. This is all I have wanted since the morning Xavier took her from me.

Her lips fall from mine, her eyes volleying back and forth waiting for me to either go with it or walk away.

"Fuck," I groan, my hands clasping her face as my lips cover hers, our teeth clashing before my tongue sweeps through and glides with hers. Her arms wrap round my neck and I let my hands roam down her body, cupping under her and lifting her into my arms, her legs wrapping round my waist. She whimpers as I spin and hold her against the door. My fingers fumble, pushing the hem of her pretty little sun dress up and around her waist. Letting my eyes fall between us, her pale blue lacy panties soaked. Hooking my finger round them, I pull them to the side and fall to my knees, one of my hands holding her in place as my tongue flicks against her clit, gliding up and down her pussy. Fuck I have missed her. My fingers tease at her entrance, plunging into her hard and fast.

"Oh," she whispers, her hips bucking against my face and I press my hand a little harder to pin her still.

My cock aches and I need her. Holding onto her ass, I stand and she makes quick work of unbuckling my belt. She places her hand on my shoulders and steadies herself as I kick my suit pants off. Fisting myself from my boxers, I line my hard, thick cock at her tight, slick opening.

Our eyes meet, both panting, her fingers digging through my shirt and into the skin of my broad shoulders and I have to clamp my hand over her mouth as I slam myself into her, my hips rocking up and stilling for just a moment to let her get used to me.

I forgot how fucking good she feels. How good her tight little pussy feels clamped around my thick cock.

"You've got to be quiet," I whisper, my lips falling to her neck as I begin moving. This is not slow and sensual. This is fucking.

Hard.

Raw.

Fucking.

My fingers dig into her hips as I piston my hips in and out of her, my cock slipping in and out with ease, coated in her arousal and my head tips back as I try and savour every single moment of this.

"He has no idea that I am in here, fucking what is his," I rasp, and she lets out a quiet moan, "but you'll never be his."

One of her hands falls from my shoulders and skims between us as she begins to rub over her clit.

"Titus," she begs, and I nip at her jaw, moving my lips lazily across to her ear.

"Yes, Little Red."

"Fuck me hard, please, I need to remember this for days," her voice cracks and my heart lurches in my chest.

I pull to the tip, seeing how her pretty little cunt stretches round me, slowly edging the tip in and out as her needy pussy grinds over me, her hips rotating as she tries to get what she needs.

"Patience Twilight," I breathe, smirking as I grip her hips tighter.

She pants, her fingers still circling over her clit when I thrust into her hard, our skin smacking as I pound into her over and over.

"Yes," she breathes, and I don't miss the tear that rolls down her cheek, her pussy tightening around me. Skimming my fingers up her body, I tug at her low neckline and pull it down so I can lock my lips round her pretty, pink nipples.

Circling my hips, I match her strokes until she gasps, her eyes rolling.

"Hold off baby," I whisper against her reddened breast.

Letting her down slowly, she winces when I pull my cock from her. I twist her round quickly, bending her over so her hands are pressed against the door, and I spread her legs, slipping two fingers into her, her hips rocking back and forth over me, her arousal dripping down my fingers and wrist.

"You're so fucking wet," I whisper, snatching my fingers from her then bending my legs slightly as I push her dress further up her back, I tease at her entrance with my cock, slowly edging into her before I fill her to the hilt, a soft whimper leaves her as I slip in and out, pounding into her hard. One of my large hands wraps round her tiny waist, the other grabs her messy bun as I pull her head back, my body leaning across her back.

"You take me so fucking well," I praise her, and her pussy tightens, "come for me," I groan as I feel my own orgasm teasing.

"Harder," she whisper-begs and I give her all I can, fucking her deep and fast.

Her hips move over my cock, meeting my every harsh thrust and I feel her clamp down over me as she orgasms.

"Shit," she whispers, her hand disappearing in-between her legs as she rubs herself while my cock is still buried deep inside of her, fucking her hard but slow now. Taking my time to make sure she has taken all she needs from me. Panic pricks at my skin when I realize I am fucking her without a condom, but that only makes my want for her grow. She is fucking mine.

"There's my good girl, you're mine," I grunt as I fill her one last time and a shiver explodes over me, my own orgasm ploughing through me like a runaway train, and I fill her with every drop of me.

We're both panting but neither of us say a single word. I slip out of her and turn her to face me. Lowering my lips over hers, I kiss her softly before I drop to my knees, lifting one of her legs over my shoulder as I swirl my fingers at her opening, dipping the tips in as I mix our arousal together, then push them deep inside of her.

"I want you full of me," I whisper, placing a soft kiss on the inside of her thigh before I let my tongue flick over her clit, then suck her into my mouth.

"King," she whispers, as I continue to fuck her with my

fingers. As I continue letting my tongue devour her, I eat her as deep as I can, her soaked pussy on my face when she comes all over my fingers once more.

"Such a greedy girl," I smirk, softly biting her clit then kissing it. "But you're my greedy girl."

I pull my fingers from her, standing slowly when I push my fingers between her plump lips.

"Clean them," my voice shakes as she keeps her eyes on mine, sucking my two fingers into her mouth.

She jumps when there is a pounding on the door.

"Amora!" Wolfe shouts and I smirk.

"She'll be out in a minute, she is busy," I groan when I feel my cock twitch as she smirks around my fingers.

"Get her out here now."

"Watch your mouth Wolfe," I bite, slipping my fingers from her hot, wet mouth before lacing my fingers in hers and leading her away to the bathroom to clean her up.

I OPEN THE BEDROOM DOOR, HOLDING AMORA'S HAND AND walking into the lounge when I feel everyone's eyes on her.

"What did I say about touching her?" I bark towards Wolfe. That rage that slowly simmered was now back and at boiling point. I let go of Amora's hand reluctantly, taking long, slow strides to where the little weasel is sitting.

He says nothing, just looks at me which aggravates me even more. Grabbing him by the collar of his shirt, I drag him up from his seat and close my fist. I throw a punch into his jaw, his head snapping to the side, and I hear Amora gasp, the sound of chairs scuffing across the floor when I feel hands on me, grabbing and dragging me back.

"Let go of him," Wolfe says softly, and they all drop me.

I step back and stand in front of Amora. I feel the eyes of his henchman on me, but they don't intimidate me. Wolfe rubs his jaw, taking his seat once more then turns his attention to his guys. "I deserved it, I laid hands on her... take your seats." He holds his hand out towards the empty seats and his guys all take their seats one by one.

"Take her out for a while, I want her back at eight," Wolfe dismisses us, and I don't hang around for a second more before I am dragging her out of that hotel room and onto the streets of London town.

CHAPTER FORTY-SIX
XAVIER

I PACE.

Back and forth.

Forth and back.

Nerves prick at me, my heart thumping in my chest and I hear my phone beep.

I stop before I look at my desk. Stepping forward I see the unknown number.

Unknown
We have eyes.

Relief swarms me and I am glad that Titus and Amora aren't in the hotel. Titus text me a little while back letting me know that she was okay and they're walking round London whilst Wolfe finishes up with a meeting.

I hate that I am doing this to her.

Hate that I am putting her through this.

Hate that I can't tell anyone what I know.

But it will all be over... soon.

Xander and Ezekiel walk into the office, taking their seats and I get ready to brief them.

Time is running out and I can't lose her.

I can't lose any of them.

CHAPTER FORTY-SEVEN
AMORA

The hours slipped by too fast and we're already back at the hotel.

I sigh as Titus leads me to the stairs that take us to the first-floor suites and I cling onto his hand a little longer.

"I miss you already."

"I'm here Little Red, you won't be by yourself with him anymore." He reaches forward and tucks a loose strand of hair behind my ear. "Did he touch you... has he..." he pauses, and I know where he is going with this. I shake my head from side to side.

"Nothing."

"Good."

"But I have no idea if I can hold him off," I whisper as we begin climbing the steps.

"It won't get that far, I promise."

"How can you be so sure?" I stop in the middle of the staircase and face him.

"Do you trust me?" his voice is low and I am hesitant. "Twilight," his voice cracks.

"I don't know who I trust anymore," I roll my lips. Harsh, but it's the truth.

"Just keep fighting him for me, I won't let him near you."

"You're not with me all the time," I shake my head.

"Then I'll camp outside your room, I'll be your shadow. I won't let him near you." He repeats his words and I swallow the thickness down.

I begin walking, slipping my hand from Titus' as he follows and he slowly falls back into bodyguard mode, always with me, five steps behind.

The door to our suite opens and Wolfe stands there with a smile on his face. "Welcome back," he wraps his arm round my shoulders as I pass him, and I can just imagine how Titus is feeling.

He leads me to the sofa, sitting me down then disappearing for a moment and returning with a bottle of water.

"Thanks..." I am a little confused, but I have come to realise you get two sides to Wolfe.

"I am sorry about earlier, I didn't mean to hurt you," he sits next to me, I stiffen as his fingers brush against the bruise.

"Don't touch her," Titus' low voice booms round the room and I hear Wolfe scoff, looking over his shoulder.

"You're dismissed," he shoos Titus away and my eyes lock on Titus'.

"You can't dismiss me, I work for Amora and Xavier, not for you."

Letting my eyes fall to my lap I sigh when I hear Titus' phone and a deep groan escapes him.

"I'll be ten minutes, do not fucking touch her," Titus orders before lifting the phone to his ear.

I hear the door click and now it's just me and Wolfe and my heart begins racing in my chest.

"Do you think I am stupid little monster?" he asks, his hand grazing over the bare skin of my thigh and my skin pricks with fear as his fingers wrap round the top of my leg, gripping harder and pinching the skin.

"No, why," I grab his wrist and try and pull his hand off me, but I can't.

"I know you fucked him," his tone is venomous.

"What?" I breathe, my eyes wide.

"You. Fucked. Him." He says slowly and emphasises every word.

"No," I shake my head from side to side.

"Tell me, why can he fuck you, but I can't?" he squeezes tighter now and I can already feel my skin beginning to bruise. "Is it because you think I wouldn't find out? I can smell it on you, I could hear you." His lip curls and he snarls, "How about I fuck you now? Let me see if you have some magical pussy that I know nothing about because it seemed like he couldn't quite get enough of you. Has this been going on between the both of you the whole time?" Tears prick my eyes, my throat burning and all I can do is shake my head again.

"So, when can I fuck you? How about tonight? Maybe I need to *show* you who you belong too because you have been mine from the moment you were dropped on my doorstep by your coward father. You are indebted to me. Me!" His voice grows louder, and I flinch. His hand moves higher up my thigh, squeezing the skin again and causing his grip to burn.

"If I catch you fucking him again, I'll destroy everyone you care about, including your bodyguard," he grits.

My body begins to tremble.

"Do. You. Understand?" He drawls out his words and I nod over and over. "Good. Now get out of my fucking sight," he lets go of my leg abruptly before pushing me away.

It takes me a moment to catch my breath, but as soon as I do, I stand and Titus walks in the room, his eyes moving between me and Wolfe.

"Is everything okay?" Titus asks.

"Everything is fine," Wolfe answers.

Titus' icy glare narrows on Wolfe. "I wasn't talking to you," before he averts his gaze to me.

"Are you okay?"

I manage to nod, completely numb.

"I just want to go to bed, will you please come with me?"

"Of course," Titus bows his head and I hear Wolfe scoff, but I ignore him.

Walking quickly, I walk into the bedroom and Titus is close behind me. The bedroom door closes softly and as soon as it has, I rush into his arms and let him envelope me in a tight embrace.

"I have no idea what I missed, but I'm not going anywhere," he mumbles into the top of my head and places a soft kiss into my hair.

"Don't ever leave me," I whisper, burying my face into his chest and I feel him inhale sharply.

"I promise, Little Red."

CHAPTER FORTY-EIGHT
AMORA

ONE MONTH LATER

IT HAD BEEN A MONTH.

I have no idea why Wolfe is dragging this whole façade out. I'm surprised he hasn't dragged me down the aisle by my hair.

A month of living with Titus five steps behind at all times. The odd finger brush whilst we were in the hallways, but I haven't let Titus near me since the night in London. Wolfe's threat was too loud for me to ignore. I couldn't put my family in harms way, and I definitely couldn't put Titus there either. He had a daughter and a life outside of this. No job was worth dying for.

Titus led me to the dinner table where I sat alone. Wolfe and Hunter were hardly here at the moment due to work and maybe that's why this whole *wedding* is being delayed but I wasn't privy to know anything. I was just the good fiancée who sat at home. I hadn't painted in over a month and I missed it, but honestly, the weight of everything was too heavy on my shoulders for me to even let any creativity seep in.

My chair is pulled out by Arlo and I thank him. I'm not waiting long until my dinner is served up. Rare steak, new potatoes and steamed vegetables. This was the first proper meal I had managed to actually eat because I haven't had much of an appetite over the last few weeks.

"Sit with me," I turn to face Titus, and he gives me a nod, pulling the chair out next to me.

His hand glides under the table and rests on my bare thigh, my insides swarming with butterflies at his touch, and it's made me realise how much I have missed it.

"Imagine we are sitting at the boat lake back home, our feet over hanging the dock with nothing but the calmness of the lake in front of us," I close my eyes for a moment in inhale deeply. "Imagine I am holding your hand, bringing it to my lips and caressing the back of it with soft, feather like kisses." I smile, my heart warming and glowing in my chest.

"That feels like a distant memory, sitting at the lake with you, our first kiss in the pouring down rain," I exhale a shaky breath and turn to face him, "that was my favourite kiss of all."

"You have nothing to compare it to."

"I have all your other kisses," I nudge him with my elbow and his mouth drops open. Letting my hand drop under the table, I grasp his fingers for just a moment before reaching for my knife and fork and cutting into my steak. My eyes widen, the smell of the fat from the meat wafting through my nose and my stomach rolls with nausea.

"I can't eat this," I drop the cutlery on the plate, covering my hands with my mouth and heave. Titus pulls the plate away and I stand quickly, rushing for the toilet that is located out by the entrance lobby.

I hover over the sink, bent over as I close my eyes and inhale through my nose and splash my face with cool water.

I hear a gentle knock on the door before it opens.

"Twilight," Titus looks at me in the reflection of the mirror.

"Don't look at me," I cover my face, the water droplets running down my wrists when my hands are pulled from my face.

"I always look at you, sickness or not," his voice is low, and my arms drop by my side.

"I've felt rough for the past week," I admit, slowly sitting on the toilet and closing my eyes to try and relieve myself of this sicky feeling that is growing by the second.

Titus' hand rests on my forehead.

"You don't feel warm, come on, let me get you to your room," but before I can answer and tell him I want to stay here, I stand abruptly, lift the toilet seat and sick up whatever is in my stomach. "It's okay," Titus whispers, his large hand rubbing the centre of my back, the other holding my hair away from my face.

This was not okay.

I was sick.

And the man that I loved with every fibre of my being was rubbing my back whilst I was throwing up.

Ground. Hole. Swallow.

LAYING IN MY BED, I BECOME TEARY AND SUDDENLY I JUST WANT my mother. Titus rubs one of them away with his thumb pad.

"What's wrong, talk to me... I can help."

"I want my mum," I wail, turning to look at him. I'm pathetic but I feel sorry for myself.

"Okay baby," he says softly, reaching into his suit trousers and slipping out his phone and suddenly, fear hits me like a fully loaded truck.

"What's the date?" I whisper, my heart racing and my mind frantic.

He looks at me confused and twists his wrist towards him and looks down at the clock face on his phone.

"The fourth," his face lifts to look at me and my eyes widen, my face paling.

"Fuck."

"What, why did you want to know the date?" I hear the panic in his voice, but I can't seem to get my words out. Every time I try, I stutter over them.

"I... erm," I rub my palms over my duvet, "I think... I... shit," my hands begin to tremble.

"Twilight, you're scaring me," and suddenly, I am scaring myself.

"My period, fuck, fuck, fuck," and now it is Titus' time to pale. "I'm late, like, late late."

"What do you need from me?"

"A test," I am frantic, and I can't seem to calm my mind down, my heart is galloping in my chest like a herd of wild horses. "How are you going to get out? No, I'll be fine, you'll be fine. Go. Please," I beg and he just nods, not looking back once before the bedroom door slams shut.

How could I have been so stupid.

"It's just stress," I repeat to myself out loud.

You hope my subconscious whispers and I let myself fall back into my pillows, covering my face with my arms.

Shit.

CHAPTER FORTY-NINE
TITUS

Jumping in the car, my heart is jack hammering in my chest. Pregnant? Surely not. We've done it twice recently, granted one without a condom... but still. Pregnant? I know hand on heart that it's only been me with her. And if she is pregnant, it's my baby. But pregnant?!

I race down the road to the closest drugs store to try and get her some tests. I panic and dial Killian because I am stressing, and I don't want the rest of the guys to know about this yet.

"Titus, you okay?" he asks and I butt in.

"Fine, I need help but this does not and I mean it, go any further than between me and you."

"Of course, shit, is everything alright?" and I hear the sound of a door closing softly.

"How many tests should I buy to see if someone is pregnant, I mean, I did all this twenty-two years ago. Has much changed? You used to get it confirmed via bloodwork with the doctor, but does that happen still? Is it different in England?" My speech is rushed, and I hear him chuckle.

"Oh dear."

"Killian, I called for help, not judgement."

"And I'm going to help you... just..."

"Please."

"He is going to kill you," and I know the bastard is smiling.

"I know, I'm going to be six feet under by the time I get back to the house," I turn my blinker on and pull off the slip road and continue to the store.

"Just get a couple of different brands, clear blue and first response are what we used. If it's negative, do another one in the morning, if its positive..."

"Shit, what if it's a false positive?"

"No such thing."

I tighten my grip round my steering wheel as I pull into the parking lot and settle on the first parking spot I see.

"I'm here, not a word."

"Lips are sealed..."

And I breathe a sigh of relief.

"Daddy," and he hangs up.

I practically fall out of my Jeep, stumbling over my own feet as I pace forward and straight into the small drug store. Opening the door, a small bell chimes over my head and I scan the small aisles and see the brands Killian mentioned. I grab two of each, swiping them off the shelves and dropping them on the desk in front of me.

The young girl's eyes are on me and for some reason it makes me panic.

"They're not for me... they're for a friend." As soon as I say it, I drag my hands down my face.

"Figured," she says sarcastically. "That'll be thirty-eight pounds and forty pence please."

My eyes widen and I choke on my own gasp.

"Expensive little darlings aren't they?" she smirks and I

am unsure if she is talking about the pregnancy tests or the kids that come after the pregnancy tests.

"They are," I nod, before throwing her two twenties.

I grab the small, white plastic bag she has packed them in, and I rush out the store ignoring whatever she mumbled as I left.

Panic sets in, not at the fact I have these tests, but the fact that I have left Amora at home, alone. If Wolfe comes back and finds her in the state she is in he will start questioning her. Slamming my car door shut, I start the engine before I have even put my seat belt on as I race down the road to get back home.

Pulling into the long and winding driveway, my heart thumps loudly in my ears, relief swarming me when I see the driveaway still empty.

Slipping the bag in the inside of my suit jacket, because I don't trust these fuckers, I enter the house quietly and head for Amora's room.

Opening the door softly, I freeze when I see Wolfe sitting on the bed next to her.

"Where have you been?" he asks, his gaze not lifting from Amora's. She is stiff, her eyes wide and pinned to me.

"Had an errand to run for Xavier," I lie smoothly and squeeze my arms by my side because I am terrified the tests will fall from the inside of jacket.

"Okay well, you will not be needed anymore this evening. Amora is unwell, so I will tend to her. Goodnight Titus."

"That's not the deal."

"It is tonight, now leave."

I see Amora nod gently and this time I stay quiet and listen. I turn, walking back out the door I just came through and walk down towards my bedroom, slamming my own door behind me. Taking the plastic bag, I place it in my bedside table and peel my jacket and shirt off me.

I am desperate to be with her, to be the one looking after her but I must step back when asked. I don't want to risk fucking this up. If she didn't nod and give me the go ahead, then I would have stayed. But she asked me to go.

And for her, I would do whatever she wanted.

Padding into my bathroom, I turn my shower on and try and wash the day off my aching body.

One thing I knew for certain; either way, whatever the outcome... I was there.

Right beside her.

Not five steps behind.

Not anymore.

———

IT'S JUST TURNED ELEVEN P.M. AND I WAS WIDE AWAKE. I HAVE spoken to Arizona briefly, but she couldn't wait to get me off the phone which gutted me a little but at the moment, I have bigger problems to worry about than my twenty-one-year-old daughter being short with me.

Turning my head slowly, I look over at the nightstand and I am desperate to take one out and go to her room. I mull it over, umming and ahhing to myself before I roll over, pull the drawer out with force and rip the box to one of the tests open, shoving the test and instructions in my pocket. I grab a tee from my closet and pull it over my head one handed and head out into the hallway. The house is silent and it unnerves me. I pause outside her room and listen for anything but it's quiet. Slowly twisting the iron doorknob, I push the door open and see Amora curled up sleeping, alone. My heart slows and I smile. Stepping into her room, I push the door behind me, letting it close quietly. Moving slowly over to the bed, I climb in behind her, letting my arm rest on top of her body and I pull her closer to me, my nose buried in her freshly washed hair and her scent of apricot and coco butter gives me my hit instantly. She stirs in my arms and my heart lurches in my chest.

"Sleep Twilight, I'll be here when you wake."

And as much as I try, my eyes fall heavy and within minutes of being close to her, I am gone.

I SLOWLY OPEN MY EYES, MY ARMS STRETCHING ABOVE MY HEAD and it takes me a moment to realise that I am in Amora's room. I reach my arm across but her side of the bed is empty. Panic swarms me but within minutes, I see her walking out of the bathroom.

"Good morning," I smile at her and she smiles back, her beautiful red hair is up in a ponytail but loose strands tumble in curls round her pretty face.

"First morning we've actually woken up together," she smirks, climbing in bed next to me and sitting crossed legged.

"It's not enough," a lazy smile creeps onto my lips, "how are you feeling?" reaching for her, my fingers trace circles on her thighs.

"Sick," she sighs, her eyes dropping to her lap.

"I have a test with me, the rest are in my room..."

I slip my hand into my pocket and pull the test out that is wrapped in the instructions.

She nods, licking her lips as she stares at the test.

"I'm scared," she admits after a while.

"You have nothing to be scared about baby, I'll be here... every step of the way."

"You will?" her brows raise, her voice is timid.

"I will." I nod, and even though I am terrified of the outcome, I would never let her know. "It's you and me Twilight."

Her fingers walk across the bedding towards the test before lifting it and sighing.

"I suppose I better..."

"Yeah," I snort a hot breath through my nose, my fingers slipping from her skin as she climbs off the bed and I instantly miss her. "Want me to wait here?" I ask and she nods. "Okay baby, I'm right here," I wink. And once I know she is in the bathroom, I sit against the headboard, my eyes pinned to the door the whole time.

The five minutes she is gone feels like hours have slowly slipped by as each second ticks past, I worry that Wolfe will walk through her bedroom door at any moment. I hear the toilet flush and my heart begins to beat that little bit harder now.

The bathroom door opens, her fingers clasped round the test but her eyes are on mine.

Each step seems to drag, the blood rushes to my ears and all I can hear is my steady heartbeat.

She stops, looking down at the test one last time before her beautiful, glassy eyes land on me.

"I'm pregnant," she just about manages to let the words escape before she breaks into choked sobs. I rush off the bed, wrapping my arms round her tiny frame and just hold her, my lips pressed to the top of her head as her tears soak through my grey tee.

She's pregnant.

She's going to be a mom.

And I'm going to be a dad.

Again.

And my thoughts instantly go to Xavier.

Shit.

He needs to know.

Just not right now.

My focus is on her.

"It's going to be okay baby," and even though I didn't know if what I was saying was even true, I found myself repeating it. Over and over.

Because I would do everything in my power to make everything be okay.

She wasn't just a job anymore.

She was so much more.

My new beginning.

My future.

My love.

WALKING ROUND THE GROUNDS, AMORA HADN'T SPOKEN, AND I was glad that Wolfe and Hunter were out for the day. It gave us both the chance to let the news sink in. This was not part of the plan, and even worse, I now have to call her father to let him know that his daughter, whom was in my care and protection is now pregnant.

With my baby.

And she is to be married off.

It's fucked up and I am a dead man walking.

Every time I go to open my mouth, the words don't come out. I have no idea what to say to her, or what to talk about to get her out of her head.

Her fingers graze the top of the long grass as we walk

through the meadow, she looks as if she is a million miles away and I wish I could get in her head just for a moment, so I knew what she was thinking.

"Where did Wolfe go last night? I thought he was staying with you?"

"Work," she shrugs, "suited me, I didn't want him there anyway."

I nod and continue following her.

"Have you told my father yet?" her voice is loud over the silent meadow and the summer breeze catches the ends of her hair, the sunlight glistening through the small gaps.

"Not yet."

She stops, spinning to face me.

"I think it needs to be done sooner rather than later given the circumstances," she tears her eyes from mine before she starts walking again.

"Want me to do it right now?" My tone is a little short with her unintentionally.

"What do you think?" she snaps, but this time she doesn't turn round to face me.

I clench my jaw, dragging my hand down my face.

I am tired.

Slipping my phone out my pocket, I falter back a few steps behind her so she can't hear me and find Xavier's name. I inhale deeply, my heart is skipping beats in my chest before swiping my thumb across the large phone screen and I wait for it to connect.

"What now?"

"We have an issue," I keep my voice low as I continue to follow Amora, my eyes fixed on her the whole time.

"What sort of issue?"

"A pretty big one..." I pause for a moment, I swear my heart is going to explode.

"Spit it the fuck out Titty."

"We need to move the timeline, this plan of yours needs to move quicker."

"And why is that?" I can hear the condescending tone dripping from his tongue.

"Amora is pregnant."

Silence.

I wait a beat or two before speaking again.

"Xavier?"

"Please don't tell me..."

"Xavier," I breathe.

"Are you about to tell me that you're the one that got *my* daughter pregnant..." his voice is low and calm and for some reason that is making me more nervous than him losing his temper.

I inhale sharply, holding my breath for just a moment then exhale a shaky one.

"Yes."

There is no other word needed than that one.

Silence fills the line before my ear is filled with harsh, ragged breathing.

"You knocked up my fucking daughter?! I hired you to protect her! Not make her a fucking mother. I swear to fucking Lucifer Titty, I am going to murder you with my own hands when all of this is over." His voice is loud, and I have to pull the speaker part of the phone away from my ear, his voice still loud enough to hear the profanity that is coming from his mouth. I mean I get it. I would react the same if I was being told that my daughter was pregnant.

"How's that going for you?" Amora shouts out, turning and gives a slow, sarcastic smile.

"Amazing," I mouth to her then shake my head from side to side.

"I am too angry to speak to you, fuck off."

The line goes dead.

"I think your father is pissed with me."

"What gave you that impression?" She smirks, then takes a seat between the long grass in the meadow.

"He told me," I shrug my shoulders up and catch up with her.

"Did he call you the C word?" she rests her hands behind her, her legs out straight in front of her and she closes one eye as she looks up at me.

"He didn't actually," I crease my brows.

"Wow, he is really angry then. He throws that C bomb around like glitter, the fact that he *didn't* call you that... well King, I would start your escape plan now," she giggles and pats the space next to her. I feel my phone buzzing in my pocket continuously. I pull it out and see numerous messages from Xavier.

> **Xavier**
> I am going to kill you.

> **Xavier**
> You're a dead man Titus.

> **Xavier**
> I suggest you think about packing up and going back home.

> **Xavier**
> How fucking dare you.

> **Xavier**
> She's my baby and now you've got her pregnant!?

Xavier
I'm going to murder you in your sleep Titty.

I sigh, switching my phone off and kneel down in front of her. I gently push her to lay back on the soft ground and I lay my head on her stomach.

"How badly is this going to fuck up the plan?" she asks, and I feel her voice vibrate through her body.

"I have no idea," and that's the truth, "your father hasn't been very forthcoming with what the *actual* plan is..."

I lift my head and turn to face her.

"Will this mean this whole arranged marriage is over?" I don't miss the sad smile that graces her lips.

"I wish I knew how to answer that question Twilight, I really do."

A heavy sigh leaves her before she flops back down, and I go back to resting on her stomach. I have no idea how long we lay here for, but by the time we decide to move, dusk is setting in.

"Do you know what I hate the most about this whole situation?" I mutter, exhaustion blanketing me.

"What?" she sleepily replies, her fingernails tickling over my head.

"That I can't love you out loud."

Her fingers stop almost instantly, and I realize why.

Love.

CHAPTER FIFTY

AMORA

THAT I CAN'T LOVE YOU OUT LOUD.

My heart shatters in my chest.

Love.

My fingers begin moving again as I try and let his words sink in.

"I hate that too," I finally muster the words to answer him.

"To watch you marry someone else..." I feel his arms tighten round my waist, "to not be able to kiss you whenever I want... I am desperate to love you for all to see, but I have to love you in secret and that's what is killing me."

"Titus," I whisper, slowly sitting up and forcing him to move his head.

"I love you, Twilight."

I feel my eyes prick with burning tears.

"I wish it could be that way... but..." a silent tear rolls down my cheek and he catches it with his thumb, swiping it away. "Just not in this life," my lip trembles.

"Baby, one life will never be enough for me and you,"

his thumb runs across my bottom lip as he kneels between my legs, his fingers wrapping round the back of my head as he holds me, so I have no other choice but to look at him.

"I'm yours Little Red, in this life, in the next... I'll be yours in every damn lifetime," his nose rubs against mine, "whether I have to be yours in secret, or not, baby, I'm yours."

"I'm yours," I clasp his face in my hands, his crystal blue eyes glistening in the sunset. "Always. I love you," I just about manage before his lips crash into mine, we hold each other in an embrace as we savour every moment of what feels like our last kiss.

We break, panting and my insides screaming with want, his thumb drags along my lip once more and I have to control myself. His hungry eyes roam over my heaving chest and as much as I want him, all of him, I can't. We can't. Placing my hand on his chest, I shake my head from side to side.

"I need to know what we're going to do..." I pause as I glide my hand down his chest before moving it over to my non-existent bump. "About this."

His eyes widen as they move from my hand to my face.

"Nothing, we're going to do nothing because this farce is going to be over and you're going to have *our* baby."

I try and swallow the lump down as the tears threaten to fall, the ground falling away beneath me and my heart obliterating in my chest. "Titus," I manage, "this..." I gesture my finger between the both of us, "it's never going to happen... the sooner we accept that, the better it will be for both of us. I'm yours... just not in this lifetime. I love you with every fibre deep inside of me but..." I sniffle, swallowing the thickness away. "I'm marrying Wolfe Knight."

And I watch as he falls back, his lips parted and I know he is hurting, but it has to be like this.

I have to break his heart, just like I have broken my own.

THE LAST FEW DAYS HAVE PASSED IN A BLUR, TITUS HAS BEEN BY MY side but neither of us have spoken a single word to each other.

I cleanse and moisturise my face when I see Titus in the doorway, glowering over at me.

"You need to meet Wolfe and Hunter downstairs... now."

I nod, my heart cracking as I stand and walk towards the man I love, but he turns away as I approach him. I stand still for just a moment and let my eyes close, imagining his fingers are laced within mine just so I get the hit I so desperately crave from him.

Inhaling deeply, I begin to walk to the dining room to join both brothers. I have no idea why I am meeting them as we haven't eaten together in weeks. Most nights I skip dinner and stay in my room, but tonight, I can't hide away.

Titus steps in front of me, his eyes meeting mine and I can't help but feel that he knows what this is about, but he is keeping me in the dark. He twists the doorknob and opens it into the room where I see my husband to be sitting there, huge grin on his face and hungry eyes.

"You look beautiful Amora, you're glowing," he stands as I take my seat next to him. "Staying away from you is getting more and more hard as the days go on, but," he exhales, "I did promise your father I wouldn't fuck you until we're married," and I choke on my own breath. "But it seems that day is going to be getting a little closer now..."

one corner of his lips lift and I see his eyes shift to Titus before they land back on me. "I have not long got off the phone with your father..." he pauses, and my pulse quickens, I sit up a little taller and let my hands fall from the table and into my lap. Hunter's eyes move between me and Titus the whole time as if he is trying to work something out. "I must say... it was an interesting call... a very interesting turn of events."

He's outed me.

He's outed us.

My palms begin to dampen, and I slowly rub them on the skirt of my dress.

"Oh really?" my voice is a little higher than normal and I hate that I can't control my nerves that are currently ripping through me.

"*Really*" he grins, his eyes darkening as he reaches for his wine. I slowly turn my head to the side and glance at Titus who looks tense, his shoulders are high, his leg is bobbing up and down and his fingers are locked together, tightly.

"Xavier demanded the wedding be brought forward, he doesn't want to wait anymore to be rid of you once and for all... so, without further ado."

And my heart drops from my chest.

"You'll be my wife next weekend, seven days to go... and I can't wait to finally fuck and claim you as my own. Titus will be gone," Wolfe's eyes trail over to Titus, "that part of the deal will be over so no more loitering bodyguard. I'll get you all to myself and trust me, I am *so* looking forward to fucking you so hard that I make you bleed. No one will ever touch you again, I'll ruin you for any other man." His hand grabs mine, tugging me towards his lips and places a kiss on the back of my hand, "Oh, little monster... the things I will do to you."

Perspiration beads on my forehead, I am desperate to face Titus because I know deep down he is reeling inside, he will be furious at the words that are coming from Wolfe's mouth.

"And then I'll get you pregnant until you can't take anymore, little Knight heirs to continue my legacy..." he drops my hand abruptly and it hits the table. "Maybe I'll share you with Hunter, you can spawn some of his children as well."

My stomach rolls and nausea creeps up my throat. I begin to panic. I force my eyes shut and swallow the bile back down.

"How does that sound?" he smiles, his eyes batting over to his brother.

"Sounds like heaven, bet she has a tight little..."

"Enough," Titus barks from the other side of the room, standing tall and walking over.

"I don't care what you do with her when I am gone, but you do not speak about her in that way," he slams his hand down on the table and all I can focus on is *I don't care what you do with her when I am gone.*

"Why are you *so* protective of *our* little monster? Hm?" Wolfe goads, elbows on the table and a smile like a Cheshire cat spreads across his weasel like face.

"Because it's my job."

"Or," Wolfe stands, walking out from the table and behind my chair so him and Titus are standing toe to toe. "Is it because you have feelings for her?"

Titus says nothing, but I can see his fists balled at his side and I know he is way past angry.

"Is it because you want to know what it is like to be

inside of her... oh wait," Wolfe's fingers curl round the back of my neck and he tightens his grip, "that's right, you have been inside of her whilst I was in the room next door."

I stiffen and I hear a deep, primal growl leave Titus.

"If I knew you were a slut, I would have just shot daddy dead," Wolfe says with amusement lacing his voice and a shiver dances up and down my spine.

"Get your fucking hands off of her," Titus barks.

"Or what?" Wolfe continues to goad him, his fingers digging deeper into my neck and I wince.

"She's still in my protection, let go of her."

Wolfe hisses, relaxing his fingers and my skin is bruised almost instantly.

"One fucking week," Wolfe steps back, sitting down at his place at the table, "I hope you spend the rest of your miserable life thinking about me fucking her, or should I say *us* fucking her," Wolfe reaches over and takes Hunter's hand.

"Watch your back Wolfe, because as soon as I'm done here, you'll have a target on your back," Titus grunts, reaching for my hand and pulling me from the table.

"Ooo," he says in a high, sarcastic tone, "I am so scared."

Titus does well to ignore him because I want to bite back and scream, but I don't have a chance because Titus drags me out the room, but before the door can shut Wolfe calls out. "You have a dress fitting tomorrow little monster, nine a.m. Don't be late," and Titus slams the door behind him.

CHAPTER FIFTY-ONE

SIX DAYS TO GO...

MY ALARM GOES OFF, BUT I AM ALREADY AWAKE. I HARDLY SLEPT A wink as I replayed the last few days on repeat in my head. The way Titus told me he loved me, then we both broke each other's hearts. Whether our motives were intentional or not, it still sucked and it still hurt. Rubbing the ache in my chest, my hand wanders down to my stomach and I rest it there. I didn't want to get rid of this baby, but how could I keep it? Wolfe wouldn't raise this baby as his own and I didn't think it was fair to bring a baby who was so loved into a world that was so cruel. They didn't deserve that. They deserved so much more. I always dreamt of being a mum, but now I am pregnant I feel nothing but dread. Because this was not how I wanted it. I wanted *so* much more when I finally fell pregnant. Guilt swarms me as I am trying to forget about this baby because thinking of anything other than that kills me a little more inside each time.

Finally dragging myself from my bed, I sigh and look

around my room. I pace towards the window and open it, letting the little breeze in and the heat knocks through and it instantly takes me breath away. Summer is in full swing and the days are sticky and humid. I choose a dusty pink tee dress that has loose sleeves but a cinched waist emphasizing my little curves that I have. Slipping on white, high-top platform converse trainers, I pull my hair into a loose ponytail.

I try not to let my emotions get the better of me when I think what this day should entail. I should be excited about going wedding dress shopping with my bridesmaids, Arabella, Hope and Faith and of course my mother and Betty. I should be getting butterflies when I try *the one* on, knowing full well my husband-to-be will be in tears as I float down the aisle like a vision that he has only ever dreamed about.

But instead, I am going with my bodyguard, Titus. Who is also the man I love, whose baby I am currently pregnant with, to be fitted for a gown that I have no say in, all to marry a man to lift the target from my father's head.

I sit at my dressing table but I can't stop my eyes from drifting to my bedroom door behind me. Titus is normally here by now. Fear claws at my throat, my stomach flipping and slowly filling with dread that something has happened to him, especially after the stand-off between him and Wolfe. Pinching my mascara from my make-up bag, I try and let my chaotic mind ease and focus on getting ready for my appointment. The sooner I can get this over with, the better.

I just finish applying a coral lip-gloss when I see Titus standing in the doorway, worry etched over his face.

The lip-gloss rolls from my fingertips as I stand and make my way over to him.

"Where were you?" I whisper because if I speak any louder, he will hear the anxiety that is lacing my voice.

"I had to sort some bits out back home..." his voice trails off and I ignore the stabbing pain that is currently slicing through my heart.

"Okay," I nod and I know I have no right to even feel anything other than regret because it was me who pushed him away but I did it for his own good. I done it because I have no other option than for this to be my new life.

"You ready to go?" he looks at his watch and his brows furrow.

"Yeah," I mumble as I walk ahead, and he is now back to being five steps behind and I don't miss the way my heart beats when he isn't close to me. It stutters in my chest.

WE SIT IN SILENCE AS TITUS DRIVES US INTO THE CITY OF LONDON. He follows his Sat Nav and we drive past my old work building and my eyes begin to well. I miss my old life; I miss the person I was and just being here in the City I love the most is just a reminder at what I have lost.

I feel his hand slip between my thighs as he gives me a soothing squeeze and I smile. But it's not a happy smile. It's one full of sadness and I am petrified that I will never get my smile back.

Titus pulls down a narrow side road before parking. Something feels off, and I don't know why but there are certain things that don't make sense. The Knights are a well-known name throughout London, yet I never have any protection other than Titus. Is this all a fabrication? Surely, I am a target to their enemies, but then again... does anyone know who I am?

"Ready?" Titus asks as he cuts the engine, his voice gravel like.

"Not really," retorting, I open the car door before Titus has a chance to.

He leads me through another alleyway and that's when I see the small, tucked away wedding boutique. I stall for a moment, just staring wide eyed at the sign.

Amora's.

"Is this a joke?" I side eye Titus and he just shakes his head from side to side as if in disbelief.

I am so over this asshole. Storming forward, rage consumes me as I push through the door.

"Ah, Amora," Wolfe is standing in the middle of the room, his eyes glistening when they land on me.

"What a pleasant surprise," I roll my eyes and stand close to Titus. "Love the name, very original."

I watch as he licks his top lip slowly. "I thought it was a kind gift, didn't you Arabella?" and my blood runs cold when I see my best friend being dragged from behind a curtain by one of his henchmen.

"Oh my god," I whisper as Wolfe grabs the top of her arm and pulls her close to him.

"Tell your friend that you thought my gift was kind," he tightens his grip on her arm.

"It was a nice gift."

I nod, "I agree, I'm sorry," I am a mumbling, hot mess and my mind is working overtime and making me overthink everything. I will do whatever I need to make sure she is safe and doesn't get hurt.

Wolfe shoves her forward and Titus steps in front of me so he can grab her and stop her falling.

"Are you okay?" I pull her from Titus and into an embrace, hot tears rolling down my cheeks.

She nods into the crook of my neck as we stay hugging.

"And let's not forget mummy dearest now..." I hear his vicious tone, my head lifting when I see my mother being walked in. Her eyes find mine straight away, and I see the relief swarm her. God, I have missed her.

"Of course, we had to bring your mum along for the big day, every little girl needs their mother on their wedding dress day."

"Mum," I sob and she gives me a gentle nod. He lets her walk over to me, her arms cocoon me, and I never want her to let go.

"I've missed you so much my love," she whispers, pulling away and cupping my face in her hands. "You look lovely," she sniffs before kissing me on the forehead.

"I've missed you more," I choke and let her wrap me in her embrace once more.

"Are you okay?" she asks me, us finally breaking apart and I see the worry in her eyes. I have no idea whether my father has told her about my pregnancy or whether he is keeping it under wraps for now. I don't want to upset her or bring her any unnecessary stress.

I nod. I don't want to speak because she will hear the crack in my voice and instantly know I am lying.

She rolls her lips and I know she knows.

She turns to Arabella who is trembling and she pulls her in for a loving hug.

"It's okay, we're all okay," my mothers gentle voice soothes as she strokes the top of Arabella's hair.

"Now that we are all reacquainted, I will let you try your dress on," Wolfe gives a sharp nod before walking out of the shop and slamming the door behind him.

Silence echoes loudly in the room and we wait until we know he has gone.

"Oh my god," I whisper, suddenly I feel breathless and my chest hurts.

"I'm just glad you're both okay," my mother's hands come up to her mouth.

"He is psycho. I don't get him..." looking over my shoulder quickly to make sure he isn't coming back, "one minute he is kind and attentive... the next..."

"He is a fucking psycho through and through. Definition of a narcissist."

"Does father know you're both here?" my eyes volley between them but she just shakes her head from side to side.

"Okay," I rub my lips together. I go to step forward when I feel Titus' fingers wrap round my wrist and pull me towards him.

"Are you sure you're okay? I had no idea about any of this," the apprehension is evident in his voice.

"I will be," a soft smile masks my face but it soon slips when it's time for me to go and try my dress on. An older lady walks out and looks me up and down. She has short, brown, bobbed hair. I would say late fifties maybe. Impeccably dressed and obviously not very fond of me by the way her eyes rake up and down my body all whilst looking down her nose.

"The dress your fiancé picked for you is just through here," she holds her hand out, showing us the way down a light hallway.

The boutique is very small, but it's beautiful. And honestly, this is the kind of shop I would have come to get my wedding dress. Obviously not this actual one because it's just been put up for me. I feel like anything to do with weddings has been tarnished by Wolfe.

The store assistant stops in front of an ivory silk dress bag.

"Are you ready to see your dress that your fiancé has chosen for you?" her thin lips curl into a smile but it seems forced.

I nod, looking over my shoulder and Titus is just staring ahead.

This is torture.

I feel heartbroken at what is about to happen, so I know he is feeling it too.

She unzips the bag slowly and my eyes bug out of my head.

It is not my style at all, and I can't stop the disappointment that surges through me like a lightning bolt.

I watch as she lifts it from the bag and hangs it on a hook to the left of me.

The bodice is mesh with boned structure, like a corset. A bra looks as if it's been sewn into the top half of the dress. It's finished off with sewn thick, white leaves that climb the bones of the corset like twisting vines.

A tulle skirt comes straight off the short, bodied corset and fans into an A-line skirt with a slit so high it's going to be up to my upper thigh.

"Isn't it just *stunning?*" she claps her hands together, her head tilting to the side.

"I wouldn't use the word stunning."

She spins quickly, glaring at me then looks me up and down in pure disgust.

"Well, your husband to be picked it out and was very insistent on you wearing it," she tuts, rolling her eyes in the back of her over worked face.

"I didn't say I wouldn't wear it... I said it wasn't stunning." I shake my head from side to side and huff.

"Well, I disagree," the snobby bitch snaps her head back around and pulls the bag off the bottom of the dress.

"You wear it then," sarcasm coats my tone.

"Amora," my mother nudges me in the ribs.

"I have no idea why Mr Knight is marrying such...."

"Such a what?" I step towards her.

Her beady eyes drag over me once more before she shoos me away.

"I am not wasting anymore of my breath on you, step into the changing room and we will get you into this dress," she unhooks the dress from the rail and pulls back the curtain to open the dressing room. I inhale deeply, stepping towards her and pulling the dress from her grip and beam at her.

"I am more than capable of dressing myself, thank you."

Entering the dressing room, I pull the curtain with force to shut it.

"Silly cow," I mutter as I unzip the back of my sundress.

"I heard that."

"That was the intention."

I hear my mother apologise profoundly.

"Mum! Stop apologizing for me, if I wanted to say sorry I would."

"She has her father's attitude," my mother continues completely ignoring me.

"Nothing wrong with that," I hear the sound of my father's voice float through the room and my heart thumps in my chest.

"Great," I shout out as my dress pools on the floor of the dressing room. Arabella stays quiet, she knows what my father is like, so she knows what's best and that's not getting involved.

"Your daughter has an attitude problem."

"Like my earlier statement, nothing wrong with that," I hear him voice back to my mother.

"There is when she is trapping off about her wedding dress."

"Has he dressed her in a fucking shit dress?" my father's voice gets louder.

"Sir, excuse me," snobby bitch calls out but he doesn't listen. He never fucking listens.

The curtain pulls back and roll my eyes as I try to cover myself.

"Dad!"

"Titty! Cover your fucking eyes. Show me the fucking dress." His voice claps round the room like thunder.

"Well *daddy* if you let me get it on, then you can see it in all its glory," and I know he doesn't miss the condescending tone that drips off my tongue.

He pushes his hand through his hair, stepping back and tugging the curtain back over.

"I swear to fucking god if he is going to make my baby look like a meringue, I am going to murder him."

"Xavier, calm down," my mother says softly to my father.

"Keep your eyes closed Titus, or actually, face the wall. You don't have the right to look at her."

"Xavier!" she shouts, and I sigh, puffing out my cheeks.

"Titus you're fine, do not face the wall!" I call out as I drop the wedding dress to the floor and step into it.

"Don't listen to her, face the fucking wall." He barks out.

I ignore the dysfunctional chaos that is currently unfolding outside the changing room and my mind flits to Titus and suddenly I am nervous about *him* seeing me in a wedding dress.

Slipping the straps up my arms, I brush my hands down across the bodice before inhaling deeply. I deny myself to look at my reflection, I don't want to see what I'll be wearing to end my life as I know it. The life that I want is one that dreams are made of. The life I am going into is a living nightmare full of darkness.

Pulling back the curtain I step out onto the floor and the loud voices suddenly lower to complete silence.

"Well," I just about manage as my eyes move slowly until they land on Titus and I watch as he swallows hard, his eyes fixated on me.

"It's a pretty dress," my mother tilts her head to the side and I know she doesn't like it but that's okay. Because neither do I.

"Is it comfortable?" Arabella asks as she looks at the boned corset.

"Not overly, but it's fine, I'll get over it... or maybe break a rib or two," I shrug my shoulders up as I look down at the dress.

"What is that?" my father points to the large slit in the dress that sits just under my groin.

"That's a skirt slit," my head rolls up and I plaster a huge, closed lip smile over my face.

"Over my dead body," he roars and storms towards the snobby woman, looking down at her and I swear he is going to explode.

"Get that fucking slit stitched up otherwise she isn't wearing it," he grits out, his eyes bugging out his head and I can see how fast his shoulders are rising and falling.

"Mr Knight requested that no changes are to be made,"

she shakes her head softly, lifting her chin up and looking down her pointy nose.

"I don't give two fucks what Mr Knight requested, I, me, hello... *me,*" he stabs himself in the chest with his finger. "I am requesting that you sew the fucking slit up or there will be no wedding. It's that simple. So, you call little Wolfie and tell him that from me. If he has a fucking problem, then he will call me. Get it done," he snaps and turns to face me, his eyes roaming up and down my body.

"Awful," he rolls his lips and inhales heavily. "Get undressed, we're going for lunch. Fuck Wolfe."

"Xavier," Titus pipes up and my father slowly turns to face him.

"What?"

"I think we should get Amora home," he nods gently to my father as if they both know something I don't.

They stare each other down for a few minutes before my father steps back. "Fine, we will go back to the house for food."

Titus nods and walks towards the door.

"I'll help you out," my mother states and Arabella follows.

Stepping back into the dressing room, I just stand and let them undress me.

And suddenly, I feel nothing but numbness.

THE RIDE HOME WAS QUIET. IT WAS JUST ME AND TITUS, BUT NO words had been exchanged. I wanted to ask him if he was okay, but I felt I lost that right. I saw the utter heartbreak on his face when he saw me stood in that wedding dress.

Realisation finally sunk in that this was nearing the end. There was no happily ever after for us.

Pulling into the carport, I open the door before Titus has even put the handbrake on.

"Amora," I hear him, but I ignore him like he has ignored me for the last half an hour.

I smile when I see my mother park next to us. She slams the car door shut, Arabella behind her and I can see my father stewing in the car.

"Ready?" I smile, linking my arm through hers as we begin walking to the main entrance of the house. Arabella linking her arm through my left arm.

"I am."

"Dad annoyed you?"

"Oh yes," she smirks, "so he can stew on it."

"It was an awkward car journey," Arabella sniggers as I open the front door.

"Welcome to my prison," I say as I open the door wide, my jaw dropping to the floor when I see Wolfe standing in the entrance hall, stark bollock naked with a petite blonde on her knees giving him a blow job. Disgust rolls deep inside of me, what a little weasel.

"What's the matter wife? Don't like seeing me getting sexual acts off someone else... oh, well... I just wanted to give you a little taste of your own medicine... doesn't it taste bitter," he smirks as he continues to throat fuck the woman.

"Not overly," I glare at him through my lashes, a slow smirk slipping onto my lips, "I mean, I am more relieved than anything."

"And why is that little monster?"

"Because losing my virginity to *that* would have been a breeze with your little wiener," I shake my head, "oh, and my father is behind me, *wiener dick*," I lift my head and continue to walk to the garden.

"What the fuck have I just walked into?" I hear my father's voice bounce from the walls and I let out a soft giggle.

Take that you little fucker.

We sit at the dinner table and the room is thick with tension. I don't know how my father refrained from planting a fist on Wolfe's jaw for being disrespectful, but then again, he already has a target on his back, we don't need anymore.

"How was the wedding dress?" Wolfe asks, lifting his eyes from his dinner plate.

"Awful, I've told your little wench that she needs to sew the slit on Amora's dress up."

"I wasn't asking you." Wolfe sneers then looks at me, "Amora?"

"Awful," I nod, taking a bite of chicken and instantly regretting it so I wash it down with water and silently pray that I won't be sick. "I don't like the dress," I just about manage.

"It's not about you though, is it?" Wolfe remarks and I pause, lifting my brows high.

"I am pretty sure it's more the bride's day than it is the grooms. I mean, most, not me, but most little girls dream of their wedding day. The flowers, the dress, the venue..." my lips twitch, "the husband."

I place my drink back on the table.

"But unfortunately, I don't get to choose any of that, because I wouldn't have chosen you but alas, here we are. So yes, the dress is awful. You chose so wrong."

"Well, I am sorry to hear that but that's the dress I want you in."

"Then the slit will be sewn up like my father requested."

Wolfe slowly turns his head to look at my father who just cocks his head to the side. My breath catches in the back of my throat when I feel Titus' hand skim over my thigh and grip tightly. I've missed the way my skin tingles, the way my heart drums in my chest at the smallest bit of contact.

"Xavier," Titus calls across the table and I see my father's eyes clock that Titus' hand has just slipped up from under the table.

I freeze and widen my eyes at the sudden loss.

"Pass the salt please."

I swear I see the life drain from my father's eyes as he chokes on his mouthful of food, but my mother let's out a little giggle and I don't miss the crimson that sparks in her cheeks, my lips twist into a smile and I like that I am blissfully unaware of what the private joke is; I will ask my mother one day, just not today.

CHAPTER FIFTY-TWO

FIVE DAYS TO GO...

Sitting at my easel, I stare at the blank canvas. I have been sat here for hours and I haven't even picked my brush up. My mind is too chaotic. It's messy and dark and I hate it. I have never felt so blocked before with my painting. This is my escape. But I can't escape this hell hole that I am living in.

I was never one for fairytales, but now I am living in complete unhappiness, all I long for is a fairytale and to be whisked away by a knight in shining armour.

But not everyone gets a happily ever after and I was one of them.

I let my hand fall to my non-existent bump and I feel my heart break. "I will always love you, little one," I whisper so only I can hear, "we will be reunited one day... but until then I just wanted you to know that I do in fact love you... very *very* much. It's just not the right time for you and me," I sniff, a tear rolling down my cheek, but I don't wipe it away. I let it fall. I want to feel the pain of my words and future actions. I want to be reminded of this day for the rest of my life.

Any ounce of happiness I felt is slowly leaving me as each day goes on bringing me one step closer to my fate.

I pick up my palette and squirt black paint onto it before losing myself into my eternal darkness.

TITUS

"I'm ready to come home now," I admit, a heavy breath leaving me as I fall onto my bed.

"Are you though?" I hear Arizona ask and I take a minute to think on my answer. On one hand yes, I am ready. Because I can't stand being in close proximity to someone I have fallen in love with and I miss my daughter and my friends. But on the other hand, no. Because I don't want to leave the woman I have fallen in love with in this shit situation that is really, nothing to do with me. She's just a job.

My chest tightens and I feel the ache burning through me.

"Yes," I groan out as I rub my chest to try and alleviate some of the ache.

"That bad over there?" I hear Arizona crashing about.

"What are you doing?" I ask, pulling the speaker part of my phone away from my ear.

"Just trying to get my computer set up for..." she pauses, "assignments."

My brows pinch and I sit up.

"Assignments? I didn't think you had anymore."

"Huh? No, I don't. Sorry dad I am exhausted. I have got to do some research and Keaton's internet is crap."

"Anywhere else you can go?" I hear her sigh.

"Well yeah, but I kind of don't want to. I sort of like being here."

"Only temporary though, right?"

"Of course, yeah! Only temporary, right," she agrees with me, but something feels off and I don't know what.

"Arizona," my tone is a little sterner now and I stand from the bed, "is everything okay? Because you know you can tell me anything," I swallow thickly.

"Yes dad, honestly, everything is fine. I'm a big enough girl, I can handle myself. Things have just been a little tense at work that's all."

"Well make sure you're having some time out, your mental health is more important than your job and I hate the thought of being thousands of miles away and you struggling with burnout because you're burning the candle at both ends."

"Dad, please," she groans in a plea.

"Okay."

"I'm sorry, I'm just..."

"Yeah, I know. Tired, exhausted, busy... I get it."

"Dad..." her voice is softer now and I hate that she feels guilty.

"It's fine Ari, look I've got to go... I'll speak to you soon."

"Bye dad, I love you."

"Love you," and I have to cut the phone off before my voice betrays me and she hears just how much I am hurting.

Tossing the phone onto the bed, I walk out the room to find Amora. I've already missed her too much today and I have five days left to soak every bit of her in before I am on a plane back home.

I wasn't ready but I also know that I don't have a choice.

This was the job.

Keep her safe, keep her protected.

And once the job was done, I fly back home.

The job was nearly done and whether I liked it or not, I had to go home.

Walking down the narrow hallways, I keep my ears out for anything that gives me a reason to get her out of this hell hole, but as predicted, the halls are deathly silent.

Pacing quietly, I pause when I round the corner of her studio. My mind flashes back to yesterday when she came out of the changing room wearing her dress. I felt the fire burning up inside my chest and causing my heart to disintegrate into nothing but ash. My eyes wouldn't leave hers, even if I tried. Realization hit me like a damn truck when her eyes settled on mine, she was really doing this. This was really happening.

The one woman I have given myself to, the one woman who brought me back from the complete loneliness of darkness was the one who wasn't mine to keep. I don't know why, for some fucked up reason I thought something would change. I thought this whole plan would somehow collapse around us and I could take her away from it all. And then, like a miracle, she was pregnant. With *my* baby and even that is being snatched away from me and I have no say in it. Because she is right. Wolfe would never accept a child that wasn't his, and I know that man well enough to know that he would make Amora's life a living hell until the day either one of them dies. And that's not fair on her.

As much as I want to be selfish about this, I can't.

Ultimately it is her choice, and she has made it.

I take a moment to calm my nerves before I enter the room to see her standing there flicking black paint onto her already black canvas.

She stiffens as I walk towards her, but with each step, my heart gallops in my chest and I swear she can hear it.

"Twilight…" I breathe, having to stop myself from wrapping my arms around her waist and nuzzling my face into her hair just so I can be filled with her scent.

"Titus," she whispers, and I know it's because if she speaks out loud, her voice will crack showing me just how much this is hurting her too.

"Are you okay?" I know it's a stupid question, but I still can't stop myself from asking.

"Not particularly, but I will be… eventually."

"You will," I take a small step forward just as she turns to face me. Her perfectly imperfect eyes find mine and I feel the air leave my lungs in an instant, leaving me gasping for breath.

"This is really happening," her glassy eyes find mine.

"Yes, Little Red…" I roll my lips, "this is really happening."

"Five days."

"Five days," I nod, ignoring the splintering pain that is currently searing through my chest.

"I wish things could be different."

"They will be, but just not in this lifetime. You're my soulmate Amora, I truly believe that you are the missing piece to my soul, the one that has been waiting for me, but we are not meant to be together in this life. Our love would be too chaotic and messy for this one. But the next one…" I close the small gap between us, cupping her face in my hands.

"I will find you," her bottom lip wobbles and a single tear rolls down her cheek, but I catch it with my thumb.

"I will find you first, Little Red, I promise. In the next life and the one after that... we will always find each other. Just not in this one," I press my forehead to hers and that's how we stand until both of us find the strength to walk away.

I was put here to love her; I knew that was part of my journey but the bigger lesson of it all was that I didn't get to love her in this life. I had to let her go, and it killed me, but I knew it had to happen. I had to turn my back and walk away.

CHAPTER FIFTY-THREE
AMORA

FOUR DAYS TO GO

My heart thrashes in my chest, I wake dripping in sweat. Sitting up it takes me a moment to calm my racing heart.

"It was just a nightmare," I whisper to the empty room but as my eyes scan and adjust I realise I am not alone.

Wolfe is sitting in the corner of my room with his eyes on me. I reach over, turning the lamp on so I can see him clearer.

"Well, hello little monster," a sickening smirk plays on his lips.

"What do you want?" my tone is sharp as I pull the duvet up round my chin.

"Thought I would watch my fiancée sleep, something so peaceful about watching you."

"You're a creep," I nibble on the inside of my bottom lip.

"Am I? Why is that?" he stands from the chair and walks slowly across the room before sitting next to me on the edge of the bed.

"Because you've sneaked in here and were watching me

sleep..." shaking my head from side to side stating the obvious.

"And?"

"It's creepy," I swallow as he edges a little closer to me and he sighs heavily and I can smell the stench of alcohol that is on his breath.

"The things I am going to do to your smart, pretty little mouth," he whispers, his thumb brushing across my bottom lip and I feel myself shudder.

"Come near me... I dare you," I challenge him, turning my head to the side so his thumb drops from my mouth.

"Don't play games little monster, you will always lose," his chin lowers and I see the evilness in his eyes as he glares up at me through his lashes.

"I'm not playing games, I warned you, I'll cut your dick off while you sleep. You don't scare me. Keep throwing me empty threats *Wolfie*, I will not submit to you."

He reaches out, grabbing a fistful of my hair and tugs my head back, hard. I ignore the burning sensation coming from the root of my hair. His lips lower to my ear and I freeze under his grasp.

"Don't keep goading me, monster. I will break and ruin you in every way possible. Especially since a little birdie has told me something you're keeping hidden from me..."

I stiffen, my eyes widen slightly, and I am praying he can't feel how quick my pulse is racing under my skin.

"Well," he nips at my ear, "that's given me the confirmation I need," his tongue flattens along my cheek as he licks me, and I try my hardest not to throw up as my stomach twists with nausea.

"So not only have you fucked him when I was promised your purity... you're also carrying his bastard child, hm?"

His grip tightens and I feel the sting in my eyes.

"Wolfe," I just about manage, my voice cracking and I hate that I am falling weak around him.

"I will rip that brat of a child straight from you myself, you're walking on a very thin line Amora... you need to watch before you slip and fall," his breath is on my face, and I let my eyes close as a tear escapes and I am mad at myself in an instant.

He lets go of me, then pushes me with force so I fall into the duvet.

"I am so angry that I could tear you to shreds," he stands from the bed and pushes his hand through his slick hair. "I promised your father I wouldn't lay a hand on you until we're married, but as soon as we say I do, I am dragging you into the doctor's office and getting your little issue rectified."

"Who said I would go with you?" I sit up, my insides trembling but I won't let him notice.

"Me!" he shouts, "I said you will go with me!"

I flinch and instantly regret it and I see the wicked grin spread on his face.

"I am going to destroy you, and trust me little monster, I am going to love every minute of it."

"Why are you calling me little monster in English now? Ashamed that I caught you out," I smirk at him and he balls his hands by his side. He comes for me, but I lean forward and spit in his face. He growls, his hand darting forward as he grabs another fistful of hair and literally drags me from the bed and pain radiates through me as my body hits the floor.

"Get off me!" I scream, my hands flying to where his grip is but all that does is make him tighten it.

"Not a fucking chance," his voice echoes as he pulls me to my feet and drags me along behind him and I am careful not to trip over my own feet.

My heart booms in my chest, each beat feeling heavier and faster and sickness rolls in my stomach at what he may do. Is he going to hurt my baby?

I try and ignore the thoughts as a cold sweat blankets me and I trip, my knees hitting the ground as I cry out.

He doesn't stop. Just continues dragging me along the hard, wooden floor.

And then I realise. I know where he is taking me.

Standing outside Titus' room, I hear a loud crash as he kicks the door down and it smashes against the wall.

"What the fuck?!" Titus growls, his feet hitting the floor with a thud. Wolfe pulls me up on my feet by the root of my hair and throws me back to the floor, my chest hitting before my face. "Fuck," Titus runs over, scooping me up and cupping my face as his eyes search to make sure I am okay. "Are you okay?" I can hear the panic in his voice and all I can do is nod, because if I speak, he will know I am lying.

"I have no idea what you two are fucking playing at but it's taking everything in me not to put a bullet through both of your heads," Wolfe's tone is vicious, and Titus lifts his gaze from mine before he pushes me behind him, so I am protected.

"I think you must be dumb," Titus' voice is shaky, and I know it's because of the rage that is no doubt bubbling inside of him.

"And why is that?" Wolfe stands with his arms crossed.

"I have asked repeatedly for you not to touch her, and so has her father." Titus stands.

"And I was promised a virgin and it seems I have been given a whore," he spits, glaring in my direction and I cower down. "Looks like no one here is good at keeping their promises, hm?" his tone is condescending. "Especially you, dear Titus who has not only fucked my wife to be but has also got her pregnant... but don't worry." Wolfe smirks, "I will be taking care of that as soon as we're married by ripping it out of her."

Titus runs for him, grabbing him round the throat and smashing his back against the wall before he lands a fist to his jaw, the crack loud and bouncing off the walls before Titus puts another on his lip.

Wolfe does nothing, just stands grinning as blood coats his teeth, Titus panting in harsh inhales.

"I knew you would snap, just proves to me how good her little cunt must be to have you throwing fists around."

"Shut the fuck up," Titus slams him into the wall once more.

"I can't wait to see what she feels like," Wolfe continues, and I stand on trembling legs as I begin to walk towards where Titus and Wolfe are.

Titus won't stop until he kills him.

I squeeze myself between them and stand in front of Wolfe.

"Enough," I whisper to Titus as his wild, dark eyes leave Wolfe and settle on mine. I repeat my words again trying to get him to snap from whatever trance he is in. Placing my hands on his bare chest, I suck in a breath as I close my eyes relishing in the feelings that are tingling through my fingers.

I gently push him back, but he doesn't move.

I try again and when I finally open my eyes his crystal blues have softened. The storm that was once thundering in the windows of his soul has gone. Relief swarms me and I push him again, this time, he steps back.

Wolfe lets out a low chuckle, wiping the blood from his lip then spitting at my feet before looking at his watch.

"Oh look, it's just gone midnight... three days little monster," and a shiver dances up my spine before he walks out the room. Once I know he was gone, I throw myself into Titus and sob uncontrollably why he holds me.

Everything I loved is slowly being ripped from me and there is nothing I can do about it.

"It's okay, I've got you..." he trails off, "I've got you," his arms wrap around me, and we don't move. He just holds me tight as his shirt absorbs my tears.

CHAPTER FIFTY-FOUR
XAVIER

THREE DAYS TO GO

SITTING IN MY OFFICE, PICTURES FLICK ACROSS MY COMPUTER screen and I see one of Amora that makes my chest tight and my heart ache.

She is three.

Sitting on a beach with a sandcastle. Her wild, red curly hair tumbles to her shoulders, her big eyes wide and full of adventure and excitement and the most beautiful smile on her face.

I tap my finger to my lips, my eyes welling as I remember the holiday well.

And that's when it hits me.

I have royally fucked up.

CHAPTER FIFTY-FIVE
TITUS

TWO DAYS TO GO

I HAVEN'T SLEPT.

My eyes red rimmed and dry and as much I feel exhausted, sleep doesn't come. I lay awake, eyes pinned to the ceiling in constant fear that he is going to hurt her. I didn't let her out of my sight, and she is safe sleeping in my arms, her head on my chest and her soft snores fill the room.

Resting my arm over her, I pull her closer to me and hold her a little tighter into my chest. My heart shatters deep inside of my ribcage at the thought of how close I am to losing her, to losing both of them.

Fuck.

She is carrying my baby, a perfect mix of the both of us but in two days I lose them both.

I never knew I wanted another child until this happened. Until her. But yet, I'll never get to be a father again all because of this fucked up situation I seem to have gotten myself completely tangled in.

The job was to protect her.

But I became infatuated with her, falling helplessly in love.

I was and will always be irrevocably in love with her. In this life, in my next and so on. My life changed the moment our eyes met in her father's office and our souls blazed with adoration for one another, entwining and tying us together in an infinite bond that would never be broken. Even in death, we would find each other until our souls are born to earth once more to begin their search for each other.

We were an everlasting love.

This just wasn't our time.

AMORA

I stir, everything aches, and I know it's because of how Wolfe handled me yesterday. My knees are bruised and grazed, my scalp is on fire and aches and my body feels like it's been hit by a freight train. Just as I am about to panic, I hear the steadiness of Titus' heartbeat under his skin that is softly singing in my ear. Pushing myself up slowly, I wince because the way my muscles radiate pain with each little move.

A small smile creeps onto my lips when I see Titus sitting upright, his eyes closed, and I am desperate to see them in all their beauty. He looks so peaceful and as much as I want to wake him up, I won't.

I gently try to move back but his arm that is wrapped round me tightens and that's when I see his eyelids flutter, his crystal blues landing on mine and my heart skips a couple of beats and my soul is soaring as I feel the connection ignite deep inside of me causing a catalyst of feelings to consume me whole.

"Morning Twilight," the grouchy rasp of his voice makes the hairs on the back of my neck stand up and my skin pebble.

"Morning," my voice floats through the empty room as Titus pulls me back towards his warm body and I curl up and let my head rest on his shoulder when I feel his soft lips brush against my forehead. I let my eyes flutter shut for just a moment as I enjoy every second of how my body reacts to him.

"Sorry if I woke you," I whispered.

"You didn't wake me Little Red, I haven't slept," he admitted, a soft sigh brushing past his lips.

"Don't worry about Wolfe, what he did yesterday..." my stomach twists but I am cut off when I am dragged from Titus' side and pulled on top of him, legs either side and I try my hardest to ignore the hard bulge that is currently hiding in his boxers.

"I don't want to talk about it," he shakes his head from side to side as his thumb brushes against my cheek.

Silence falls between the both of us as his other hand rests on my hip, his fingers dancing over my skin in small circles.

"I feel like I am being punished for something," I admit, my eyes gazing into his.

"Baby, you're not being punished. We have just fallen into an unfortunate situation."

"It's not just a situation though, is it?"

He says nothing and pulls his eyes from me.

"I'm being married off, to a man I loathe and wish dead every minute of every day. I have two days, two days until I say, *'I do'* and once those two words pass my lips, my life is over. The future I have pictured from the moment I met you is slowly slipping out of my grasp. Living on a ranch with you, our kids running round and living their best lives as they make mud pies and dig for treasure. I'll come out onto the wrap around porch telling you all that dinner is ready and then there's you. Sweaty and beautiful in the dusk of the evening, walking hand in hand with our children after working on *your* ranch that you have always dreamt of. I would move across the world for you, just because I would never want to know what it was like to not have you in my life. But now..." I pause and my head falls forward, my hands resting on the warm skin of his chest as his heart begins to race under my tingling fingertips.

"You will always be with me, always etched in my heart Twilight. But we won't be living out our dreams," his fingers graze against my jaw, his head tilting slightly as his fingers continue down my neck, down my sternum until they eventual trace across my stomach and I feel my heart tremble in my chest.

Lifting my hand from his skin, I place it over his as we sit in silence dreaming of the *what if's*.

CHAPTER FIFTY-SIX

AMORA

ONE DAY TO GO

STANDING ON A SMALL PLATFORM, I GAZE INTO THE MIRROR, BUT my mind is elsewhere. The bitch of Satan was fixing the hem of my dress and making sure everything was perfect for tomorrow.

Tomorrow.

My stomach rolls with nausea and I close my eyes to try and not even think about what my life is about to become.

"Are you okay?" I hear Titus' voice and a small smile pulls at my lips.

"I will be," I inhale deeply and let my eyes focus back on the mirror.

The dress looks better now it fits me correctly, and the slit has been sewn up so it's not as revealing.

"There," she claps her hands together loudly and I jump. "Happy?"

"Not particularly..." I roll my eyes and then let them roam up and down my body. "It'll do, but I think maybe the dress should have been black seeing as I'll be entering a mourning period."

She tsks, shaking her head from side to side as she walks away.

Poisonous little dwarf.

"I think I hate her more than Wolfe," I smirk, turning to face Titus. "So?"

He stands, hands fisted deep into his pockets as he walks towards me, and I can see the pain that tarnishes his beautiful face.

"It pains me to say it but..."

I nod.

Because I know what he wants to say.

"Keep the words to yourself," tears fill my eyes and I have to look away. I slowly turn and look back to myself and just take a moment.

This is it.

The beginning of the end.

I'M SITTING IN MY STUDIO WHEN TITUS WALKS IN AND BREAKS ME away from my painting. My creative flow is still not one hundred percent back, but I felt the tingles in my fingers today.

"Your mom is on the phone," he gives me a lopsided smile and passes it to me and my brows furrow.

"Mum?"

"Hey darling, I just wanted to call and see if you were okay?"

I sigh.

"I wouldn't say I was okay..." I look to Titus.

"I wish things didn't have to be this way, but please be

rest assured that I have made your father pay. I am so disappointed in him, and I am so sorry that we—and yes it is we because I am also your mother—but I am Amora, I'm sorry that we have put you through this. This is not the way I expected to watch my baby girl get married. I dreamt of the perfect day, the perfect dress and the perfect man..." she trails off.

"So did I Mum, but it seems neither of us are going to get that dream." My tone is curt, and I feel the disappointment surge through me.

"Your friends have been calling for updates..." and I hear the light-heartedness in her voice.

"That's nice of them," I shake my head, "Mum... I know you think you're helping but you're not. At all. I've been dealt a shitty hand, I'll get over it so stop trying to appease your guilt with all this bullshit."

"Amora... I..."

"Mum, please. I love you, and dad..." I pause, "but just accept what is happening. The deal is done."

"Daddy will fix it," she whispers down the phone.

"And I've just been given a unicorn," I shrug my shoulders up and I can feel the burn in my throat intensifying. "I'll see you tomorrow." I cut the phone off before she even has a chance to respond and give it back to Titus. "Sorry about that," I let my head fall forward and sigh.

"Nothing to apologize about, Little Red." He smiles, tucking his phone inside his jacket.

"How's your daughter?" I ask, turning back to face my canvas.

"Weird," he admits, dragging a stool across and sitting down next to me, his eyes focused on the canvas.

"Why?" I ask, turning my attention to my painting.

"She is just being..."

"Distant?"

"Hm," his voice rumbles in his throat, "I wouldn't say distant."

"No?"

"No," he shakes his head from side to side, "it's like..." he pauses for a moment and I turn to face him and I see the pained expression that's slowly being painted onto his face. "She can't wait to get me off the phone. It's always been me and her, but now... it's like she is proving that she doesn't need me. Making me doubt everything I thought I knew about her." He sighs heavily and it's as if he has the weight of the world sitting on his shoulders.

I reach across, slipping my hand onto his thigh and give him a tight-lipped smile.

"I know she is busy with her internship; I get that... but it's just like she knows how to cope without me."

Now it was my turn to sigh.

"She's a young woman... she is trying to make a dent in her world and whether you like it or not big guy... she doesn't need you. Maybe she didn't want to hurt your feelings by telling you that, but now you're out the country... well, she can breathe."

His lips part as if he wants to say something, but he soon closes his mouth and just rubs his lips together.

"I know that came across really harsh but take it from a twenty-five-year-old with a father that likes to suffocate her... in the best way possible but he needs to let me find myself in this black and white world until I find the small bit of colour needed to light my world up."

I pause and dig my nails gently into his thick thigh.

"Like I found you, you showed me just how beautiful this world actually is. My very own kaleidoscope. I never knew life could be this pretty until you. You took my mediocre black and white world and painted it with a medley of colours, but I can only see them with you. Nothing looks as good when we're apart but when you're with me, I see everything so..." My eyes settle on his and my heart gallops in my chest, "vividly."

His large hand rests on top of mine and the corner of his mouth pulls into a slow smirk.

"I have always been a little... *overprotective*." A low chuckle escapes him.

"Aren't all fathers?" I lean into him and he envelopes me with his arm, holding me close to him.

"But after Sharon walked out... it was only me and her, and the guys of course. I would have never made it through the first twenty-one years without them. Sleepless nights, colic, teething, her first steps, first day at school..." he tightens his grip, "they've been there every step of the way." His lips find the top of my head and he stills. "She broke me in a way I never thought was possible but then I found you and everything slipped into place. All of this needed to happen for me to be able to realize just what love actually felt like."

I slowly sit up, my wide eyes on his. Feeling his large hand cup my cheek, I lean into him.

"I love you Amora, with every fiber of myself. You fixed me without even realizing it. And I know after tomorrow, I'll have to love you from a far, but just know I will never stop loving you."

"I love you, Titus." I choke placing both hands on his face as I move from my stool and climb into his lap, legs either side of his as I slip my tongue into his mouth, a low groan vibrating through him as my hands drop from his face and rest on his chest just so I can feel his steady heartbeat under my fingers.

Our kiss deepens, his hands skimming down my side and under the hem of my dress as he pushes it up around my waist, but he stops, his eyes volleying between mine.

"I need you," I whisper, my forehead pressing against his.

I hitch a breath when his teeth nip at my jaw, my neck, before his lips press against my collar bone and his fingers skim over the front of my thong, gently rubbing over my already throbbing clit.

Bucking my hips forward, he strokes me again as his other hand tugs the neckline of my dress down, popping my full breast from my bra and his hot, wet mouth is locked around my rosy nipple as he sucks and licks.

My breath shudders in my chest as pleasure ripples through me, my arousal pooling in my lace underwear.

"So wet,' he murmurs against my sensitive skin as he hooks his fingers round the thin material that is stopping him from getting what he wants. What I need. Teasing at my opening, two fingers stretch and dip inside of me causing me to gasp.

"Titus," I whisper, my eyes lifting from him for just a moment to check the doorway.

"I've got you," he whispers back as my hips rock forward, silently begging for him to fill me. My lips crash down onto his, my hands resting on his thighs behind me as his fingers pump in and out of my slowly and I feel so consumed with pleasure that my eyes roll in the back of my head.

Panic causes me to freeze when I hear a noise rattle behind us.

"Baby, eyes on me... focus on me," he reassures me as

his fingers curl deep inside of me, stroking me slowly and working my body up.

"Make me forget, just for a moment... make me forget what my life is about to become," I say quietly, my throat burning as a tear escapes and rolls down my cheek.

He doesn't say anything, just seals his word with a slow, deep kiss and my skin explodes with goosebumps and my heart sings in my chest to a song that only me and him can hear.

Lifting me gently, he makes quick work to unbutton his suit trousers and I feel the thick head of his cock rubbing and teasing at my entrance.

Ever so slowly he glides me down onto him and my pussy stretches around him until I am full of him.

Locking my arms round his neck, my hips begin rocking over him building myself up as I give him all of me.

"I'll never forget just how good you feel," his lips brush against my ear as he wraps his arms round my waist, his hips lifting and rocking into me, meeting my every move.

Our teeth clash, lips meet and our tongues dance together as I begin to slow but Titus keeps moving, not stopping as he thrusts deep inside of me, his fingers slowly glide down my sides and dig into the skin on my hip as they wrap tightly round me.

"Keep going," I beg, panting as I break away from our kiss and he works my body, lifting me up and down as he slips in and out of my aching core. My fingers trail down between my legs as I rub them gently over my sensitive clit, my pussy tightening as I move with him, the head of his cock rubbing the aching spot that I so desperately need touched.

Just as I feel the prickle of pleasure begin to coat my skin, Titus stands, my legs wrapping round his waist as he presses me against the cool wall behind us. I tighten my grip round him, his hands skim underneath me, his fingers digging into the bare skin of my ass. He slips out of me to the tip, slowly teasing with gentle thrusts and I can feel the burn radiating through me, heat blooming between my legs and I can hear just how wet I am.

"I'm close," I close my eyes when I feel his lips on my neck.

"I love fucking you," Titus pants as he pulls back then slams into me hard.

"Shit," I whisper, my fingers digging into his shoulders, "do that again," I plead, my body beginning to tremble as he pulls to the tip and holds it for just a moment before rocking his hips forward hard.

"Fuck me Titus, hard and fast," I cry out, pleasure rippling through me and I don't care if we get caught in this moment.

His perfect, thick cock slips in and out of me with ease, a delicious, burning ache brewing deep inside of me as I feel the pressure teasing as he fucks me fast, my back hitting against the wall on each thrust.

"Oh," I whimper, "Titus," I breathe as my head dips forward, but Titus' hand leaves my ass and is up round my throat within half a second.

"Look at me as you come, Little Red," his fingers wrap at the base of my throat and I have no idea what he has done to me but I smile, my orgasm teetering as I give a gentle stroke over my clit as he pounds into me one last time and I explode around him, biting on my bottom lip to stifle my moan and ignoring that I drew blood as I feel his cock pulse inside of me as his orgasm rips through him, his head tipping back as he continues to fuck me hard.

"Fuck, baby," he groans, pinning me to the wall with his

hips and cupping my face with his hands as we both pant, catching our breaths.

"I'm not ready for tomorrow," I admit, locking my hands round his neck and holding him tightly.

"Neither am I baby, but it's out of our control."

"At least we have today," I give a sad smile.

And he nods.

"At least we have today," he repeats, his mouth slanting over mine as we lose ourselves in each other once more and all the worry of tomorrow slowly slips away.

CHAPTER FIFTY-SEVEN
TITUS

WEDDING DAY

I IGNORE THE SICKLY FEELING THAT ROLLS THROUGH ME. I STAYED with Amora last night. Wolfe was away on business, but Hunter made himself known most of the evening. The control I had to have to not let my hand rest on her non-existent bump was torture. I have to convince myself that there is no baby because if I let my mind actually accept that she is pregnant, I will destroy everything that Xavier has worked so hard on.

It had just turned twelve and Wolfe and Amora were to be married at dusk and I ignore the searing pain of my heartbreak.

Twilight.

My favorite time of day and the reason for her nickname and I can't help but think that sick fuck knows that.

He isn't stupid, he knows we sneak around but that's what I don't understand. No other man would allow it. He is aggressive and possessive, but he does nothing to stop it happening. If roles were reversed, I would have outed me weeks ago.

The whole thing is iffy, and I have said that from the beginning.

The bathroom door goes, and Amora walks out wrapped in a towel as she walks across the room.

"You okay?" I ask as she keeps her head down.

We have hardly spoken this morning and I don't know what to say or ask. I know it's because of what today is, but the thought of us spending our last day together not speaking is killing me.

"Fine," she forces a smile on her face as she sits down at her dressing table.

I sigh, my eyes drifting to her wedding dress that is hanging up.

"What time is your mom coming over?" I try my luck asking her something else.

"She's not. Wolfe has said no one is allowed over." She rubs her lips together before she lets her head fall forward and into her hands.

"Where is he?" I stand and anger boils my blood.

"Titus, leave it... I'm not your problem anymore," she sniffles, and she rubs her red rimmed eyes.

I pace over to her, pulling her up and wrapping her in my embrace.

"Yesterday I was... but not today," her voice cracks. "I wish it was yesterday again, but yesterday is gone."

Inhaling deeply, I gently push her away from me and cup her face in my hands.

"Yes, yesterday is gone, but not to me. I will go back to yesterday for the rest of my life because from today, you're not mine anymore and the thought of living every day hereafter destroys me." I just about manage before my voice trembles. I edge forward, my lips pressing to her forehead, and I linger for just a moment, because being this close to her is killing me.

I step back and wipe her tears.

"Don't waste any more of your tears on him, Twilight," I give her a cheeky smile even though I am dying inside.

She nods, sniffing then turns away before she disappears into her dressing room. I step back, sitting on the edge of the bed once more and I wait.

My phone vibrates in my pocket, and I smile when I see Kaleb's name.

"Hey, long time no speak," I sigh, widening my legs and resting my elbows on my knees as I lean forward.

"You've been a busy boy," I can hear the humor in his voice.

"That I have," I smirk.

"How are you feeling... when do you fly? I'll pick you up from the airport."

"Flight is at eight-twenty tonight." And just saying that out loud makes my chest ache. "So, I'll be in about eleven-twenty your time, but I can cab it, don't stress." I'm very nonchalant. I've missed my friends but honestly, I just want to sit and reflect on the last month and then cradle a whiskey when I am at home so I can just learn to live with my new normal. A life without her.

"Don't be stupid, I'll be there. I'll bring Connie too."

Scrubbing my face, I nod as if he can see me. "Okay, cool."

"Hope all goes well today... few more hours and it'll be over."

"If only you knew," I scoffed and my eyes lifted to her, standing in a strapless white bra and satin, white panties.

"I'll see ya later," I swallow the thickness and cut the phone off without hearing if he even said bye.

"You're killing me," I admit, and those three words can be used in so many different contexts with how I am feeling right about now.

"Sorry," her cheeks blush and my heart races in my chest. "I need help in my dress," she rubs her lips together.

"Of course," I stand, and I don't even try to hide my erection in my pants. I want her to see what she has done to me.

Her eyes widen and her cheeks darken with crimson.

"Don't be embarrassed Little Red, it's all for you, you've seen it all before."

I unhook her wedding dress and discard the bag it's been sitting in, letting it pool on the floor just in front of her feet, I hold my hand out for her to take so she can steady herself as she steps inside of it. But before I help her into her dress, I kneel in front of her and look up at her through my lashes, a slow smirk gracing my face and her cheeks redden again. Pressing my lips over her thighs, I place soft butterfly kisses against her pale skin, grazing them against the front of her satin panties, kissing and nipping at her sensitive flesh through the material, my hands wrapped round her slim hips.

"Titus."

"Twilight," I groan against her covered pussy and my skin tingles.

Slipping her panties to the side, I don't give her a minute to say anything as I swipe my tongue through her folds, and I feel her shudder under my grip. I am desperate to fuck her, but I needed to taste her, to savour her as if she was my last meal.

Her knee bends over my shoulder, and I bury myself in

her soaked folds, my tongue flicking and flattening against her clit as she begins to ride my face.

"Oh," she moans, and I know she is getting close, her fingers are clawing into my shoulders as she balances herself.

"Not yet baby," I groan as I stand and move behind her, my feet wide as I straddle the dress that's on the floor.

"Pick your dress up," I whisper, and she bends in front. Wrapping my fingers round her waist I pull her peachy ass into me, grinding my hips so she can feel how she makes me feel.

"Titus," she breathes, and I roll her up so my lips are next to her ear.

"I crave you all the time," one of my hands glides down between her thighs and I slip a finger straight inside of her, "it seems you crave me too Little Red," I groan as I pump into her slowly.

"One last time..." her voice is quiet.

"One last time," I nip at her ear and step back expecting her to follow but she doesn't. She bends down again, and I see the wet patch soaking through her panties from her arousal making my cock stiffen even more.

She pulls her dress up and slips her arms through the straps before holding it in place.

My brows furrow for a moment but I think I know where she is going with this and thrill flashes through me.

"Can you zip me up?" she looks over her shoulder at me and I can see the fire igniting in her beautiful eyes.

I step forward, clutching the zip with trembling hands and tug it up in one move.

"Thank you," she smiles, turning forward and walking towards the foot of the bed.

"Now fuck me," she pouts as she looks at me again,

bending slowly and placing her hands into the comforter of the bed.

I know we shouldn't, but she makes me feral.

I unbuckle my pants as I walk towards her and discard them to the floor before I grab the skirt of her dress and push it up and over her hips. Teasing my finger down her ass cheeks and into the side of her panties, I push two fingers deep inside of her as I stretch her, my other hand wrapped round my aching cock as I glide my hand up and down as I finger her.

Once I know she is ready for me, I hook her panties and drag them over fully to the side and expose her completely as I slip my tip into her soaked pussy and slam forward causing her to cry out.

"Quiet Little Red," I hush her, "we don't want him coming in and seeing me fuck his fiancée in her wedding dress, do we?" I growl, one hand curled round her hip as I drive into her hard and fast with relentless pounds. Her cunt clenches around me and her moans fill the room. I'm not going to last long and neither is she.

"Titus, fuck," she cries out as I spread her cheeks and watch my thick cock stretch her and slip in and out with ease.

"Your pussy looks so good full of my cock, you're such a good girl. You take me so well, Twilight. You were made for me," I praise her on a moan and tease my thumb at her puckered little asshole.

I feel her freeze and a low chuckle rips through me.

"I'm just teasing baby, but fuck I would have loved to have taken that away from him too," and as soon as the words are off my tongue, I feel my rage brewing and I need to calm myself down. Tightening my grip round her hip, my thumb dips into her tight hole and I hear the vibration of a moan slip past her lips, and it turns me on so god damn much.

"You like the thought of that don't you baby, me filling every hole of yours so he can't be the first."

"Yes," she breathes.

"Say the word baby, I'll take it. I'll take it and brand you as mine."

"Take it Titus, take it all," she cries out and I slam into her hard.

Slowing my hips, I slip out of her and push two fingers inside of her and coat my fingers in her arousal.

"I'm so close," she whimpers, and I grin as I pull out of her and rub her tight asshole with it, using it as lube.

I do it again making sure that my cock and her ass are ready, my cock throbbing and my own release is impending. As soon as I'm in her, I'll explode.

I slip a finger into her ass and she stiffens. "Relax baby, you're doing so well," I praise her as I pump in and out of her before slipping a second finger in. "You're being such a good girl for me," my voice is low and her hips begin moving back and forth over my fingers.

Looking down, I admire the view before pulling out of her and teasing the head of my cock at her tight opening.

"Relax baby, I promise this'll feel so good," I hum, sinking my teeth into my bottom lip as I edge into her slowly and gently.

"Shit, Titus, slowly..." she cries out and I rub soft circles over her hip bone trying to distract her.

"There's a good girl, you're taking me so well," I moan, my whole body tensing as I slip a little further into her as my other hand cups her pussy before slipping two fingers inside of her, working her up.

"Oh," her pussy tightens around me.

"There we go," I smile as I fill her with one last thrust then let my fingers fall from her hot, wet pussy. "Fuck, baby, I wish you could see how good you look," I moan, both hands on her hips as I slowly move in and out of her in gentle, short, strokes.

"Titus," she pants, and she lifts one of her legs, so her knee is resting on the edge of the bed and I slip in deeper, my eyes rolling in the back of my head. "I need more," she whispers, her eyes meeting mine as she looks over her shoulder at me and I do as she asks. Teasing two fingers at her opening, I fuck her hard but slow, riding into her and I don't stop until she is a trembling mess beneath me as I snatch an orgasm from her and I follow, pumping all of me into her virgin ass and I lose it as I pound into her twice with hard thrusts.

Slipping out of her gently, I hear her hiss as she falls forward on the bed and I cover her back over with her satin panties and I watch as my arousal drips from her. I crash beside her, resting up on my elbow as I brush my fingers across her cheeks.

"Are you okay?" I ask, my eyes on hers the whole time.

"I am, I am perfect, Titus... thank you," she mumbles and my heart swells in my chest.

"Don't thank me, Twilight." I lean forward and place a soft kiss on her lips.

"It was the perfect goodbye," she pushes up and lets her skirt fall and my heart cracks.

"It was the perfect goodbye," I whisper as she disappears into the bathroom and closes the door behind her.

She sits all pretty at her dressing table as she brushes through her wavy, red hair. I watch as she styles it into a low bun, fastening it in place with slider clips. She tugs a few curly strands from her hair, and they fall to frame her face.

She really is the definition of beautiful. Finishing her look with a bright red lipstick that pops against her ivory skin, she looks every bit bride.

I am lost in thought when I hear the bedroom door bang open and I stand instantly, moving to where Amora is as I try to guard her.

"It's bad luck to see the bride before the wedding," I snarl, and I notice that he isn't alone. An impeccably dressed doctor rounds the door frame and stands with a black, leather doctor's bag.

"Get on the bed Amora," Wolfe snaps and commands and I hold my hand out indicating for her to not move.

"She's getting ready."

"And I don't give a shit, bed, now," Wolfe's voice booms round the room and I watch as Amora flinches.

"Why?" She asks as she stands up and steps to the side of me, revealing herself fully and I watch as Wolfe's eyes sweep over her but there is nothing. No emotion, no admiration or adoration... nothing.

"I want the doctor to check if you're *actually* pregnant and you're not pulling a little stunt." He glowers at her, his eyes hooded.

"Why would I lie?" her tone is sharp, but she still moves towards her bed.

"I don't know Amora... why would you?" sarcasm drips from Wolfe's tone and it takes all the strength I have not to fly at him.

Amora lays down, her head turning to look at the doctor who is walking over to her sheepishly. I follow.

"How are you, Amora?" The doctor asks as he indicates for her to lift her dress.

"I'm okay," her voice is small, and I hate that he is putting her through this.

She eyes the room and I try and block as much of her as I can from Wolfe's seedy eyes.

"Don't hide on my behalf little monster, I'll be seeing it all very soon anyway," his voice fills the room and I even get shivers dancing up and down my spine at his seediness. I ignore the blood that is currently thrashing in my ears at his words and just focus on Amora.

I look at her and she is laying with her wedding dress bunched up round her chest.

"You could have complimented your bride before you done this to her," I growl, my hands fisted into my suit pants.

"But I would be lying," Wolfe shrugs and I close my eyes and count down from five because each word that comes out of this prick's mouth is pushing me one step closer to strangling him.

"I am just going to have a little feel round of your stomach, is that okay?" he asks with a kind voice, and she nods.

After a few moments of silence, I hear the doctor ruffle around in his bag.

"She is definitely pregnant, I would say around five-six weeks," he nods in Wolfe's direction and Amora begins to pull her dress back down.

"Ah, ah, ah," Wolfe makes himself seen as he thunders across the floor. He reaches for the doctor's shoulder and gives him a sinister and calculated look and my fucking blood runs cold.

The doctor returns the look with a curt nod.

"It's time to rip that baby out of you now, I want you *bleeding* with the loss of *his* child as you walk down that fucking aisle to marry me. I don't even care if you bleed out into the skirt of your dress, it'll just show everyone that you weren't pure and that you are a fraud."

"Don't you fucking dare," I turn, rushing for him as I shove him back into the wall, hearing a loud thud as his slim body hits it.

"Do it," Wolfe smirks and I hear Amora shouting for him to stop.

"Fucking make him stop, or I will," I pull Wolfe from the wall before slamming him back into it.

"Over my dead body," he grins at me, his hollow and soulless eyes are nothing but a dark emptiness.

I twist him round and throw him to the floor before I kick him in the stomach, blow after blow.

"Please, no," I hear her plead and I snap my head round and run for the doctor who is just about to put his hands on her. I shove him hard, making him lose his balance as he falls and hits his head on the bedside unit and knocking him out cold.

"Shit," I pant, and Amora's eyes are wide, her face paling as she stares at the lifeless doctor. "Little Red, eyes on me," I say softly, and she turns to face me and I let out a sigh of relief. I hear Wolfe groaning behind me but before I can turn around, he is on my back, punching me with hard blows in the side of my head. I try and shrug him off me, but he clings on and the dull pain that is currently radiating through me makes me think my head is being split open. I lift my arms up and rip his hands from around my neck and throw him to the ground and he cries out as his body slams against the floor.

I kneel over him, grabbing him by the front of his shirt as I lay punch after punch into his face.

"Do you know how long I have wanted to do this to you," I grit as I connect my fist with his face again and he just smirks with a bloody grin. I fall back onto my knees, panting and I can feel the blood tricking down the side of my face. "You're not fucking worth it." I spit on him and slowly stand, my legs trembling, and I feel the adrenaline coursing through my body. I turn and face Amora, and she looks petrified.

"It's okay," I soothe as I stagger over to the bed, my busted and bloody hand staining the sheets as I rest it.

I watch as Wolfe stands and wipes the corner of his mouth, his chest rising and falling fast.

"I will get that baby out of her, I'm not having my wife carrying a child that isn't mine," he stumbles forward. "Then I am going to fuck her until she is pregnant with my heir. She will be nothing more than a sex toy to me and my brother and once I am done with her, I'll throw her out like the worthless piece of shit she is. Or maybe I'll kill her, at least that way she'll be with her baby because that's the only way she'll get to meet it." He snarls and my stomach twists. I stand, clenching my fists by my side.

"Amora," my voice is steady, "get out of the room, now." And for the first time since being with her, that's the only command I have ever given her.

I hear her scrambling behind me, and she runs out of the room without looking back. I sigh in relief, my shoulders sagging, and he catches me off guard in that one moment.

He launches himself at me, his hands round my throat as he squeezes the life out of me slowly.

My eyes widen when I see Hunter approaching slowly and I begin to panic knowing he must have passed Amora in the hallway.

Shit.

I grab Wolfe's hand, trying to pull them away from my throat but the cunt has such a tight grip. My eyes begin to narrow, the noises around me echoing and suddenly all I can hear is *Chasing Cars – Sleeping at last* with images of everyone I love.

Arizona.

Amora.

Kaleb, Keaton, Nate, Killian, Connie and Reese.

My family.

At least I'll die knowing I tried.

That's all I can do right? *Try.*

I did what I promised.

I protected her to my last, dying, breath.

I squeeze my eyes shut and my lungs burn as they beg for air. I kick out in one last attempt to live. Kicking Wolfe straight in the stomach, he falls to the floor, winded. I gasp for air, coughing and sucking in as much oxygen as I can to fill my starved lungs.

Hunter glares at me and I stand tall, getting a second wind. I see something shiny in his hand and it takes me a moment to realize it's a knife.

My blood runs cold and thrashes through my veins, my heartbeat pumping in my ears. It's not long before Wolfe is back on his feet and he turns to face his brother, giving him a sickening glare.

"Night night fucker," Wolfe grits and just as panic

begins to set in, Hunter rushes towards me and passes me the knife.

I freeze, my eyes on him and he gives me a nod. "I've always been on your side," his voice is low, and I hear Wolfe roar, racing towards me and Hunter and I move at him with force, my hand jolting forward as the knife slips into his stomach and I see the pain shatter through him. I retract the knife instantly, letting it slip from my grasp and I feel numb as I watch him fall to the floor, his hand pressed against his wound and he laughs a menacing laugh, shaking his head from side to side.

"First time with a knife?" he mocks me and slowly stands, "It's going to take more than that..." but my eyes widen when I see Wolfe fall to the floor in a heap and Hunter is holding the freshly bloodied knife.

I am in shock, my eyes pinned to a lifeless Wolfe, and I slowly lift my head to look at Hunter.

"Hunter," my voice trembles.

"It's the only way this would end. He wouldn't have stopped, and I couldn't stand to witness how he was with Amora and what he threatened to do to her. I was angry at Xavier, but it wasn't his fault. He was tipped off. I knew that. I struck a deal with Xavier; I was always on your side." He steps towards me and holds out his hand to shake mine.

I look down at it, my stomach rolling with nausea when I see his brother's blood coating it.

"Sorry," he says with a grimace as he rubs his hand down his jeans then holds it back out. I accept his handshake, the whole time my mind is trying to catch up with what the fuck happened.

"The police will be here soon, this is on me... now go and find her," he steps back, dropping the knife to the floor and he slowly sits down next to his brother's body.

"I'm sorry for your loss," I whisper, and he gives a soft nod, his hand resting on Wolfe's back.

"Some things have to come to an end, family or not..." his voice is full of gravel, and I step out of the room not looking back.

I needed to find Amora.

CHAPTER FIFTY-EIGHT
AMORA

WEDDING DAY

I RUN DOWN THE STAIRS AND SEE MY FATHER STANDING THERE.

"Amora?"

"Daddy," I throw myself at him and his arms wrap around me tightly.

"What's the matter?"

"Wolfe and Titus are fighting."

I hear my father sigh.

"Let them fight, they need to get it out of their system."

I pull away from him and my expression hardens.

"What?" I snap.

"Trust me, they'll be fine, now come, we have to go..." my father wraps his fingers round my wrist and drags me down the driveway with me kicking and screaming behind him.

I swallow the large lump that is burning in my throat, my eyes are red rimmed and bloodshot, but I refuse to cry.

Not today.

We stand in front of large, dark wood arched doors and my heart is stuttering in my chest.

My arm is linked through my father's, and he holds onto me tightly.

The sound of music begins to play, and it sounds like a death march.

"You look beautiful, Amora," he says quietly as the doors begin to slowly open and I drop my head and keep my eyes pinned to the floor. I can't look up. I don't want to.

I don't want to look and see Wolfe standing there. It had been forty minutes since we left the house where Titus and Wolfe were fighting, but my father assured me both men were okay and Wolfe was waiting for me at the altar. I ignored the heartbreak that was currently consuming me with each step I took, bringing me closer to my fate.

I really thought my father was playing the joker. Never in my wildest dreams did I think he would do this to me.

I count in my head slowly, *one, two, three, four...*

"I'm going to fucking kill that little wanker," I hear my father curse under his breath, and I snap my head up to see Titus standing at the altar, bruised and bloody but he was there.

Not Wolfe.

"Titus?" I whisper as we approach him, my father's grip tightening on me.

"Twilight," he smiles and my eyes roam over his beautiful but beaten and swollen face.

He's here.

"What are you doing here?" my voice is tight as I look behind me expecting to see Wolfe barrelling down the aisle at any minute. I feel everyone staring and my cheeks begin to redden.

"I couldn't let him have you, you're mine Little Red, yesterday wasn't enough for me to have for the rest of my life. I needed today and tomorrow too."

I pull my hand from my father's with force and step up towards Titus, climbing the two steps so I am now standing in front of him.

"Don't make me beat you under the eyes of God Titty," my father growls stepping towards us.

"There has been a change of plan..." Titus says with that cheeky smirk and looks at the vicar who looks utterly confused.

"Twilight?" Titus says softly and my heart melts in my chest, "Shall we?"

My eyes fill with tears, and I nod over and over.

"Yes," I mumble, nibbling on my bottom lip to try and stop the tears falling.

"You had to fuck up the plan. My well executed plan and you've fucked it up..." My father turns round, looking at the stunning church ceiling and he shakes his head in disappointment, "again."

He sighs, looking out onto the church and clicks his fingers and I see men standing from the pews one by one.

"Go and search the house," he commands, and the guys run out of the building, and I look at my father confused.

"I'll explain later... now, come on. We have shit to sort out." He holds his hand up and twirls his fingers. He turns back round to face me, stepping forward and climbing the steps as he places a soft kiss on my cheek.

"I love you, Amora," he says softly and quietly so only I can hear, and a lone tear rolls down my cheek as I watch my father turn towards Titus, his hand resting on Titus' chest before he pats it gently. "You have my blessing, Titty," he lets his head drop and spins, stepping away and sitting next to my mother who is crying happy tears, Betty passing her a tissue whilst dabbing her own eyes. My eyes seek out my brothers and pride swarms them which makes my skin tingle.

"Are you sure about this?" I whisper as I focus my all on Titus and excitement and anxiousness courses through me.

"I have never been surer, wife."

I bite the inside of my cheek when the vicar looks at both of us with a confused expression on his face before addressing the room.

"Dearly beloved, we're gathered here today…"

EPILOGUE

AMORA

My head rests on Titus' chest and I feel at peace. His fingers skim up and down my bare back as we lay in silence after consummating our whirlwind marriage. I have no idea what happened yesterday, nor do I want to, I am just grateful that I am laying in his arms. Tied to him forever, legally.

I let my fingers trace over his chest in small circles and I hear the deep intake of breath he fills his lungs with.

"Is this a dream?" I crane my neck up to look at him and his thumb brushes over my bottom lip.

"No Twilight, this isn't a dream," his voice is low and full of haze as his lips stroke across mine and I melt my body against his. I smile against his lips as his large hand rests on my lower belly.

"It feels real now... I didn't want to think about our baby but now," he pauses and his beautiful blue eyes volley back and forth from mine. "Now I can get excited, I didn't want to love someone I was destined to lose."

"Our baby..." I blink back the tears as my heart flutters in my chest.

"Our baby," he beams at me as his lips crash into mine once more.

———

We walk hand in hand down the back streets of London and I feel free. Free from the life I felt chained to. Free from the life I was meant to live. But here I am, my fingers linked through his and so fiercely in love with this man it scares me.

We stop outside *Harrods,* and I look up at Titus, my brows furrowing with confusion.

"We don't have wedding rings, Little Red." He leans in, his arm wrapping round my back as he pulls us body to body and his nose rubs against mine. "I want the world to see you're mine," he kisses me softly before dragging me into the shop and my insides blaze with want for him.

He leads me to a counter, and I see the iconic *Cartier* sign. My heart thumps in my chest.

"Titus, I would be happy with a *Haribo* ring," I nudge into him and my eyes widen as I see the prices in front of me.

"I know you would baby, but you deserve so much more than a *Haribo* ring." He winks and the sales lady practically skips towards him with pound signs flashing in her opal eyes.

"How may I help you?" she asks, her hands behind her back as she beams at Titus.

After an hour, we both have matching gold, thin bands wrapped around our ring fingers.

"Are we reckless?" I squeeze his hand as we make our way back to where Titus had parked.

"Absolutely," he grins, leading me across the road when a gap appears.

"How will your daughter take it?" I can't help but ask as we step back onto the pavement.

"We will deal with that when I am home," and the calmness in his voice eases me.

"I want to come home with you, I don't want to stay here, and I won't ask you to stay here when your friends and family are back in New York."

He stops suddenly, spinning to face me and I see the look of shock on his face.

"What about your family and friends?" he asks, a hard expression etched on his face.

"They'll survive without me, it's time I take my life into my own hands and do what I want. I need to spread my wings and find my freedom," I shrug and Titus laughs, embracing me on the busy pavement as he kisses me.

We've not been home long when my father seeks us out in the library. I was lost in a book and Titus was on his phone trying to rebook his flight after he missed it.

None of his friends know we got married.

None of his friends know that I am pregnant, and anxiety cripples me at them finding out.

"Amora can you and Titty join us in the dining room for dinner?" he asks softly as he leans up against the door frame. My eyes float to Titus who gives me a soft nod. I haven't spoken to my father once since he walked me down the aisle but I know we have to talk at some point so he can tell me what the fuck had happened over the last few weeks.

"Okay," I stand, holding my hand out for Titus to take and a rush of love explodes through me as he links his fingers through mine.

"Fucking hell," my father grunts under his breath and I can't help the giggle that escapes me.

Nerves rattle inside of me when I walk into the dining room and see my mother, Xander, Ezekiel and Betty all sitting there. I'm not mad at Betty. I could never be mad at her. I give her a small smile as I take my seat next to her and her frail hand lifts and cups over the top of mine when I rest it on the table.

"I missed you," she just about manages, and I can see the tears dancing in her eyes.

"I missed you too."

"Did you miss me?" my father asks as he takes his seat at the head of table.

"No," I turn to face him and smile, Titus shuffles next to me and I see his shoulders move as he laughs quietly.

"Charming."

"We're glad you're back," Xander pipes up and I can see the guilt masking his face and my heart constricts in my chest.

I throw my brothers a tight smile. I wasn't quite ready to forgive Xander yet. Ezekiel I was never mad at. I honestly think he was in the dark, much like me.

My mother's eyes are glued to me, and I give her a soft nod.

"I think there are a few things that need to be addressed," my father clears his throat.

"Do you?" my mother snaps at my father and I roll my lips.

"Royal, please..." my father drops his head, closing his eyes.

"What?" she acts confused.

"I fucked up, I know. I've apologised..." he pauses,

looking round the room, "god knows I've apologised," he growls, and I look down into my lap.

Titus' hand sneaks into my lap and rests on my thigh.

"Words mean nothing, you've got to prove it which you still haven't," she shakes her head from side to side and reaches for her red wine and shakes her head from side to side.

"Red..." my father's jaw tightens, and his fists clutch at the white table sheet.

"Temper temper," she tuts in disgust, and I don't miss the way her lip slightly curls at the corner of her mouth. She's playing him.

"Right," his voice booms as he claps his hands together loudly. "All shut the fuck up and let me explain."

Xander puffs his cheeks out and Ezekiel just sits and listens, his eyes fixed on my father. Titus' grip tightens on my thigh, and I let out a deep exhale.

"Do you all really think I would have just given Amora, my daughter, my baby girl away to that fuck wit?"

"Well... you did," Ezekiel pipes up and my dad shoots him a death stare.

"Not out of choice!" he pushes his hand through his hair in frustration.

"It wasn't out of love was it?" my mother snipes at him and my eyes widen as I reach for my water.

"Royal I swear to fucking lucifer," he side eyes my mother and she shrugs her shoulders up. "Please, let me just speak," he whines, and I can see how deflated he is becoming.

"Dad..." I say after a moment, "go ahead... tell us all your side of the story," and I'm not being sarcastic or condescending, I want him to tell it. He has something to say so he should be able to tell us all what is on his mind.

"Thank you darling," he smiles softly at me, and I feel my heart warm in my chest.

"The truth is... The Knight Brothers *did* want Amora because I killed their father. Rightly so, they wanted blood as I'm sure you would boys..." he pauses and turns his attention to Xander and Ezekiel and they both nod in agreement.

"Right," he nods back, "but one day when I was trying to find anything to get them off the scent of Amora, I was approached by someone high up in the police force. I have never had dealings with them before, I've never had to. I was always clean in my job; I had people working for me so never got caught out... until Bartholomew Knight." He stops for a moment, licking his top lip, wetting it.

"Please, continue," my mother goads him but he ignores her.

"They wanted the Knight brothers; they came to *me* for help so I took that as an advantage. I gave Amora which in turn gave them The Knight Brothers. It wasn't a decision that I made lightly, I lost a lot of sleep because I just didn't see how the deal seemed fair or how it was going to help me. After a week, I met with them again and told them I would take the deal, but with that handshake went my job. They had everything on me. All the jobs, the clean ups... even your mate's little problem with the rockstar was pulled up," he gazes at Titus for a moment. "They used blackmail and promised that I wouldn't see the inside of a jail cell if I agreed to help them. My slate would be wiped clean. So, I took it. Too much hung over me, over us as a family and I hate that I somehow got each and every one of you involved and wrapped up in this lifestyle. Before I met my wife..." he looks at my mother with so much adoration I feel tears pricking at the back of my eyes, "I didn't care for anything, but as soon as I fell in love, everything shifted somehow. The jobs just didn't become jobs anymore. Each life I took laid as a heavy burden on my shoulders knowing I had taken a father, a mother, a child, a grandparent... I had blood on my hands, and it didn't matter how much I tried to get it off, I couldn't. I was tarnished with death." He sighs and his body turns to face me, his arms stretched across the table, and I placed my hand over his.

"I'm sorry that I had to use you as the pawn in this fucked up game of chess, but it needed to be done. I knew I wanted Titus here; I knew he would go above and beyond to look out for you because he was a father himself..." my father's warm glare turns ice cold as he focuses on Titus. "Yet I didn't expect him to knock you up then marry you," he grits, and I hear Xander cough and Ezekiel spits his wine out all over the table.

"What!?" they both say in unison and my eyes widen.

"Surpriseeee," I say in a high tone and force a smile on my face.

"Focus guys," my father rolls his eyes in an over exaggerated manner and bangs his hand on the table, so everyone looks at him again.

"The plan was for the police to grab Wolfe from the church and deal with him. We managed to get Hunter on side from the very beginning. He wasn't made for that life; he wasn't cut from the same cloth as Wolfe and Bartholomew. He was different. He was kind and wanted to help. If everything had gone to plan," my father pauses and side eyes Titus, "Amora was never going to be in any real danger because Hunter was always going to be our eyes and ears whilst she was there. I just needed Titus there as a *just in case*. I just never expected him to kill his brother... well, so we thought."

The colour from my face drains and I feel nauseous suddenly.

"When the police went and searched the place, Wolfe's body was missing."

I watch as Titus stiffens in his seat, he swallows hard.

"So is Wolfe still out there?" The panic is evident in my voice.

"Honestly?" my father says softly, "I have no idea, but we just need to focus on what is here and now. This hasn't been easy, and it was a well-executed plan until good old Titty here," my father leans over and smacks Titus hard on the back causing him to nearly cough up a lung, "had to interfere and fuck up the plan. Didn't you?"

Titus puffs out his cheeks, sitting tall in his chair.

"But," my father finally averts his gaze, "all that matters is that you're here, you're safe and I am so fucking sorry for putting you through literal hell. I don't know if you'll ever forgive me, but please know Amora, darling... I would have burned the fucking world to ashes to get you back from him. It was all a ploy, and it worked but I am sorry that you were used as bait." And I can see how crushed he is, his voice cracks and his eyes glass over.

"Daddy," I whisper, my voice trembling as I stand up and throw my arms around his shoulders as he still sits down, holding onto him as I whisper into his ear, "I forgive you."

He sniffs, curling his arm up and placing his hand on my shoulder as we stay in the position.

I slowly stand and my father's eyes fall to my stomach.

"And I'm so glad this little one didn't get harmed, because I was ready to rip Wolfe from limb to limb if he even tried," and I stiffen when I hear Titus clear his throat.

"What?" my father growls.

"That's why I fought him... he tried to..." Titus coughs and shuffles in his seat. My father says nothing but knows exactly what Titus is getting at and I feel a cold shiver blanket me. "Hunter handed me the knife, I stabbed him, but he still got back up and he just fell to the floor..."

My father's eyes close and I see him inhale slowly.

"Did you check to see if he was *actually* dead?" My father asks and Titus pales.

"There was so much blood... I assumed..." he leans back in his chair and my eyes pin to the man I love. "I just wanted to get to Amora, I wanted to be waiting for her at the top of the aisle..." he shakes his head from side to side as if disappointment is currently eating him up inside.

"Titus," my father's voice is soft, "don't beat yourself up over this. You done the right thing, you done your job... you protected Amora." He gives a small smile. "Thank you, son," he slowly nods at Titus and I take that as my cue to step back, taking my place next to my husband.

They finally found their respect for each other.

And it was because of me and our baby.

Because neither of them would have let anything happen to me or them.

We all fall into a form of easy and light chatter when I see my mother get up and nestle herself in my father's lap.

"I am still mad at you..." she whispers against his lips, "but I forgive you," and I see my father deflate at having his wife back on his side. I watch as my father whispers something in my mother's ear and she giggles like a schoolgirl.

Gross.

"Well, seeing as we're sharing..." I clear my throat, my heart galloping in my chest and all eyes lift and settle on me.

"What is it?" My mother asks, her brows furrowed.

"I'm moving to New York."

The room falls silent, and I can hear the low rumble in my father's throat fill the room. I wince, panic coursing through me when a slow smile pulls on his face.

"Looks like the Archibalds are relocating!" His voice booms round the room.

"What the fuck?" I hear Titus shout and my father lets out a loud, rumbling laugh.

"You can't get rid of me that easily, Titty. I'm your father-in-law," he winks at Titus then wraps his arms round my mother and suddenly, all feels right in my life.

Every single piece of it.

TITUS

We step off the plane at JFK and as he promised, Kaleb was standing there waiting for us.

"You ready Twilight," she nods, her hand tightening in mine. I know she is nervous, fuck, I am nervous but we both know this is the right move.

We have a week to ourselves before my father-in-law— also known as Satan—moves to New York.

I see Connie standing next to him literally jumping from foot to foot with excitement and my smile widens.

"Don't be nervous, Little Red," I whisper to her as we close the gap between us and my friends.

"Titus," Kaleb booms as he wraps his arms around me and pats me on the back.

"Hey bud," I smile as I embrace him and it's not until now that I realise quite how much I have missed him.

I pull back then envelope Connie in my arms.

"Good to see you Titus, damn, we missed you." She steps back and her eyes roam over my face, "England looks good on you."

I smile before looking down at Amora and my thumb brushes over between her thumb and index finger.

"It does, doesn't it," I smile before turning my attention back to my friends. "Guys, this is Amora. Amora, this is Kaleb and Connie."

Amora blushes as she holds her hand out for Kaleb, but he reaches for her and pulls her in, squeezing her but she doesn't let go of my hand.

"Hey Red, how are you? So good to meet the girl that thawed my best friend's ice heart." He chuckles and then Connie sweeps in for a hug.

"I'm sorry, we're huggers," she beams as she links her arm through Amora's and walks off. I catch her looking over her shoulder at me and she gives me a sweet smile.

"So, you fell in love."

"Man, did I," I laugh as Kaleb wraps his arm round my shoulders. "I fell so god damn hard."

"How do you think Arizona is going to take the news?"

"I have no fucking idea," I roll my lips and I feel a pang of anxiety slice through me.

I have no fucking idea.

We pull up outside a bar just down the street and I pinch my brows.

"Why are we here?" I ask and I look out the window at the bar we had my leaving drinks and lunch in.

"The guys are in here, they didn't want to wait till later," Kaleb shrugs, cutting the engine. I can hear Connie chatting away to Amora and all she does is smile. Fuck, her cheeks must be aching.

I hop out the car and rush to Amora's side as I take her hand and lead her onto the sidewalk.

"Sorry about this... I had no idea," I throw her an apologetic shrug and she gives me a wink.

"Don't apologise, I can't wait to meet everyone," she pushes onto her toes and gives me a kiss on the cheek.

"Come on love birds, let's go," Kaleb calls as his fingers find Connie's and we follow them into the bar.

I spot Keaton, Killian, Reese and Nate straight away. Keaton's eyes widen and he looks shocked to see me, but I have no idea why and that makes my stomach bottom out and uneasiness swarms me.

"Titus," Killian calls out, standing from the booth and shaking my hand, gripping it firmly.

"Nice to see you buddy, I hope all is well," my voice is loud over the Friday evening chatter and Killian just nods. Nate holds his hand up, pushing his glasses up his nose and I know that's as much as I am going to get from him tonight.

Keaton stays seated and smiles when my eyes land on him.

"Do I not get a proper hello?" I smirk as I wait for him to stand and after a while he does, but not without making it very clear he feels awkward.

"Hey man," Keaton squeezes my shoulder then holds his hand out for Amora. "Are you going to introduce me?" he tilts his head towards my wife.

"This is Amora, my wife. Amora, this is Keaton" I wrap my arm around her waist and pull her into me and I can feel their eyes burning into me. "Oh, and Keaton." I call out, "I think you may have put a dud condom in my bag as Amora is also pregnant."

And that's when I see everyone's faces, their eyes wide and tension is thick in the air.

"What the fuck?!" I hear Arizona's voice slice through me, and I freeze.

ARIZONA

I am numb.

I have already been forgotten by one parent and now I am going to be replaced by another.

No one is going to give a shit about poor, little Arizona.

Sure, I wanted my dad to find love again but not with a girl a little older than me. Even worse, he married her and knocked her up. Worse than that!? He told his friends before *me*.

But don't worry daddy... seems I'm not the only one who kept a secret.

Switching my laptop on and making sure the door is bolted, I open up my webchat.

TallDarkandHandsome has entered the chat.

I smile.

My favourite fan.

YourGoodGirl: *Good evening handsome.*

I type on my keyboard as I give myself a once over in the mirror. Red, laced bralette, a matching suspender belt with ivory stockings and crotchless panties.

Just like he wanted.

I wasn't in the right frame of mind for tonight, but at the same time, I needed out of my head, and this was guaranteed to help.

I glance over at my toys laid out on the bed and excitement thrills me.

TallDarkandHandsome: *Evening Vixen.*

Okay, so I'm not a doctor.

Far from it.

The only thing I have in common with a doctor is I see a lot of people daily.

But enough about that for now.

Now was time for my revenge and Mr *TallDarkandHandsome* was the perfect antidote for that.

Like I said, they weren't the only ones with a secret.

Betrayal was best served hot with a side of your dad's best friend.

THE END

The Betrayal, book three in the Illicit Love Series will follow Arizona and Keaton.
This is an age gap, dad's best friend and forbidden love interconnected standalone.

Titus, Amora, Kaleb, Connie, Nate, Killian, Reese, Royal and even Xavier... yes, that grumpy bastard will not leave me alone, but at least he gets to retire... right?

If you want to read Xavier and Royal's happily ever after, you can find them here:

http://mybook.to/XavierSL

ACKNOWLEDGMENTS

My readers, thank you for reading The Loathing. I hope you loved Amora and Titus's story and enjoyed seeing a few familiar faces.

To my book bloggers, thank you for everything you do. Sharing my cover reveals, making and sharing edits and teasers for my stories, the recommendations of my books, the Reels, the TikTok videos and edits.

You will never know how much your support means to me. It means the world to me. Thank you, thank you. I am forever grateful.

My BETA's, Carrie, Jordan and Holly thank you for reading my first draft of The Loathing, you will never know how much you helped shape this story and how much I appreciated your feedback and thoughts. Thank you for helping me with the American terms and slang throughout for Titus and his friends dialogue.

Robyn, my PA. My friend. My dark and twisted sister. My otter. Thank you for putting up with me and not leaving me. I love you.

Please don't leave me.

Ever.

Lea, my editor. Thank you so much for doing such an amazing job like always, so grateful for you.

Leanne, once again you smashed this cover out of the park. I am so grateful that I messaged you back in 2018, and thank you for sticking with me, and for putting up with my indecisiveness.

My posies, Sophie and Harriet, thank you for joining my team and doing everything you do. I would be lost without you.
    I know I have made friends for life.
    Love you.

Lastly, my husband. I wouldn't have started this journey if it wasn't for you. Thank you for believing in me and more importantly pushing me to not give up and to take the leap. None of this would have been possible without you.

If you enjoyed The Loathing, please tell your friends and share on your social media platforms, and please, if you can, be sure to leave a review.

Love you all x

Printed in Great Britain
by Amazon

33642863R00263